MW01147675

The Very
Best Of
The Best
Of Secrets
Volume 2

On Newsstands Now:

TRUE STORY
and
TRUE CONFESSIONS
Magazines

True Story and *True Confessions* are the world's largest and best-selling women's romance magazines. They offer true-to-life stories to which women can relate.

Since 1919, the iconic *True Story* has been an extraordinary publication. The magazine gets its inspiration from the hearts and minds of women, and touches on those things in life that a woman holds close to her heart, like love, loss, family and friendship.

True Confessions, a cherished classic first published in 1922, looks into women's souls and reveals their deepest secrets.

To subscribe, please visit our website:
www.TrueRenditionsLLC.com or call **(212) 922-9244**

To find the TRUES at your local store, please visit:
www.WheresMyMagazine.com

The Very Best Of The Best Of Secrets

Volume 2

From the Editors
Of *True Story* And
True Confessions

Published by True Renditions, LLC

True Renditions, LLC
105 E. 34th Street, Suite 141
New York, NY 10016

Copyright @ 2015 by True Renditions, LLC

All rights reserved. No part of this book may be reproduced or transmitted in any form or by any electronic means, without the written permission of the publisher, except where permitted by law.

Visit us on the web at www.truerenditionsllc.com.

Contents

THIS BOY BELONGS
TO NOBODY

There comes a point in every mother's life when she feels unable to face one more runny nose or messy diaper. It wasn't so long ago when I was at that point. I felt if I didn't talk to some "real" people soon, I'd turn into a raving lunatic.

Don't get me wrong. I love kids. I chose to stay home with mine while they were small, even though a second income would have been quite welcome at times. It was important to me to be the guiding force in their young lives, and besides, it was fun watching them grow and develop. It's just as well that I felt that way, too, because Zach, my husband, would have insisted on it.

Of course, I always knew that my turn was coming. Once the youngest was in school I could do what I wanted—join the other career women, make a fulfilling contribution to the world. In the meantime, while I was at home, I supplemented my husband's income by baby-sitting. It wasn't much harder to care for someone else's kids than it was to care for my own. And it was only for a few years—just until our second son was in school. When he was four, I began making my plans. Once he was in kindergarten, I'd go to school and start my new life.

That was the year Brennan came into our lives. Brennan was the child of Zach's old high-school buddy, Chandler. He and his wife were killed in a car crash when Brennan was only two months old. There were no close relatives, and he needed a home so badly. We fell in love with him right away, and he became part of our family instantly. We adopted Brennan, and then I had another five years to wait to begin my career.

If I do say so myself, I was one of the best baby-sitters around. I gave all my kids a lot of love and care. Sometimes more than they got at home from a tired mother who'd worked all day. Let's face it, though, talking to little ones every day can make you crazy. I couldn't wait for Brennan to start kindergarten so I could get on with my life.

Of course, all my mothers thought I was completely crazy to envy them for having jobs.

"You don't know how lucky you are," my sister-in-law sighed. "You set your own schedule and no one tells you what to do. If you want to eat lunch at a different time every day, you can. And if you don't want to vacuum you can just skip it and relax."

Sure, and if two toddlers were fighting and the baby spilled his

1

cereal and one of the kids had a stomachache, life was just marvelous. And it always seemed like all the kids got sick at the same time. Have you ever tried keeping straight the medications for six different kids to be given at different times in different doses? In addition, there was always one difficult child each year. Like Aidan, my colic baby.

Aidan's mother was very young, just eighteen, and she was raising him by herself. I never knew who his father was. Sometimes it's hard not to interfere in the way other people raise their kids, and it was especially hard in Kirsten's case. I tried to remember that a child that screams all the time is awfully hard on the nerves, especially for a first-time mother. Still, Kirsten didn't help matters by being so impatient with him.

"I just can't stand his screaming," she told me one morning. "Nothing will shut him up. I have to put him in the back bedroom and shut the door so I can hear the television!"

I bit my tongue and tried not to say what I felt. It wouldn't help Aidan any. Kirsten told me once that her parents helped her out financially every week, and I got the impression that if it weren't for this generous allowance, she probably wouldn't have kept Aidan.

He was a little sweetie when he wasn't crying. But then he usually had his real crying spells in the evening, so I missed most of them. I'd already suggested that she talk to her pediatrician about his formula—I had this pet theory that colic babies were allergic to something they were eating—but she didn't follow my advice. Aidan was barely three months old when she switched him from formula to whole milk.

"Formula's too expensive," she complained. Of course, she didn't seem to mind spending money at the bar she went out to every weekend.

"Really!" I fumed to Zach. "Too cheap to spend a few extra dollars a week on formula, but she can go barhopping all the time. And I notice she certainly doesn't skimp on her clothes. Aidan doesn't have any decent clothes that I've ever seen. He's dressed in garage-sale stuff, which would be fine, except she doesn't even keep him very clean. Poor little guy."

"If she's mistreating him, then report her to the child-welfare agency," Zach told me.

"She doesn't actually mistreat him that I know of," I admitted. "It's just that she doesn't seem to care for him enough. She never pays him any attention."

Zach smiled and gave me a quick hug. "Not everybody can be as good a mother as you. She's young yet. Give her a chance."

I agreed that perhaps I was being too judgmental with Kirsten, so I decided to avoid that. It wasn't until she started bringing me

2

bottles of soda for Aidan that I really blew up at her.

"Do you want to stunt him mentally and physically forever?" I demanded. "What kind of nourishment do you suppose he can get out of this junk?"

"Well, he likes it," she said defensively.

I ignored her and continued. "Kirsten, I'll tell you one thing right now. You take this baby to a doctor and find out what is wrong with him and how to take care of him properly, or I'll notify the child-welfare agency!"

I don't know if she was bothered by my threat or just decided she didn't want to chance losing the money her parents were giving her for Aidan, but for once she did what I told her. Soon Aidan was on a special non-milk formula, and he was like a different baby. He even let me cuddle him and he started smiling and laughing.

Of course, Kirsten didn't turn into a perfect mother instantly, but at least she kept him a little cleaner. She still went out to bars a lot, and it bothered me that I never saw her give him any affection. Aidan was an early walker and took his first steps alone by the time he was eight months old. Kirsten didn't seem excited at all when I told her about it.

"Now he'll be into everything," she complained bitterly, and I found myself biting my tongue again.

Shortly after that, Brennan started kindergarten and I stopped baby-sitting. It was Aidan I hated to let go more than any other of my kids. Now that I had a half day free, however, I wasn't going to waste any more time. I filled the free hours taking secretarial courses in preparation for when Brennan was in school full-time. It was challenging and fun to finally spend a portion of my day in the company of adults, and I loved it. Oh, sure, I missed the quiet times with my little ones and their amusing behavior, but I sure didn't miss those runny noses and dirty diapers!

Over the next year, I occasionally saw Kirsten and Aidan around town. He forgot me soon, of course, and was quiet whenever I tried to talk to him, his huge eyes looking back at me solemnly. It seemed that every time Kirsten and I talked, she had a different baby-sitter. The latest was a high-school girl free for the summer. Each time I saw Aidan, I felt a twinge of guilt over my "abandonment" of him. But I firmly squelched it. After all, he wasn't my responsibility. I'd waited a long time for this—it was my turn now!

By the time Brennan started first grade, I'd finished all my classes and started job hunting. It was discouraging at first, but I finally got a job in a small real-estate office as a receptionist and typist.

Now I found out why my mothers had been so tired at the end of every day. Even though my job was a lot of fun and I loved it, by the end of the eight hours I was ready for a little relaxation. Instead, when I got home there was all the housework waiting for me, supper to make, and at least one load of laundry to keep me from getting buried in it. On top of all this, I needed to spend some time with the boys so they wouldn't feel neglected.

They weren't giving me much help around the house, either. Zach had just opened up his own business, a gas station and convenience store, and he was spending long hours trying to establish himself. After working twelve-hour days, he was so exhausted when he got home that I hated to ask for help. The boys, however, were a different story. They were so used to Mom being home and doing everything for them that it was quite a shock when I suddenly expected help.

I found myself turning into a real nag. Then, feeling bad about it, I'd end up doing everything myself anyway. After a few months of this, the house was increasingly messy, and I was getting desperate. I considered going on strike at home to wake my family up to my plight, but I didn't want to have to go that far. I loved them, and I wanted them to help me because they loved me.

About this time, I read that Kirsten's parents were killed in a bad apartment-building fire. Evidently she got a big insurance settlement, because she quit her job right away. Aidan didn't seem to benefit from it though. She never stayed home with him, and whenever I saw him he was with one teenager or another.

Summertime brought a little relief to my own problems at home. It seemed to me that the boys were gradually learning to do more for themselves. I made an effort not to nag so much and to praise their accomplishments. Even Zach seemed to be accepting my new role, and he commented on it on one of his rare evenings at home.

We were sitting on the couch, me reading while he was watching a movie. During a break, he leaned over and gave me a kiss.

"What's that for?" I smiled at him.

"You're doing a terrific job, Brenda," he told me. "I thought things around here would be awful when you went to work, but you seem to have them under control now. I'm proud of you."

I looked around our home. So it wasn't spotlessly clean. It was lived in and comfortable. Our oldest son was at the movies with some friends, and for once the two younger ones were playing a game without fighting. Life was definitely looking up. Around nine o'clock the phone rang.

"Hello, is this Mrs. Nicholls?" a female voice asked.

"Yes, can I help you?"

"You don't know me, but my name is Clara Alders. I'm baby-sitting for Kirsten Chambers."

"Yes, Clara, what can I do for you?" I asked.

"Well, I don't know. That is, I was supposed to watch Aidan all

4

weekend. Well, it's getting late now and Kirsten hasn't come home yet. She's always told me if I had trouble to call you, and I really don't know what to do," she explained.

"When did she say she'd be back?" I was already feeling annoyed.

"She told me she'd be here around noon today, and I've been waiting. My mom's called several times to see if she can pick me up yet, but—"

I felt like screaming. It wasn't my problem! I'd raised my children responsibly. I didn't need this.

I didn't scream, of course. I went down to Kirsten's apartment and took over, assuring Clara that I'd leave a note for Kirsten to find telling her that Aidan was with me.

Her parents came to get her, and I sympathized with her mother, who said to me, "I didn't want her to take a weekend sitting job anyway. And now this! What's the matter with that woman, anyway?"

They left, and I turned to Aidan. He had been sitting quietly on a chair the whole time, watching us solemnly with those beautiful eyes. I tried to get him to show me where his clothes were, but he wouldn't talk. So I went into the bedroom he shared with his mother and started going through drawers hunting for his things.

Then I realized what had happened. Most of the drawers were completely empty except for a few containing Aidan's things. I opened the closet. It held only a few older dresses and a pair of worn shoes. Almost all of Kirsten's things were gone.

Aidan didn't have many clothes, and they were fairly worn, but I packed them all in a grocery sack and took them with me. I left a note as I had promised Clara, but I didn't really expect to hear from Kirsten. It looked to me like she was gone for good.

I drove Aidan home and fixed a cot for him next to Brennan's bed. The entire time, he still hadn't said one word. He settled down to sleep at once, and Zach and I discussed the situation.

"I don't care if you decide to keep him here or not, Brenda," Zach said. "But I do think you should call the police tomorrow. Kirsten can't be allowed to do this. If she doesn't want him, I'm sure there are plenty of people who would take him. He's a real cute kid."

I looked at Zach quickly. He'd had the same look in his eyes when Brennan came to us.

"No, Zach! We decided we could only afford to raise three kids. I will not give up my job to raise another child," I insisted.

"I didn't say it should be us," he protested guiltily.

"Just so I've made myself clear," I threatened.

"Don't worry. I know it wouldn't be fair to ask you to give up your job," he said and kissed me.

5

It was two o'clock in the morning when Aidan started screaming. I was out of bed in an instant, and rushing into Brennan's room, I took him in my arms. His eyes were wide with fright, and he acted as though he didn't see or hear me. His little body was as stiff as a board when I tried to hold him close. He screamed for fifteen minutes, by which time everyone in the house was awake.

Zach shooed the boys back to bed, explaining the situation in low tones. I finally calmed Aidan down and put him in bed with us. At three o'clock it happened again. And at four-thirty. Zach normally got up at five anyway, so that time, as Aidan fell into an exhausted sleep, we stayed up and I fixed Zach breakfast.

After he left, I waited on the rest of the family to wake up and thought about Aidan. His screaming fits reminded me a little of the colic attacks we'd gone through when he was a newborn. He was completely out of control. Not once in any of his screaming sessions had he spoken a word. As a matter of fact, Aidan hadn't said anything since I'd picked him up the night before.

I did some quick figuring in my head. Aidan had been eight months old when I quit baby-sitting. That had been almost two years ago, which made him around two and a half years old. Surely he could talk! At that age my kids were impossible to shut up! Maybe, though, he was just too scared to talk. After all, he didn't know us at all anymore, and his mother was gone. That had to be traumatic.

Matthew, my oldest, was thirteen, and I paid him twenty dollars a week to watch his two younger brothers while I worked. I bribed him with extra money to watch Aidan also, and left while Aidan was still sleeping. But all day the memory of his screams haunted me, and at lunch I called Matthew.

"He's okay, Mom," Matthew reassured me. "But he's real quiet. He won't play or eat or anything. Just sits on the floor and watches TV. He hasn't talked or cried at all. It's kind of weird."

After I hung up, I was more worried than ever, and the afternoon passed slowly for me. On the way home, I stopped by Kirsten's apartment. The door was still locked as I'd left it, and there was no answer to my knock. On impulse, I knocked on the apartment next door. It was opened by a young woman in blue jeans and a tank top holding a young child.

"Hi, can I help you?" she asked in a friendly voice.

I explained who I was and the girl, who told me her name was Allie, invited me in. Her apartment presented quite a contrast to Kirsten's, even though they were almost identical. Although small and cluttered with baby things, it was cheery and had many homey touches that made it an inviting place to visit.

"I don't really know Kirsten that well," Allie explained, inviting me to sit down. "We've only lived here six months. When we first moved in, she was really friendly to me. But after a while I realized I was being used as an unpaid baby-sitter. She'd run to the store, and then she'd be gone all evening. I started feeling like I had two kids, not one. Then the time she did that and didn't get back until the next day, I really blew up. I haven't seen much of her since."

"Did you see her leave Friday?" I asked.

"Yes, she was with some guy and they were putting her suitcases in his car. She told me she was moving and they were taking a load of stuff in the car. They were going to rent a truck and come back for the rest of her stuff and Aidan. I never gave it a second thought. She was always leaving him for one reason or another."

"Do you know who the man was?"

Allie smiled. "I never could keep up with Kirsten's men. There was always one or another around." She stopped, and then added, "I didn't mean that like it sounded. It's none of my business how anyone else lives their life."

"I'm going to have to notify the child-welfare agency about Aidan," I told her. "Do you mind if I tell them to talk to you?"

"Not at all. I can't believe she just went off and left him like that. I mean, she wasn't that great of a mother, but to abandon him. Maybe she was in an accident."

"Maybe." I didn't believe it, but it was a possibility. "I have to be going now. Thanks for talking to me, Allie."

"Sure. Let me know what happens, will you? Aidan is such a little sweetie."

"Allie?" I thought of something.

"Yes?" she looked up curiously.

"Can Aidan talk?" I asked.

"I've never heard him say one word," she admitted. "I tried to talk to Kirsten about it, because to tell you the truth I'd about decided he was either deaf or learning disabled. But she wouldn't listen to me. She just said he was a slow learner. He should be talking a lot by now, shouldn't he?"

I nodded. "Yes, he should."

When I arrived home, the house was in an uproar. I could hear Aidan's screams as I got out of the car.

"Matthew, what on earth is going on?" I demanded as soon as I got inside.

"Mom, he won't do anything you tell him to. He was sitting right on top of the TV. I told him to move back three times and he wouldn't, so I pulled him back. I wasn't rough, Mom, honest I wasn't!"

"I know, Matt, where is he?" I asked.

"In the bathroom."

Aidan was wedged into a tiny space between the sink and hamper. His face was beet red, his eyes were wild, and he was still screaming.

"Aidan, come here," I urged. "Come on, baby, it's all right."

He ignored me, and I clapped my hands loudly above his head. He didn't see it coming, and he didn't even flinch. I pulled him into my arms and sat on the toilet rocking him back and forth, murmuring soothing words. At first he held himself stiff, but gradually he relaxed. His screams turned into sobs, then whimpers.

While I comforted him, my mind was racing. It was obvious now that Aidan was deaf. That explained his silence and lack of response. What I didn't understand was when it had happened. I had baby-sat for him in my home until he was eight months old, and he'd certainly had his hearing until then. He'd even said a few words. What had happened?

When his sobs subsided, I carried him out into the living room. I started to set him down on the sofa, but his arms tightened around my neck, so instead I sat with him.

Matthew was still watching television, and he turned to me as I sat down. "Gosh, Mom, what's the matter with him, anyway? He doesn't say anything, and he never listens to what you tell him. Do I have to watch him tomorrow?"

"He can't hear you, Matthew," I explained.

"You're kidding!" he exclaimed.

"No, I'm not. He's deaf."

"Gosh, poor kid." Matthew looked at him guiltily. "No wonder he's so scared. I'm sorry I complained. I'll watch him for you tomorrow if you want me to."

"Thank you, sweetheart, but I don't think that will be necessary. I'm going to call the police in a few minutes and see what they can do."

I sat rocking Aidan and humming softly to him. Slowly his grip around my neck loosened and his breathing evened out.

"Did he take a nap today, Matt?" I asked.

"No, he wouldn't do anything except sit in front of the TV. He didn't eat, either." When I was sure Aidan was asleep, I carefully laid him on the couch. "I'm going to make some phone calls, Matthew. Where are Brennan and John?"

"They're down at the school playing ball," he said. "I told them to be back in an hour."

"Thanks, Matt, you're a good kid." I tousled his hair.

"Aw, Mom!" He turned back to the television and I noted his red ears with amusement.

I really had no idea who to call about an abandoned child, so

8

I phoned the number listed in the book for non-emergency police business. I explained the situation, and after that it was easy. The woman on the other end took care of everything.

"I'll notify the appropriate authorities and send someone over as soon as possible. Does the child have any close relatives that you know of?" she asked.

"No, his grandparents were killed in a fire a few months ago. His mother was an only child. I don't know if she has any aunts or uncles," I said.

When I finished my call, I checked the time. I couldn't believe how late it was. Zach always came home for a quick supper before he returned to the shop for the late shift. I only had half an hour before he was due home.

Moving quickly, I tore open a box of frozen chicken and stuffed it into the oven. By the time Zach came in all tired out from his day, I had a truly modern dinner ready—frozen chicken, instant mashed potatoes with canned gravy, brown-and-serve rolls, and frozen corn. The only "real" food was the salad from our garden!

Thank goodness none of my men were picky eaters! Zach made a slight face at the potatoes and gravy, but made no comment other than, "Busy day?"

I told him first about Aidan's deafness, then gave a brief account of my visit to Allie's apartment and my call to the police. Aidan was still sleeping and Zach glanced into the living room to make sure he hadn't woken up before asking in a low tone of voice, "Did she say what will happen to him?"

"You don't have to whisper, Zach. I told you, he can't hear anything. The woman just said she'd send over someone from Family Services."

"Maybe he should stay with us. Just for a while until they decide," he suggested. "It's not good for a kid to move around a lot."

"Zach, we talked about this last night," I reminded him.

"Just until they find a family for him," he coaxed.

"I don't think that's such a good idea. I'd have to get a sitter for him, and—"

"I don't really mind doing it for a while, Mom," Matthew interrupted.

"Let him stay, Mom," ten-year-old John chimed in, adding his pleas. "He needs a place to stay, and we've got plenty of room."

Since we live in a three-bedroom house, I wasn't sure where he got this. But I ignored that and listed the logical solutions instead.

"Look, guys, I know he needs a place to stay, but they'll put him in a nice foster home with a good family. And as cute as Aidan is, he'll be adopted as soon as it's legally possible," I assured them.

9

"Not with his handicap, Mom," Matthew put in. "Lots of people don't want a special kid."

I couldn't argue with that, but I didn't let it stop me. "Look, don't you think that I have enough to do without taking on the care of a toddler? I just got settled into my job and organized around here. Who's going to do the extra work?" I asked them all.

"How much work can a two-year-old be?" Zach replied.

I gave him a withering look. "That's the dumbest thing you've ever said to me. A two-year-old is twice the work of a six-year-old, ten-year-old, and a thirteen-year-old combined. I should know—I've raised three!"

Zach grinned at my outburst. "I meant to say that we'll all pitch in and help, so the extra work doesn't fall on you. Won't we, kids?"

Brennan had been silent during most of the talk, but now he tugged at my sleeve. "Mom?"

"What?" I asked.

"I'd really like to have Aidan here. Then I wouldn't be the littlest and I could pretend I have a little brother. I'll share all my stuff with him, honest."

He was so sincere, I couldn't turn him down. I raised my hands in surrender. "Okay, okay! I'll talk to the welfare agency about being foster parents for Aidan. But that doesn't mean they'll let us. And I want everyone to remember that this is just temporary, okay?"

They all agreed, but I still had an uneasy feeling about it. Zach left for work, and I was soon busy straightening the house for our visitor. For once, the boys started the dishes without arguing, and I settled on the couch to enjoy a few minutes of peace and quiet. Soon Aidan woke up and I took him out to the kitchen to fix his supper.

"We'll do it, Mom," Matthew told me, taking him from me.

"Give him some chicken and potatoes," I told them. "He can have applesauce afterward."

I had only been on the couch a few minutes when I heard earth-shattering screams from the other room. I rushed in and found Aidan in the middle of the floor, his face screwed up tightly, screaming loudly. A plate of food sat on the table, and Matthew was trying to coax him back into the high chair.

"Cook!" Aidan yelled.

The boys and I looked at each other in amazement. We might not understand it, but it was definitely a word.

"What does he want, Mom?" John asked.

"I'm not sure." I tried to talk above the cries coming from the little boy. "Let's see if we can find out." Picking him up, I started for the cupboards. Opening one, I started pointing to different items.

"Peanut butter? Soup? Cookies?" I said out loud.

The cries stopped, and once again he spoke. "Cook!"

"He wants a cookie, Mom," Brennan cried.

Aidan was trying to reach the cookies in the cupboard, so I took them down and sat them on the counter.

"First, young man, you have to eat your supper," I told him, reaching for his plate.

His little face crinkled comically before he let out a roar of outrage. I gathered him in my arms and held him so his face was near mine. As he opened his mouth to scream again, I blew hard in his face. It took him by surprise, and his mouth closed as he tried to get his breath back.

I grinned at him and said firmly, showing him his plate then the cookies, "Supper first, then dessert."

With no further fuss, Aidan settled in his chair for supper.

While he ate, I tried to get a belated look at the paper. Shortly the doorbell rang.

"Mom!" Matthew yelled in a voice guaranteed to be heard throughout the neighborhood. "Your welfare lady is here!"

Mrs. Theodore, as she introduced herself, was a friendly woman in her mid-forties. I explained that Aidan was eating a late supper since he'd slept through ours.

"Good." She smiled. "That'll give us a chance to discuss his background. Tell me everything you know about him."

I told her about Kirsten, including the information Allie had given me about a "move."

"Tell me, Brenda, do you think she meant to abandon him?" Mrs. Theodore asked.

I hesitated. "I certainly never thought she was blessed with an overabundance of love for Aidan. But I wouldn't have thought she would do this. Still, she told Allie they'd be back for the rest of the stuff in a truck and get Aidan then. There isn't enough stuff in that apartment to put into a station wagon, let alone a truck. Yes, I think she abandoned him," I finally said.

We were interrupted just then by Brennan, who bounded into the room. "Mom, Aidan ate all of his supper. Can he have a cook?"

"Yes, he may. But keep him in the high chair," I said.

Mrs. Theodore gave me a puzzled look. "A cook?"

"Cook," I explained, "is the only word Aidan has spoken since we picked him up last night. We figured out pretty easily it means cookie."

"Surely the child knows how to talk. Didn't you tell me he's two and a half years old?" she asked.

"I'm fairly sure that Aidan is deaf," I told her then.

She looked a bit surprised.

"He wasn't born deaf," I went on.

"You're sure?"

11

"I baby-sat for Aidan until he was eight months old. He reacted to all the normal noises and made sounds like all infants. I'm sure."

She made a notation in her notebook, and then snapped it shut. "We'll see that he has a thorough checkup."

"Mrs. Theodore," I began. I was ready to ask about caring for Aidan, but we were interrupted again. This time by the entrance of John, holding a scrubbed-clean Aidan by the hand.

"Hi, Mom. I cleaned him up for you," he announced, leading Aidan over to my chair. "Did you ask yet?" he whispered in my ear, loud enough for the whole room to hear.

"Mrs. Theodore, this is my middle son, John." Then I turned to him as he nodded politely and replied in a whisper that matched his, "No, I didn't. Why don't you get lost so I can?"

He grinned sheepishly and left the room.

"Ask me what?" Mrs. Theodore said.

"My family wants to keep Aidan with us for the time being, until a permanent home can be found. He seems to like it here, and he's so insecure," I added.

Mrs. Theodore looked around the room, and then nodded slowly. "Yes, I think that could be arranged. We'll have to do a quick home study, and there'll be lots of paperwork, but we should be able to work everything out. I can give you a list of approved sitters to take care of him while you work."

"I was planning on Matthew. He's very responsible," I said.

"I'm sure he is, but the department has certain requirements where these kids are concerned, and one of them is that anyone who cares for them has to be over eighteen." Her smile softened the words, but I began to feel cornered.

The rest of the visit was spent filling out forms—the preliminary work—and making lists of things I needed to do. Right before she left, she gave me a list of approved sitters and told me she'd call and let me know when their doctor could see Aidan.

After Mrs. Theodore left, I called a few of the sitters on the list. After three tries, I managed to find one who agreed to take Aidan the following day. Her name was Melody.

By the time Zach got home at ten, all of us were already in bed. I, for one, was exhausted.

The screaming started at midnight this time. Aidan would scream for ten or fifteen minutes, then I would rock him for another twenty or thirty. After that he slept an hour. Then the whole thing started again. By morning, I was a wreck. Zach left, and I fixed the boys an early breakfast since we were all awake.

"Gosh, Mom. Is he going to do this all the time?" John complained. "I couldn't hardly sleep!"

I fixed my sons with a warning look. "You all voted to keep him here. Now put up with it!"

On my way to work, I regretted my words. I shouldn't have taken my lack of sleep out on them.

Before I left Aidan with the new sitter, I chatted with her a few minutes, explaining his special problems. Melody seemed quite understanding and gentle, so I felt a little better, until I started to leave and Aidan attached himself to me screaming.

"Go on," she motioned, and from years of experience, I knew that once the "mother" was out of sight, the child usually calmed down. I left, but it was harder than I'd thought it could be.

One of the things I liked about my job was the informal atmosphere in the office. My hours were flexible. If I needed time off to take one of my sons to the doctor, I could make it up the next day and someone would arrange to cover the phones for me. Still, I didn't like to take advantage, so it was with some hesitancy that I approached my boss that afternoon about taking some time off.

I explained about deciding to keep Aidan temporarily, and then, drawing a deep breath, said, "He's going to have to see a doctor, then probably a specialist. And I'm sure I'm going to have to make at least one visit to the welfare office to fill out forms."

Mr. Cameron frowned slightly. "Are you sure you're not taking on too much, Brenda? With three sons of your own and a full-time job, you surely don't need anything else to do." He smiled then and added, "Of course you can have the time off. Just try not to spread yourself too thin, okay?"

I couldn't be offended—since I felt that he could be right—so I smiled back and agreed to take it easy. But I found that was easier said than done.

When I picked Aidan up at the sitter's, Melody looked as exhausted as I felt. When he saw me, Aidan came running and grabbed hold of my leg as if he'd never let go.

"Did he scream long?" I asked, half afraid to hear the answer.

"Only most of the day," she replied wearily.

I groaned. "I am so sorry. He doesn't seem to have been taught anything, does he?"

"I did notice that the only way he has of making his wishes known is screaming. I'm all for teaching him that's completely unacceptable. How about you?" she asked.

"How can we teach him when he doesn't understand?"

Melody shrugged helplessly, and I left, thanking her again for putting up with him.

After supper was over that evening, I asked Matthew to watch the kids and drove over to the library. I was hoping to find some books on deafness in children. After looking the subject up, I entered the appropriate aisle and came face to face with Melody!

We looked at each other in amazement, and then burst out laughing.

"Here," she whispered, handing me half of her books. "We'll split them up. Maybe one of them will help!"

While I was out at the library, Mrs. Theodore called, leaving a message that I was to take Aidan to their doctor the following morning at ten o'clock.

"That's crazy," I fumed. "I can't just take time off from work without notice!"

"Well, Mom, that's what she said," Matthew, repeated patiently.

"This isn't going to work," I said to no one in particular.

"Mom!" my three sons all yelled at once.

"Okay. I said I'd try, so I'll try," I promised.

I went into my bedroom and dialed Mrs. Theodore's home number. A child answered the phone, and I heard her yell, "Mom!" When she came on the line, I was ready.

"Mrs. Theodore, you're a working mother, aren't you?" I asked.

"Yes," she answered, sounding puzzled.

"Then you understand the fine line we walk between our families and our jobs. My family comes first with me, of course. But I have to consider my job, too. My boss is extremely lenient about time off, but I need to give him some warning so he can reschedule. I can't just walk in at nine o'clock and then announce I will be leaving in an hour!" I blurted out.

She sighed. "I really did try to schedule you later, but Dr. Thrush is going out of town Thursday for a medical conference, and he's really booked up. I wanted him to see Aidan before he left so he could refer us to some specialists."

Her voice sounded tired, and I felt ashamed of myself. After all, she did have a family, too, and I had just interrupted their time together.

"Okay," I replied. "I'll see what I can do. I'm sorry I bothered you at home."

"That's all right, it's part of the job." She laughed. "I think it just got me out of helping do the dishes. Want to talk a little longer?"

"No, I'd better try to get hold of my boss. Thanks anyway."

I called Mr. Cameron at home and explained the situation to him. He was very understanding, but I felt bad about it. I wanted to be Superwoman—able to handle my job and family with no conflicts and neither one suffering at the expense of the other. Instead, my life seemed to be a series of compromises I didn't like making.

The next day I took Aidan to the doctor. It was only the first trip

14

of many. Over the next month I took more time off than I care to think about. Mr. Cameron was still very nice about it. But since I wanted to make my time up, I found myself working later hours trying to get the work done, then going home and rushing around frantically to keep my home in order.

The screaming fits had slowed down to one or two a week at first. Then as Aidan felt more secure, they stopped altogether. None of the doctors we'd seen had been able to find a physical reason for them. Dr. Thrush, back from the convention, shook his head. "Children do have nightmares," he said. I tried to imagine what a two-year-old would have nightmares about, and I didn't like what came to mind.

The news about Aidan's deafness was both good and bad. The good news was that tubes were surgically implanted, and it was hoped that in time he would recover full use of his hearing. The bad news was that his hearing loss had been caused by repeated blows to his head. It was unknown if there had been other damage. We'd just have to wait and see.

As Aidan settled in with us, the tantrums became few and far between also. Melody and I read all the books in the library, and between us we started teaching Aidan as best as we could. Still, I reminded my family regularly that this was just a temporary solution. The authorities had been unable to find Kirsten, so meanwhile Aidan was in limbo. Officially, the state had custody.

By the end of the month, the extra strain was starting to show on me. I felt like I was losing control of my temper. I snapped at anyone who got in my way. I guess mainly I was just tired. The promised help from Zach and the boys hadn't been forthcoming, and I just didn't feel up to the extra work having Aidan with us caused.

I was taking a load of clothes out of the dryer late one night when Zach got home.

"Hi, honey." He came up behind me and put his arms around me, nuzzling my neck. I pulled away, gave him a quick kiss, then turned back to fold the clothes.

"How was your day?" I asked, concentrating on my work and longing for bed.

"So-so. At least we were busy." He put his arms around me again and whispered in my ear, "Want to fool around, pretty lady?"

In fifteen years of marriage, Zach and I had always had a terrific sex life, and I could count on one hand the times I'd turned down an offer like that. I sighed. I was so tired, all I really wanted to do was sleep. Still, it had been a while.

"Let me finish this. I'll be there in a minute," I said.

"Come on, now. This can wait," he teased.

"No, Zach. If I don't do them now they'll wrinkle," I snapped.

"Fine." He released me abruptly. Stepping back he said sarcastically, "Do I need an appointment around here or what? All I'm asking is a few minutes of your time. It's been a long day, and I wanted some time with my wife. If the laundry is more important than me, forget it!"

He turned away angrily, and something snapped inside me.

"Don't make me out to be the villain here, Zachary!" I yelled at his back. He turned, surprised. "Sure you're tired, and your day hasn't been too great. So you come home and want to fool around. Well, so do I! But when you don't have any clothes to wear, who do you blame?" I accused him. "So when we're through having fun, you go to sleep, and I get to come down and redo this laundry which I could have done within ten minutes. I'm tired, too, you know. I want this day to end!"

"No one told you that you have to work!" he said defensively.

"I'm a person, Zach, not a robot. I need to grow and expand. Did you marry me to have a built-in housekeeper or for myself? As long as you're not inconvenienced, who cares what I want or need, is that it? You and the boys decided we should keep Aidan," I rushed on, "and promised to help with the extra work involved with a two-year-old. So far it's all fallen on me. I was doing just fine juggling my life until you made that decision. Well, I can't do it anymore. You take charge of everything now, and see how you do!"

I started crying then as I shoved past him, and he grabbed me and pulled me into his arms, holding me while the sobs shook my body.

"Hey, Brenda," he said softly, and smoothed my hair and rocked me like I did Aidan. "I'm sorry, honey. I didn't realize."

I couldn't stop crying. It was as if all the past weeks had fallen in on me. Gently he led me to bed and undressed me like a child.

"Sleep, sweetheart, it's all right," he whispered, holding me lovingly until I fell asleep.

When I woke up it was light out, and I was stunned to see that the clock said ten. There was a note leaning on it. I called in sick for you, it read. Aidan is at the sitter's. Get some rest. I love you, Zach.

Slowly, I got out of bed and put my robe on, then wandered into the kitchen. The house was so still! I made myself a pot of coffee and went into the laundry room. The laundry was gone, and I checked the drawers and discovered someone had folded it and put it away. I got my coffee and climbed back into bed, deciding I had some decisions to make. First, though, I'd just rest a little more.

When I woke up again, the clock said five-thirty. What was the matter with me? I got up and went into the kitchen. Matthew was washing dishes and John was drying them.

"Hi, Mom, do you feel better?" Matthew asked.

"Yes, I do. Why didn't you wake me up when you got home from school?"

16

"Dad said to let you sleep," John told me.

I went out into the living room and was amazed again. All the clutter had been picked up and someone had vacuumed and dusted. Zach and Brennan were sitting on the floor playing a card game, and Aidan was flipping through a book.

"Hi, Brenda." Zach came over and kissed me. "How are you feeling?"

"Fine. Why aren't you at work?"

"We'll talk about it later. Now we're going to have a family meeting. Are you hungry first?" he asked.

It had been twenty-four hours since I'd eaten, and I was suddenly starving. "Yes!" I exclaimed, and started for the kitchen. But Zach stopped me.

"Here, sit down. Matthew, bring Mom her food," he called.

Not five minutes later, Matthew brought in a plate containing a hamburger and French fries. It was steaming hot.

Zach laughed at my look of surprise. "We went to the fast-food place on our way home. After we bought your new present."

He looked at me expectantly as if I should be able to guess. I looked at my hot dinner.

"Oh, Zach. Not a microwave?"

He grinned, and I pushed back my plate and raced into the kitchen. The next few minutes were busy ones, as the boys proudly showed me all the features of the microwave oven they'd chosen. It was a crowd of happy children that followed me back to the living room to watch me eat.

"You shouldn't have, Zach. We can't really afford it," I said.

"It wasn't just for you, honey. We have no intention of letting you work yourself to death anymore, do we, guys? And if we're going to help with the meals, we need all the help we can get! Right, men?"

They all shook their heads vigorously.

"It's time we really learned to help run this house. After all, it's our home, too," Zach went on. "All you have to do is work out a schedule and we'll follow it, right?"

"Right, Dad!" the boys chimed in.

I smiled at them. "I love you all. Thank you."

The boys grinned back sheepishly. "Ah, Mom!" they said.

"Go on, now," Zach told them. "Mom and I want to talk."

The two oldest burst out of the room, but Brennan stayed where he was. He looked so sad I wondered what was the matter, but Zach whispered something into his ear and he left, too, moving slowly, not like himself at all.

"What's wrong with Brennan?" I asked.

"I'm not sure. I think he's worried about you. You know how

17

sensitive he is." Zach shrugged. "Now, let's talk."

I pushed my plate back, and settled myself into a comfortable chair. "What about?"

"Us, our family. Aidan." Zach paused and watched him playing busily with his blocks. Then he looked back at me. "I owe you an apology."

"Zach—"

"No, I do," he interrupted. "I've always had the attitude that your job is something you want to do, not have to do. Therefore, you should be willing to 'pay' for having it. Maybe I've felt a little threatened by it. I want you to need me and sometimes I don't think you do anymore," he admitted.

"Zach, I'll always need you!" I said.

He kissed me and held me tightly. "I know that, deep down inside. I'm sorry, Brenda, I haven't been fair. I want you to be happy, and I realize you need this job to challenge you and help you grow as a person."

"Thank you, honey. I really do," I told him.

"I guess I've been a little jealous of your job for other reasons, too. I want you to be happy because of me and our children—not some outside influences. I've been really selfish, Brenda. And another thing," he went on. "You were right last night. The boys and I talked you into taking Aidan, but we left you to handle all the responsibility of it. That's not fair to you. You were right—three kids are enough. I called Mrs. Theodore and asked her to place Aidan in another foster home. They're making arrangements now."

I watched Aidan trying to knock over the tower he'd just built, and then said, "Zach, that's not necessary. You were right, too. It's not good for him to be moved all the time."

"No, but we're really not being fair to him now, either. Kirsten hasn't been heard from. In a year he'll be considered adoptable. There are lots of foster parents looking for a child they can adopt for good. It's not right to let him get so attached to us when he could be with a family who wants him permanently. I told the boys," he added.

It was a valid point, and I couldn't argue it. But later, when I was putting Aidan to bed, I had a lump in my throat that wouldn't go away. And when I went upstairs again to tuck the boys in, Brennan was still much quieter than usual.

"What's the matter, honey?" I asked.

"Nothing," he mumbled.

"You sure?" I persisted.

"I'm just thinking. Can't a guy think?"

"Sure, baby." I kissed him lightly, but he rolled away.

"I don't need a good-night kiss. I'm too old," he told me.

I left the room, sighing. My baby was growing fast!

After the boys were all in bed, Zach and I enjoyed a quiet evening together and I vowed that we'd do it more often. It had been too long since we'd spent time together.

We'd been sleeping only a half an hour or so when a noise in the kitchen woke me. I looked at Zach who was sleeping soundly, then slipped quietly out of bed. Maybe one of the boys was sick.

Brennan was in the kitchen making himself a peanut-butter sandwich by the light of the refrigerator. He jumped guiltily when he saw me.

"What on earth are you doing, honey?" I scolded gently.

"I'm making breakfast. I'm going away," he said.

"Going away! Why?" I asked.

"Because."

"Because why? Don't you love us anymore?"

"Yes," he said shakily, and a tear rolled down his cheek.

All grown up or not, I scooped him into my arms. "Come on, kiddo, let's talk."

I took him into the living room, and we cuddled in the big chair together. "Now, what's this all about?"

"Well," he sniffed, "Daddy said we had to send Aidan back 'cause you're so tired and he's causing you too much work. I'm adopted, too, and I thought maybe if I left, you wouldn't be so unhappy 'cause you wouldn't have so much to do. Then you could keep Aidan here. He's just little and I'm big enough to take care of myself now." His voice quavered a bit, and I hugged him to me.

"Oh, Brennan! You're our son. Just like Matthew and John. We chose you, and we love you very much. You can't leave us—you're family!" I told him.

"But, Mom, we all chose Aidan, too. I thought he was part of the family. Don't you love him?" he asked me.

I didn't really know how to deal with his six-year-old logic, so I held him and assured him we loved Aidan, and eventually he fell into an exhausted sleep.

It was a good thing I'd caught up on my sleep that day, because after I put Brennan to bed, I lay awake thinking for the longest time.

The next day, I went back to work as usual. I felt like a fraud. Everyone was so nice to me, when the only thing wrong had been a lack of sleep and emotional exhaustion. During my lunch hour, I called Mrs. Theodore to talk to her about Aidan's departure.

That night, our new schedule worked well. The microwave was going to be a great timesaver in the kitchen, and the boys were willing helpers. After supper, John washed dishes and Brennan and Matthew put them away while Zach and I relaxed in the living room.

19

When they were done, I called them all in.

"I want to talk to you all," I said, picking Aidan up from the corner where he was picking lint off the carpet and depositing him on Zach's lap.

"First of all, I owe you all an apology." They all looked at me as though I'd lost my mind, so I went on. "I wanted a challenging career, but I expected everything else in my life to be perfect, too. I've been trying to act like Superwoman, and when I couldn't I've blamed it on my family. I forgot that what really counts is us—together. I love my work, but I love you all more. My work is important for me, but you guys are my life. We're a family, and I've been trying to carry the whole load instead of sharing it with those I love, the way families should. When I couldn't do everything, I took it out on all of you. I'm sorry."

I didn't know if much of what I'd been saying the kids understood, but Zach took my hand and held it tightly.

"Now, there's another thing," I continued. "This family voted to let another person in to love—Aidan. Well, once you're part of a family, there's no leaving, ever. So I talked to Mrs. Theodore today, and she says when the waiting period is over, we can adopt Aidan permanently."

"Hurray!" the boys yelled, jumping up and down, and pandemonium reigned for a while.

Brennan ran over to me and gave me a big hug. "Thanks, Mom," he said, his eyes shining.

"Thank you, sweetheart." I hugged him back.

Later in bed, Zach turned to me and demanded, "What changed your mind?"

I told him about what Brennan had said last night, and explained how I felt we were losing him along with Aidan. "Besides," I added, "three's an uneven number. Now four, that's a family!"

Zach just laughed and pulled me close.

It's been a year now since we adopted Aidan. In that time he's regained his hearing, and the doctors have assured us that he shows no signs of being mentally impaired by the beatings that caused his deafness in the first place. Every time I look at that sweet child and think of how he was treated, I hope I never see Kirsten again— because she would definitely be sorry to see me.

Things aren't absolutely perfect, of course. The boys and Zach don't always remember the schedule and their promises, and sometimes I can be a bit of a nag. But a perfect life would probably be boring anyway.

And Aidan couldn't be better. He'll talk your ears off now if you'll let him. Soon he'll be starting nursery school and he's already started to read a little. With three older brothers coaching him, he's had no trouble!

I can't believe I was ever willing to let this loving child out of our family. But Aidan's ours now, and nothing will ever separate him from us. Today he is a bright, mischievous little boy, and those beautiful eyes of his no longer mirror fear and sadness. Now they are filled with love.

THE END

STILL IN LOVE
WITH MY EX!

I took a lot of time getting ready for John's visit, choosing my dress carefully, fussing with my hair and makeup. I certainly hadn't cared how I looked during those last bleak months before the breakup of our marriage. I'd been locked away in a prison of grief and bitter loneliness, so that nothing else seemed to matter.

It was pride, I told myself now. I wanted him to see how well I was getting along without him and I hoped he'd tell Terri, his new wife! I wouldn't admit, even to myself, the hope his telephone call had stirred in me. He'd asked to come see me about a business matter, but that could be an excuse. Maybe he really wanted to see me.

My heart raced and my hand shook so hard I could hardly get my lipstick on straight, thinking that maybe at last he was seeing Terri as she really was, and realizing what he'd given up for her.

I hated Terri, not only because she'd taken John from me, but also because of the way she'd done it. She was a mother herself, a divorcée with a little boy the age my Dougie would have been. Yet she'd had so little feeling for me, losing my only child so suddenly and dreadfully, that she hadn't hesitated to steal my husband. While I was still wandering around in a daze of grief, unable to care about anything much less fight for it, she'd gone after John, using every trick she knew to land him.

She even had the nerve to tell me it was my fault, the day she and John came to ask me to give him his freedom. I can still remember my outraged shock at the suddenness of it. I know they say a wife is the last to know when her husband's involved with another woman, and that's the way it was with me. I knew Terri Barnes by sight, the way everybody knew everybody else in Forest Glen, our little suburban town, but that was all. I hadn't been impressed enough with what I saw to want to know her any better.

Not that I had anything against her, but she was one of those women who seem to come alive only when there's a man around.

I'd first seen her at John's garage. She drove an old car that seemed to need a lot of attention, according to Harris Landon, John's young helper. Looking back, I wondered if he'd been trying to warn me the day I stopped for gasoline and saw Terri talking to John, kidding with him while he put gas in her car.

"Has John taken over your job, Harris?" I asked. "I thought the pumps were your department."

"I thought so, too, but Mrs. Barnes won't let anybody but Mr. Meyer do anything for her," he said. "I'll tell him you're here."

I told him not to bother, that I'd stop on my way back from the supermarket. John didn't even see me, though I drove right by him on the way out. He seemed absorbed in what Terri was saying, but it never crossed my mind that he could have any real interest in her. He'd built a good business by being pleasantly attentive to all his customers.

It just showed how much I knew about the man I married. It was like a nightmare, hearing John say, "I know you don't care any more, Laurel. For a long time now, you haven't even known I was alive."

Since Dougie's death, he meant. I was too hurt by his callous selfishness to answer. Maybe he could forget the tragedy of that black day when Dougie, watching eagerly for his daddy to come home, had darted into the street directly into the path of a car coming from the other direction. John had forgotten, if he could put another woman's child in his own son's place.

Worst of all, he hadn't even had the decency to come to me alone. I knew how John hated unpleasantness of any kind. Maybe he figured I wouldn't make a scene in front of Terri. Well, he was right. I was filled with disgust, hearing him say, "Terri and I never meant to hurt you. It was just one of those things."

"If this is what you want," I told him coldly, "I won't stand in your way."

Through the ordeal of the divorce, it helped a little to know I had the sympathy of my neighbors, especially the women. Mary Barton, whose husband owns the only dress shop in Forest Glen, and Alice Laney, the druggist's wife, told me about the bills Terri had run up for clothes and cosmetics.

"She was counting on John to pay them," Alice said. "She knew he was doing all right. Even with the new garage opening up, John gets most of the business."

"I doubt if he'll get as much now," Mary said. "People around here don't like the way he's treated Laurel."

My friends predicted the marriage wouldn't last. "John will be begging you to take him back when he comes to his senses," Erin Waldrop, my best friend, said.

The court awarded me the house and furniture, and John was ordered to send monthly checks for my support. Surprisingly, I hadn't cared too much about my getting the house, but when I heard that Terri was terribly disappointed about its being given to me, I got a thrill of satisfaction, knowing I'd been right about her. She was greedy and grasping and stupid besides, thinking she could take another woman's husband and not pay in some way.

23

After that, I was conscious of a sense of power whenever I thought of the house. It was something I had that Terri wanted and couldn't take, the way she'd taken John.

It was my hatred of Terri that made me come alive again and start rebuilding my shattered life. I'd show her and John that they didn't matter to me.

Living alone, without the problem of making a living, I had time on my hands, and I decided I'd put it to good use. I cleaned my house until it shone. Then I started on the yard. I weeded, mowed, and fertilized until the lawn was a green velvet carpet and the flowerbeds a blaze of color. The neighbors told me it was so beautiful it looked like a picture in a magazine.

It gave me a lift, too, when I saw how the outdoor exercise hardened my muscles and made my figure firm and slim again. I had to take in my clothes to make them fit, and I made myself a few new dresses besides. Then, with a new hairdo and makeup, I knew I didn't look like the same person I'd been a few months before.

My friends were delighted with the change in me. "I'm so proud of the way you've adjusted," Erin told me. "You've certainly proved you've got what it takes."

"To live alone and like it?" I asked, feeling pleased with myself.

"You know that's not what I mean," she said. "You've made the best of a bad situation. But you won't have to live alone, not for long."

"Sounds interesting," I murmured. "Tell me more."

"Oh, stop it," she said, laughing. "I'm not expecting you to rush out and get married tomorrow. We both know it's not that easy, not in Forest Glen anyway. You have to make opportunities to meet the right man, then work at the business of landing him."

"Like Terri?" I meant to say it lightly, but just thinking of her made the words come out hard.

Erin looked startled. "Of course not! I wouldn't think of comparing you with Terri. You've got so much more—brains and character as well as looks."

But she's got John! I didn't say it out loud, though I thought at first I must have, I was thinking it so hard. Maybe Erin had forgotten her prediction that John would come back to me, but I hadn't. It was what I was living for. Time had softened the resentment I'd felt toward him, leaving only the memory of the love we'd shared, the sweet, tender moments and the wild, passionate kisses. With my new glowing health came an awakening of longing for that lost love. More and more often I was conscious of a deep regret that I'd turned John over to that woman without a struggle.

As my longing for John grew, my hatred of Terri increased. I'd met her face to face only once since the divorce. It was in the supermarket. She looked at me blankly at first, then her eyes widened in startled recognition. I stared at her coldly, noting that she'd let herself go. Her hair looked drab, and she'd lost her look of well-dressed, well-groomed smartness.

I'd heard she'd stopped her visits to the beauty parlor, and I hoped it was because John had put his foot down. It couldn't be easy for him to keep up two homes and pay the bills of somebody as extravagant as Terri. My check came every month, though not as promptly as at first. Once it arrived two weeks late, with a note of apology from John. He'd had some bills that had to be taken care of.

Terri's bills, I thought resentfully. If he expected any sympathy from me about that, well, he could consider himself lucky that I didn't make a fuss over my check being late. . . .

And then I got the call from John, asking to see me. It was almost eight o'clock by the time I finished getting dressed. I took a last look at myself in the mirror and hurried into the living room just as the door chimes sounded.

John was thinner, and he didn't look happy. He was wearing the gray suit I'd always liked, but in the harsh glare of the porch light I could see that his shirt was badly ironed, with a scorched place on the collar.

"Come in, John," I said, giving him a warm, welcoming smile. I was trying to be calm, but I couldn't help the way my heartbeat quickened when I saw how his face brightened at the warmth of my greeting.

"Thank you," he said, glancing around the room and then back to me. "Everything looks terrific, and you—you're prettier than ever, Laurel." He hesitated, and then blurted, "I've wanted to come before, but I didn't quite dare."

"Why, John?" I asked shakily.

"Because of what I did to you," he said. "I couldn't blame you, I guess, if you turned me down now."

Looking back, I wonder how I could have been such a fool, taking it for granted there was only one thing he could mean—that he still loved me. That was what hurt so, the way I threw myself at him, saying, "Ask me, John! I'll never turn you down."

I came back to earth hard, hearing the things he was saying in a voice that was filled with gratitude, not love. "You're wonderful, Laurel, taking it like this," he said. "I told Terri you'd be reasonable, that you wouldn't hold a grudge. Wait till I tell her you're willing to help us get on our feet."

Sick with humiliation, I realized it was money he wanted to talk about. Wonderful, was I? Why didn't he say what he really meant—that I was a fool, so in love with the man who'd thrown me aside I'd let him get away with anything.

I'd been a fool, all right, giving him a chance to humiliate me a second time. But I wouldn't be any more. John was crazy if he thought I'd take a cut in my support checks so he and Terri could have things easier.

I told him all that and a lot more, lashing out at him furiously. "The fact that you're having a hard time doesn't excuse you from your obligation to me," I told him. "You wanted Terri and you got her. Now that you've discovered what she is, don't come whining to me and expect me to do without so she can have the luxuries she thinks she's entitled to."

Anger blazed in his eyes. "Leave Terri out of this," he said. "It's not fair to blame her. She tries hard. It's not her fault that she's not a good manager like you. She's—well, in some ways she's like a child. She loves nice things, and sometimes she gets in over her head without meaning to. But she's not a gold digger. She loves me and needs me, the way you never did. You're too self-sufficient to need any man!"

"Looks like I'd better be," I said bitterly. "I suppose you mean I can get a job and support myself. So could Terri, though I don't suppose that has occurred to either of you—"

"You're wrong," John cut in. "She wanted to. But how could she? Her place is at home with Ron. He needs her."

And no one needed me. I was speechless before this final bit of unthinking cruelty. But John had already realized his mistake. The last shred of hope faded from his eyes and his shoulders sagged. "I'm sorry," he said. "I won't bother you again."

I cried for a long time after he left. For the love and happiness we'd once had as a family, or that I'd thought we had. John had just told me he'd never loved me—at least not the way he loved Terri. My love for him died finally then. But not my hate. It was stronger than ever, because it was all I had left to cling to.

The next morning I told Erin what had happened. Oh, not that I'd been ready to take John back. That was too painful even to think about. Just about what he had wanted and the way I'd turned him down.

I was so sure of her wholehearted sympathy that I waited confidently for her to tell me I was right. So I was disappointed when she said, "I've heard that John's having a hard struggle. He's lost a lot of his business to the new garage."

It sounded as if she was sorry for him, as if she thought I was too hard on him. "Because of me, I suppose," I said. "Maybe you think I should have done what he asked."

I felt a little foolish when I saw her look of surprise. "What gave you that idea?" she said. "Anyway, it's your business, not mine."

It wasn't enough to reassure me. I couldn't get over the idea that she was silently criticizing me, thinking I was hard-hearted. I didn't say any more, and I left soon afterward. But a few days later something happened to strengthen the feeling I had.

Erin and I were talking, and she mentioned casually that Forest Glen was growing, especially the business section. "With all these new stores opening up," she said, "we soon won't need to go into the city for anything. Besides, it makes jobs for people who live out here."

I thought of the new branch bank, the restaurant, the hardware store, as well as the real-estate office where Erin's husband, Vincent, worked. They were building a block of new stores, so there was no knowing what might develop next.

Erin told me about one new business. Vincent had just leased one of the stores to a man from the city who was putting in a decorator's shop. It would carry materials for draperies and slipcovers, as well as ready-made ones.

I didn't know why she was so enthusiastic about it, not until she told me, almost too casually, that the new owner was looking for an assistant. When I said it ought to be easy enough to find one, she said, "But it won't. Mr. Bingam is looking for someone special. Fairly young, but with experience, preferably in decorating her own home. She must have good taste, be capable of advising people about their decorating problems, and be able to manage the shop when he's away."

She stopped, looking as if she expected me to say something. When I didn't, she drew a long breath. "Vincent and I couldn't help thinking how well you fitted the description, Laurel. When Mr. Bingam asked Vincent if he knew anybody, he thought of you right away."

A wave of suspicion flamed through me, deepening when Erin seemed to avoid meeting my eyes. "Why?" I asked flatly. Then I added, "As if I didn't know! Oh, I've known from the first that Vincent was on John's side. They've always been friendly. Besides, men stick together. But for you to turn against me, too—"

I stopped. Erin's face had a puzzled look. "I'm not on John's side, Laurel," she said. "I don't know whether you'll believe me or not, you're so touchy and suspicious lately, but I wasn't even thinking of John. I was thinking of you, and of the lift you'd get from an interesting job. Now I'm convinced you need it, and not for the money either. You need something to distract you from this obsession you've developed about John and Terri."

"Thanks," I said stiffly, "but I'm really not in the market for a job."

Erin didn't mention it again. I didn't give her an opportunity to. Since she obviously felt I was a bore, obsessed by my troubles, I stopped dropping in for coffee and a chat, the way we'd done every day for years. She visited me a few times, and then gave up. We spoke pleasantly when we met outdoors, but I couldn't even pretend to feel close to her any more.

The other neighbors followed Erin's lead. They were outwardly friendly enough, but a little too polite. I began to feel that they were silently criticizing me. So I withdrew more and more from everybody, feeling it was better to be alone than with people whose sympathy was so fickle.

Keeping house for one person couldn't take all my time, and neither could reading and watching TV. When I found myself getting restless, I'd go for a walk. Usually I went to the cemetery, where I'd sit beside Dougie's grave, brooding and reliving the tragedy. I knew people would say I was only torturing myself. Maybe I was. But at least I hadn't forgotten my little boy, the way his father had.

Sometimes on my way home I'd pass by the apartment development where John lived, and it would give me a grim sort of lift to see how dingy it looked. A drainage ditch ran along the edge of the development, and it was filled with muddy water each rain. Swarms of noisy children were always playing around it, wading and sailing their boats and bickering among themselves.

I never paid any attention to them until the day one of the children separated himself from the yelling pack and streaked across the yard without looking where he was going, bumping into me with a jolt that sent him sprawling. He looked up at me with scared gray eyes, and I saw that he was only about five. He clutched a skinny, bedraggled kitten in his arms, and both the boy and the kitten were soaking wet and covered with mud.

I looked at the mud on my freshly cleaned dress, then at the child. He was looking at it, too. "I—I didn't mean to do it," he explained. "I was trying to get away before they got him again."

He looked down at the struggling, frightened kitten, then back at me hopefully. I couldn't scold him, he looked so pathetic in faded jeans and a too-short T-shirt, plastered wetly to his body.

"You shouldn't have been playing in that dirty water," I said, helping him to his feet. "Why were they trying to take the kitten away from you? Does it belong to one of them?"

He shook his head, scowling. "No, they were trying to drown him, 'cause he's a stray. I was trying to pull him out when one of 'em pushed me in the water. But I got him, and I'm going to keep him." He looked defiantly at the children who were standing silently together, waiting for me to leave. "He can't be a stray if he's mine, can he?"

"No," I said, smiling. "He's a lucky kitten to find a home with you. I'll walk you to your door," I added, sneaking another look at the waiting boys.

"Gee, thanks," he said, giving me a smile of such genuine friendliness that I felt an almost painful stirring of warmth and tenderness—even after I knew who he was. . . .

When he led me to the apartment building I knew was John's, when he told me his name, Ron Barnes, I stood staring at him, unwilling to believe he could be Terri's child.

"What's the matter?" I heard him say. "You look so funny. Do you feel bad?"

I nodded. "Yes, I guess I do," I said. "I'd better be going. Run in and let your mother change your clothes before you catch cold."

"She's not here. I can do it myself," he added. "I fix my lunch every day."

"You mean you're alone here every day?" I must have sounded as shocked as I felt. He looked at me warily and edged toward the door.

"I promised I wouldn't tell. Good-bye," he said, scuttling inside like a scared rabbit.

It was none of my business, I kept telling myself. But I couldn't stop thinking about that child. He could have drowned in that ditch! People who took parenthood so lightly had no right to a child. They should be reported to the authorities.

I told myself that was my reason for going back again and again to see Ron. It was my duty as a citizen, as a woman interested in the welfare of children, to discover and report a case of neglect.

I was kidding myself, of course. I had to admit finally that it wasn't duty that drew me, or even my hatred of Ron's parents and a desire to punish them. It was Ron himself, and the love I'd come to feel for him. It was seeing his face light up at the sight of me, watching him run breathlessly to meet me, begging to know what I'd brought him. We'd play with the kitten, who was filling out and getting bright eyed and frisky, or we'd go to the movie, a few blocks away.

It was easy to satisfy the curiosity of the only neighbor who seemed to notice by telling her I was a relative. She didn't ask any more questions. She just said she was glad to know there was somebody who took an interest in Ron.

I'd long ago decided that Ron really was neglected. Terri was never home. Then why didn't I report it? Because I knew I'd lose him. Whether his mother was ordered to take better care of him, or whether he was placed in a foster home, I would never see him again. Even though I knew my attitude was selfish, I couldn't give up the only source of happiness that I had left.

Ron was an exceptional child. He had an active imagination and was delighted with the fairy stories I told him. He was fond of make-believe, maybe because he was a lonely child. He called me his fairy godmother. "Fairy godmothers are real as long as you keep them a secret," he told me gravely. "I haven't told anybody about you, not even Mommy or Daddy. If I did, it would break the spell and you'd disappear and you wouldn't come back any more."

His little freckled face looked solemn and very earnest when he asked, "Where do you go when you disappear? To a castle?"

"Yes," I answered, going along with the game. "It's not a big castle, just big enough for a little boy and his fairy godmother. Would you like to see it?"

He nodded eagerly, his eyes bright with excitement, when I promised I'd take him the next day. "Can Moses come, too?" he asked.

I nodded, smiling at the name he'd given his kitten. "Because I rescued him from the water," he'd explained.

It was the first of many happy days we spent together at my house. The house seemed to come alive again with the chatter and laughter of a child to fill its stillness, with fingerprints and scuff marks to mar its barren neatness. But the greatest change was in me, with a child to fill the emptiness in my heart and give me something to build my life around. I'd feel warm and contented as we sat at the kitchen table together with cookies and milk, watching Moses lap his milk from a bowl on the floor.

Yes, I knew the chance I was taking, letting myself love a child who wasn't mine. But it was too late to be sensible. I knew when I brought Dougie's electric train from the attic, and all the other things I'd thought I could never allow another child to touch, just how much Ron had come to mean to me. You can't stop loving just by telling yourself your love is unwise.

Besides, why should I? How could it be wrong to give love and happiness to a lonely child? Seeing his face light up with awed delight when he saw the toys, watching him play with them, happily absorbed for hours sometimes, I knew he was happy with me, and certainly a lot safer than he'd been before.

I should have known my contentment was built on a shaky foundation. I was lonelier than ever the times I couldn't have Ron with me. Once he didn't meet me for two days, and I was frantic with worry.

The third day I walked over, my heart leaped with joy when I saw his small, sturdy figure on the playground. I'd started to cross the busy street running beside it when Ron spied me and ran to meet me. My shriek of warning stopped him from darting into the traffic. I was shaking so when I reached the other side of the street and gathered him into my arms that I sank down weakly on the grass.

"Hasn't anybody told you not to cross the street alone?" I gasped.

He nodded. "Daddy did. Mommy, too. But I was so glad when I saw you, I forgot."

He'd had a cold, he went on to explain, and his mother had stayed home with him. But he was all well today.

So she was gone again! Was John blind, or didn't he care how Terri was behaving? I'd always been scornful of people who asked children prying questions, but worry over Ron drove me to ask him where his mother had gone.

It was obvious that he didn't know. He just accepted it, the way children accept the things they don't understand. "She brings me candy when she comes home," he said. Then he put his hand trustingly in mine. "Can we go play with the train?"

"We certainly can," I answered. "We've got a new book, too, with stories and a lot of pictures."

It was so wonderful to have Ron back after the separation from him! I knew I couldn't pretend to myself any more. I wanted this child for my own, to keep always. I loved him far more than his own mother did, and I could give him a far better home. He'd be the most important thing in the world to me.

It was harder than usual to take him home that day. The time slipped away from me, so that it was almost dusk when I said good-bye to him in front of his door.

I'd gone only a few steps when a yellow convertible drove up and stopped. I caught a flash of blond hair and moved quickly on when I recognized Terri. I didn't know the man who was with her. He was a stocky, middle-aged man, well dressed and prosperous looking.

I didn't want Terri to see me, so I stood very still in the next doorway while the man got out of the car and went around to help her out. But I needn't have worried about her seeing me. She was leaning heavily against the man, who was supporting her with his arm. Drunk! I thought, watching them disappear inside together.

I was almost sick as I turned and walked rapidly away, thinking of Ron in that apartment, wondering how many times he'd seen his mother come home like that. If I told the proper authorities how unfit she was to have his custody and how little his stepfather cared about him . . . .

I told myself I mustn't hope, but I couldn't help it. My heart beat crazily with excitement. I didn't know anything about the law, but if it came out that I'd been caring for the child—that I loved him and he loved me—surely that would count heavily in a court of law.

I wonder if anybody ever worked harder at anything than I did, after that day, to win Ron's love. It was all I thought about. I bought him presents, gave him treats, took him to the zoo—anything I could think of that might please him. I gave him my time, energy, and complete devotion, only to find it wasn't enough.

Oh, Ron loved me, but it wasn't the kind of love I wanted. I was his friend, a part of the world of make-believe, but not his real world. He'd accepted my friendship gratefully, and I'd filled a lack in his life. But he wasn't mine. I learned that with shattering suddenness one night.

I'd kept Ron later than usual, and I sensed his restlessness. The days were shorter by then, and a drizzle of rain, with overcast skies, made it look later than it was. Ron's attention wandered from the story I was reading and he looked worried. "Maybe Mommy's home," he said, peering out of the window. "I better go home."

I felt a sharp stab of jealousy. "Don't you like it here?" I asked. He nodded.

"Then how would you like to stay here for always?" I went on. "You could have the room with the bunnies on the wall, and the swing, and all the toys and picture books for your very own."

His eyes brightened with interest, I noticed. He looked thoughtful, as if he was turning the idea over in his mind. My heart lifted on a wave of excited hope when he said, "I guess maybe I'd like it." He smiled. "Moses could play in the backyard, couldn't he?"

I laughed happily. "That's right. And I'd get you a puppy, too."

"Gee, that'd be great," he said. "Daddy likes dogs, but he says we haven't room for one. I bet he'll like to live in this house. Mommy, too."

I bit my lip, a little worried that he'd misunderstood me. I had to explain to him, gently and patiently, that Mommy and Daddy wouldn't be coming. I should have been warned by the stunned look on his face, but I hurried on, telling him about all the fun we'd have. I don't think he heard any of it, though, after my first words. I stopped when I saw that he was looking at me with wide, frightened eyes, backing away from me as if I were a monster.

"No," he said, bursting into tears. "I want to go home. I want Mommy and Daddy."

Nothing I could say made any difference. There was nothing for me to do but admit defeat. I had to take him home, my heart heavy with the knowledge of how completely I'd failed. He was so relieved to be home he could hardly take time to tell me good-bye.

After that heartbreaking experience, I knew I had to stop seeing Ron and try to forget him. The next day I took down the swing and put away the toys. But it wasn't so easy to put away the memories. The quiet and the loneliness were even harder to bear, now that I'd known a brief period of happiness and hope and the feeling of being needed. The restlessness was worse, too.

One morning, about a week later, I knew I had to do something—anything that would use up some of my restless energy and help distract my mind. I was having breakfast when I noticed how thin and worn the kitchen curtains were getting, and I decided to go down to the new decorating shop and look at material for new ones.

There were a number of customers in the shop when I got there, waiting for Mr. Bingam, the owner, to wait on them. He was busy with Kathy Stillman, who'd just bought the old Hightower place, and at the same time he was trying to keep an eye on everybody who came in. I'd been in the shop only once, on opening day, and I didn't expect him to remember me, so I was surprised to hear him say, "Good morning, Mrs. Meyer. Please make yourself at home. I'll wait on you as soon as I can."

"He means if I ever make up my mind," Kathy said, laughing. "Am I glad to see you, Laurel! Come tell me what to buy that'll go with my furniture. Then Mr. Bingam can take care of these other people before they get tired of waiting and walk out."

Mr. Bingam looked relieved when I agreed, and by the time he'd taken care of his other customers I'd helped Kathy choose fabrics for slipcovers and curtains for her whole house, and I'd figured from her measurements how much of everything she'd need. It was a good-sized order, and he thanked me for my help. By that time the shop was empty of customers, and he invited us to have coffee with him. Kathy had to leave, but I accepted.

Over the coffee, we got acquainted, and I found myself liking him. He was about thirty, lean and thin faced, with steady gray eyes. There was a wryly humorous twist to his mouth as he told me about the trouble he was having getting someone to help him in the shop. "The right person could make her own job, name her own salary as soon as the profits justified it. Someone like you," he added.

"Like me? But you don't know me," I objected.

"I don't have to," he told me. "I saw how you stepped in and took hold of things. Besides, I'm a pretty good judge of people. I wish you'd give it a try. I've got a feeling we'd work well together."

It had been a long time since a man looked at me admiringly. I was flattered by the eager way he waited for my answer—till I reminded myself that he needed help badly.

"I'll have to think it over," I told him, not wanting to be rushed into a hasty decision.

He looked disappointed, but he said, "Of course. Take all the time you want." Then he added, "Just so you say yes. I've been so tied down I hardly see my family. My young son is in bed by the time I get home at night and still asleep sometimes when I leave in the morning. I live in the city, you know."

I didn't know—or that he had a family either. Not that I was interested, I told myself, wondering why I felt so depressed as I got up to leave. "Don't go yet," he begged, looking so disappointed I agreed to stay long enough to have another cup of coffee. "I won't even talk about business," he assured me.

There was no opportunity to talk at all, the way people kept coming in. His coffee got cold, though he tried to drink it in moments snatched between waiting on customers. Finally I left, knowing he'd been right when he said he needed help.

I was outside before I thought of the curtain material I'd come for. But I didn't go back. I saw people going in and out of the new restaurant and was surprised to realize it was after twelve. On a sudden impulse I decided I'd have lunch there. It would be a change from eating at home alone.

It was the rush hour, and I had to take a small table in the back and wait my turn to be served. It was a long, tiresome wait. Wedged in my corner, I couldn't see anybody I knew, or anything but the tops of the waitresses' heads. One of them has hair the color of Terri's, I thought idly. Then a group of people got up to leave and I saw that it was Terri.

Stunned and incredulous, I stared at her, trying to adjust my mind to what I saw. Terri, the gold digger, the selfish home wrecker, working as a waitress. It didn't make sense!

Or maybe it did, I thought, watching her smiling good-bye to the people who were leaving, seeing her pick up the tip they left. Whether she preferred this to taking care of her home and child, or whatever her reason was, Terri was taking care of herself.She hadn't seen me. She was smiling when she came to take my order, but her smile faded abruptly and she stared at me.

"There's no need to look like that," I said. "Whether you believe me or not, I didn't plan this meeting. I'm very surprised to find you working here."

Her face reddened. "Why should you be surprised?" Her voice was hard with dislike. "Did you think I was the kind who could sit and fold my hands while John killed himself with overwork, keeping his place open day and night, trying to scrape up the money to pay you and still leave enough for us to scrape by on? You're willing to make him do that, but I'm not!"

I tried to keep calm, but my hand shook with resentment. "I know how you hate it that John has to send me money," I said. "But you knew when you married him how it would be. Remember that the court decided how much he should send me. The decision was based on his earnings."

"On his earnings then!" Her voice rose, shrill with bitterness, then sank again when several people glanced at us curiously. "But that was before you turned people against him, so that a lot of them stopped giving him their business."

"That's not true," I said.

But there was no stopping her. "Believe me, he wouldn't have asked you for help if he hadn't needed it," she went on. "When you turned him down, I told him he ought to ask the court to reduce it. But he wouldn't."

"No?" I took a puff on my cigarette, and then stubbed it out. "So he sent you to work instead? You'll have to do better than that, Terri. I know John. Besides, he told me he wouldn't agree for you to leave your child."

I knew, when I saw her scared, trapped expression that I'd hit home. She wet her lips nervously. "He—he doesn't know it," she said. "You needn't look at me like that. If you think I want to leave Ron, if you think I don't worry about him. . . . But what can I do? I worry when I see him needing things, too. I was scared at first, but it's worked out fine. He's a good kid, smart, too."

She stopped suddenly. "Maybe you'll tell John," she went on, her voice defiant. "Well, I can't help it if you do. I did the best I could."

"Why should I tell him?" I stood up. "Never mind taking my order. I'm not hungry, after all."

I wondered, as I made my way out, if Terri could possibly be telling the truth. I hadn't thought of it before, but she had problems, too. However you looked at it, it was a bad situation—two women dependent on one man. Then I told myself not to be a fool. Terri had brought her troubles on herself. If the going was tougher than she'd bargained for, it wasn't my fault.

Once outside, I walked along aimlessly, caught up in my thoughts. I didn't even notice the direction I was taking until I found myself across the street from Ron's playground. I was about to turn away when I noticed a child playing with a kitten in the grassy section between the sidewalk and the busy street. It was Ron. I felt my heart pound with worry.

I started to go to him, then stopped, remembering how I'd promised myself I'd leave him alone. After I'd battled so to forget him, why should I risk being hurt again? After all, he wasn't playing in the street. He could take care of himself. His own mother said so. She wasn't worried about him, so why should I be? Why couldn't I turn my back on him and walk away?

I don't know. I like to think that God sent me there that day—made me hesitate as long as I did. I was turning to go when I heard Ron cry, "Moses, come back!" I whirled to see the kitten dart into the street, chasing the ball they'd been playing with.

35

Horrified, I tried to call to Ron to stay where he was. Even if I had, even if he'd heard me, it wouldn't have made any difference. The child's dash to rescue his pet was instinctive. Just as I acted instinctively to try to save Ron. I don't have any clear memory of what I did. I only remember the horror I felt, watching him run out in the street and snatch up his kitten, totally unaware of the car bearing down on him. . . .

I was still screaming his name—and Dougie's, too—when the dark mist of pain cleared a little and I realized I was in a hospital room. A nurse was bending over me, adjusting a tube that was attached to my arm and to a bottle suspended above my head.

"Ron?" I whispered weakly.

The nurse turned her head quickly. "The little boy's fine," she told me. "You saved him, Mrs. Meyer."

After that, she told me the bare facts—that I'd reached Ron and thrown him and his kitten clear of the car. I knew, of course, that I'd been hurt. But the nurse wouldn't answer my questions. The doctor told me later about the concussion and the two fractured ribs, and I knew about the cuts and bruises. But I was going to be all right, he told me.

Later that day Terri came to see me. Her face was swollen with crying. "I had to see you," she choked. "I've been nearly out of my mind, thinking maybe I'd never get a chance to thank you, or to ask you to forgive me for the awful things I said."

"There's nothing to forgive," I said, realizing it was true. Realizing, too, that I didn't hate Terri any more.

She went on to tell me that she'd quit her job. "From now on I won't leave Ron, no matter what happens. As John said, and Mr. Hess, too, there's no job in the world as important as taking care of him."

I must have looked puzzled, because she explained that Mr. Hess was her boss. "He's short of help, but he said I was right to quit. He was worried about Ron being alone so much. He met him one day when I got sick on the job and he brought me home. But you're not interested in all this," she broke off guiltily. "I'd better go."

"Wait," I said. "This Mr. Hess—is he stocky and middle aged? Does he drive a yellow convertible?"

She nodded, looking surprised. "How did you know? Do you know him?"

"No," I said. And before I could say any more, a nurse came in and Terri had to leave.

After she'd gone, I lay thinking about Terri and John, happy in the feeling of freedom it gave me to know I didn't hate them. I was seeing things more clearly now, realizing I'd been wrong in saying Terri stole my husband. He went willingly, perhaps because she gave him something I'd failed to give. I remembered the indulgent pride in his voice when he said she was like a child, and the critical way he'd called me self-sufficient. That should have told me a great deal. Terri was the kind of woman he wanted, and I wasn't. That was what he really meant. His need was for a woman who would look up to him.

Perhaps it was true that in my grief I'd shut him out, instead of turning to him for help. But there was no sense in telling myself that alone was the reason for the breakup of our marriage. Neither of us had cared enough to save it. John had recognized this. I was the one who'd fought it, but only because of hurt pride. And that same wounded pride had turned me into a hate-driven creature, obsessed with the desire for revenge. No wonder I'd driven my friends away!

But I hadn't, I found. I'd shut them out, but they were still there, waiting for me to want them again.

There were telephone calls, flowers, gifts, and a stream of visitors. It was wonderful to see Erin and Vincent, and to watch their delighted surprise at finding me looking so well.

"You'll get no sympathy from me," Vincent growled, pretending disgust. "You look better than when you went in, practically a new person."

"I am a new person," I said.

I knew how true it was when John came to thank me for saving Ron. It didn't hurt a bit. I could put him, and Ron, too, in their proper places at last—as Terri's husband and child. I'd loved Ron, but it had been a possessive love. I still loved him, but in a different way, wanting only his happiness.

I was touched when John told me not to worry about money. He'd take care of the bills. He said it bravely and cheerfully, but he looked so thin and tired and anxious I knew he must have been wondering how.

"I'm not worrying," I told him. "My insurance will take care of most of it, and I've saved quite a bit of the money you've sent. Actually, I've been thinking I could do on less. If the job I've been offered works out, I'll probably be able to support myself entirely."

Even though he protested, I could see the relief in his eyes, and the startled respect. It told me plainer than words what a load he'd carried.

But it was Gerald Bingam's visit that did the most for me. There was no mistaking the anxious concern in his face when he came in, or the glow of relief when he saw me sitting in a chair beside the window. He didn't mention the job that first day. He stayed only a few minutes. But he came back the next day and the next, until I began to expect him at a certain time each day. It worried me, the way I looked forward to it. I'd only be letting myself in for more heartache if I let myself become emotionally dependent on a married man.

It was the day before I left the hospital that I learned the truth about Gerald. He was talking about Reg, his six-year-old son. "He sounds adorable," I said. "I'd like to see him." Then suddenly I was telling him about Dougie, the child I'd lost.

He listened quietly, and I felt the warmth of his sympathy. "I knew you'd been hurt, too," he said. "When my wife died two years ago, I thought I couldn't go on. But I had to, because of Reg. I couldn't let him down, or my mother either. She's been caring for him."

I hope I managed to hide the surge of relief that went through me. I wasn't so immature that I believed myself in love with Gerald, but I was happy that I could continue my friendship with him with a clear conscience.

As soon as I had recovered completely, I went to work for him. The job worked out so well! It gave me a whole new interest in life, as well as an opportunity to get to know Gerald better. In the months that followed, we gained in mutual respect for one another, and then that respect changed into a wonderful growing warmth.

Finally, one weekend, Gerald asked me to meet his mother and little boy. He said his mother wanted me to come for dinner, and that Reg was getting very curious about the "nice lady" he'd heard so much about.

I was scared, but thrilled. By then I knew what Gerald meant to me, but I realized our future together depended on the success of that visit.

It couldn't have been a nicer, happier day. Mrs. Bingam and I took to each other right away, and after Reg got over his first shyness, he warmed up to me and wouldn't let me out of his sight.

After that, I visited Gerald's home often. Six months after I'd gone to work for him, he asked me to marry him, and there were no doubts or fears in my mind when I accepted him. Our love had grown slowly and surely, and I knew it was strong enough to weather any test that might be given it.

I am the most grateful woman in the world that I can write such a happy ending to my story. By now, secure in Gerald's love, I can sincerely wish John and Terri every happiness in their marriage. I want them to get along, for their own sakes as well as Ron's.

Perhaps that's the most wonderful thing Gerald has done for me—he's freed me from bitterness and the heavy burden of false pride. He's taught me that the most important things in the world are our love and the life we're going to build together.

THE END

MY HUSBAND'S MISSING!
Run away, or foul play?

Even though we had gone through it all so many times, the detective was still patient with me.

"Of course we'll keep looking, Mrs. Kerry, but perhaps the time has come to consider alternatives," he said.

I knew, though, that what he was really saying was: "Yes, we'll keep looking for your missing husband, even though we have no leads, we don't know what happened to him, and we don't think there was a robbery because there was no sign of a struggle. We'll keep looking, even though we honestly think he deserted you and the kids, and isn't it about time you faced facts?"

I wondered whether it was professional ethics that prevented him from coming right out with it, or whether he didn't want me to break down in front of him.

Whatever he thought, he was wrong! I shouldered my purse, thanked him politely, and left. I doubted I would be back again. I had been to the police for the last time. Now I would find Jim myself.

All the way home, as one part of my mind was carefully counting the baby-sitter money for Laurie, another part was hearing the words spoken by Jim's parents and my own, by his boss at work, and by most of our friends and neighbors: "Husbands skip every day of the week. So maybe he didn't leave a note. Most don't. Face it, Wendy, he's left you, so get on with your life."

But Jim didn't walk out on me. I knew as surely as I knew the sun would rise tomorrow morning that if he was able to come home, he would. If he was going to desert me, there would have been some warning, some lessening of the rapport between us—and there had not been.

I pulled into the driveway, and the kids—Bobby, Jamie, and Nicole, my youngest—came running to meet me.

"Mommy, did they find Daddy yet?" Bobby asked.

"Not yet, honey, but don't worry. He'll come home soon," I said. There was no use telling them the police were no longer trying very hard. Jim Kerry's disappearance was yesterday's problem now. There were more urgent things to occupy their time.

Laurie followed the kids out. She looked at me with one eyebrow raised in a question. I shook my head slightly, so the kids wouldn't notice, but she caught the gesture and showed her sympathy. I held out the baby-sitting money. She pushed it back at me. "Don't be silly, Wendy," she said. "You need it more than I do, and if you don't, then use it to get out and treat yourself to a movie before you break down completely."

I almost did break down, right then and there, at her kind words, but instead I scooped little Nicole into my arms and carried her into the house, taking comfort from her soft hair, so like Jim's, and her sparkly personality, also like her father's.

By the time the kids were asleep that evening, I was truly close to breaking down. Laurie was a shrewd judge of my feelings. I made a cup of coffee and wandered outside to the patio to think.

Hours later, almost the whole night later, in fact—I still could not convince myself of what almost everyone was saying. If Jim had left me, why would he call the night before his disappearance, laughing and joking as usual, ending up with the "I miss you" I looked forward to each time he called when he was out of town on business?

The people who ran the motel where he had stayed that last night agreed with me. Their faith in him had been one of the bright spots in the whole nightmare. He always stayed there when he was in that town. "He's a family man. I can tell," the manager told me. "Take a man away from his home, put him in a strange town, give him a motel room and, if he's the kind to take a little action on the side, he will. I see it all the time, and Jim Kerry never strayed. Every time he paid his bill, I could see that he was eager to be home, and it was no different that last day."

I came to the same conclusion I did every time I thought things through: Something terrible had happened to Jim. Someone had dragged him from his car in such a way that it left no evidence of force, or someone robbed him in town, left him for dead, and drove the car to its place in the country where the police finally found it by the side of the road. No, that was wrong. Jim had driven the car there himself; his fingerprints were on the steering wheel.

But what had happened? Where was he now? My head ached with it. I realized then that the first signs of morning were creeping into the black of night. The kids would be up soon. I wished for a moment that I didn't have to worry about them. Then I could go and look for Jim myself. I took back the thought as soon as it popped into my mind. If Jim was dead—and he very well could be—I would have nothing of him ever again except our children. I got up slowly, like a very old woman, and went in for a few winks of sleep before they woke me up.

During the day, something kept nagging at me. Something from that night on the patio. It couldn't be about Jim—I had merely gone around and around everything I knew. It was something else, something new, something to do with the kids. And then it hit me with the force of a blow. If anyone was going to find Jim, it was going to

40

be me! And I couldn't look for him because I had three small children to consider—unless I took them with me.

I began to tremble as an idea took shape in my mind. It had been there all along really, only I hadn't seen it until that second. Neither my parents nor Jim's would consider baby-sitting while I went on a fool's errand. Neither set of parents had approved of our marriage in the first place. They had predicted doom, and had frowned at the wedding instead of crying tears of joy. It had been their voices the police had heard when they could find no evidence of foul play. It had been their dark thoughts about our marriage that helped paint a picture of a husband who would desert his family. There would be no help there, nor would I ask. They had done damage enough.

Maybe that was why Jim and I were so close. We both knew it was the two of us together, with no one to help from either side. Consequently, we relied on each other, and eventually we developed a closeness that needed few others to sustain our life together. That was another thing. The police thought we looked like a couple having problems because we had no large circle of friends. They didn't know we didn't need lots of friends. The very few people we knew well, Laurie and her husband among them, were steadfast in the belief that Jim had not deserted me. But what were so few voices against a whole community of voices saying he ran away?

When I told Laurie of my plan, she nodded. "I'd watch the kids if I could, Wendy," she said, "but I'm a teacher and school won't be out for another week."

"Just knowing you care is something, Laurie," I assured her. "If someone didn't believe me, I'd go crazy."

"I'll keep an eye on the house," she promised. "Don't worry about a thing. I'll even field the bill collectors for you—tell them you went on a round-the-world tour."

I smiled. Trust Laurie to make a joke out of something very unfunny. Without Jim's paycheck, we were fast approaching an economic crisis. Our lawyer was the first to try to make me face what he called facts. He suggested I divorce Jim.

"You can't collect his life insurance without evidence that he's legally dead, and that's seven years down the road," he said. "The house is in both your names—everything is—and your hands are tied legally. You can't find a job that will support the kids and you and keep the house, and you can't sell anything without him here to agree to the sale.

"But if you divorce him, citing desertion, you can get the house and some other things put in your name as part of the divorce settlement, and you can sell it and find something else less expensive."

He saw the tears in my eyes, but went on mercilessly. "Face it, Mrs. Kerry. Much as you believe your husband will come back, if he doesn't return within a very few months, or if the police don't discover for sure that he's dead—" He paused for his words to take effect. "You are going to lose your home and everything you possess. You must take steps before it's too late."

Now the clock was against me, along with everything else. If I failed to find Jim or to determine that he was dead, I would have no choice but to go ahead with the lawyer's advice.

Laurie was watching me, puzzled. "Just what are you going to do, Wendy? How will you manage with the kids? Motels cost a bundle, and you can't leave them alone while you go running around."

"I'm going to sell the car and the station wagon," I told her. "The police brought the car home once they were through with it. With the money, I'm going to buy a van, one of those camping things, and we will simply move in. I'll tell the kids it's a vacation. For them, it will be. School's almost over for the year."

It was easy to trade the car and station wagon in on a camping van. The salesman knew the value of what I was trading, and he knew he was getting the best of the deal. I didn't care. I only wanted to take possession and get out of there.

We bought groceries and stocked the small larder. We went through our closets and took whatever clothes were most practical. Nothing dressy, nothing unessential. I permitted the children to take one toy apiece. The boys were pretty sulky about that, but Nicole was content with her favorite doll.

The day finally came that we were ready to leave. Three couples came to wave good-bye. Their faces were grave, concern written all over them. Laurie, evidently a spokesman of some sort, shoved something into my hand.

"Here, Wendy, this is for you," she said. "I'm sorry it's not more, but it's all we could scrape up on short notice."

I looked in my hand. Five hundred dollars lay there.

Laurie's husband took out his wallet, withdrew something, and handed it to me. Clearing his throat, he said, "It's our gasoline credit card. I wouldn't feel right, knowing you and the kids might be stranded somewhere, maybe in trouble, and with no way to keep going. Use it, and don't worry about paying us back. If you can someday, fine—if not, that's all right, too."

I wanted to say no to everything they were doing. It wasn't their problem. It wasn't their crazy idea. But, looking at that money and the credit card nestled in my hand, I felt a terrible fear and knew for the first time just what an enormous task I had set for myself. The money seemed to shrink before my eyes, and the size of my search grew. I shoved it all in my purse and hugged them each in turn. Then the kids and I climbed into the van and we pulled out.

We went to the motel first, for that was the last place Jim had been known to talk to anyone. I sighed. I knew what would happen because I had talked to the manager and his wife before. They were sympathetic, they believed me, but there was only so much that they knew. But I went there anyway, because I could think of no place else to start.

They were no help, other than being supportive of what I was doing. "I always said he didn't skip. He wasn't the type. I hope you find him, dear," the woman told me. Her eyes said she didn't think I would. Why should I, when the police couldn't?

Nevertheless, we stayed two days, more to get used to living in the van than for any other reason. There was a small campground not far from the motel, and we stayed there. The kids got to know the owners of the motel, who always had cookies in a huge jar for the children of their guests, and they helped themselves liberally. The last night we were treated to dinner at their house. I wondered if it would be the last good meal we would have, for the tiny stove in the camper was adequate only for the bare necessities, and no way could our funds stretch to cover meals in restaurants.

Then we cruised over the road Jim usually drove coming home. It was strange. It was as if Jim was there beside me, pointing out all the landmarks in this road he knew so well from many business trips, but that I had never seen before. It was because I knew Jim so well, of course, that I could see through his eyes, hear what he would say, know what he would comment about the passing scenery. I felt comforted, and surer than ever that he was alive.

It was a busy highway, though there were times when ours was the only car in sight. I realized it would not have been hard for someone to overcome Jim without witnesses, but it would have to be quick. I shook my head. That was foolish thinking so I stopped, but then realized it wasn't foolish at all—it was why I was here, to think about Jim, to think like him, to see more than the police had seen. I saw now that something could have happened to him. The police had said otherwise. In broad daylight, on a busy highway, they had said it was impossible. They were wrong. Unlikely, yes. Impossible, no.

We reached the spot where the car had been found. I pulled over, but soon had to continue on because of the press of traffic. Jim's car had been pulled off completely. The police thought it proof that he had abandoned it. Perhaps he had simply known the traffic patterns of the highway and pulled so far over to avoid being rear-ended.

There was a roadside rest area a little way up, still within sight of the place, and I pulled in there. The kids got out and stretched and took out their toys to play.

It wasn't a big rest area, just a couple of picnic tables, a cabin housing restrooms and a place to fill a bottle with water. We were the only people there. I defined an area where the kids could play, then brought one of the folding chairs from the top of the van, one of the few luxuries I had indulged in on the advice of some camper friends. I now appreciated it because I could sit there, sipping clear, cold water, and think—except nothing came to me except the rhythmic, almost hypnotic noise of the passing traffic.

Had Jim ever stopped here, I wondered, during his frequent trips? I decided not. He would be in too much of a hurry to get home to want to stop at all. I knew that about him. Glancing at the children, I knew it even more surely. Even if Jim and I had had a problem, he would have come home to his children. If there had been some need in him to get away from me, he would have arranged it in such a way that he could still see them, for they were so important to him. No, I was now more convinced than ever that Jim had not deserted us. He was either in trouble—or he was dead.

I watched the cars passing, the trucks, the campers like mine, all the stream of traffic. One large truck pulled into the rest stop and the driver got out and stretched. "Mind if I join you?" he called. "Got to take a break once in a while, and it gets pretty lonely on the road."

I motioned to him to sit, and he lowered himself onto a nearby bench. "Nice day."

I agreed that it was, and there didn't seem to be much more to say. He watched the kids playing. "They yours?"

"Yes."

"Nice-looking kids. I have three of my own."

"Do you miss them when you're driving?" I asked.

He nodded. "I miss them like crazy, but a guy's got to make a living."

Like Jim, I thought, who never wanted to leave, but had a job that required it.

We sat in companionable silence after that, until the trucker finished his can of soda and tossed it into the trashcan. "Well, I've got to get to the city," he said. "Got to unload this truck early tomorrow morning, and I don't want to drive all night, so I'd better get cracking."

A spark of curiosity was lit in me. "Is that where you're headed?"

He laughed as he got up. "Lady, you must not be from around here or you'd know that everyone on this highway is headed there. This isn't the East, you know, where everything is built up. Out here, where else is there for all those cars and trucks to be headed except to the city? And that's a good two hundred miles from here, and I'd better get going. Nice talking to you."

I watched the traffic closer after that. He was right. The majority of cars and trucks were on the same side of the highway as I was, and they were all headed the same way the truck was. The other side of the highway was almost empty. Something struck a chord. The police had not found Jim, or his body, or anything to tell what had happened. Perhaps it was because they looked in the wrong place. They didn't extend their search to the city.

That thought led to others. Why hadn't Jim stopped in this rest area instead of on the side of the road as he had done? Because his way was blocked and he had no choice? Because he stopped to help someone stalled by the side of the road? Jim was always helping stalled motorists, a repayment for the times he had been helped himself. Could he have stopped one time too many—have chosen someone laying a trap for an unwary driver? And would they have been in a hurry to complete whatever it was they had in mind, anxious to get their victim out of sight before another car came along?

If all my suppositions were correct, where would they have taken him? Where would they have finally disposed of him, or of his body? I got up and put the folding chair back on the top of the van. I knew now where our next stop would be. We would follow that truck and all the other cars and trucks to the city.

The kids were more than ready to leave. They were tired of playing. I had not told them about their father's car being found nearby. The road had no meaning for them at all. They crawled into the back and soon fell asleep with the drone of the tires and the late afternoon sun bouncing off the windows of the van. I was glad. I needed the time to think, to plan.

What do you do when you're looking for a needle in a haystack and you can't even be sure you have the right haystack? It was a large city. When we reached the outskirts of the city hours later, with darkness hanging over everything, it was all I could do to find a place to camp, let alone think ahead to tomorrow's work.

"You going to stay long?" the campground manager asked.

I hesitated. "I don't know. It depends—"

"You want the spot by the day or the week?" he cut in.

Something made me take it by the week. It was cheaper, and I doubted we could cover an entire city in less time than that.

I started with the hospitals the next day. The local police had contacted police departments in all the neighboring states, so it would only be wasted time to talk to them. But the hospitals hadn't had anyone by that name, or anyone who looked like Jim about the time he disappeared.

I went back a second time after remembering something. About three weeks after Jim's disappearance, some of his traveler's checks were cashed. I swore the handwriting on them wasn't his, but the police didn't think it meant anything. In their eyes, it pointed still more strongly to the possibility that he had deserted me. He left all his clothes, his suitcases, everything that would remind him of his old life in the car, but he remembered to take his money.

The checks had been cashed in the city. Someone had communicated with Jim in order to have those checks. But the hospitals were no more helpful the second time. The people I spoke to were patient and careful and looked like they were concerned, but I was sure they thought I was crazy.

I started in on the hotels, motels, and campgrounds—every sort of place I could think of that a person might stay. If he was in the city, he had to sleep somewhere. As I went from place to place I tried to think of some reason Jim might have left us. Then I realized what I was doing—agreeing with everyone else—and I stopped thinking at all and simply became like a robot ferreting out facts. Only there were no facts to find. Jim had vanished off the face of the earth as surely as if he had never existed at all.

"Mommy, this isn't a fun vacation," Jamie complained.

"He's right," Bobby chimed in. "You said we were going to do things, go to nice places. All we've done is ride around and wait in the van while you go talk to a bunch of people."

"When are we going to do something we want to do?" Jamie asked.

I sighed. The kids were right, and I didn't blame them for their rebellion. "Okay, you have a point," I said. "I guess it has been my vacation more than yours. Let's take tomorrow to do what you want. Where do you want to go? Any ideas?"

Oh, did they have ideas! I didn't realize how much they had noticed of the city as I drove around. They wanted to see the zoo, the arcades, the park, and everything else all at the same time.

"Whoa! We can't fit all that into one day," I said. "What say we start with the park? We can have a picnic lunch there with ice cream for dessert, and then go through the zoo in the afternoon. It's only across the street from the park."

That plan seemed to satisfy them, so the next morning we set off. Their cheerful voices told me I was right to take this precious time for them. After all, what would Jim's and my marriage mean if our children learned only unhappiness?

The children ran and chased each other through the wide open spaces of the park while I sunned myself on a blanket spread on the grass. As the sun crawled slowly across the sky I began noticing things—the police, strolling inconspicuously along the paths, elderly people on benches, the joggers, the lovers—and my heart turned over at the memory of Jim and me in just such a role. And there were the poor people of the city—the men in torn jackets and shabby hats, some of them with a small bottle sticking from a back pocket, and the ones who looked lost, without hope. Vacant, unhappy eyes in surprisingly young faces.

As the day wound to a close and the last zoo animal was tucked away for the night, we walked back through the park to where the van was parked. The people were almost all gone, I noticed, the last few homeless men hurrying away. Where did they go? The police were watching them seemingly casually, but making sure they didn't stay for the night. I shivered. A park at night could be a dangerous place for them as well as for me, even though its lushness must be inviting to a homeless man.

Where did all those lonely men go? The answer to that question was suddenly very important. There must be places for people like them to sleep, to eat. Places for people with no money. Jim would not have money if he were still alive. Even if he had left willingly, his money would have run out long ago, and it was difficult to find jobs. How could he survive? Suddenly, I had to know the answer to that question.

I made sure the boys were safe in the van then, with Nicole clinging to me, I stopped one of the policemen. "Excuse me," I said.

He looked at me politely.

"I was wondering—I know it sounds crazy," I stammered, "but I've been watching all day, and I just wondered where all those men go at night. The—the ones who look like they don't have any home—"

The policeman shrugged. "Some of them sleep in alleys."

"What about the rest? What other place is there for them to go?"

The policeman was very patient. "A lot of them get taken in by the church missions, soup kitchens, halfway houses. There are a number of places like that—in what you might call the slum district of the city. Those men come here during the day to get away from that area, but at night they have to go back."

I nodded. "I just wondered. Thanks," I said.

"Most people don't even see them," the policeman said, sounding almost embarrassed by his obvious concern. "It's like they're invisible. . . ."

He was right. If I hadn't been sitting waiting for the kids, I would not have noticed them, either. A chance, a coincidence, had made them become visible at just the time when I was becoming discouraged, at a dead end. Now I had somewhere else to look. I would look in a part of the city I had ignored before.

The very first place we went the next morning, I met Reverend Hayes. He was old enough to be my grandfather and one of the hardest-working men I had ever met with enough love to encompass all the destitute people who came through his place every day and still have plenty left over for the kids and me.

"It's quite a task you've set for yourself," he said after I'd told him my story. "It's not really safe for a woman and three children to wander around here, even in the middle of the day."

"I know, but I'm going to look every place I can," I said.

He waved his hand. "I know that, and I commend your courage, but it's still dangerous. I was just thinking that maybe I can help. There are women here who can watch your children while I take you around. I know the area well. You don't. We can probably accomplish in a day or two what it would take weeks to do by yourself."

I sagged as some of the burden I was carrying was lifted from me by his kindness. Tears were becoming so frequent lately!

The kids were more than happy to be the center of attention of a group of middle-aged women in the mission, and our van was soon parked safely in back where they could keep an eye on it. Reverend Hayes and I set out to check every dive and beer joint in the district.

By the end of that first day, I was discouraged as well as thoroughly depressed from the sight of so much human unhappiness. Reverend Hayes was sympathetic. "I'm used to it, Wendy, but I know you aren't, and you are under a tremendous strain. Maybe tomorrow. . . ."

When we arrived early the next morning, we set off as soon as the kids were settled and the van was parked once again in its safe place. We talked to a lot of people, saw a lot of empty alleys, looked into too many blank eyes.

It was almost noon when Reverend Hayes suggested we break for lunch. "There's one more place near here," he said. "I know the people who run it. They serve lunch, which most places don't. Maybe we can beg a meal."

"All right, but then let's go back," I said. "I don't think I can take any more of this, and it isn't doing any good. No one we talked to has even a remote idea about Jim. Maybe it was a wild goose chase, after all."

He nodded. "I understand. After this place, we'll go back, but now everyone knows to watch for your husband, and that's something."

It was a place where men came and went on a daily basis. There were beds, there was food, and there were no questions asked. First come, first served. The man in charge was doubtful when we told him why we were there.

"I'm afraid we can't be of much help," he said. "We don't know the people who come through here. Some wouldn't come if we got too nosy. But feel free to look around. It's the wrong time of day, though. We empty out pretty much during the day. In a few hours, you'll see more people around."

48

It was with a sinking feeling that I made my way to the kitchen. From there, I could glance through the door and see men at the tables, eating.

And there he was! At first, for a few heart-stopping moments, I could not believe it was really Jim. I almost didn't recognize him. He had changed so much since I last saw him. His hair was long and there were the shaggy beginnings of a beard. It looked like it had been cut, then let go again, as if he despaired of ever keeping it neat. But it was Jim—my Jim, my husband!

I went to him, forgetting Reverend Hayes, forgetting where I was, and forgetting everything except that my search was over. I walked quietly, carefully. I don't know why, except that after such a long time, after not knowing whether I would ever see him again, I was afraid in some part of me that he might vanish before my eyes if I made any noise, or he'd run if I spoke. Then I gathered my courage.

"Jim," I said.

He didn't look at me. His eyes were blank.

"Jim. It's me, Wendy!" Something was terribly wrong. There was no recognition in his eyes. There was no love, no hate, nothing at all. He shifted uneasily in his seat, looked around at the others in the room, then back at me.

"I'm not angry with you, Jim. I just want to know why. Why did you go? Why did you leave me?" I asked.

He reached for a roll and chewed thoroughly before answering. His eyes were just as blank as before. "I'm sorry, lady, but I don't know you," he said.

The sun was filtering in, the world was still turning, but Jim—my Jim—was sitting there saying he wasn't my Jim.

Could I be wrong? Could I have made some terrible mistake? I peered closer and knew this stranger was my husband.

Amnesia? I had heard of it. Could that be the answer? Jim's eyes were truly empty, not evasive as if he didn't want to face the wife he had left. We stared at each other carefully over the aluminum dinner plate, and there seemed to be nothing to say. He finished his meal. I was afraid he would take the plate and hand it politely to the cleaning woman and just as politely walk out of my life. I couldn't let that happen!

I sat beside him. He moved slightly away from me. He was alert, like a hunted rabbit, but he stayed where he was. I had to be very careful. "I know you. You are Jim Kerry," I said.

He was listening, but trying to appear as if he wasn't. He was waiting for something. I plunged ahead. "You are my husband."

He shrank away and looked nervously over his shoulder. "Lady, I don't know you." He got up. He was leaving!

49

I reached out, touched his sleeve, held him back. He couldn't go now, not after all I had been through! "Please!" I exclaimed.

He didn't like the attention we were attracting. He sank back onto the bench.

"Please come into the back room and hear what I have to say," I begged him. "That's all, nothing more, just listen—please." It was an eternity before he moved, then he nodded, and I was able to breathe again.

In the back room, in the presence of Reverend Hayes and the man from the mission, I talked to Jim. Only it wasn't Jim, it was a stranger—a person I didn't know and who didn't know me, who didn't know anything at all except that he could get three meals a day and a place to sleep if he came to this address every day at the right times.

"Don't you want to know about yourself?" I asked.

He nodded. He was unable to answer any questions as to who he was and where he came from. He was afraid of us, but he could not manufacture a past to explain himself. He admitted he had amnesia. "But I don't think I'm the man you say," he muttered. "I don't know you at all."

I looked at Reverend Hayes for help and he said, "It's obvious you need help, whoever you are."

Jim nodded, watching Reverend Hayes like he wouldn't watch me. It was easier for him to talk to the minister than to me. It hurt, but I tried to accept that I frightened him, while Reverend Hayes belonged in his new life.

"What do you know, Jim?" Reverend Hayes was deliberately using his name, I was sure, trying to establish some link with us.

"Nothing. One day I woke up in an alley," Jim said. "I had bruises all over me. The sky was bright. It hurt my eyes. I was cold. I've been here ever since."

Reverend Hayes nodded. "He was probably beaten," he murmured to me. "Beaten and robbed and dumped in the alley by the men who waylaid his car." He took my arm. "It seems to me we need two things right now. To get Jim clean and into some better clothes, and we need a doctor, someone who knows a lot more about amnesia than any of us."

"Can we go back to the mission? The children are there. They'll want to see their father," I said.

Jim cringed and backed away. I could have bitten my tongue. Jim, who loved kids so much, would not know his own children, not if he had no memory of ever having them. What a terrible thing those people had done to him!

Reverend Hayes smoothed things over sensing Jim's sudden fear.

"Maybe that's not such a good idea right away, Wendy. Give him a little time to get his bearings. A little rest, a checkup, then there's time enough to think of other things."

Jim relaxed. They took him away to clean him up, and later he was admitted to a hospital for a thorough exam. It gave me time to think.

Reverend Hayes and a psychiatrist talked to me privately at the hospital. The kids were in a waiting room, promising to be good. I crossed my fingers. Their patience was wearing thin, and they didn't know we had found their daddy. It would be cruel to tell them so, then turn around and say they couldn't see him.

"Can you get someone to take care of the children for a while?" the psychiatrist asked. "Jim should only have to deal with one thing at a time. He didn't know he had a wife. That's enough for now, to get used to being married, without trying to be a father to three children too young to understand what happened."

I said cautiously, "Maybe I know someone. I have a neighbor who might manage. She's a teacher, and she's on vacation now."

Laurie was almost hysterical when I called, but when she finally took in all that I told her, she came through like a trooper. "Of course we'll take the kids," she said. "We'll be there as soon as we can make it, and don't worry about a thing. You always said Jim would come home to you, and now you must believe that his memory will come back. Have faith, Wendy. God would not have let you find Jim if he wasn't going to be all right eventually."

How many coincidences had led me here? Maybe Laurie was right. I hung up the phone and cried a little, and then I wiped the tears away and got the kids ready. They were more than happy to be finished with this strange vacation, and Laurie was like a second mother. I wouldn't have to worry about them. I could concentrate on Jim.

Reverend Hayes arranged for Jim and me to use a cabin owned by a friend of his, a place he went sometimes when he needed to get away and think. We drove the van there, Jim beside me, immersed in his own thoughts, lost to me as completely as if he was in another world. Would he ever return? Would the Jim who married me ever find his way home?

"Are the children nice?" he'd ask sometimes during our stay at the cabin. Not "our" children. Just children in a neutral sense, belonging to someone else, or to no one at all.

I tried to jog his memory. "Do you remember the vacation we took to the mountains one year?" I asked. All I got in return was a polite, remote stare, but no comment because that vacation was lost to him.

51

Finally, after a week, I broached the subject of going home. I could no longer stand the isolation. "Jim, would you like to go home? The doctor said you are in good health now, and your memory might return sooner in familiar surroundings."

There was uneasiness at my words, nervousness in the twisting of his hands, but eventually an answer. "I guess so," he said. No enthusiasm, but an answer.

We called Reverend Hayes and told him we were going home. He probably thought things were going splendidly since we'd made such a decision. The psychiatrist who stopped by occasionally knew there had been no progress at all, but she was optimistic. It would only be a matter of time. Jim's agreement to go home at all was a step in the right direction, she pointed out. I wasn't so sure. It was merely a lack of anything else to do, a gesture of defeat on his part.

I called Laurie and told her the situation. She understood. "Don't worry about a thing, Wendy," she said. "I'll make sure the kids aren't around when you get here. We'll make more plans for them than you can imagine. We'll keep them so busy they won't realize there's anyone living in your house. That'll give you two a little time before they come dive-bombing in on you."

"Thanks, Laurie. You'll never know how much you've meant to me," I said.

"Brace yourself, kid. It's not over yet. But now you can see the light at the end of the tunnel," she told me.

Jim prowled about the house restlessly when we got home. He touched things, then took his hands away without actually lifting anything from its place, the way someone might do in a museum, admiring things in an impersonal way.

"It's a pretty house," he said.

"We chose most of the things together. I suppose you don't remember," I said.

He said nothing, just paused at a wall where we had framed pictures of all of us—the kids, the important and some of the not-so-important events in our lives. His eyes went to a picture of him laughing, a fishing rod in one hand. "That's me." He sounded surprised, as if he didn't really believe he was Jim Kerry until that moment.

He peered closer to see the pictures of the kids. I backed away, giving him this moment to reacquaint himself with them. "I'll be in the kitchen. You look around all you want," I said gently. But I listened for footsteps and I watched from the corner of my eye for his shadow to move away from that picture gallery and it stayed. Something about the pictures held him captive, but when he came in the kitchen later, there was no smile of recognition. Nothing. Just that same polite, blank stare of one stranger accepting another stranger's hospitality.

The kids didn't realize we were home. True to her word, Laurie and her husband must have kept them hopping for we didn't even hear their voices in the yard next door. Jim spent much time on the patio, as if afraid to venture farther and expose himself to the world. It was completely screened, surrounded by the fences and plants we had chosen so carefully to give us privacy in the close-knit world of our neighborhood.

After several days, however, Laurie must have run out of places to take the kids. I heard them playing beyond the patio. The boys were teasing Nicole, as usual, sailing their Frisbee over her head, leading her on a wild goose chase, never letting her catch it. I could hear the aggravation in her voice.

"You dumb old boys. You think you're so smart. Well, I have my own Frisbee, and I can play with it if I want to."

"No, you can't. It's at home, and the house is locked," Jamie said.

"I don't care. I'm getting it," she said.

Jim paid no attention to her pattering footsteps. He wouldn't know it was his daughter who had spoken the words that drifted over the fence.

Nicole rounded the corner and her footsteps stopped as she caught sight of us. "Mommy, you did come home! You left us alone with Laurie." Her voice was accusing. Then her gaze went to her father. She said nothing, and the two of them looked at each other for a long time, and then she went to him as naturally as only a little child could and raised her arms to be lifted up. I held my breath. "Hi, Daddy. You were gone a long time," she said.

I shouldn't have worried. I should have realized that even if Jim didn't know his own daughter, nothing could erase that love of children—all children—that he had. He scooped her up and smiled uncertainly as she nestled contentedly in his arms for a few moments, then struggled to get down. "I want my Frisbee. Will you get it?"

Jim looked at me uneasily, and then fielded the question. "I'm tired. You get it." It was the sort of thing any father might say to his child, or to any child at all.

Nicole returned a few moments later with it and went back to play in the yard. She never mentioned seeing her father. In her little-girl mind, he had merely been on a trip and he went on trips all the time. The boys never realized Jim was home.

But Nicole refused to sleep in Laurie's house that night. Laurie brought her over apologetically. "I'm sorry, Wendy, but if I made a fuss about it, she d spill the beans and the whole wide world would know Jim is back."

It was bedtime. We tucked her in together, Jim and I, in the old way, the way we always had when he had been home. She insisted on it, telling us in advance each and every detail, from Jim's reading her a story, to brushing her teeth, to tucking her favorite doll in beside her so she could listen, too. Jim played along. He often turned puzzled eyes to her, but there was still no recognition.

I tossed and turned that night, tormented and disturbed. Jim was in the room next to mine. Obviously, he still could not accept sharing a bedroom.

It was late when I finally gave up trying to sleep. I slipped from my bed and wandered about the house. My aimless footsteps eventually led me to Nicole's room. Jim was there, gazing down at her. He didn't know I was there, and I pulled back into the shadows. I watched as he touched her forehead, stroking a wisp of hair away from her closed eyes.

Then he bent over her quickly, a sudden frown crossing his forehead, and he peered closely. Something was wrong! I was suddenly scared.

He placed his hand on her forehead, and then I saw her face and the unmistakable signs of illness. She was hot, sweaty, and there was an ominous redness about her skin that hadn't been there only a few short hours before. I panicked and was about to run to her when she opened her eyes and looked at Jim.

"Daddy, I don't feel good," she murmured.

"I'll get you some water," he said.

He moved, and I pulled myself back into the shadows again. He brought her the water, and she gulped it thirstily. He took the glass then and I came into the room. I could no longer remain a spectator if Nicole might be ill.

"What's the matter, Jim? What's wrong with her?" I asked.

He looked at me, not like a stranger at all, but as someone to help him. "I don't know, but she feels so hot."

We turned together to stare at our daughter. Something was truly wrong and it had come upon her so suddenly. "Maybe we should take her to the emergency room. Oh, Jim, if anything happens to her, I don't think I'll be able to stand it," I said.

I never was good in a crisis, always depending on Jim to carry me through. Now his voice crackled with authority. "It's not necessary yet. She's not all that sick." Then he turned sternly to Nicole, looking just like the Jim I knew and loved. "What did you have to eat yesterday, young lady? Have you had any strawberries?"

Of course! Nicole was terribly allergic to strawberries, and the smallest serving would give just such a flush to her face and make her terribly sick. Her head went down, only her eyes peeping at him in utter despair. She knew she wasn't supposed to eat strawberries. "Only a little bit in the ice cream," she said.

Without a word, I ran to the medicine cabinet where we kept the prescription for just such an emergency, and soon a dose was inside her. We waited, not saying anything, not looking at each other, until the fever finally disappeared and the rashlike flush began to slowly recede and she slept.

Shadows grew and time lengthened to something that had no meaning as we stood there. I made the first move.

"Jim?"

"Yes?"

"You knew about Nicole's allergy. You remembered. I forgot, but you remembered," I said.

The clock ticked long seconds before he said anything, but when he did I could hear clearly the agony of a man whose life has been torn from him and who is looking desperately for all those stolen yesterdays. I heard Jim—my Jim—say, "That's all I remember. Just that one thing! Nothing more, nothing at all! Why? Why can't I remember?"

"It will come, Jim. The rest will come. I know that now," I said.

He took a ragged breath, then turned to me in a sudden desperate hope that his next words might be the truth. "She gets sick easily, doesn't she? She gets sick a lot. There have been other nights like this one, haven't there?"

He was asking, begging me to tell him he truly remembered those other nights that he wasn't guessing about them. "Yes, she does!" I cried. "We used to joke about the way she never gets sick except in the middle of the night!"

I put my face in my hands and began to weep because the memories were still there and he wanted those memories now. He was not yet Jim, not completely, but he was not that stranger, either. He would make the long trip back to us, to me, and to my love. He would have his yesterdays again—all of them—and we would have tomorrow.

Slowly but surely, the more time Jim spent in the house—touching, seeing, and being so close to the things and people he'd loved—his memory returned to him. Each day seemed to bring a new recollection, and sometimes he'd come to me like a young boy excited by a new discovery.

There are still times, even now, that Jim hesitates when someone asks him a question. He'll get a troubled look in his eyes for a second, but then he's all right. I just hold him closer after those times, reassuring him that my love for him will always be there—the love I've always had for my Jim, my husband.

THE END

55

EVERY WOMAN'S DESIRE

The first time I met Rudy Sherwin, I felt sorry for him. I was late for work at the Nolan Wholesale Company—where I'm a secretary—because I had stopped by Rudy's Repairs, his machine repair shop, to see about a broken computer that had been left there. Belinda, one of the new clerks at my office, had taken the firm's machine there and had been unable to retrieve it.

"If I don't get the computer back, Mrs. Harlan said she's going to fire me," Belinda wailed to me after work yesterday. "But every time I go there, the place is closed or the owner tap dances around the date it'll be ready. Will you march in there and demand it back, Jen?"

I'm hardly the marching or demanding type, but I told her I'd give it a try. I figured I'd explain the situation, insist upon the computer's return, and if it was still broken, simply take it to another repair shop.

That was easier said than done. The first thing that met my eyes as the door closed behind me was this rugged-looking guy, surrounded by computers and other electronic equipment, sitting at his desk feeding a baby. His eyes swept over me with a harried, tired look.

"I can tell from your face that I've got another disgruntled customer," he said. "What can I do for you?"

He stuck a pacifier in the baby's mouth, strapped her into an infant seat, and then strolled over to me. I couldn't quite hide my smile when I noticed he had a spot of baby food on his shirt.

"I need my company's computer back," I said.

He ran a hand through his hair and studied me. "Any chance you could give me a break? I've been through a rough time the last couple of months—a personal problem—and I'm behind on everything."

"Could you promise it to me by five?"

He groaned. "I'd love to, but every time I get going on something, the baby cries or wants attention. You see, my wife—oh, forget it." He looked irritated and began searching through his inventory for the claim number I showed him. The phone rang and the baby began to cry. He gave me a pleading look. "Could you take care of her while I get the phone?"

Why not? I thought, and slipped behind the counter and picked the baby up.

"Her name's Lauren," he called. "Mine's Rudy."

"Hello, Lauren," I said, settling her into my arms. She couldn't have been more than two months old.

"Support her head," Rudy admonished, and I did so awkwardly. I'm not exactly great with kids since I've never been around any. Lauren must have sensed it because she kept screaming at the top of her lungs.

"Here, let me show you," Rudy said, hanging up the phone and coming over to where I was struggling with the squirming baby. Lauren went into her father's arms with a sob that turned into a hiccup as he began jiggling her around. "You learn the knack after a while," he said.

"Where's her mother?" I asked. I regretted the question the moment it left my lips. It wasn't any of my business.

Rudy stopped bouncing the baby and stared at me. "She left some time ago." His mouth straightened into an angry line.

"I'm sorry," I said quickly.

"Don't be. It was the best thing that ever happened to me." He began looking for my claim slip again, rocking the baby in his arm as he did so.

"Don't you have a relative or anyone who can help?" I asked. It was obvious from the mess that things weren't going too smoothly.

"I had a babysitter until last week, but I haven't been able to replace her. I've been trying to take care of Lauren and run the shop, too. I had an assistant until a few days ago. I found him overcharging on the work and pocketing the extra cash. I had to let him go." He sighed and shook his head. "It's not easy being a single parent."

Maybe it was simply that he looked so tired and beat, but suddenly I said, "I can come back at noon and take care of Lauren while you work on my computer."

"Would you?" he asked. "That's the nicest offer I've had in a long time."

"I'll be glad to do it," I said, heading for the door.

"Hey, what's your name?" Rudy called.

"Jennifer—Jen," I replied.

Belinda, her face tight with worry, cornered me the moment I walked into the office. "Did you get it? Mrs. Harlan has already been on my tail about it this morning."

"I'll get it at noon," I said.

Belinda smiled. "Thanks," she said. "I tried to cover for you, but I think Mrs. Harlan noticed you were late."

It was my turn to smile now. I wasn't too worried. When you've worked for a company for ten years, they'll hardly let you go because you're late one morning out of many. Still, Mrs. Harlan, the office supervisor, called it to my attention when she marched through with a batch of reports. "It's not a good example for the younger girls," she said.

"It couldn't be helped," I replied. I turned back to my typing slightly annoyed—not because she'd taken me to task for my lateness, I deserved that—it was the dig about my age.

"What's the matter?" my friend Denise asked later on our coffee break.

"Mrs. Harlan was giving me a hard time," I answered. Denise was so pretty, I could hardly believe she'd never been married. It was a whole different ball game with me.

"How about going to Wilco's with Dara and me tonight?" Denise asked. "There's going to be a country-western band, and they're offering a special on steak sandwiches."

Wilco's was a bar down the road and it was usually packed on Friday nights. "I can't," I replied. "I didn't have a very good time there last time." I stirred some cream into my coffee.

"It didn't have to be that way." Denise studied me. "You acted too uptight, too cautious. You frightened away half the guys that sat down at our table." Her warm smile took the sting from her words.

I took a swallow of coffee. "I couldn't help it. I came across like I always do. Whenever I meet a guy there, my tongue trips over my words and I feel like the village idiot." I shrugged. "I can't help but think he's simply looking me over for a tumble into bed."

Denise laughed. "Maybe he is, but would that be so terrible? You know, at our age we can't afford to save ourselves for some miracle that may never happen."

"You have a point," I replied. "I just don't feel comfortable at Wilco's. It isn't my style."

"It wasn't mine either, until I realized the guys weren't exactly beating my door down and I wasn't getting any younger. I decided it was more important to connect with someone even for a night or two than not at all."

A defensive tone crept into her voice. I understood the loneliness and restlessness that drove her back to Wilco's time and again—I'd felt it myself many times. "It's okay for you, Denise," I reassured her. "I just can't get into the bar routine."

"Is it because of your looks? If you'd get your hair styled and wear more makeup, you could improve your appearance a hundred percent." She was talking fast, cramming the words in quickly because she was afraid of hurting my feelings.

I smiled, trying to relieve her of guilt. "It's not my appearance, Denise. I've been unattractive all my life. I can handle that. I don't need some guy drooling all over me to make me feel like a worthwhile person, honest."

"So why not give Wilco's one more chance?" Denise persisted. "Sometimes if you risk, you gain. Besides, you don't want to spend your birthday alone, do you?"

I shook my head. Today was my thirtieth birthday. Dirty thirty, I thought, when you're unmarried and haven't had a date in two years. But I knew Wilco's would only make me feel worse. I'd falter through all those awkward conversations, or try to look more appealing than I was, knowing most of those guys were only looking for a one-night stand.

I sighed. "Wilco's is out, but we can get together tomorrow and celebrate."

"Okay," Denise replied, "but if you change your mind, call me."

"Sure," I said, knowing I wouldn't.

Back in the office, I began stacking folders to file. I did it automatically, thinking over Denise's words. Maybe I was too cautious. Maybe I did scare guys away. But I wanted something more than a quick affair. I might be plain Jennifer Lisa Gordon, but I still clung to my pride and my dreams. I wanted to get married to some nice guy, have a couple of kids, and make a home for the people I loved.

I'd come from a loving family myself. My parents had married late in life, but they'd welcomed me with open arms even though Mom was forty-five and Dad was fifty-three at the time of my birth. I'd always felt a little different when I was growing up because my parents were as old as most kids' grandparents. Maybe that's one reason I had so much trouble talking to people my own age. Even so, my childhood had been full of sugar cookies and warm hugs, so it was only natural I would want moments like those with a family of my own.

That urge for a family had gotten stronger in the last year since both my parents had died. Mom passed away from a heart attack and Dad followed six months later. I really felt sad and lonely without them, even though they had both lived good, long lives. How I longed to be married and wrapped up in a family of my own! Even that screaming baby I'd held this morning had felt wonderful in my arms. I could hardly wait to pick her up again and cuddle her.

You don't lose those desires simply because you don't look like a beauty queen. What I had told Denise about my appearance and being able to handle it wasn't really true. Even her comments, made with the best intentions, hurt.

"Pretty is as pretty does," my mother used to say when I'd voice doubts or unhappiness about my looks. So, like so many plain girls, I concentrated on learning to be pretty in other ways. I was always the one that volunteered to paint the sets for the school play, take over a baby-sitting chore so my friend could go to the prom, or I'd type the notes for the student council.

Oh, growing up had been hard. For a moment, an ache crept

into my throat as I remembered all the humiliation that came with being plain: the team games where I was always the last chosen, the dances where I sat against the wall with a bright smile pasted on my face while I prayed for one boy to ask me to dance, the weddings I'd attended as the bridesmaid and never the bride.

No, I didn't need a man to drool over me or even fill my head with delicious compliments. I simply needed one to put his arms around me and say he loved me for the kind of person I was and not for the face I presented to the world. You certainly didn't meet that kind of man at Wilco's, but the thought didn't make me feel any better as I went about my office duties that morning.

Rudy Sherwin met me with a finger to his lips when I showed up at his shop at noon. "I've got Lauren sleeping," he said, "and I've almost got your computer fixed. Why don't you have a seat? I should be done in about fifteen minutes."

I looked around at the terrible clutter of the office and shook my head. "Listen, I'm a trained secretary, and if you'll give me a sketch of your invoice and filing system, maybe I can make some sense of it."

"Would you? That would be terrific," he said. He briefly described how he ran the business part of his shop.

I thought the task would be a fairly simple operation, but I'd barely skimmed the surface by the time I had to leave.

"I can't take a chance on being late twice in one day." I told him. "You can send the repair bill to my firm."

He wrote down the name and address. "I'd really like to repay you for all your help today," he began. "Unfortunately, when my wife left, she took off with all the cash assets, so how about dinner at my house tonight?"

"You don't owe me anything." I was suddenly conscious that, underneath the sadness and worry in his face, there was an attractive man.

"It's not such a great deal," he said. "Lauren will be there adding her voice to the merriment, and if you don't come I'll probably settle for another bologna sandwich. You don't want to be responsible for my malnourishment, do you?"

I laughed. "Heaven forbid! I'll be there. What time?"

What did I have to lose? At home, all that waited for me was a lonely meal in front of the television. Instead, I could be with Rudy and Lauren, pretending that I was like all the other girls in the world who were pretty enough to attract someone like Rudy. What if he was asking me to come for dinner because he felt he owed me something? For once I'd take Denise's advice and throw caution to the wind. I'd have this one evening with Rudy and pretend I was an ordinary girl on a date.

I didn't regret it a bit as I helped Rudy feed Lauren, give her a bath, and then tuck her into bed. "She really is a darling baby," I said as we tiptoed out of her room. "I just can't understand how her mother could leave her."

Rudy turned around and studied me for a moment. "It's a long story. Maybe we'll get to it tonight. In the meantime, I think I smell the meat loaf. It should be almost done."

He hurried to the kitchen, settled me on a stool with a glass of wine, and began coating the meat loaf with mashed potatoes. "Now we pour this can of mushroom soup over it and we have instant gravy. Not a bad touch, huh?"

"It's wonderful, but don't you want me to help?" I asked as he began chopping cucumbers and tomatoes for a salad.

He smiled at me and shook his head. "I'm an old hand in the kitchen. Erica didn't have a domestic bone in her body."

I could hear the pain in his voice.

Rudy stopped chopping. "I don't want to talk about her now. I want you to tell me about yourself."

Maybe it was because I knew the situation wasn't for real, that Rudy was simply repaying a favor, that made me relax and talk without worrying about the impression I was making or whether he thought I was ugly.

"There's not much to tell," I said. "I was born and raised right here in Dallas and after high school I went to secretarial school."

"And then you went to work for the Nolan Wholesale Company?"

I smiled. "Yes, but it sounds so boring to say I've worked at the same company for over a decade. It doesn't seem that long."

He pulled out my chair, lit a candle that was stuck in a wine bottle, and said, "There's probably a lot of stick-to-itiveness in you. That's a nice quality."

I felt myself responding to him almost against my will, not because he was so good-looking, but because he seemed to really want to know about me. Before I quite knew how it happened, I was telling him about my parents—the years I'd spent taking care of them and their recent deaths.

"I suppose that's why you never married," he said, and I think I could have reached across the table and hugged him right then.

"That had something to do with it," I agreed, "but now tell me about yourself."

Throughout dinner, I listened as Rudy talked about his childhood in a small town, the trade school he attended, and his decision to settle in Dallas because he could buy his repair shop for a reasonable sum. "I'd saved a lot of money working in construction one year," he explained.

"And then you married Erica," I said tentatively.

"Yeah, I married Erica. What a mistake," he said with a bitter laugh. "Hey, don't look so upset. Our marriage was over long before she had Lauren."

"Well, tell me about it," I urged him. I wanted to know why there was so much pain in his voice.

"I'll tell you about Erica this one time, and then I don't ever want to talk about her again. I met her while I was going to trade school. She was one of the prettiest girls I'd ever seen. She had the face of an angel and hair that framed her face like a cloud." He shook his head.

"She wasn't an angel, though. She was more like a devil. I just didn't know it until after we got married. I don't want to go into everything she did, but it was plenty—other men, other beds." He glanced across at me, a haunted look in his eyes. "I don't even know if Lauren's my baby—not that it makes any difference. I wanted her anyway—which is more than I can say for her mother."

"But why did Erica get pregnant if she didn't want a baby?" I asked softly.

"A mistake. Erica didn't plan on having Lauren, but I found out she was pregnant before she could get rid of her." His mouth hardened. "Not that she hadn't already made plans. I agreed to give her all our savings if she'd go through with the pregnancy."

"You paid her to have Lauren!" I couldn't keep the disbelief, the shock out of my voice.

"You might say that. Unfortunately, the savings account wasn't enough for Erica. She swiped all the money out of the business account, too, before she left town. That's why everything's going to hell at the shop." Something hard and unyielding showed in the set of his jaw, the anger in his eyes. "I guess it was worth it. I got Lauren and filed for a no-fault divorce. Erica agreed to that and signed the papers while she was still in the hospital."

His voice trailed away and then he said, "It's funny. I thought having Lauren might wake Erica up to some basic truths about life, but she didn't even want to see the baby." He looked angry. "Not that it would have meant anything. There were too many ugly memories for Erica and me to begin again."

"I'm sorry," I said. "I can tell you still haven't worked your way through it."

"I better have!" he said in a loud voice. He stared at me as if weighing his words. "I made up my mind after Erica that I'd never let another woman get that close to me ever again, to turn me inside out, make me vulnerable. Right now, I'm scared of long-term relationships." A long silence followed his words. Then he smiled and said, "But what about you? We haven't discussed your love life yet."

"There's nothing to discuss," I said curtly. "I've never been in

62

love and never expect to be." I looked away from the pity I knew I'd see in his eyes.

"I think it's time for me to go," I blurted out, jumping up from the table and rushing across the room for the coat I'd thrown over the back of the sofa. I pulled it on, grabbed for my purse, and whirled around to see that Rudy had followed me across the room.

"Say, wait a minute," he said. "What's wrong? How have I offended you?"

I began walking away. "You wouldn't understand." I had to get away from him, from the warmth in his eyes and the nearness of him reaching out to me.

"Don't go," he said quietly. Gently taking my arm, he forced me to turn around and meet his eyes with my own. "Don't get defensive with me. We were having a good time only a few minutes ago. I talked with you about things I wouldn't normally discuss with anyone. You can return the favor and give me a little of yourself, can't you?"

He had such a caring look in his eyes that I felt something break inside of me. Before I knew what was happening, I was telling him all about growing up, how awkward I felt in places like Wilco's, and how it felt to be thirty years old, unmarried, and with no chance that I ever would be.

The next thing I knew, Rudy's arms were around me and he was patting my back like I was five years old. "There, go ahead and cry it out. You know something, Jenny, I don't think any less of you because you shared that with me. If you really want to know, I think more of you."

I had told him my name was Jennifer—or Jen, for short—but he insisted on calling me Jenny. He handed me his handkerchief and led me to the sofa.

"Now you sit here," he said, "and I'm going to get us some coffee. While we're drinking it, we're going to discuss our plans for the rest of the weekend."

Rudy's plans included trying to catch up with all his work at the shop and I fell in with those plans as naturally and happily as breathing. Before long, I was spending all my lunch hours and most of my weekends with Rudy at his shop, or at his house or mine with Lauren. We'd managed to find a reliable baby-sitter for the daytime, but the rest of the time the baby spent with Rudy or me.

I was losing my heart to her, too—especially when she stared up at me with her big eyes, or held out her chubby arms, begging to be picked up. Not that Rudy and I were anything more than friends—we weren't. We simply spent lots of time together because it was convenient and nice. I suppose Rudy didn't feel threatened by me since I asked and expected nothing from him. Also, I wasn't so naïve as to think that anyone who looked or acted like Rudy would ever give any serious thought to a romance with me. I knew my limitations and that all I'd ever be to him was a friend.

Still, Denise couldn't resist a couple of comments when she stopped by on a Saturday to find me feeding Lauren for the third week in a row.

"You've got that baby again," she said in an accusing voice. "As much time as you spend with her and that guy, you should move in with them."

"It's not that kind of a relationship," I explained. Denise had never met Rudy, but I'd told her all about him.

"You mean you're practically living in his pocket, doing all the bookkeeping for his shop, and taking care of his daughter, and there's nothing more to it than that?" she asked.

"Yes, that's all there is to it," I said.

"No hugs, no kisses, no nothing?" she continued.

I didn't answer.

"I don't mean to come down so hard on you," Denise said apologetically, "but it seems to me like you're doing all the giving and this Rudy's doing all the taking."

"It's not like that at all," I protested. "I'm glad to give him my time, and even that little bit of money I lent him wasn't anything to me. In fact, he's already given it back."

"I can see there's no use talking to you about him," Denise said. "Just be careful, Jen. You're so inexperienced with guys, in spite of your age. Now take me. I won't flip out if I get involved with someone and it goes up in smoke."

"Maybe I won't, either," I said. "Besides, I told you I'm not involved with him."

She shook her head. "Oh, yes, you are, and in the worst way— with your heart."

I spent the rest of the afternoon stewing over Denise's words. By the time Rudy dropped by to pick up Lauren, I couldn't hide my state of mind.

"Hey, why the gloomy face?" he joked. "Has someone been ruffling your feathers?"

"You might say that," I snapped.

He picked up Lauren, kissed her, and walked over to me. "You are crabby. I'll bet that's because you've been spending too much time with the monster here," he teased. "Tell you what. I'll ask the baby-sitter if she'd take Lauren for the evening, and then I'll take you out to dinner and dancing. Is that a good deal for a lovely lady?"

He smiled at me with such warmth that I felt weak.

"It's a deal I can't pass up," I said. I felt an unbearable excitement

64

that Rudy was going to take me out on a real date. This might be a chance for him to see me as a woman—it might mean the turning point in our relationship.

The night was more wonderful than anything I could have imagined. First, there was steak and lobster at a restaurant furnished with antiques and Tiffany lamps turned so low, I could hardly see Rudy's face across the table. Later, he took me to a nightclub where we danced to slow, romantic songs. We danced the way lovers dance: my arms tight around his neck, his arms around my waist. I felt wrapped in a golden haze of happiness as we moved together on the floor. How could we only be friends when he made me feel like this? Denise was right: I had lost my heart to Rudy and it was too late to get it back.

After a time, I looked into his eyes to find him smiling at me. Then his lips touched mine and my knees went weak as we kissed. I knew there was never going to be anyone as important as Rudy Sherwin in my life. He seemed as shaken as I was when our kiss finally ended. "Let's get out of here," he said in a hoarse voice.

As we walked to the car, Rudy held on to my arm possessively. When we were finally settled inside, he held me close, covering my lips, hair, and eyes with wonderful kisses.

At last, he pulled away. "You're so sweet," he said, "and I want you so much, but this is all so crazy."

He gave me a quick kiss when we got to the door of my apartment. "I'm going to take a rain check on our usual coffee," he said.

"But why?" I asked, not understanding. I wanted so much to spend more thrilling moments in his arms.

Rudy kissed my forehead. "If I come in now, I won't leave. I don't think you're ready for that yet. I don't even know if I am." He cupped my face, tilted my chin, and looked into my eyes. "Jenny, I need time to think. I'm so mixed up about my feelings right now. I need some space. Can you give me a couple of weeks to straighten out the mess in my head?"

I swallowed and my mouth felt dry. Was I losing him before I ever even had him? "I can give you time, Rudy. Do you want me to skip the lunch hours as well as the evenings?" I asked quietly.

He nodded. "I know you don't understand, Jenny, but I need some time to be alone—completely alone. It'll only be for a short time."

"Sure," I said and watched him disappear down the stairs.

The ache in my throat was threatening to strangle me. I didn't know what had gone wrong between us, but the tears were streaming down my cheeks by the time I managed to let myself into the apartment. Everything had seemed so perfect only a few hours before, and now my wonderful date with Rudy had turned into a disaster. All because of those few desperate kisses, he needed space—space to think about us, space to forget me, space to decide my role in his life in the cold light of day. I shed the first of many hot, bitter tears that night.

I was a mess during the next two weeks. I didn't only miss Rudy, but Lauren, too. My arms ached to hold the baby, and I wondered each day how much she'd changed and what new thing she had learned. I guess I was pretty edgy about the whole turn of events because I let Denise talk me into going to Wilco's with her. That's how lonely I was without Rudy—how much I missed his companionship. At the last minute, though, I changed my mind.

"I better not," I told Denise. "Rudy might show up at my place, and I'd hate it if I missed him."

"You're impossible," Denise snapped. "No wonder he treats you like he does. He takes you for granted and then pulls a crummy trick on you like disappearing for the last two weeks."

"It goes with the relationship. I couldn't be any other way with him." I felt the sting of tears behind my eyes.

"You're such a fool," she scolded. She narrowed her eyes at me. "I've got the solution to this whole problem. You pick up the phone, call your precious Rudy, and invite him to the company party next week. Then I'm taking you in hand so that when he shows up, you'll be such a knockout he won't know what's hit him."

I gave her a doubtful glance. I wasn't sure what Denise had in mind, but I didn't see how I could be any more miserable than I already was. Once a year, Nolan Wholesale had a ceremony where they handed out awards to the top salespeople. Afterward, there was dinner and dancing at a nice restaurant with a banquet room.

I blew my nose and made the phone call, my heart turning over at the sound of Rudy's voice.

"Jenny!" he said cheerfully. "I've just been thinking about you. I think I've got my head on straight at last, and I'm looking forward to your company party. I'll be there."

After a few more minutes of chatter about Lauren and her latest accomplishments, I hung up with a lump in my throat as big as a walnut.

"He's coming," I said, turning back to Denise.

Immediately, my friend began outlining her plan for all the improvements she was going to help me make in my appearance. "We'll both take that Friday off, and I'll go with you to the salon and shopping. For God's sake, take my advice for once."

I did my best to take Denise's suggestions, but somehow I wasn't convinced. "I don't know," I said when I saw the picture she produced from a magazine about hairstyles. "I like my hair long and natural and I think Rudy does, too."

"Honey, you would look great with curls," Denise insisted. "We'll get the stylist to cut more hair around your face and give you a perm."

I let her talk me into that, but I drew the line at the bleach job she had in mind. "No, the perm is a big enough change," I insisted, "and I'm not sure that's an improvement." I had a head full of curls when we left the beauty parlor, but I didn't quite know what to do with them.

Denise also had plenty of ideas about the kind of dress I needed. "You should wear something tighter and lower, Jenny. You've got the cleavage, so why not show it?"

I twisted in front of the dressing-room mirror trying to imagine what Rudy would think of me in a low-cut dress that hugged my hips seductively.

"Buy it," Denise advised. "I love that shade of red on you."

"I don't know," I said, hesitant. "I've never worn anything so revealing in my life. I'm not sure I can carry it off, Denise. It's not the real me."

She wrinkled her forehead, annoyance showing in her eyes. "Sure, it is. Once I do your face, you'll be a knockout. We're going to show that Rudy you're no slouch."

"Maybe Rudy likes my face the way it is," I said as I slipped off the dress.

"How could he? You wear no more makeup than a twelve-year-old girl. It's time to grow up and show Rudy you're a woman."

"Maybe." I wasn't really convinced, but I bought the dress and all the accessories Denise said I needed to go with it.

Later, back at Denise's apartment, I showered and then she began making up my face. When she was done, I stared at myself in the mirror.

"Don't you think that's a little too much eye shadow?" I asked.

"Absolutely not! And don't you dare try to rub off any of that lipstick," Denise warned good-naturedly. She took the tissue from my hand and motioned me toward the door. "Go get dressed while I take my shower. Quit worrying about your face. You look awesome!"

Denise didn't have a date for the party, but she planned on making contact with some of the out-of-town salesmen who would show up. I had to admit she looked great. Somehow lots of makeup and low-cut dresses did more for her than me.

But I kept my opinions to myself all the way to The Yellow Rose, the place where the party was. Denise darted ahead of me when we got inside.

"I don't want to miss the cocktail hour, and I want you to meet Rudy by yourself," she explained. "Isn't that him over there?" she asked, leaving me alone.

Rudy was waiting outside the party room, looking more wonderful than ever in a nice sports coat and slacks. When he saw me, he came to meet me with an astonished expression upon his face. I guess my appearance was anything but what he expected.

"Well, do you like it?" I asked in a timid voice. I wanted so much to be beautiful for him—to be the woman he wanted me to be.

"You certainly look different," he said.

He took my arm and we headed toward the party room.

I glanced up at him and caught my breath when I saw the expression in his eyes.

"You don't think I look good," I accused. "You think I'm ugly—too ugly for you to love." I yanked my arm away and ran down the corridor—away from the party, and away from Rudy's mocking eyes.

When I got outside, I could hear Rudy's feet pounding on the pavement behind me. But the only place for me to escape to was a supermarket across the street. My side aching, my breath coming in gasps, I fled through the traffic and shoved myself through the supermarket doors.

I grabbed a cart and leaned against it for a moment until I caught my breath. Then I sensed Rudy behind me even before I turned to face him. I recognized the spicy scent of his aftershave lotion.

"You idiot," he said loudly. "You could have been killed running across the street like that."

"A lot you would have cared," I muttered. Out of desperation, I began pushing the cart down the produce aisle—anything to get away from him—but he followed. "Why don't you leave me alone?" I asked, stopping at the tomatoes. I picked up a couple of them and placed them into the basket.

"You might as well get decent ones," Rudy said, taking one of the tomatoes out and putting another one in.

"I can make my own decisions, thank you!" I announced and started pushing the cart again. There was this awful pressure in my chest that seemed to be squeezing the breath out of me.

Rudy stopped the cart with his hand. "I'm beginning to wonder. Whose bright idea was it that you show up tonight looking like a cheap slut?" He glared at me and shook his head. "Look at you, Jenny." He turned me around until I was staring into a large, round mirror that aided in catching shoplifters. "Is that the girl I've known for the last six months?" There was irritation mixed with sadness in his voice.

As I stared at myself in the mirror, I realized how I must have seemed to him—an ugly girl trying to make herself into something she wasn't.

"You're right, I look like a freak!" I cried, turning on him in a fury. "Why don't you go away and leave me alone like you've done the last two weeks? It's obvious you don't think I'm good for anything except to keep your books and feed your baby!"

I could tell by the way his face drained of color that I had hurt him. For a moment, I felt small and mean, but then I thought about the way he'd made me stare at myself in the mirror and I pushed the cart up and down the aisles like a madwoman.

Rudy cornered me in the meat department. I was trying to decide between pork chops and hamburger, but the packages were blurred before me. The stern line of his jaw told me he had himself under control again.

"Look, Jenny, let's be reasonable," he began. "I know you're mad, but the whole point is that you don't have to dress or wear makeup like that to impress me. I liked you just the way you were."

The tenderness in his voice brought the sting of tears to my eyes. In a minute I'd be throwing myself in his arms and we'd be right back where we started from—nowhere.

But he wouldn't stop. "You see, Jenny, you're so pretty inside that it radiates to the outside. When you try to make yourself into something you're not—like tonight—it simply takes the edge off all that radiance. To me, you're beautiful like whole-wheat bread, a mountain stream, lightning in the sky, stars—"

That did it. I was in his arms, my head buried against his chest, and he was stroking my hair with a gentle hand. "Let's pay for those groceries and get out of here," Rudy said quietly. "I've got a few more things to say to you."

We lined up behind an old woman with just a few items in her shopping cart. "I hope I've got enough money," she mumbled. I didn't know if she was talking to me, Rudy, or herself. She kept counting the coins in a frayed change purse as the cashier added up her groceries.

"Fifteen dollars and twenty cents," the checker said, holding out his hand.

The woman counted out all of her money.

"You're still two dollars and fifteen cents short," the checker said.

"Here," I said on impulse and shoved the additional money into his hands. When I saw the stubborn tilt to the old woman's chin, I touched her shoulder and said, "I've left my money at home lots of times. Someday I'll be in your spot and you can lend me some."

She looked at me with grateful eyes and took a pencil from her purse. "Well, I do thank you, dear. If you'll write down your name and address, I'll see you get your money back."

I didn't protest—I knew a little something about pride myself.

The woman left and Rudy began helping me stack my own groceries on the counter. "You know," he said, reaching for a can of corn and putting his lips close to my ear, "I think the reason I love you is because of things like what you just did."

For a moment, I thought I hadn't heard right. But when I looked into Rudy's eyes, I saw he meant it.

"I love you, too, Rudy," I said.

The next thing I knew, he was kissing me right there at the checkout counter, with six smiling customers lined up behind us.

"Come on, folks, I don't have all night," the cashier complained. Rudy and I broke apart, laughing.

Rudy waited until after we got out of the supermarket and were back at my apartment before he asked me to marry him. I'd also had time to wash the makeup off and put on my usual jeans and T-shirt.

"Now, that's the way I like you," he said, "and as soon as some of that curl comes out of your hair, it'll be as pretty as ever." He patted the sofa next to him. "As they say in the movies, what are you doing for the rest of your life?" He stroked my hair and held me close.

"Spending it with you, I hope."

"That's kind of what I had in mind," he said.

I sat up straight and stared at him. "I thought you were never going to let yourself get involved with a woman again."

He smiled. "That was before I met you, Jenny, and found someone to trust. I don't think you'll ever let me down."

"No, I won't," I promised and gave myself up to the pleasure of his kiss.

THE END

MOM KILLS MY SEX LIFE!
She scares away my friends

It was eight o'clock. He'd said he would call me, and if a boy is going to call you for a date, he calls before eight o'clock, doesn't he?

My folks were in the living room, watching TV. I sat in the dimly lit hallway, on the little gossip bench, staring at the silent, hateful phone.

Ring, I said silently.

Then a kind of loneliness welled up inside of me and my eyes filled with tears.

Please—please ring!

From behind the closed door to the living room, I heard my mom laugh softly at something somebody had said on the television. I could see the bright light from the little lamp my daddy always used, making a thin, yellow line under the door. Daddy always brought work home with him from his jewelry store—watches and clocks to be fixed, rings to be mounted.

Thinking about my folks made me feel a little guilty, and I stood up and switched off the lamp by the phone.

Okay, I told myself. So he isn't going to call. He wasn't so much, anyway. Just a boy. Like all the others. Just a boy who said he'd call me and didn't.

"Danica," Mom called, "come and see this, honey. You'll love this new comedy team!" I heard her laugh again, like a little girl. "Daddy," she said softly to my father, "honey, ask her to come in here. I'll fix us some sandwiches."

I stood there in the dark. Then I closed my eyes until everything was completely shut from my view. I didn't want to see it. The familiar little gossip bench, the big clock that had been my mom's grandmother's, the hall table where we always put the mail. I didn't want to see it, because I didn't want to be here—didn't want to live here—didn't want to belong to them.

"Danica!" Daddy called. "Honey, what are you doing? You there, Danica?"

I pushed open the big, sliding living room door and looked at him. He sat in his favorite chair, with the light shining down on his nice, silver-brown hair. He smiled at me, and like always, I felt guilty. Guilty for having thought, even for a second, that I didn't want to be a part of Mom and Daddy.

I sat down on the couch and watched the people on the show, laughing when I was supposed to, slumping down and looking comfortable. In a little while, Mom came in with the sandwiches.

"I thought you had a date tonight, sweetie," she said. She handed me a sandwich. "Didn't you say something about that new boy over at Karnville? My—he's certainly been giving you a chase, hasn't he?" She winked at Daddy. "She's only been out of high school three weeks and already, she's practically engaged!"

"I'm not engaged!" I said, louder than I'd meant to. "I never said I was engaged. I—I'm not even seeing that boy anymore. We—we broke up."

"Broke up!" Mom set the tray of sandwiches down and looked at me. "But, Danica—I thought you said he was so nice! I was hoping we could have him over for supper this Saturday night." She looked at Daddy. "Your father was going to close the store early and everything."

I stood up. "Well, he won't have to. Like I said—we broke up. After all, I only had those four dates with him. It—it's too far for him to drive clear over here from Karnville, Mom. He drives an old car and—well, it just didn't work out, that's all."

I watched my mother's face when I said that. I was afraid, like I always was, that maybe I'd hurt her. Every time I broke up with a boy, it was always the same pattern. The boys were almost always new in town, or visiting, or guys from a little town near us who didn't know me very well. I'd date them, and then somebody would tell them about my mom, and then we'd break up.

Sometimes it would get as far as their coming to the house. They'd meet my folks, see my mom, and then there'd be some kind of a fight, usually on our next date. I knew these boys just picked a fight with me as an excuse to get rid of me. Not many boys wanted to tie up with a girl who has a midget for a mother.

Midget.

Later, as I lay in bed, the sounds of my folks' gentle laughter and the voices from the TV set floating up the stairs, I said that word over and over again in my head.

Usually, I didn't let myself say it. Or even think about it. It was like—well, like I was somehow being unkind or disloyal to my mom. She never used that word. Neither did Daddy. They were so much in love and so happy and secure that they probably never even thought about it!

But it's true, I thought, staring up at the dark ceiling. It's true! That's what Mom is—she's a midget. A freak. That doesn't mean she isn't kind and good and the best mother a girl ever had. It just means she's—well—different.

When I was little, I didn't realize that. And even when I did finally see that my mom was so much tinier than other kids' mothers,

I didn't think much about it. My daddy was real short—about five-two—and his brothers were all short, with small hands and feet. I remember my mother's father before he died—he was small, but no smaller than my best girlfriend's grandfather was.

In grade school, I was always the littlest kid in the class, and I liked that. On the playground, the big girls used to baby me, and most of my teachers treated me like I was something special. My arms and legs were skinny then, and lots of times, a teacher would sit me in a special place in the classroom, away from the window drafts, so I wouldn't catch cold.

Then when I was nine or so, I suddenly realized that I'd grown taller than my mom had. I remember we were sitting at the supper table—Mom, Daddy, and I. I got up and stood by Mom, helping her scrape dishes, and when I said something to her, I had to look down at her.

"Mommy," I said, my voice frightened, "Mommy, I'm bigger than you are!"

"Sure you are," Mom said calmly, taking a plate from me. "You're shooting up like a sprout! If Daddy does well this week, we'll have to see about a new winter coat for you."

I touched the top of my head, like I wanted to stop myself from growing. "But—but I don't want to be big! I want to be little—like you!"

Mom smiled at me. "You won't be horsy, Danica, if that's what's worrying you." She looked at Daddy, her eyes veiled. "You'll be just right. Small and delicate, the way you should be."

The way you should be. Gradually, I began to realize that my mom wasn't the way she should be. Sometime before I reached junior high, I must've realized that my mom was different. Not different inside, because she wasn't. She had my Brownie troop in after school, and I had slumber parties, and all my girlfriends loved her. It was just on the outside that she was different. She was only the size of the kids in the fourth or fifth grade.

But that didn't matter. My folks had lived in Smallville all their lives, and nobody seemed to think anything about it. Mom was really active in our church, and she belonged to a bridge club, and at the annual flower show, Mom's roses nearly always won. I never really felt different, or afraid, or ashamed.

Until I was in junior high. Then a new boy came to school and asked me for a date. I'd never had a date before—nobody in my crowd had—and I was so thrilled that right away, I told all my girlfriends. One girl, Audrey Slocombe, was jealous. Not of me, but of the fact that this new boy had asked me for a date.

"I'm not allowed to date," she said peevishly. "Or wear lipstick, either. Not until I'm thirteen. My mother says nice girls don't."

I stared at her. Nobody had ever before hinted to me that I wasn't nice, that I wasn't just like all the other nice girls who lived in old-fashioned houses on shady streets, and who had birthday parties and new bikes and whose fathers belonged to the men's club.

Then, with a kind of new, feminine wisdom, I realized that Audrey was just being nasty. What she really wanted was for this new boy, with the sharp clothes and the big-city accent and the stories of how it was to live in a big city, to ask her, instead of me, for a date.

That date—I can't even remember the boy's name—was the turning point in my life. The boy didn't come. He was supposed to pick me up at my locker, and he didn't come.

When I saw him at school the next day, like a foolish, naive little girl, I stopped him in the hallway and asked him pointblank why he'd asked me for a date and then hadn't shown up.

"Listen," he said, his voice harsh, "where I come from, kids start going steady really young. I've looked over the crop here, and you seemed to be the cutest. I figured I'd date you a few times, then ask you to be my girl."

My heart soared. "Then why didn't you come to my locker? I don't know for sure if my folks would let me go steady, but they might let me date you." I said it calmly, as if it were my natural right to have this boy want me for his steady. After all, everything else that was nice had always come to me, hadn't it? A new doll, a birthday party, playmates, plenty of good food to eat, a nice house to live in.

"I can't go out with you," the boy said, his eyes cold. "One of your girlfriends told me that your old lady's a freak. A midget."

It was as if I'd been struck in the face.

Freaks—midgets—they'd always been the funny people who came to the county fair. A tattooed lady, two tiny, painted little people standing next to the fattest lady in the world . . . I'd never thought of my mom like that. Mom—in her apron, in her kitchen, in her garden, sitting beside me at church, cooking supper, putting an extra pillow on my bed so a girlfriend could spend the night with me.

But from then on, that's how I thought of her. Oh, not openly—not so she'd ever, ever guess. But way deep down inside of me. And when I started dating, the pattern began. I never went out with town boys. Some of them asked me, but I didn't want to date them, because I knew they might date me and even kiss me, but they'd never ask me to marry them. And after all, wasn't that what every girl wanted? To be married and have a home and family?

I wanted that. Maybe I wanted it more than most girls, because I wanted to prove to the world that it didn't make any difference that I had a mother who was a midget. I'd read lots of books on midgets—

ever since I first heard the word from that boy at school—and I knew that midgets usually have normal children, and that the condition isn't inherited or anything like that. It's caused by a glandular disorder. My grandparents had been normal. My mom's younger brother was normal. And I was normal. It wouldn't have any bearing on my future—or my children.

But the boys in town didn't know that. I'd imagine what they thought—Sure, date Danica, but man, don't get too involved. I mean, don't even think about getting serious. You want your kids to turn out to be freaks? You want her mother at your wedding, like something out of a sideshow? Sure, be nice to her mother, but for a mother-in-law? Well, you just don't do that kind of thing. You pick a girl who has normal folks when you think about marriage.

When I was a junior in high school, an old Army base was reopened near our little town. There were lots of young soldiers stationed there—boys not much older than I was. Most of them were nice, decent, and lonely. I didn't go out with the ones who weren't aboveboard.

There was Nate, a boy from Chicago. I went with him for three weeks. We fought a lot, once we'd decided we were in love. Sure, I was jealous of him. He was tall and broad shouldered, with beautiful, dark eyes and soft, curly hair. I was afraid that maybe he was seeing somebody else—that he didn't really love me.

He was supposed to come to church with me on a Sunday morning and meet my folks. Then I was to go to Chicago with him and stay at his married sister's and meet his parents. But that never happened.

The night before he was to meet my parents, we had a terrible fight. It ended up with my slapping his face, hard. He got up and left me sitting on the park bench where we'd been arguing.

I never saw him again. I knew, deep in my heart, that somebody from town had told him about my mom. To save himself from the embarrassment of meeting my mother, he'd picked a fight with me. He'd deliberately broken up with me.

Oh, older boys weren't as blunt as that kid in junior high had been. More experienced boys didn't say, "I hear your old lady's a freak, so it's all off, honey." They did other things. They picked fights with me, broke it off with me before they had to face the ordeal of looking down at my mom and seeing what she was.

Then in the middle of my senior year, the Army camp was deactivated. The soldiers were all transferred to another base, and our town slowed down to its normal, sleepy pace once again. All of a sudden, there weren't any new guys for me to meet. Now, there were just the kids I'd grown up with—the kids who already knew all about me.

Somehow, I felt that with a guy who didn't know about my

mother or me, I could win. If a guy got as far as proposing to me, and then met my mother, things would be okay.

So when the camp was emptied and closed, I just stopped dating. Mom worried about me, but as always, I was very careful not to hurt her. Like when I had a fight with Scott, the last soldier I'd dated. I told Mom that there'd been another girl in New York, where he was from, and that she'd written to him, breaking us up. Mom just looked worried and sorry for me, but not too much so—just the way a regular mother would.

Then when my parents felt I should be over Scott and start dating again, I told them that I wanted to make the honor roll at school. I told them that I had to stick to my books and there just wasn't enough time for dating. They didn't seem worried—they didn't seem to think that was so unusual. After all, I still had a social life. I went to the movies with my girlfriends and had slumber parties, and once in a while, I'd date a local boy, just to keep my folks from suspecting that I was ashamed.

A few months before graduation I began writing to a girl in Lake George, a town about two hundred miles away. I subscribed to a teen magazine, and I'd gotten this girl's name out of the pen-pal section. When I wrote to her, she answered right away, and before long, we were friends.

It was nice having a friend like Sharon. I didn't tell her about my mother—I didn't lie to her, but I just didn't tell her the whole truth. I told her that I didn't date much, that I'd had boyfriends before and had been hurt by them. Now, I just studied hard, helped my mom at home, and went to the movies with my girlfriends.

Sharon didn't tell me so, but I knew she was really popular. She sent me a picture of herself, and she had a great body and was really pretty, with nice, long blond hair. She sent me photos of herself with at least ten different guys.

This is Ethan, she'd write. I met him at the skating rink. We all skate a lot here. Like I told you, this is strictly a resort town, and in the winter, it's really dead. In the summer, though. . . .

Finally, she wrote and asked me to come visit her. At first, I tried to think of ways to tell her that I just couldn't. I didn't want to meet her. I didn't want to have to tell her the truth about myself. I didn't want to have to ask her to come visit me and then see the shock her face would show. After all, I had lots of girlfriends right here in town. And they were used to my mom and the way she was. But a strange girl, a girl who'd never thought about anybody having a mother like mine—well, she'd probably react like all the guys from out of town had.

Then I met Robbie, and I wrote to Sharon and told her that I couldn't possibly come, that I was in love and couldn't bear to leave this guy. I'd been graduated from high school about a week when I met him. He'd come to Karnville to work for his uncle, and I'd met him through a girlfriend of mine. I always felt terribly nervous with him, like I was sitting on a keg of dynamite or something, and we had lots of arguments. But I was so used to having arguments with my boyfriends that I didn't think twice about it.

Then last night—Saturday night—we'd had a really bad fight. But Robbie had said that he'd call me. Now it was Sunday—and nearly midnight. He hadn't called. So he'd dropped me. Somebody had finally told him about Mom, and, of course, he'd dumped me.

Actually, it was my daddy's idea that I take Sharon up on her offer to visit. "You've been mooning around here for three weeks, Danica," he told me one night. "You don't have to get a job if you don't want to, honey. You could go to nursing school—or maybe even college. I don't think I could swing four years, but you could try a semester or two, see how you like it, see if you can get a scholarship."

"No," I said, shaking my head, scared he'd see the hurt in my eyes, "I don't want to go anywhere, Daddy."

I'd made up my mind when Robbie didn't phone me that it wasn't going to happen again. I was through worrying about boys. Okay, so I wouldn't get married. No boy in town would get serious about me, and I wasn't going to chase after out-of-town boys anymore. I had a nice home, and wonderful folks; I didn't need to get married.

I looked at my dad. "I'll get a job here in town. Typing or something. Maybe clerking."

He patted my hand. "Why don't you wait till fall, honey? Then you can work for me a few hours each day, keeping the books. Later on, you can begin selling. It'd give me more time off; your mother and I thought we might join a bowling team this winter. If you were there taking care of the store for me, it'd be a big help."

Why, I wondered suddenly, why is everything in the world so easy for me—even getting a job? Everything except the one thing I really want—finding a boy to love, one who loves me back.

"I'll tell you what," Daddy said. "You take a little vacation— write that girl and ask her mother to call us collect. We'll talk about your visiting her. Then in the fall, you can settle down and begin working for me."

When I wrote Sharon, I warned her that I wouldn't want to date while I was there. She wrote me back special delivery.

It's okay, Danica, she wrote, I know how hurt you are about Robbie. You didn't tell me, but I guess you two broke up. You don't have to date. Just come. We've got plenty of room.

The night Sharon's mother called my mother and the two of them talked, I stood there holding my breath. I was scared to death that Mom would say something about the fact that I'd broken up with an awful lot of boys, or that she was different from most women. But, of course, she didn't say any of those things. I guess Mom just figured that most girls fought with their boyfriends, and I know that she didn't consider herself really any different from anybody else.

So I went to Sharon's. I felt free for the first time in my life—nobody there would know that I'd lost a lot of boyfriends because of Mom. And nobody would know about Mom—and what she was.

My daddy, bless him, gave me three hundred dollars to buy some cute summer clothes with. I washed my hair the night before I was to go, and Mom did it up for me. She stood on a stool to reach me, expertly twisting my hair around her tiny fingers until she'd styled it just so.

My folks went to the bus station with me, and when I bent down to kiss my mom, I felt a sudden stab of guilt.

"Look, Daddy," Mom said, "she's still a baby—why, I believe she's homesick already!"

I smiled at them. I didn't want them to know that I was glad to be going away—if only for two weeks. Okay, so I wouldn't date, but all the same, it'd be wonderful to just be a normal girl, like everybody else.

To get to Lake George took nearly seven hours. It really was only at the other end of the state, but this bus was one of those slow jobs, stopping to let country people out in front of their farms and things like that.

Actually, I didn't mind the long trip. It was part of my two weeks of freedom. And every time somebody new got on the bus, I found myself smiling in a friendly, open way. One lady even offered to share her lunch with me, and after she got off, one man told me all about his troubles with his wife. They both looked at me as if I was sweet and kind and interested. But I wasn't. I wasn't any of those things. I listened to them talk, because it was so darned sweet to have strangers talk to me without my having to be scared that they'd later see me on the street with my mom.

"Why, isn't that the nice girl we met yesterday? Who's that with her? Her mother? But—how awful! Why, look how little that woman is! She's some kind of dwarf, isn't she?"

But now, nobody would talk that way—not for two long, wonderful weeks!

I closed my eyes after our one o'clock lunch stop, and I didn't open them again until somebody gently shook my shoulder and said, "This is Lake George, honey."

I sat up and stared at the bus driver. Then I hurriedly grabbed my suitcase and kind of stumbled out of the bus.

I looked around the big station, panic growing in me. The town was bigger than I'd thought. The station looked new, and lots of people in shorts and sports clothes were rushing around.

She's expecting you, I told myself, so don't flip! You've got Sharon's phone number, so just call her. She and her parents are probably on their way here right now to get you.

I walked around the station, looking for a phone booth. Then, as I passed the wide-open doors, I heard someone honk a horn. I peered out into the bright, hot sunshine, and a girl with blond hair sitting in a long, shiny white convertible waved at me. I walked toward her, still not sure. Then she motioned for me to come.

"Hey!" she said. "Danica, hop in!" She smiled. "I'd know you anywhere! But I didn't think you'd be so tiny and cute!"

I slid into the seat beside her. She took off right away, the tires squealing, weaving in and out of the downtown traffic. She glanced at me briefly. "Gee," she said warmly, "I thought you'd be some kind of a goon! I mean, a swell kid, but creepy to look at—you know. But you sounded so interesting that I still wanted you to come, gooney or not!"

I grinned and laughed, feeling just wonderful. "Why'd you think I'd be like that?"

She shrugged. "Oh, all the guys you were always breaking up with."

I looked out the window at the long, white hood of the car. "Well, it looks like you've got yourself a guy who's crazy about you! Gee, does he let you drive his car very often?"

Her eyes widened. "What? Oh, this is my car, honey—a present from dear old Mommy and Daddy when I graduated last June."

That put a different light on everything. I didn't say much after that, even when we pulled up the long, tree-lined driveway that circled the big, white house.

"Well, here it is," Sharon said, her mouth twisting a little. "Cozy little dump, isn't it? Come on—let's change clothes and go down into town and get some lunch."

I touched her arm. "Sharon," I said, "I—I guess I might as well tell you. I didn't know you—well, that you lived in a house like this. My folks—we aren't rich, Sharon. I hope I don't—I hope I don't embarrass you. I mean, my clothes—and I've only got a little spending money. . . ."

She looked at me, her eyes narrowing. "What's this—the poor-but-proud bit?" She took my hand. "Listen, Danica, I don't care if your folks have money. Maybe when you get a big whiff of my folks, you'll be happier with your own." She hopped out of the car, smiling brightly. "Only trouble is, you probably won't get to even see my honorable parents. They're in—let's see—Vegas, I think. Soaking up some sun from the sunlamps hung over the dice tables, no doubt."

I followed her into the big house. The wall-to-wall carpeting was as thick and soft as a feather pillow, and the house seemed shady and cool and crisply clean.

"Hey," Sharon said, yelling into the silence, "I'm home! My friend's here, too! We won't be home for supper, though, so go neck with Ray or something." She started up the broad, circular white staircase, and I followed after her, clutching my suitcase in both my hands.

"Who were you talking to?"

She giggled, pushing open a door that led into a charming bedroom. "Just Mary," she said. "She's supposed to be our housekeeper, but actually, she's a sort of combination baby-sitter and spy. She gets mad when I tell her that I know she necks with Ray. He's the milkman—and he's married."

I sat on the edge of the high, ruffled bed. "You mean that your folks won't be here all the time I'm here?" I asked, surprised.

She grinned at me. "That's right—just you and me and old Mary. She won't say much, though, because I always threaten to call Ray's wife and tell her about the time I caught her and Ray in the kitchen together!"

I laughed and fell back on the bed. Sharon flopped down beside me, and we talked for a long time. Just girl talk—about music and boys and complexion problems and stuff like that. But there was a kind of loneliness about Sharon—I could tell she really was glad to have me there with her.

We finally decided it would be more fun if I slept in her room, instead of taking the guestroom. We talked for a while longer then, and finally, we got around to the subject of parents.

"Mine just aren't around," Sharon said, her eyes suddenly filled with bitterness. "My dad's a big wheel in town—real estate—and my mom loves to travel. She thinks the biggest deal in the world is a Concorde flight with champagne, and her new fur coat on the back of her first-class seat. She didn't even come to my graduation. That's why they gave me the car—guilt atonement, the psych books say." She shrugged. "Anyway, you've probably got troubles at home, too. No girl breaks up with that many guys unless her folks are in on it somehow."

I flushed. "I'd rather not talk about that," I said. But I could tell by the wise look in her eyes that Sharon knew it had been about my folks, after all. And it had been! Without their even knowing it, they'd split up my relationships time after time after time.

Because of Mom.

Because of what she was.

It was really something that night. Sharon and I changed clothes, and then we drove back downtown for lunch. At the drive-in, about ten boys hooted and honked when Sharon expertly swooshed into the driveway of the place. They crawled out of their flashy cars and came over and started kidding around with us.

Sharon introduced me, and I looked at them, smiling, my mind working. They looked young and a bit overfed and kind of babyish. Rich boys is what they were—very spoiled, trying to act big. I didn't want to date any of them. I knew if even one of them knew about Mom—why, I could just imagine the fat blond one, with the crewcut and expensive clothes—why, he'd probably treat me just like that kid in junior high had!

Then suddenly, Sharon tossed her empty milkshake cup out the car window, stepped on the gas, and we took off. We sped along for a while, and finally, she turned and smiled at me.

"You passed the test, Danica."

"What test?"

She made a right turn. Ahead of us, I could see lights and a lot of parked cars. "You didn't go for those jerky boys. Shows you're used to better things—like what I'll show you at the rink."

I didn't answer her. She thought I'd been kidding about not wanting to date! She must've thought that I hadn't really meant it!

On an impulse, I almost told her about my mom right then and there. But then I stopped myself. After all, it was true that Sharon was unhappy because of her parents. But to be neglected was one thing. To be ashamed—like I was—was quite another.

I'd never been to a skating rink before. At home, we didn't have one. This place was packed with kids—skating, horsing around by the refreshment stand—and the music from the loudspeaker was blaring.

"Gee," I said, impressed. "All the girls are wearing those tiny little miniskirts that are in again! I feel like such a fashion 'don't!'"

"Relax," Sharon said.

A little later, we changed into our skates and rolled out onto the big, polished floor.

"What do we do now?" I asked, a kind of shyness and excitement in me suddenly.

"We skate."

Sharon grabbed my hand then, and the next thing I knew, we were out on the circular, slick floor. I hadn't skated since I was a little kid, but it wasn't too hard. I stayed on my feet, at least. Sharon looked straight ahead of her, not smiling, just skating gracefully to the loud music, pulling me along with her.

Suddenly, two boys skated up next to us. Sharon didn't even look at them, but I did. One was tall and slender, and the other one—the

81

one who was grinning at me with warm, dark eyes and a crooked smile—was short and broad shouldered. He wore a white polo shirt that set off his beautifully tanned arms and neck and face.

Finally, he slipped his arm under mine and the other boy took Sharon's arm. We skated along in silence for a while. Then Sharon and the other boy separated from us and began doing some really cool moves.

"Want to slow-skate?" the guy with me asked.

I shook my head. All my resolutions about not getting involved with anyone were dissolving fast. This boy obviously liked me—I could tell that by the look in his eyes. And he was cute—just the kind of guy I'd always been attracted to—not so tall as to make me look like a shrimp, with big, broad shoulders and dark hair and eyes.

"I'm new at this," I said, almost stumbling.

His strong hand steadied me. "New at being with a guy? Or new at skating?"

He led me off the floor, his arm around me. I felt my face flush with a mixture of shyness and excitement. He was very sure of himself.

"You sit here," he said, smiling down at me. "I'll get us a couple of sodas."

When he came back, he introduced himself. "I'm Kieran Shaughnessy," he said. "I work as a waiter over at the resort hotel." He glanced over at Sharon, out on the floor. "You and your girlfriend slumming again?"

I sipped my soda and looked up at him. "I don't understand."

"I haven't seen you around before, but I know who she is. When her folks come home—which isn't often—they sometimes have dinner up at the hotel where my buddy and I work. I don't imagine they'd like the idea of her dating a waiter." He smiled at me, and my heart began beating fast and hard. "And I don't suppose your folks would, either."

He thinks I'm a rich girl, I thought kind of dazedly. He thinks I'm just like Sharon!

"Just the same," he said, bending over to take off my skates, "why don't you go out with me, anyway? Sharon and Brad have a kind of standing date—every night." He shrugged. "After all, Brad and I will be leaving here at the end of the summer. We're from Philadelphia. We read about this place and decided to try to get jobs here for the summer."

Sharon and Brad were skating toward us just then, their arms around each other.

"Well," Sharon said, "looks like you've got yourself a guy, Danica!"

"Danica." Kieran looked down at me and smiled. "Nice name.

Nice name—nice girl. Poor little rich girl." He took my hand and pulled me to my feet. "You taking Sharon's car, Brad?"

Brad nodded. Kieran held my hand, and we walked out of there together. My mind was spinning so that I couldn't think straight. I climbed into Kieran's beat-up old car and it felt like home. I wasn't used to big, fancy cars like Sharon's.

"It's not much," Kieran said when he finally got it started, "but it beats walking."

We drove to a diner for sandwiches and sodas, and Kieran did most of the talking. That was fine with me. I was scared he'd ask me about my folks. He'd just naturally assumed that I'd met Sharon at the boarding school where she'd gone her senior year, when I told him we were friends and I was visiting her.

Well, I told myself, let him think that. Let him think that, for no matter how much you like each other, you won't be able to write to him later, anyway. Let him think it's because your folks are rich and they wouldn't approve of him—a coal miner's son. Even if that's kind of insulting, it's better than having things get up to the point of having to let him meet your folks!

He didn't kiss me good night, and that kind of surprised me. When we got home, Brad and Sharon were sitting in Sharon's car, out in front of the big, white house. I saw them go into a long clinch. Then Sharon got out of her car and Brad followed her. They met us by the front door, and Sharon took my hand.

"Come on, Danica," she said, smiling, her blond hair tousled, her face flushed. "If we don't get in pretty soon, I'll miss the nightly call from my folks. They always call me just to check on me."

I said good night to Kieran and Brad and walked into the house with her. When we got to the top of the stairs, the phone rang. I went into the bedroom and undressed, trying not to hear what Sharon said. But I couldn't help overhearing some of it. She told either her mother or her father that she'd been to a girlfriend's and had just gotten back. She said that I was very sweet and nice and we were having a lovely time. Then she came back into the bedroom, her hands trembling.

"I don't know what it is," she said bitterly, "but I always feel ashamed about my folks. When I talk to them on the phone, I feel ashamed because I lie to them. And when I'm out with Brad, I feel ashamed because I know he thinks I'm a poor, tossed-aside rich kid whose folks don't give a damn about her!"

I crawled into bed. I felt almost the same way. Of course, my folks loved me, but I felt ashamed when I talked to them, because I'd lied so many times about why I didn't want to date or why I'd broken up with boys. And with Kieran, I'd felt a sense of shame, too. Because I didn't dare tell him the truth about myself.

I met Mary the next morning. She really wasn't so bad. Though I expect she felt that Sharon and I were a handful. Sharon was never around for meals, and she acted like Mary was always in the way. I tried to be nice to Mary, though, and I decided that the trouble was that Sharon resented her. What Sharon really wanted was for her mom to be a stay-at-home mom. But she wasn't, and that was that. Just as I wanted my mom to be normal. But she wasn't, and there really wasn't much that I, or anyone, could do about it.

Sharon and I dated Kieran and Brad that next night, and the night after that. We went skating the first night, and the second night we went swimming in the big, cool, moonlit lake. It was wonderful to be with Kieran—he was full of fun and there was a kindness and sweetness about him that I loved. But still, he hadn't kissed me. Sharon kept teasing me about that, saying that I ought to grab him and kiss him real good. But I didn't want to get too involved. The truth was, I already cared too much about him. And in another ten days, I'd be going home, and that would be the end of my vacation, the end of my freedom.

A couple of days that week, Sharon and I drove up to the big hotel and had lunch. The boys were there, working in the dining room, and Kieran kept looking at me as he served the customers, his brown eyes warm.

He loves me, too, I kept thinking. I know he does! If he didn't really care about me, he'd have made a fast pass at me or something. Kieran isn't a kid who's never been around—it isn't that he's too shy to kiss me. It's because he thinks I'm too good for him. Out of his class. That's a laugh!

That next night, Kieran and I had a date alone. Sharon had to stay home because her folks were going from Las Vegas to Los Angeles and they wanted to call her early before their plane left. Her dad had some kind of business deal to close, and they'd be gone for another two weeks or so. She and Brad had planned to talk by phone that night, but that was all.

So for the first time, Kieran and I were really alone for the whole evening. That first night, we'd only had time to get acquainted. Now, though, we knew enough about each other—enough so that we didn't have to make small talk. Of course, the things that Kieran knew about me were kind of shadowy. I'd told him that my dad owned a store, which was true, and that my folks were pretty strict with me, which was true. The rest he just concluded himself.

We'd gone for a swim, and afterward, we rested on the empty, soft beach together. Kieran talked about his folks—about how much fun it was to be part of a big family. Finally, he turned to me.

"I'm really not at all ashamed of being poor, Danica. I guess I

84

ought to be making excuses to you. But if you could only understand—if you'd only understand what it is not to have a whole lot, and yet have everything. . . ."

No, I thought bitterly. I don't understand. I only understand the part about not having a whole lot.

Before we left, Kieran kissed me. I don't think he meant to. He reached for his towel, and his hand accidentally brushed my arm, and then suddenly, his arms were around me. It wasn't a kiss that came from politeness or trying to act big or be smart, or because it was the thing to do. It was a kiss that came from want and need and love. I knew that as soon as Kieran's lips touched mine. And I knew a lot more. This was different—different from the other boys I'd dated. With them, even when they kissed me, I'd be thinking, Now maybe I've got somebody! Maybe he won't be startled or shaken or horrified when he sees my mom!

But with Kieran, I didn't think at all. I just felt. I just clung to him and knew dimly that it was very warm and wonderful there in his arms, the soft sand beneath our bare feet, and the summer stars bright and silvery overhead.

"Danica," he said, his voice hoarse, "maybe if I talked to your folks—I could find another kind of job."

"No," I said, moving away from him. "I—I don't want you talking to them, Kieran! Please, we don't have many more days left. Let's just chalk this off to a summer love affair."

He looked at me for a long time, and then he picked up his towel. "Okay," he said, his voice hard. "Funny, that's just the same routine Sharon gives Brad. He's in love with her, you know. It isn't just a big joke with him. But she's scared of what her folks might think."

That night, I wanted to confide in Sharon so badly that I ached. Lying there next to her in that big, soft, frilly bed, knowing that she probably felt as I did, I wanted to talk about it.

But I didn't. After all, her problem wasn't really the same as mine at all. She was afraid that her folks would try to stop her marriage. I was afraid that Kieran would leave me if he ever met my mother.

The next couple of days we double-dated again—skating, swimming, and a picnic on Sunday. The housekeeper, Mary, didn't bother too much with us. After all, Sharon and I were eighteen, and we always managed to get in on time.

Every night that next week, Kieran kissed me good night. Sometimes it would be in the backseat of Sharon's car as we parked in front of that big, lonely white house. Sometimes it would be at the beach, or in the old car that Kieran owned. And sometimes, as Kieran took my skates off, he'd look up at me, his eyes so bleak and full of want that it would mean more than a kiss.

We loved each other. We hadn't said the words, and yet each of us knew. And we had only two more days left.

There was something else I thought about, lying in bed next to Sharon. After she'd gone to sleep, I'd think about Kieran, about how kind he was, how gentle and hardworking, and what a wonderful husband he'd make. There had never been any mean words between us. Never any arguments. And that was strange for me. Always before, when I'd gone with a boy, there'd been fights.

And thinking about it, I began to realize that perhaps those fights and nasty words had happened not because somebody had told the boy about my mother, but because I'd been so ashamed. I'd known that the boy would drop me as soon as he saw her, so I'd picked a fight in order to avoid having the same cruel words said to me that had been said once before. Because I'd never been able to forget that boy in junior high—the one who'd said my mom was a freak.

But with Kieran, there hadn't been that pressure. I'd known all along that our courtship would never get to the place where I'd have to take him home to meet my parents, and so there'd never been any tension or fighting. I'd known all along that what we had was just for a little while—and I'd wanted it to be good and kind and right the whole time.

And it was—so right, in fact, that on the last night I spent with him, I suddenly began to cry. We'd left Brad and Sharon at the rink, and when Kieran drove me back to Sharon's, she and Brad weren't there yet. I didn't have a house key, so Kieran and I sat in his car.

"Danica," he said softly, his voice strained, "you could call your folks—ask them to let you stay a few more days. Maybe—maybe we could work something out." He turned to me. "Or do you want to go home? Maybe you don't feel like I do."

I didn't look at him. "I have to go home, Kieran," I said. "I—we're going on a trip. To Los Angeles. I have to go home." It was surprising how easily the lie came to my lips. I got out of the car then and went up to the porch. I could see the headlights of Sharon's car round the curve of the drive. In a few seconds, she got out of the car and Brad got into the old car with Kieran.

I didn't look back. I went into the house with Sharon and followed her up the stairs.

When we were in bed, she suddenly took my hand. "Kieran loves you," she said softly. "I haven't told him anything about you. I—I won't even talk to Brad about you. I guess I can understand, Danica. I know you've got some reason for not wanting to see Kieran again. It's your business." She turned over and buried her face in her pillow. "If only I had the guts to stand up to my folks! If only I weren't so scared of what they'd say and do!"

I sat up and looked down at her. "Maybe you don't know," I said. "You've never tried talking to them, have you?"

She looked up at me. "They'd—they'd try to stop it. They'd cut off all my allowance."

I said softly, "If you're afraid to be poor, Sharon, then you aren't worth worrying about."

Kieran called me from the hotel the next morning, but I told Sharon to tell him that my bus had already left. I packed my things, and Sharon drove me to the bus station. Our good-bye was very quiet and strangely sad, not at all like our hello had been.

As my bus pulled out, I pressed my face up against the cool glass of the window. I could see Sharon standing there, her clothes bright and expensive looking, her hair gleaming in the sunlight.

You fool, I thought. To give up the boy you love because you're afraid of being poor! If that were the only thing that stood between Kieran and me. . . .

I wanted to sleep on the trip back, but I couldn't. I kept thinking of Kieran—how sweet he'd been, the way he'd held me and kissed me, the way he'd talked about his folks, the fierce pride that he'd shown whenever he spoke of them.

And then the old guilt would come washing over me. Now I felt sure that I'd always managed to break up my romances myself, before the boys got a chance to meet my mother. And yet, if they could only have understood—if Kieran could only understand that underneath, I was as proud of my mom as he was of his—ashamed and proud at the same time. Because she'd never let what was wrong with her stop her from leading a happy, secure kind of life. Because she'd never hidden or tried to stay out of things or been ashamed. And yet she must've been ashamed. There must've been times when she was ashamed and when she'd known that I was ashamed of her.

Suddenly, I wondered if I'd fooled her at all—if she'd really believed that I'd broken up with those boys for the reasons I'd given her. Maybe she'd known that I'd lied to her all along, known that I'd been ashamed to bring them home. Maybe she'd even known that I'd picked fights just so that they wouldn't have to see her.

I'd thought Mom and Daddy would be at the bus station to meet me, but they weren't. I got off the bus, and then I had a soda in the corner drugstore. I walked home, down the familiar, shady streets, lugging my heavy suitcase.

I was home. I'd never take another vacation like this again. No matter what—I'd never try to hide from the truth again. I owed my folks that much, at least. Maybe I'd never meet another boy like Kieran, but if I did, the very first thing I'd say to him would be, "Look, my mom's different. She never grew up. She grew up in her mind and her heart, but not in her body. If you want to measure her by the size of her warmth, her goodness, her kindness, her humor, or the touch of her little hand on your arm when you've been sick or scared or lonely—then she's ten feet tall. If you want to measure her by her bravery, her calmness, her ability to go right on living as though God hadn't made her different—then she's a giant. But if you just hear about her or glance at her—then she's a misfit. A freak. Something to snicker at. Something to whisper about. Something to run from."

Dear God, I don't want that shame! I don't want to see my mom's face turn pale, or her eyes dim with shame, or her tiny hands tremble with resignation and despair!

So maybe that was a part of it—a big part of my fear. Because I didn't want my mom hurt. I didn't want to be hurt, and I didn't want my mom to be hurt, either!

I rounded the corner of Elmwood and Church, and I looked up, holding my heavy suitcase with one hand and shading my eyes against the bright, sinking sun with the other.

And then I stopped dead in my tracks.

Kieran's old car was parked in front of my house!

At first, I wanted to run. I thought crazily, If I don't go into the house, maybe he'll go away. He's already seen my mom—so it's too late. Too late for me to beg him not to go to my parents' house. By this time, he's seen her and he's over the first, awful shock, and by now, he's politely making excuses. Tell Danica I'll write to her. Tell her I'll call her. Tell her I was just passing by and maybe the next time I'm around. . . .

And then I thought of Mom. Somehow, I had to let her know that I was sorry—sorry for having cheated her out of the loyalty that I owed her.

I began to run, pulling at my suitcase. I reached the cement steps that led up to our house, and I left my suitcase there and hurried up to the porch, pushing open the front door.

The house was silent. I stood there, my heart pounding with dread and with a new, fierce sense of protection. I planned to walk into the room where they were, put my arm around Mom, tell Kieran that it was all right, that he could call me or write me later—that it had only been for fun. Make it easy for him. Make it easy for Mom, too.

I heard the laugh then. My mom's gentle and soft laugh. The sound came from the kitchen. I walked slowly through the dim hallway, past the table where the mail was left, past the telephone, past the proud old clock, to the kitchen door. Then I took a deep breath and pushed it open.

They were sitting at the kitchen table. The three of them—Kieran, my dad, and my mother. Mom was passing around a big plate of cookies, and Dad was working on a watch. Kieran looked up at me, and then very slowly, he smiled.

"I beat you here," he said simply. He took a cookie from the plate Mom held. "I called you at Sharon's this morning to tell you that I quit my job. I'm on my way home."

I moved toward the table, trying to make my voice calm. "Well," I said, "it was nice of you to stop by, Kieran."

Kieran and my dad looked at each other. Then Daddy stood up, clearing his throat. "Your mother and I are going bowling," he said, very formally, his voice very strange, like he was acting in some kind of play. "We'll be home later, Danica."

I watched as Mom and Daddy filed out of the kitchen. Mom kissed me briefly on the cheek, standing up on her tiptoes. "You look tanned," she said. "I must send some of my roses to Sharon's mother. She must've taken good care of you. You look tanned—and pretty."

I stared at Kieran. He was sipping his lemonade, his eyes watching me. I went over and sat down in Mom's chair.

"Well?" I said, folding my hands. "When do you leave? You can leave now, Kieran. If you leave right now, I can make an excuse for you. I can tell them you had to be home by morning or something."

He shook his head. "You're a fibber, honey. An awful fibber." He grinned at me then. "Did you know that Brad bought Sharon a ring this morning? And that a half an hour after you left, she called her folks and told them she and Brad were getting married? She kissed all that money good-bye, and they leave for Brad's folks' house tonight."

"That's nice," I said steadily. "That's wonderful." I looked into his eyes. "But they're different, Kieran. They aren't us. Their problem isn't the same as ours."

For just a second, his eyes clouded with a kind of love and understanding. Then he put his hand over mine. "Stop running, Danica. Your mom never ran. Sure, our problem's different. You don't have to give up your allowance to marry me." He leaned over, and his lips touched my cheek. "Your dad's got a great ring," he said. "He told me he'll let me have it on credit. I can have it now, and when I start working back home, I can send him the payments." His hand tightened on mine. "What do you say, honey? Want to stop running? It's only a shadow that's been chasing you, Danica. Believe me, it's nothing real."

And looking at him, I knew suddenly that he was right. Only one boy had ever insulted my mother. Because the rest had never even gotten a chance to.

Somehow, I'd thought that I was different—that my mom was different. But we weren't.

If a boy loves you, he doesn't care if your mother or dad don't talk like everybody else, or look like everybody else. If he loves you, that's all that matters. He loves you.

Who was I to say that my life had been rough? I'd had love, a decent home, and parents who loved me. Maybe kids like Sharon— kids who were lonely and unloved—maybe they were the ones who were running from something concrete. Not just a shadow. And if Sharon could push that kind of ugliness away and look forward to a new life, then surely, I could, too.

My hand pressed Kieran's. "Drink your lemonade," I said. "I'm all packed. My suitcase is out on the front walk. I guess I'd better meet your folks before we get married. Maybe your mother won't like me."

He grinned at me. "She'll like you. She'll like your whole family. I called her a little while ago. I told her that you were something special—a lot like your mom. But you just had to grow up a little in order to realize it."

And that's just what I did.

Kieran, bless him, taught me to grow up, and to realize that I'm the luckiest girl in the world.

And if you use the same tape measure that God does, we're giants—Mom and Dad, and Kieran and me!

THE END

I WAS A WIDOW
FOR AN HOUR!

I laid down on the couch with a cold washcloth on my forehead and a martyred expression on my face. Dr. Gardiner had assured me these terrible headaches I suffered periodically were due to nerves rather than a brain tumor or some other frightening condition—but that knowledge didn't make it hurt any less.

I shut my eyes and tried to relax as I waited for my pain pills to do their job. Mother used to get headaches, too. I can still remember, as a little girl, how I'd tiptoe through the darkened front room back in Wallington, listening to Mama's low moans, terrified that she was going to die. She never blamed her headaches on her nerves, though—she insisted they came on because my brothers and I made her life so hard. Well, I'd vowed way back then that I'd never even get married—let alone have kids, because it obviously wasn't much fun.

Naturally, I forgot all about that when I fell in love with Sam Clifford. We were married just after I graduated from high school and now, fourteen years later, I had four kids, and my very own headaches—just like Mom. There's Billy, in junior high, John, eleven, Aidan, nine, and Dylan, my baby, who just turned six. They're great kids—don't get me wrong, and I love them dearly. But on days like this, I know exactly how Mama must have felt. . . .

It started early this morning at breakfast. Aidan spilled tomato juice all over his favorite sweatshirt, and refused to change.

"You can't go to school like that," I argued. "It looks terrible! What will your teacher think?"

"Teachers never think—they just talk," quipped Aidan, with his smart-aleck grin.

John came down while I was bawling Aidan out for being sassy. He was still tousled from sleep, wearing old patched jeans and a faded, threadbare shirt. He eyed Aidan critically. "Yuck, that's gross—what is it?"

"Tomato juice—shut up!" snapped Aidan.

"It looks like you had a bloody nose," Dylan volunteered.

"Dylan, stop that kind of talk! We're eating!" I said sharply.

John slumped into his chair, poured milk on his cereal, and stirred it aimlessly for a while. For the next twenty minutes or so, our "conversation" consisted of: "Elbows off the table." "Don't talk with your mouth full." "Stop fighting—playing in your cereal— wiping your nose on your sleeve—kicking your brother under the table." "Go upstairs this minute and change your shirt—comb your hair—brush your teeth—look for your homework." "Which one of you poured oatmeal in the cat dish—dropped his lunch money in the dishwasher—left dirty socks on the dining room table?" "You're going to miss the bus—end up in the principal's office again—get a good smack—have to repeat fifth grade if you don't shape up."

Now, if that doesn't sound like twenty minutes worth of inspiring conversation, bear in mind that each sentence was repeated at least six times. At seven-thirty they all dashed out to catch the bus. I went upstairs to wake Billy, whose bus left at eight-fifteen.

As I looked in his room, I winced. A decorator might have characterized the theme as "casual"—but a civil defense officer would probably have called it a disaster area. There were clothes, books, apple cores, and sports equipment strewn from one end to the other. The scent of old gym shoes was overwhelming. Taking a deep breath, I waded in and flung open the window.

"Time to get up, don't forget to change your underwear, and be sure and make your bed," I announced very quickly, trying not to inhale. I hurried back out to the hallway and shut the door. A moment later, I heard Billy's feet hit the floor. Simultaneously, the house vibrated with the sound of rock music. I groaned, cursing the day we'd let him use his paper route earnings to buy that stereo.

When Billy left for school, I got down to housecleaning. Sam would be home tonight and I wanted everything to look nice. By noon, I'd scrubbed, waxed, polished, and dusted from the kitchen out to the front hall. I'd intended to spend the afternoon doing the upstairs, but by one o'clock, I felt the first faint stirrings of a headache. By three, when the boys came thumping into the house and out again, leaving a trail of cookie crumbs, baseball gloves, and books, I felt like my head was clamped in a gigantic vise.

Outside, I heard kids arguing noisily about a bicycle pump. Sitting up slowly, I squinted at the clock. Almost three-thirty now, so the medicine should take effect pretty soon, I thought with relief. As I pressed the cold washcloth against my head again, my eyes fell on the sheet of paper I'd left on the desk. I remembered the twinkle in Dr. Gardiner's eyes last week, when he assured me for the umpteenth time that there was nothing wrong with me.

"Angie Clifford, there's nothing the matter with your head that a little bit of old-fashioned common sense wouldn't cure! We've done all the tests, and you and I both know your headaches only happen when you get yourself all worked up over trivial things." He smiled, a bit smugly, it seemed to me. "Now, the next time you feel one of these headaches starting to take hold, I want you to sit down and make a list of all the things that bother you. Once you see it there in front of you, in black and white, you'll realize how really silly most of your worries are."

A wave of depression washed over me as I stared at the catalog of my woes.

Number one: Teacher conference next Thursday about Aidan. Well, there was no way Dr. Gardiner, or anyone else, could regard that as trivial! Aidan was a bright child, everyone agreed on that. But for some reason, he couldn't make head or tail of his studies. For three years now, we'd been conferring with the teachers, the principal, even the school psychologist. So far, everybody blamed everybody else for Aidan's problems.

Now they were telling us Aidan suffered from a learning disability—well, obviously, the child wasn't learning, wasn't that clear from the beginning? But no, this was a new theory, the specialist, Mr. Villanueve, insisted. They'd done tests and now they wanted to discuss the results with Sam and me. But I'd been to enough conferences to know what to expect. Sam would end up losing his temper, Mr. Villanueve would shout a lot, and I'd leave in tears, as usual. Aidan would go right on staring at his reading assignments, as if they were written in a foreign language.

Number two: Money. What family doesn't rank that pretty high on the list these days? Sam had a decent job as a salesman for a farm implement firm, but even so, inflation made it hard going. Let's see—I'd promised myself I'd send Aidan to a special reading clinic this summer. My car needed new tires, and the dentist had called last week to say Billy needed braces right away, unless we wanted him to grow front teeth like a beaver.

Number three: Sam's mother is threatening to visit for three weeks, along with his Aunt Rita. Also, I think the dog is pregnant again. The pain pill was starting to make everything hazy, but not hazy enough to allow me to ignore that. I felt a tight knot of tension at the base of my skull.

Number four: Sam is on the road for the fifth time this month. Aside from the dentist and Aidan's teacher, I haven't had a conversation for days that didn't center on peanut butter or table manners. Oh, no, I take that back. There were several chats with Mrs. Daly from next door about the dog getting in her garden and about Dylan throwing mud at her garage door, and about the construction project in our yard.

"It's a sailboat," I'd explained as reasonably as I could. "Sam and the boys are building a sailboat, just a small one." But she'd regarded it suspiciously, hinting vaguely about zoning ordinances. To tell the truth, I almost wished she were right and the city would come some afternoon and haul it away. After all, there's something definitely

93

lacking when your husband is out selling manure spreaders all week, and then comes home only to talk of spars and jibs and mizzens!

Angrily, I shook my head. No, Dr. Gardiner, I've written it all down—and I don't feel one bit better. In fact, I could fill two more pages without any effort at all! I sighed. My headaches were real because my problems were real. If Dr. Gardiner could step into my shoes for about two minutes, he'd have a headache, too!

A small sound made me turn. Dylan stood in the doorway with the same concerned expression I'd worn as a kid. "Mom, do you—"

"It's all right, honey," I assured him quickly. I laid the washcloth down and forced myself to smile. "I'm fine. I was just resting for a few minutes."

"Yeah, I know, just another headache," he said impatiently. My spirits sank even lower. At least, when my mom used to suffer, everyone pitied her and worried a lot. "What I want to know," Dylan went on, frowning, "is when are you and Dad going to buy the camper so we can go on vacation with the Jansens?"

I groaned and mentally added "vacation" to my list of problems. Mike and Laura Jansen and their two sons had been our best friends for years—when they suggested that all of us drive out west in July, it had sounded like a great idea—that is, until I started calculating motel and restaurant expenses. Sam had half-jokingly suggested we buy a camper. Now, the boys wouldn't let us forget it.

"—because Chet Dubin says his uncle has one for sale," Dylan went on. "I told him we'd probably buy it."

I pressed the washcloth against my forehead once more and shut my eyes. My headache had faded now, but the coldness felt pleasant. I might as well pamper myself—nobody else does, I thought with a twinge of resentment.

"—so his uncle is driving it over tonight for you to see it," Dylan concluded with a businesslike nod.

"Oh, no!" I sat up with a jerk. "Dylan, whatever made you tell him that? We're not going to buy a camper. Why, we hardly have enough money to buy next week's groceries!"

"But, Mom—"

"No! Honey, there's no way we can afford a camper. Besides, who knows if we could even get gas for it these days."

"Well, for Pete's sake, Mom, you don't have to holler!" Dylan gave an injured sigh and rolled his eyes in exasperation. "Then can I at least have a guinea pig?" he continued. "Chet wants to sell me his for six dollars. He says he'll give me the cage free."

I shook my head wearily. "No. No guinea pigs—no camper. Probably no vacation, either. That's the trouble with you kids—you think we're made of money!"

Dylan ambled away dejectedly. I glanced at the clock again. Almost four. Sam should be home in another hour unless he ran into a lot of traffic. I took a deep breath and stood up, waiting cautiously to see if my head would tolerate the motion.

"Time to start supper," I announced to nobody in particular. I went out to the kitchen and began chopping onions and peppers and celery. Thank goodness my family didn't have gourmet tastes. A pot of chili and fresh baked corn bread pleased Sam and the kids as much as a fancy steak dinner.

I had the chili simmering on the stove and was finishing the corn bread batter, when the doorbell rang. "Just a minute!" I yelled, sliding the pan into the oven and burning my wrist. Darn, if this was Chet Dubin's uncle with the camper, I was going to positively wring Dylan's neck! I splashed cold water hurriedly on my arm and was still drying my hands as I opened the door.

A policeman stood there, looking grim and tall and very, very official. The sailboat—that was the first thought that flashed through my mind. Mrs. Daly had made good on her threat. She'd called and complained that we were building an unauthorized eyesore out in our yard. But then, as the man stared at me, his expression a mixture of formality and sympathy, I knew it was about Sam. My hand flew to my mouth.

"Oh, my God! Something's happened to my husband, hasn't it?"

He nodded grimly and led me over to the sofa. "You're Mrs. Clifford?" he asked gently. "Mrs. Sam Clifford?"

I nodded mutely.

"There's been a shooting incident, Mrs. Clifford. A sniper in a motel parking lot. Your husband was badly injured. He's at General Hospital, over in Lynbrook."

I choked back a sob. "I've got to go to him! My car keys—where did I put my car keys?"

"No." He put his hand on my arm. "I'll drive you. It will be faster."

As his words sank in, I felt myself grow numb. There was no hope for Sam then. All this man could offer me was the chance to see him for a moment before he died. Lynbrook was thirty-five miles away. But it wasn't even in Sam's sales territory. What on earth had he been doing in Lynbrook? And why on earth would anyone want to shoot my husband?

"Yes, of course. Thank you," I mumbled, following the policeman out to his car.

"Mom—Mom, what's wrong?" Billy bounded up on the porch, his face nearly as white as mine.

Swallowing hard, I forced myself to speak calmly. "Your father has been hurt, Billy. I'm going to the hospital and you'll have to take care of you brothers." I hugged him hard. "I'll call you, honey. I'll call you as soon as I find out—" My voice trailed off in a sob.

"We'd better hurry, ma'am," the trooper whispered. "The doctor said to get there as fast as possible."

The siren screamed as we sped across town and onto the interstate, heading north to Lynbrook. "I still don't understand," I said, dazed. "Sam was in the southern part of the state. What was he doing in Lynbrook?"

I saw the officer's jaw muscles tighten and there was pity in his eyes as he regarded me. For a long moment, he was silent. Then he cleared his throat, obviously embarrassed.

"Look—uh—Mrs. Clifford, you seem like a real nice lady and I'd—uh—I'd hate for you to run into the reporters and have them asking you questions without you knowing all the facts." He hesitated nervously. "You see, there was a woman involved." For a moment, my mind refused to acknowledge his implication. I stared at him stupidly. He was shaking his head.

"I sure hate to be telling you this, Mrs. Clifford. But apparently, your husband had gone to the motel to meet this—uh—this other woman. They checked in about noon, according to the desk clerk. And—uh—the woman's husband must have found out. He was waiting in a parked car, and when your husband came out, well. . . ." His voice trailed off uncertainly. For a moment, the only sound in the car was the roar of the powerful engine and the wailing siren. But as realization sank in, the shock was like someone hitting me hard in the pit of my stomach. For a moment, I just sat there, hardly able to breathe.

Everything grew dark and sort of blurry. I felt a cold sweat break out on my forehead. I thought I was going to faint. But as I shut my eyes, my mind flashed back to a scene fifteen years before—an ugly scene with Sam's mother.

Sam and I had just gotten engaged that day. I'd insisted that we go to his mother's to tell her our happy news. It was a small, shabby house in a marginal neighborhood. Sam's dad had walked out on his family when Sam was a child, and his mother had never forgiven him—or any man. Sam had moved out as soon as he was old enough to get a job.

"Why live with someone who hates me and doesn't bother to conceal it?" he'd said bitterly. Anyway, I'd insisted on going to Mrs. Clifford's house to show her my engagement ring. We were sitting in her kitchen, I'd just told her about our wedding plans. Dimly, I heard her voice, harsh and bitter, echoing in my mind.

"If you marry him, Angie, you're a bigger fool than I thought!"

she told me then, her voice cutting through my happiness. "Sure, he says he loves you. Sam's father told me that, too. But do you know how long love lasts?" She laughed harshly. "Wait until the first baby comes, honey—that's when a man's eyes stray to other girls— younger, prettier girls who don't smell of formula and diapers."

Sam had sat there, grim-faced and silent, his fists clenched into tight knots. I was in tears as we left. Sam had been right. His mother was a horrid, embittered old woman with an evil, poisonous tongue. Even though Sam comforted me and told me not to be upset, the incident took some of the joy from our wedding day. Not that I'd believed one word she told me, of course. Like I said, Sam was a family man all the way. Never, for one moment, had I ever suspected him of being unfaithful. Until now. . . .

The policeman gave me a worried glance. "Are you okay, ma'am? You look awfully pale—is there anything I can do?"

I shook my head to make it stop spinning. "I'm all right," I said weakly. We were nearing the outskirts of Lynbrook now, going nearly seventy miles an hour, weaving in and out of rush hour traffic. Motorists stared at us as we passed.

The memory came back of a day almost thirteen years ago, when Sam and I had driven this route at breakneck speed, too, only the highway hadn't been four lanes then. Only the mercy of God had carried us safely around the trucks and Sunday drivers who clogged the road. I was eight and a half months pregnant with Billy, and suddenly, with no warning, things began to go wrong, terribly wrong. I was hemorrhaging badly—so badly, we didn't dare wait for the ambulance.

Leaning on his horn, Sam rushed me to the hospital. By the time we arrived, I was unconscious from loss of blood. Thank God, Billy was delivered safely by Cesarean section a few minutes later. If we'd waited, they told us, my son would have died, and I might have, too. Sam had been wonderful during my recovery. He'd taken time off from work and he wouldn't even let me lift a finger around the house. All my friends marveled at what a considerate, doting husband he was, what a loving father he was to Billy.

"Why you'd think the boy was made of solid gold, the way that man treats him," my father said gruffly.

But I'd just smiled at my husband, sharing his feelings completely. And later, as our other boys were born, Sam had been every bit as proud and happy as he was with Billy. On Sundays, we'd all go to church together, and Sam would march us up to the very first pew, nodding and smiling to people all the way up the aisle, proud as a peacock to show off his family.

The church—oh, how would I ever face my friends, or our

pastor? The policeman was right; the reporters would have a field day with this, eagerly digging out all the ugly sordid details for the morning edition. Would it be on the TV news at six?

The policeman hadn't said if there were TV reporters at the scene, but there probably were. I buried my face in my hands, and felt the wave of anger flooding over me, eating at my heart like acid. How could Sam have done this to me?

Then, once again, I saw an image of his mother, her face etched in bitter, unforgiving hatred. She lived alone with her humiliation and resentment. Was this how I, too, would end up? I shuddered and suddenly my anger faded away in a surge of compassion for my husband. No matter what he'd done, I'd learn to forgive him. Please God, don't let him die, I prayed. I love him—we'll work it out—we'll make a fresh start. Just don't let him die.

The trooper reached over and touched my shoulder. "Almost there now," he said. "Try and stay calm."

Then we were pulling into the emergency entrance. He led me down the corridor to the elevator, then down a hall to the intensive care ward. As we approached the room, a nurse intercepted us, her tight-lipped expression telling me without words that we were too late.

"I'm sorry, Mrs. Clifford—he's gone."

"I—I want to see him," I whispered. "Please, give me at least that much."

"I'm afraid that wouldn't be wise right now," she said frowning. "You must realize, his face—the gun—well, he's really quite unrecognizable."

I winced but still I stood there, refusing to accept.

"Oh, all right," she said with a sigh. "But I'll have to phone Dr. Miller. I can't take responsibility for this myself." She bustled officiously down the hall toward the nurses' station. Then, before anyone could stop me, I threw open the door and rushed in. His body was covered by a sheet, all but his left arm, which hung lifeless at his side. Tears flooded my eyes as I recognized the wristwatch I'd given him for his birthday last year. Then, suddenly, my heart began to pound wildly and I stared at his hand, unable to speak.

"What is it?" The policeman was at my side, reaching me as I started to collapse.

"That scar," I whispered hoarsely, pointing at the man's hand. There was an ugly purplish scar across the back of his hand from the base of his thumb all the way to his wrist. "My husband doesn't have a scar like that."

The first thing I did was call home to tell the boys they could stop worrying. When Sam answered the phone himself, my facade of calm gave way. All I could do was sob hysterically. The policeman drove me back home, and I rushed to my beloved husband's arms, embracing him, tears streaming down my face. The boys clustered around, trying to hug us both and even our fat little beagle sensing that a celebration was in progress, jumped around noisily.

Another police car pulled up. As the officer talked to us, the pieces of the puzzle finally began to fall into place. A fingerprint check identified the dead man as Richie Buschinski, an ex-convict with a criminal record that stretched for years. His last crime was a break-in at the motel where Sam had spent the previous night.

"When I woke up this morning, my door was jimmied open. I discovered that my watch and wallet were missing," Sam explained. "The desk clerk told me several other rooms had been burglarized, too. He called the police and promised me I'd be notified if my things were recovered." Sam shrugged. "There wasn't much I could do—I contacted my credit card companies to report the theft." He turned to me apologetically. "I never even thought to call and tell you, honey. It didn't seem that important at the time. I just went on my way, hoping the stuff might turn up in a pawn shop somewhere."

"It turned up, all right," the tall policeman said wryly. "He was using your driver's license and credit cards at the motel where he was shot. When we identified him from your papers, I'm afraid we scared your wife half to death."

"Aw, come on, Angie." Sam put his arm around me. "You never believed for one minute that I'd be fooling around with some other woman, did you?"

"Of course not." I'd never tell Sam, of course. But I'd hold forever in my heart the knowledge that my love for him had been tested—and that it had been strong enough to survive. . . .

Billy finally managed to get my attention. "You got four phone calls from some guy while you were gone, Mom," he reported. "He wants you to call him back right away about a camper, or something. Here, I wrote it down." He handed me a piece of paper with a phone number scrawled on it. I turned the paper over and saw the list I'd begun writing that afternoon when my headache started. Just as Dr. Gardiner said, the problems now seemed insignificant.

"Does this mean we're buying the camper, Mom?" Dylan asked, his eyes shining.

I grinned happily. "Who knows?" I told him. "It won't hurt to look at it."

Several months have passed. I haven't had any tension headaches lately. Sam is still on the road more than I like, and Aidan's last report card showed little improvement in reading and math, but he's working with a tutor now. Our dentist bill threatens to put us in debt for the rest of our lives. But it doesn't upset me as much as it used to. That one afternoon of violence and terror will always haunt me—but in a strange way, I'm grateful. For I appreciate now how precious my husband and family are to me. That makes everything else a lot easier to handle.

THE END

TEENS GONE WILD!
Idle hands turn deadly

James Vincent said it best that night at Sunset Beach. I never heard James talk much before, but that night he sort of spoke for all of us.

"I don't know about you guys," he said, his eyes glittering in the moonlight, his face pale and pinched from the cold sea wind, "but I get mad. I see all these people riding in their shiny cars, laying down the cash for new houses and stuff. I get mad when I see them watering their lawns and sitting there grinning and slurping drinks in the sun. They're sitting on top of the world. They want something, they go out and get it. They're so damn fat and proud of themselves—so proud of being grown-up and safe and respectable. And me—I ain't got no world at all. Sometimes I feel like a third shoe. I don't know, I get mad, just plain mad. I want to wreck those fancy cars, tear down those fancy houses!"

A long silence followed James's speech. I didn't know if the goose pimples on my arms came from the cold or the helpless feeling of anger and doom that his words sent through me. I shivered and wanted to be a little girl again, so I could put off what was sure to come.

James was talking about grown-ups. He was talking about his folks and mine and Marty's—all of our folks. The hatred and contempt for them in his words drew us closer together in the war that is always going on between young and old—the war between those who have yet to take their places in the world and those who have already done so.

We were a teenage gang. The papers called us juvenile delinquents, and I guess they thought calling us that explained everything about us. But it didn't explain anything at all.

Take Marty, for instance. People might say there was no reason for him to hate the world the way he did. Marty's folks were rich. They lived in one of the biggest houses in Fords. His dad owned two cars, and he was some kind of bigwig in the county government. Marty had all the cash he needed. He even had his own car, as soon as he was old enough to drive. He had his designer jeans specially made, and his jacket wasn't cheap horsehide, like most of the other guys, but pure black calf. I used to think he was really hot in that outfit. But then I hooked up with Jeremy when Christina came along.

How poor Christina Wright ever became a juvenile delinquent, I'll never know. Her folks weren't rich, but they had enough. They

101

lived in one of the newest housing developments in town. Her dad was a lawyer who made a good living. Christina was an only child and her folks worshiped her. She could have anything she wanted with no questions asked. She was a beautiful girl, and she looked good with Marty.

Jeremy Floyd was for me. I used to think I went for the model type like Marty, with his long hair, nice clothes, and perfect profile. Jeremy wasn't slick and handsome at all. He was a poor kid, like me, and he worked on a garbage truck most of his spare time. But he had a quiet way about him, not loud and bragging like Marty. You got the feeling that Jeremy thought about things a lot, even though he didn't say what he thought. He had an anger burning in his heart, like all of us—but Marty's anger was all for show; Jeremy's anger was private, just for himself.

James Vincent was a skinny, pale-faced little guy who tried to strut like Marty, but couldn't quite make it. He was Marty's yes-man. When Marty sneered, James sneered; when he said spit, James spit. James came from a big, poor family like me, and there was just no place for him at home.

There was Melanie Anderson, who came from a house full of girls, of whom she was the youngest and the ugliest. Melanie had a body like Jessica Simpson and a face like—well, she was ugly. She bought her way into the gang with her body. I don't know how far she went, and I didn't figure it was my business to try and find out. All Melanie asked for was a kind word and the right to be with us. Even Jeremy's eyes glittered suspiciously when he looked at her, but Melanie wasn't the sort of person I could be jealous of. I only felt sorry for her.

And there was me, Stacy Brown, just an ordinary kid with a snub nose and a few freckles, brown eyes that matched the in-between shade of my hair, and a clear complexion that needed no makeup. You'll see dozens like me around any high school—not too bright and not too dumb, not homely but no raving beauty, either. I lived in the poor section of town, in a run-down old house that was soaked with the smell of fertilizer from a feed mill next door. It was always a grim joke of mine that the fertilizer must have been effective because there were eight of us kids born in that tiny house. There were always two or three of us missing—and one of those was always me. I stayed away from the smells of fertilizer, diapers, and sweaty clothes until I absolutely had to come back. Mom and Dad were only too glad to have me out of their way.

Other kids came into the gang and then drifted away after a time, but we six stayed on, almost always together. We started trouble with little things, like hanging around a candy store after school, messing around, jeering at the customers, trying to drown our boredom in a lot of noise. There was no place to go and nothing to do until suppertime. Soon we began meeting after supper, too. Our families didn't seem to care when we came home.

At last the owner of the candy store kicked us out. He told us he'd call the cops if we came back, and he meant it. But we had plenty of energy to work off somewhere, and for kids with a desire for trouble, the new housing developments were made to order. Rows and rows of new houses were going up at the edge of town. At night, the streets of bare, unfinished homes were as silent as bombed-out cities. There were dangerous rafters to walk on, shiny tools to steal, and night watchmen to dodge.

At first it was just the spookiness of the place that attracted us. But then after we had been chased off a few times by night watchmen, it got to be a game. We'd move in on the houses like commandos, crawling and slipping from shadow to shadow. We'd steal plumbing and nails and light fixtures from right under the noses of the watchmen. We had no use for the stuff, and we'd throw it away as soon as we stole it. It was the excitement of the game—ducking the watchmen and the police prowl cars—that kept us going back. There was one special night watchman who was waiting for us—an old guy with a grizzly beard and a mean voice. We loved to get him shook up.

We did other things, too. One morning, just before school began, Marty called the principal's office. Disguising his voice, he told them a bomb had been planted in the school. Such excitement! The school was evacuated. The cops and detectives came to search every inch of the building. Of course, there was no bomb, but it sure took the boredom out of the day for us. Then the idea caught on. Kids from other schools picked it up and used it. Nobody was prouder than Marty at the furor. The papers called it "hoodlumism," and all kinds of bigwigs had their say about the juvenile delinquents who were turning Fords into a terrible place. Even Marty's old man made a statement that was spread all over the front pages—about how parents ought to pay more attention to their kids.

Marty was bitter about that. "He's got some nerve talking," he said. "I ain't seen him at home for two weeks."

"What's the matter, Marty?" Jeremy kidded. "Don't you like your old man? They say he's quite a guy."

"Like him?" Marty's face flushed red, and he bit his tongue. He turned away, saying only, "Yeah, he's quite a guy—and he'll be the first to tell you."

That night, feeling important because of the big play our bomb scare was getting, we moved in on the housing development where the night watchman was waiting for us. We planned to give him a few runs for his money—but he had us cased that night. He jumped out of a closet in a house we were stripping of light fixtures. He stabbed his flashlight at us and held a gun on us. "This is to show you I can catch you when I want to," he said grimly. "Next time I'll shoot first. Now, you kids get out of here and stay out!"

We hopped into Marty's car and roared away, laughing and yelling. But the sight of the gun glinting in the light of the flashlight still filled my mind, and a feeling of doom weighed on me.

We drove to Sunset Beach, piled out of the car, and raced down the beach until we lost our breath and fell on the sand. We lay there on our backs, looking up at the stars. That was when James started talking. "I just get mad," he said. "I don't know why I get mad. I want to tear down their stupid houses!"

Marty stood up and faced the sea, the wind rushing through his hair. We looked up at him, and I could see Christina's face all troubled and adoring. He looked handsome, all right—but then, that was just what I didn't like about Marty. He was always posing like he was a model or something. "I'll have them all crawling someday," he said. "I'll show them."

Jeremy chuckled. "Like your old man."

Marty whirled around. "To hell with my old man!" he spit out.

"He gives you anything you want," said Jeremy. "He's a big shot."

Marty sat down. His face was hard. "I'll tell you something about my old man," he said. "He's so big and respectable, talking all that bull about honor and hard work and stuff. I used to believe him, too. I used to want to be like him. But then I found out how he got his money and his important job. The first of every month, the real big boys come to see my old man. They wear flashy clothes and they have rods under their armpits. They tell my old man what to do and what to say and what to think. And he takes it. He's scared stiff of them. He owes them everything he's got. He thinks I don't know, but I hid in the bushes one night and listened. Big? He couldn't hold his job or his money one minute without those guys. He's got no right to tell me anything."

The night closed in on us. We shivered. "Wow!" James breathed.

Marty lay down on the sand and put his face in his arms. "My old lady and my old man haven't slept in the same room since I was ten years old," he said, his voice suddenly small and scared, like a little boy's. "They hate each other's guts. She knows what he is. Big? He's big, all right—about as big as a cockroach."

We lay there looking up at the black sky, stunned by Marty's tortured words. Understanding what it had cost him to tell us, we felt drawn to one another, comrades in a hostile and suspicious world.

"All the time," murmured Melanie, "they tell me at home not to mind because I ain't pretty like my sisters. All my sisters talk about is becoming models or movie stars. If you ain't got a pretty face, you're out. I used to try all those soaps and lotions that the advertisements say will make you beautiful. But with me, it don't work. I'll show them, though. I got talent. I know I can sing. I've got a good figure, and with the right lights and makeup, anybody can look pretty on television. Lots of singers I see on TV aren't pretty at all, but they got talent."

"I don't see anything wrong with your looks," I lied.

Melanie turned to me and smiled. "My figure ain't bad," she said.

"I know," I said. "I'm not pretty, and I don't particularly care about it. I suppose, in their way, when they find the time, my mom and dad like each other—after all, look how many kids they've got. But me, I just don't want to go home. Out here I'm somebody, I'm part of something. Home is like a department-store basement."

Jeremy grinned at me. "You're pretty enough for me," he said gallantly.

I took his hand. "What about you, Jeremy? What's your complaint?"

He shrugged. "I don't know," he said. "I just got a nervous feeling inside me like I want to explode, like there's no time to do all the things I want to do. I never had a bike or an electric train or new clothes that fit me. Nothing. Never any money. I always thought that when I grew up and went to work, I'd get the things I want. But now it looks like it'll be the Army. Maybe I'll come out alive and maybe I won't. It's an even toss. I get the feeling that I'm in a trap and can't get out. I just get so nervous that I want to reach out and break something."

"That's how I feel, too," James said.

Christina whispered, "I'm scared. If our parents heard us talking like this, they'd die."

We smiled at her. Marty leaned over and brushed his lips against her hair. Christina was our baby. Not that she was the youngest, because I was. But there was no hardness in Christina, and she was always scared. I sometimes got the feeling that she came along with us on our exploits just because she wanted to be scared. I wondered why such a protected, frightened child was with us. But she didn't say.

As we lay there on the cold sand, a warm feeling of friendship washed over us. It was the first time we'd really talked about ourselves, and it gave us a deep satisfaction to know that we could. It was a better feeling than we'd ever gotten from our wild exploits. Shyly, Melanie began to sing. Soothed by her song, we closed our eyes and held hands. Ah, how good it was to have friends!

Two flashlights stabbed through the darkness and we sat up quickly. Two policemen were coming down the beach toward us, spread far apart as if they were closing in on an armed enemy. "All right, kids, break it up!" one of them commanded harshly.

"Holy crap," Marty said, "why?"

"Move on, move on."

"This is a public place," Jeremy said. "And we got rights, just the same as anybody else. We ain't doing anything."

"That's what you say," the first policeman growled. "One more word and I'll haul you all in. Now get home where you belong."

Christina begged, "Let's do what they say. Please."

Marty swore softly and picked himself up. We trudged up the beach, followed by the policemen. A moment ago we had felt so good, so full of comradeship and at peace with ourselves—but now our stomachs were twisted with shame and anger. The police followed us to the car and watched as we climbed in. "Now go home and behave," one of them said. "You kids stay out of trouble, get it?"

Marty muttered something under his breath and drove away. Jeremy smashed his fist against the back of the seat.

"What the hell do they expect us to do?" he snarled. "Do something wrong and they hunt you. Do nothing wrong and they hunt you anyway!"

I put my hand on his to soothe him. "Why did they do that?" Christina asked. "We weren't doing anything wrong. I don't understand why they chased us that way."

James hissed, "I'd like to blow something up!"

And then Marty said, "Why don't we?" We all looked at him. Marty kept his eyes on the road, but he was grinning widely.

"Huh?" James grunted.

"Just what I said," Marty said. "Let's make those cops work for their money. Let's go and blow up that house we were in tonight."

"You're crazy," Jeremy said.

"No, I'm not," Marty said. "I watched the workers blowing up tree stumps. I know where they keep the dynamite."

"That's pretty major," Jeremy warned.

"Scared?" Marty taunted.

"What the hell," James agreed. "Those houses don't belong to anybody yet. I'm with you, Marty. I want to see the big boom. It'll be awesome, man!"

"Look," I said, "We can't go tearing down everything in sight just because we're mad."

Marty whirled at me, almost losing control of the car. "What kind of world do you live in, girl? What the hell's everybody doing

106

but tearing things down all the time? What have they got bombs and guns for? Like the real big guys told my old man, you get no prizes for playing nice!"

"Let's go!" crowed James.

I looked to Jeremy for support, but he was just staring straight ahead. I could see he was still burning from the treatment we'd had at Sunset Beach.

We drove to a point a half-mile from the development. Marty pulled the car up near a tree, switched off the lights, and we walked to the edge of the dark houses, where we hid in the bushes.

"You guys go along that line of houses and draw the watchman away from the supply shack," Marty said. "Tease him up to the other end, and then get away and come back here. I'll get the stuff and then you can watch while I set it off. I know just where it is."

Jeremy and James moved out, and a few moments later we heard them rattling some boards up at the other end. The door of the supply shack opened and the watchman, cursing and searching the night with his flashlight, lumbered up the muddy street. Marty slithered off to the supply shack. We girls waited in silence, our hearts pounding, until Jeremy and James crawled up beside us. Then Marty appeared, breathless but grinning proudly. He was holding a stick of dynamite with a long fuse.

"This is it!" he said in a hoarse whisper. "Let's go!" He scrambled out of the ditch. There was nothing for us to do but follow him.

We ran across the field and crept back into the house where the watchman had caught us earlier. We gathered in a circle around Marty as he lit a match. He held the flame about an inch from the dynamite, while he grinned excitedly and looked at each of us in turn. Nobody grinned back. My heart was beating wildly. I tried to catch Jeremy's eye, but he was staring at the tiny flame as if he were hypnotized.

Then Marty lit the fuse. "This one's going to be huge!" he said. "Let's get out of here!" He tossed the dynamite through a hole in the unfinished floor. Everyone scrambled for the door. It was pitch-dark, and I could barely see their dim figures as they ran out into the night. Then I fell.

There was a loud crash as a stack of lumber fell to the floor beside me. A figure stopped in the doorway, turned, and helped me to my feet. It was Jeremy. "Damn!" he said. "Let's get out of here before we get blown to bits!"

We caught up with the others at the edge of the field. "What was all the racket?" Marty asked angrily. "You ruined everything! The watchman must have heard it, and he'll get there in time to pinch off the fuse!"

"Better hope he does," Jeremy said. "Because if he's in that house when it goes off—"

Suddenly the night was torn open by a tremendous explosion. I felt as if someone had pushed me. A taste of lead filled my mouth. When I opened my eyes, I saw that the row of houses was lit up with a red glow.

"Damn!" yelled James.

I could see Marty's eyes glittering in the light from the blast. Jeremy said nothing. I reached for his hand, but he pulled it away—then he reached for mine and squeezed it so hard it hurt. Then we heard shouts and the far-off howl of a squad car's siren. The fire engine sirens began to moan. Cars raced past us toward the blast. We ran to the ditch alongside the road to hide. Soon a couple of fire engines came rocketing by. The peaceful night had suddenly turned into a mad, screaming hell.

Then we saw an ambulance screaming down the road, and my heart turned to lead. "Come on, guys," Marty said shakily. "Let's get out of here!"

Nobody moved except Jeremy. He got up and started back toward the commotion. "You crazy?" Marty exploded. "Come back here!"

"No," Jeremy said. "I got to find out what happened to the old guy." He disappeared into the shadows. Marty started to go but nobody followed, so he came back and lay in the ditch with us and waited. Soon the ambulance came back down the road, going even faster.

When Jeremy slipped back into the ditch, his face was gray. "Well?" I asked.

"That was him in the ambulance," Jeremy said. "He was in the house when—when the blast went off. He might be dead. Nobody seemed to know."

Christina threw up. Then she began laughing and crying hysterically. Marty took her by the shoulders and shook her viciously. "Shut up! You want the cops to come down on us?"

"I want to go home," she cried. "Don't you understand? We just killed a man!"

Marty clapped his hand over her mouth. "My God," he growled, "let's get her out of here!" We climbed into the car, and I got into the backseat with Christina. Marty drove without lights, cut down some back roads, and soon merged with the traffic on the main highway. He finally pulled up in the parking lot behind the theater, which was our regular meeting place, and cut the motor. He climbed into the backseat and knelt near Christina.

"Listen, baby," he told her, "pull yourself together. We're all in this thing together. Now calm down. If everybody plays it cool, nothing will happen."

Christina struggled to get out of the car, but we held on to her. "I'm through," she sobbed. "Can't you see what we did?"

108

"Now listen," Marty begged. "We didn't want to blow up the old guy. It was an accident."

"No," Christina cried. "It's wrong. We've got to tell. I'll never be able to live with myself if we don't tell!"

"She's out of her mind! Talk to her, somebody, for God's sake!" Marty pleaded.

We took turns talking to Christina. We all felt sick about what had happened, but it seemed to us that all we could do was remain calm and stick together. If we didn't talk, nobody would find out what we'd done; maybe the whole thing would blow over. We prayed that the old man had not been killed.

Christina calmed down a bit and seemed to listen to reason. Marty shook his head in relief. He put his arm around her. "Easy, easy, baby, that's better," he soothed. But she shrank away. "Come on," said Marty. "I guess we could all use some coffee."

We drove down the highway to a diner and filed into a booth in the back. Marty and the boys brought hot coffee and doughnuts from the counter. We ate in silence. Christina's eyes were red-rimmed. The boys were tense and grim. I didn't dare talk to Jeremy. His eyes were filled with fury, and I could see it was anger against himself, against me, against Marty—against the whole world. Melanie looked stunned and her face was uglier than ever.

Two boys were sitting at the counter, watching us with half-closed eyes. We'd seen them before. They belonged to a gang from a nearby town. With a bold, bored look, they took in Christina, myself, and finally Melanie. "Hey, big hips," one of them said. "Come on over. We'll cheer you up."

That was all our guys needed. They were nervous and angry already. They sprang to their feet and walked to the counter. "The girls like it where they are," Jeremy said tensely. "But we thought we'd come over."

Marty sneered, "Wanna cheer us up?"

One of the boys rose quickly, head forward, and plunged headlong into Marty's belly. Then Jeremy stepped in and knocked the boy back across the counter, and James leaped on him, shouting. Marty got up and took on the other one. In a moment, fists were flying.

The manager and counterman came running to rip the boys apart. "Now get out of here, all of you!" shouted the manager. "You kids are ruining this place. Don't come back!"

The other boys left first, and we girls hung our heads and followed. The pair climbed into their car. One of them leaned out and told us, "We'll be back tonight. And this time there'll be more of us. We'll find you!" And then they roared away.

"They'll be back, all right," James said.

"Let's round up some more guys and wait for them," Marty suggested.

"I've got no stomach for any more," Jeremy said.

I begged, "Please, let's go home. The night's been bad enough as it is."

"I want to go home," Melanie said wildly. Christina leaned her head against Marty's car and wept. We climbed in and Marty drove us all home. He dropped me off first, and as he drove away I could hear Christina sobbing loudly all the way down the street.

The smell of the house hit me when I opened the back door— sweat, old clothes, the garbage that hadn't been thrown out yet. But somehow, that night, the smell was comforting. It was eleven o'clock and the whole family was sleeping.

I tiptoed through the living room, where my two older brothers and a sister slept, and crept up the creaky stairs to the attic. In one room, Mom and Dad and the two youngest slept. I slept in the other room. I took off my clothes and slipped into bed beside my sister. I lay awake, trembling, staring at the moonlight that filtered through the window. I wanted to think. I wanted to come to some kind of decision, but I couldn't collect my thoughts. Somehow I fell asleep.

The next morning was Saturday. I raced to the corner store before breakfast and got a paper. I found what I was looking for on the second page. The watchman had been badly burned and cut by flying timber. He was still in a state of shock, but he'd live. The police were investigating the outrage.

But I found another story I wasn't looking for. The blast made second-page news because on the front page, big as life, was a photo of stunned parents looking down at the crumpled figure of a girl in the bushes. The girl was Christina. She'd been attacked and beaten just outside her house. The attackers had smashed her head against a rock until she was dead.

Girl Brutally Murdered, Teen Gang Wars Suspected, the headlines read.

A reporter had interviewed Christina's parents. "We knew she was running around with a wild bunch of kids," Mrs. Wright had wailed, "but she wouldn't tell us who they were." Numb with grief, Mr. Wright had said, "She was our only child. We never could say 'no' to her. Why couldn't we say no? Why? Why?"

I went to sit on the steps behind the store. For a moment I thought I was dreaming, but another look at the paper brought me back to reality. As far as I was concerned, there was no doubt how it had happened. The boys at the diner had come back with their gang. They had trailed Marty's car and jumped Christina after Marty had let her off.

I was filled with rage. That gang had to get what was coming to them. But how? Should I tell what I knew to the police? They had never helped us before, why should they help us now? I had always thought of cops as enemies who pushed us around, as they'd done at Sunset Beach.

Then a chill went through me. Weren't all of us in danger? Hadn't those guys sworn to hunt us all down, one by one? We were all in for the same fate as Christina, unless I went to the police. But the police, I knew, would not stop at our story of what had happened at the diner. They would ask questions. Before they were through with us, they'd know everything. They'd find out about our part in the explosion!

I realized that going to the police meant making a clean confession of everything. It meant being prepared to take the consequences, and those consequences would fall not just on me, but on all the others. I didn't know what to do. I wished there were someone strong who could tell me what to do. I'd always worked everything out for myself, but now I needed help. I wondered—should I tell my parents what I knew? Would they be able to advise me?

I went home. Dad was not there. He was never there. With a family of eight kids to support, he had to take on extra jobs. He worked all day Saturday in a gas station. Had Dad been at home, I think I would I have gone to him and told him the whole story. But he wasn't there.

Mom was home, of course. She was never anywhere else. The baby was lying in the carriage with a bottle propped in his mouth, and Mom was racing back and forth from him to her pile of ironing. Two-year-old Vicky was yelling because three-year-old David had taken her doll, but Mom had no time for her troubles. The older boys were racing in and out, jumping on the furniture.

I pitched in with the housework, hoping to rescue a quiet moment for a talk with Mom. But a quiet moment never came. "Mom," I said at last, forgetting about my need for privacy, "I've got something I want to talk to you about."

Mom was diapering the baby. "Go ahead," she said, "go out with your friends. I can manage."

"That's not what I mean," I said.

She jumped to the stove. The stew was boiling over. "Really," she said, "sometimes I get more things done when I'm by myself. You can go out."

I shouted, "I don't want to go out! I want to talk to you!"

Mom only half heard. "Well," she said, "then you just go right ahead and talk."

I closed my eyes and said numbly, "You've got to stop for a minute. Please. I can't talk unless you stop and listen."

Mom looked up. "My gosh," she said, "you'd think I had nothing to do around here. You just talk away. I'll listen." At that moment, five of the kids came running into the house, demanding their lunch. The big boys strode in and began slamming the refrigerator door.

I gave up. I walked out of the house, knowing that it would take Mom only two seconds to forget that she was supposed to be listening to what I wanted to say.

I roamed the streets all afternoon, trying to decide what to do. I saw some policemen, and their faces seemed so hard and unfeeling that my heart fell. The stores and the sidewalks were crowded with busy people. Everyone seemed to have a place to go. I felt like an outcast. I remembered what James had said.

Why wasn't there a place for teenagers like me and my friends? We were neither here nor there, neither adults nor kids—it was as if we were in the waiting room, outside the door of life.

I passed candy stores and pool hall and playgrounds, and I saw other teenagers like myself. They were all swaggering and loud, and they were watching one another to see what impression they were making. They were all killing time—murdering valuable minutes, precious years. They had nothing else to do.

I knew Jeremy was working on the garbage truck that day, so I walked over to the city garage and waited for him to get off. Jeremy would know what to do. He spotted me from the truck when it pulled in. He swung off and walked toward me, his face tight and pale. "Hello, Stacy," he said in a low voice.

"You saw the papers?" I asked.

"Yes."

"What are we going to do, Jeremy?"

He shook his head. "I don't know."

"It was the boys in the diner, you know," I told him.

"Maybe," he said, giving me a strange look. "There's no proof of that."

"They said they'd get us," I reminded him. "You and me and all the rest of us are next, unless we do something about it."

"There's nothing we can do," he said.

"We can go to the police."

"You know what that means?" he asked me. "By the time the cops got through with us, they'd have the lowdown on the bombing and the night watchman, too."

"But we're in danger!" I cried.

He turned and took my shoulders in his hands. "Stacy, listen. Maybe it was that gang, and maybe it wasn't. If they just wanted to rough Christina up, they could have done that without killing her. Somebody lost his head, and those guys have been in the game too long for that. We've got to be sure."

"No," I said. "You're scared, Jeremy. You're just trying to find a way out."

"Sure, I'm scared," he told me. "But when I make up my mind what to do, it won't be because I'm scared or I want anybody to protect me. It'll be because I've decided for myself the right thing to do."

"Let's get everybody together tonight," I begged. "We can talk it over and decide what to do."

He shook his head. "It'll have to be without me, Stacy. I'm through."

I stared at him.

"I've been doing a lot of thinking," he said. "I've been trying to figure where I fit in. And it's not with that gang. What I've got to do, I've got to do by myself."

I backed away from him. "Does that mean you're through with me, too?"

He didn't look at me. "I hope not," he said. "You and me—that's something else I've got to figure out."

"Great!" I said sarcastically. "You'll let me know when you've got this all figured out, won't you?"

The trouble in his eyes deepened. "Don't make fun of me, Stacy!"

I softened. "Look, Jeremy, there's something else on your mind, something you're not telling me about. What is it?"

For a moment, his mouth opened as if to say something, but then he clamped it shut. He turned away. "I've got to work this out for myself," he said.

"All right," I said angrily. "While you're working this out for yourself, I'll be working it out with the others. I'm getting them all together at nine tonight in the parking lot behind the theater. If you've got any guts or any feeling of friendship left, you'll be there. If not, so long!" I turned and left him.

I went to a phone booth and called Marty. A maid answered the phone and called him. Marty's voice was muffled; he must have been cupping the phone with his hand.

"Have you heard?" I asked.

"Yeah," he whispered. "Awful! She wouldn't let me drop her off at her door. Made me leave her two blocks from her house. I shouldn't have done it."

"Listen," I told him, "I'm calling everybody together tonight at nine behind the theater, usual place."

"What the hell for?" he asked.

"We've got to figure out what to do."

"There's only one thing to do—lay low!"

I was furious. Were they all cowards? "Now look," I said, "I'm all for going to the cops. If you've got any better ideas, you'd better come tonight and bring them with you."

"All right," Marty said. "I'll be there."

"Good!" I snapped. "You call James and bring him along."

I hung up and walked over to Melanie's house. Her sisters were sitting on the front porch. Their hair was all thorny with curlers and sweat was pouring off their faces. They didn't look so much like movie stars to me.

"Melanie home?"

One of the sisters shrugged. "She's sick, up in her room. Go on up."

I walked past them into the house. It seemed to be empty. I went up the stairs and knocked on Melanie's door. A ghostly voice asked, "Who's there?"

"It's Stacy."

"Go away. I don't feel so good."

"You'll feel worse unless you let me in," I whispered hoarsely.

The door creaked open, and Melanie let me in. Her face was blotched from crying and she looked ugly and a little crazy. I told her about the meeting that night.

"No," she whispered. "I'm scared."

"So am I," I told her, "that's why you've gotta be there."

She shook her head. "I'm not moving out of this house." She went to her bed and lay down. Her shoulders heaved. For a moment I was angry. I wished that I, too, could crawl into bed and hide from everything. But then I felt sorry for Melanie. I left the room, closing the door gently behind me. We'd have to decide without her.

I walked the streets. I didn't go home for supper. As I walked and thought, anger came over me again. Frightened kids, that's all we were! Marty and Jeremy and Melanie, they only wanted to back out, to lie low. Yet we knew things that could help bring Christina's killers to justice. If we had any real feeling of friendship, there would be no hesitation about telling what we knew, even if it meant getting ourselves in a lot of trouble.

I knew then what I had to do. That was when I really grew up for good. The police had to be told. But first I had to convince the others. I couldn't do it alone, because they were involved, and I couldn't be an informer. I prayed that Jeremy wouldn't let me down, that he'd show up—but I had the feeling that he wouldn't be there. I felt dread in my heart without knowing why.

At nine, the parking lot was filled with cars. I waited at the far end of the lot for Marty's car to show up. No one else was there. I gave up on Melanie and Jeremy, but I figured James would come with

114

Marty. At fifteen minutes after nine, Marty's car pulled in through the lines of cars and jerked to a stop. I went over and climbed in. Marty was alone. "Where's James?" I asked him, puzzled.

He didn't look at me. "He couldn't come," he said. Suddenly, I knew Marty was lying. He had never called James. But what difference did that make? James would just echo Marty. My mind was already made up anyway.

"All right," I said. "It doesn't make any difference. I'm going to the police, Marty, and tell them what I know. I think you ought to come with me."

Marty didn't look up, but stared at the wheel. "Suppose I say no?" he said.

"Then I'll go anyway," I said. "I figure that it's the only right thing to do. Whoever killed Christina has got to be brought in, and we've got to do whatever we can to help."

Marty never moved. Then all at once, he sighed. I never heard anyone sigh with such weariness. "I figured you'd think that," he said. "I guess there's only one way." Slowly, he sat up in his seat and turned to me. I heard a sharp, familiar click. I looked down to see a long switchblade gleaming in his hand.

I knew the truth before he spoke it, in that split second I looked up from the knife into his agonized eyes. But the truth came too late. His fingers gripped the back of my neck and held me with the iron grip of panic and despair and madness. His words came slowly, each one dripping with pain.

"Christina wanted to tell the police about the bombing," he said. "I tried to make her see sense, but she got all goody-goody. I begged, I argued. Stacy, I got on my knees to her last night—me! But all she did was cry and cry. I couldn't stand her crying. I didn't want to kill her, but I lost my head. Do you understand?"

Marty leaned closer. His eyes were black and narrow. "Last night I lost my head. But now I know what I'm doing. The stakes are even higher now. I'm sorry. I like you, Stacy. Once I liked you a lot. But I can't let you go to the cops."

The blade flashed. I screamed and tried to pull away. There was a hot slash across my arm, and I knew the blade had drawn blood. But Marty's fingers slipped off my neck, and my hand found the door handle. I threw my body against the door and plunged out of the car into the darkness and onto the rough gravel.

I sprang to my feet and ran. I ducked between the cars, gasping for breath, my lungs too empty to scream for help. I could feel the hot, wet blood on my arm and I could hear footsteps behind me.

Marty grabbed my arm. I tore away and rolled over the hood of a car. But my ankle turned as I hit the ground and I sank to my knees.

Gravel showered on my face as Marty's feet dug in near me. I saw his arm go up. I threw myself on my face and screamed.

The knife never fell. I heard the thud of a fist on flesh, the stamping of feet in the gravel—and the knife clattered to the ground near my hand.

I looked up. Jeremy and Marty were slugging at each other with desperation and murderous fury. Jeremy came through with a smashing blow on Marty's nose. Marty's face went blank, surprised. Then Jeremy hit again. His fist crashed into Marty's jaw. Marty groaned and then, like in a slow-motion movie, he crumpled to the ground.

Jeremy stood over him, his shoulders heaving. Marty stirred, tried to get up, but Jeremy kicked him. He groaned and lay there silently. "You all right?" Jeremy asked, taking the knife from me.

I inspected my arm. "It's a nasty cut, but it's not too deep," I told him.

Jeremy dragged Marty to the car, pushed him into the backseat, and climbed in after him. "Get in and drive," he ordered me. "We're going to the police station."

Somehow I managed to collect myself and remember my two driving lessons. I jerked and stalled my way out of the parking lot and drove to the police station. When we pulled to a stop in front of it, I fainted.

Later, sitting in the station, waiting for the police to round up the rest of our gang, Jeremy told me, "I thought it was Marty. That's what's been killing me all day. I just didn't want to believe it. He was arguing with Christina before he dropped me off, and I could see he was getting panicky—and the way Christina was killed, only a panicky guy could have done it. I couldn't see the guys from the diner doing something like that. No, I had the feeling it was Marty, but I kept trying to talk myself out of it. I didn't know what to do."

"But you came," I said with a sigh.

"Yeah," he said. "I came—almost too late. I wanted to ask Marty myself. I had to be sure, before going to the cops." He shook his head. "I almost didn't make it in time. I guess I did it all wrong. We should have gone to the police right away, like you said. I've always been fighting my own fights, figuring things out for myself—maybe that's wrong. Maybe that's why they've got cops."

Jeremy's hand closed on mine, and we were both silent.

Well, that's how it happened. The trial was in all the newspapers—it's history to most people. Marty was sent to prison for life—he'll be up for parole in twenty years or so. There was talk about his old man trying to bribe the jury, but if he did, I guess it didn't work. The last time I saw Marty's father, he was an old, broken man who had lost his job, his wife, and his son—and who looked as if he didn't understand what had happened to him.

Jeremy and James got three years in the reformatory for their part in the bombing, but Jeremy's sentence was cut to one year because of his bringing Marty in. Melanie and I were put on parole, and we still have to report to juvenile court every month.

I wish I could say our folks were a big help, but they weren't. They were dazed and shocked; they didn't know what to say or do. Oh, they stuck by us, all right—they were loyal. But they didn't know how to make things any better. I guess if they'd known that, all this wouldn't have happened.

I hear that the churches and the civic associations in Fords are getting together with the school board to try and fight juvenile delinquency. That's fine. I just hope they know what they're doing. I hope that instead of fighting kids, they fight poverty and boredom and neglect by parents. And whatever program they work out, I hope they give the kids a part in running it.

I'm not trying to excuse myself. I'm not blaming anybody but myself for what happened to me. But it would help those fighters of juvenile delinquency a lot to realize that a person goes through a sort of no-man's-land in the teenage years. Those are the years when he leaves childhood behind, but still isn't allowed to take a place in the world. No, the world isn't ready for anybody until he's at least twenty, except maybe to put a gun in his hand and send him to war.

But most kids are ready for a lot before they're twenty. They can work, fight, make love, get into trouble—and they can think, too. They can see what's wrong with the world, and what's right with it. They know the difference between right and wrong. And most kids, if they're given half a chance, will do the right thing. But they have to do something—they have to have the chance. That's why there's got to be a place for them to do all the things that will help the world get better, not tear the world down.

That's the way I feel. Jeremy feels the same way. He writes me once a week. In a couple of months he'll be out, and we'll be together again—this time, I hope, to build something good.

THE END

117

"YOU BELONG TO ME!"
No man will look at you now

As the momentum of the swing carried my four-year-old daughter to what must have seemed to her to be dizzying heights, she called out, "Mommy, see how high I can go!" She was leaning back so that her hair swung free like a shimmering curtain, and, tilting her face up toward the sun, she laughed in carefree delight.

It takes so little to make her happy, I thought. A surge of fierce protectiveness shot through me, and I found myself wishing there was some way I could shield her from the harsh realities of life.

As the swing began to slow down, Carla jumped from it lightly and skipped over to the monkey bars. Just watching her was a pleasure. She was a small, slender child, and she moved so gracefully.

"Come play with me," she called, scrambling to the top of the bars.

Well, why not? The park was almost deserted, except for a few other children with their mothers, and a tall man taking pictures with a complicated-looking camera. If I wanted to climb around on the monkey bars with my little girl, it was nobody else's business, anyway. I got up from the bench where I'd been sitting and ran to join her, glad that I was wearing jeans and sneakers.

Carla's active imagination invented many different games for us to play. First we were princesses in a castle, then pirates on a ship, then monkeys in a tree with tigers prowling below. After a while, however, I noticed that she seemed to be slowing down, and I decided it was time for lunch and a nap.

"What do you say we start home?" I suggested.

A shadow crossed her face. "Will Daddy be there?"

A flash of anger shot through me at the thought of what Peter's violent temper was doing to our child. I had a sudden, unpleasant recollection of the scene last night—when he had returned from a week on the road. The first thing he'd done was complain because I didn't have a meal ready for him, despite the fact that I'd had no idea when to expect him. He'd also failed to consider that I had very little in the apartment with which to fix a meat-and-potato man's meal.

Peter was a long-distance truck driver, and when he went on a run he always left me with barely enough money to get by on. Because I'd become an expert at cutting corners, I was able to fix simple, nourishing meals for Carla and me. But I often worried about what would happen if an emergency came up. If Carla ever got sick, I wouldn't even have the money to take her to a doctor.

"When a man comes home after a long trip, he's got a right to expect a decent meal," Peter had grumbled, and I'd known that anything I said in my defense would only fuel his anger. Then he'd started in, grilling me about everything that had happened since he'd been away. Where had I gone? Had I spoken to anyone? Although I'd never given him any reason to doubt my faithfulness, he seemed to think all I did was run around with men while he was gone.

His accusations were ridiculous and he knew it. I couldn't have done half of what he accused me of, even if I'd wanted to—which I didn't—with a four-year-old child to care for and no money. Besides, living this way, subjected to constant verbal and sometimes physical abuse, had taken something from me. I'd been attractive as a teenager. But now at twenty-four, I'd become so thin and had such a washed-out, frightened look that I doubted any man would give me a second glance. My only good feature was my hair, which was as fine as Carla's and pale gold. I wore it long and straight.

I'd managed to maintain an outward calm as I'd denied his accusations, but inside I was raging. Finally, when Peter hadn't been able to get a rise out of me, he'd stormed out of the apartment, muttering that he was going someplace else to eat. When he'd come stumbling home sometime in the early hours of the morning, he'd been too drunk to do anything except fall into bed.

Carla and I had tiptoed around in the morning, being as quiet as possible. I'd tried to make a game of it as we'd dressed and eaten breakfast in silence. Then we'd slipped out to go to the park while Peter was still sleeping off the effects of his night out.

The park was my refuge, and I took Carla there almost every sunny day. Since we had no money, it was almost the only entertainment available to us, and it offered an escape from the drab loneliness of our small apartment. On cold or rainy days we often went to the library, where there was a weekly story hour and a special children's room. Or sometimes we went to the indoor shopping mall a few blocks from the park.

Though we couldn't afford to buy anything there, the two of us could still admire all the wonders displayed in the store windows. We'd make up silly little fantasies about what we'd buy if we were rich. Maybe it sounds as if we spent a lot of time pretending and daydreaming, but I felt that I had to do all I could to counteract what Peter's constant bullying and irritability was doing to Carla. Besides, it also gave me a slight escape from my own unhappiness.

But apparently my efforts to protect Carla hadn't been completely successful. There was actual fear on her sweet face when she asked, "Will Daddy be there?"

I felt like a knife was twisting in my heart, but I forced myself to say calmly, "No, darling, Daddy won't be home." I knew he'd have gone down to the terminal to check in with the dispatcher, and that should keep him away from the apartment for a while. And if Peter gave me some grocery money when he came home, I could fix him a nice dinner, which, I hoped, would put him in a better mood.

Carla slipped her hand into mine and skipped along beside me. When we passed the ice-cream stand, she turned to look at it longingly. She'd learned not to ask for anything, but it still hurt me to know that I couldn't even afford to buy her an ice cream in the park.

We had almost reached the park exit when the man I'd seen earlier with the camera approached us. At first I thought he was talking to someone else when he stepped up and said, "Excuse me. Can I talk with you?"

I looked around to see who he meant before I realized he was speaking to me. I wasn't used to being approached by strange men— in the park or anywhere else. I gripped Carla's hand a little tighter, wondering if I should just keep walking.

But there were other people in sight, and anyway, he didn't look at all frightening. And there was something about him that caught my attention. His eyes had an expression that seemed to invite trust, and his thick hair was disheveled, as if he had a habit of running his hands through it absentmindedly.

I realized that he was holding out a small white business card to me, and I took it because I didn't know what else to do. "Carter Photographic Supplies," it read, and below that was an address in the shopping mall.

"I'm Reese Carter," he introduced himself.

"Darlene Ventor," I responded automatically.

"I'm glad to meet you. You may have seen my shop in the mall."

"I—I think so." I had a vague recollection of a camera shop where Carla and I sometimes stopped to look at the photographs of baby animals in the window. "What can I do for you?" I asked. Probably he was passing out discount coupons on film developing, or something like that.

"As you can see, I'm a photographer," he said, raising the camera case, which hung from his shoulder. "Actually, I'm not a professional, but since I own a camera and supply shop, I like to fool around with photography as a hobby. Anyway, I saw you and your little girl on the monkey bars. And, well, I couldn't help taking a few shots. I hope you don't mind."

"No, I guess not," I replied uncertainly. "But why are you telling me this?"

"If the pictures come out as good as I think they will, I'd like to enter them in an amateur photography contest that the newspaper is sponsoring," he explained. "Would you have any objections to that?"

"Why, no," I said, suddenly self-consciously aware of my faded jeans, my face devoid of any makeup, and my tangled hair. I tried to smooth it down with my hand as I said only half jokingly, "You should have told us you wanted to take our picture. We'd have tried to look a little better."

"No, that would have spoiled it all," he disagreed. "Part of the charm was that you weren't aware you were being photographed. If I'd told you ahead of time, it would have made you nervous."

I realized that was true. If I'd known he was taking pictures of us, I'd have been self-conscious about our little pretend games. "Well," I said, "I hope the pictures turn out well and that you win the contest."

All at once I was aware of what Peter would think if he happened to drive by and see me talking to a stranger. No matter how innocent the encounter was, he'd be convinced that all his suspicions were confirmed. "We have to go now," I mumbled, handing the card back and brushing past him. "Good luck with the contest," I called over my shoulder, trying to make up for my abrupt departure.

"If I win I'll split the prize money with you," he called back. "And if you'd like to see the pictures, drop by the shop sometime next week."

As Carla and I hurried home, I found that I actually felt guilty over that brief conversation in the park. That's when I realized the deep effect Peter's continuous accusations were having on me. What kind of life is this, I wondered, with me feeling as if I've done something wrong if I even speak to a man? And with Carla fearful about going home because her father might be there?

Fortunately, Peter was still out when we got there, so Carla and I were able to have a peaceful lunch. After I put her down for her nap, I poured myself a cup of coffee and just sat at the kitchen table, thinking about my life.

Maybe if I'd stood up to Peter right from the beginning, things would have been different. But when I'd married him, right out of high school, I'd naively accepted his high-handedness. I was too young and inexperienced to understand that there was something drastically wrong with a marriage in which one partner dominated the other to such a degree. After all, he was ten years older than me, and when he'd assumed complete control over every facet of our relationship, I'd just thought he was being a good husband.

Eventually, as I'd matured, I'd begun to feel closed in by his bossiness and overbearing attitude. But by now, the pattern was set. My attempts to assert my independence only caused trouble.

As if he was determined to maintain control over me, Peter started acting suspicious and he became irrationally jealous. When he'd return from a run, he'd ask searching questions about what I'd done while he was away, and he became angry if my answers didn't satisfy him. The first few times I was taken completely by surprise when his questions took on a frightening tone.

"What did you do while I was gone?" he'd ask casually.

"Nothing much. I went for a walk with Carla a couple of times."

"For a walk? Where?"

"No place in particular," I'd reply. "Just for a walk."

"You must have walked someplace," he'd insist. "Why are you being so evasive?"

"Peter, come on! I'm not being evasive. I just didn't go anyplace worth mentioning. We walked to the park once, and another time to the mall," I told him.

"Did you talk to anyone?" he persisted.

If I said no he'd accuse me of lying, and if I said yes he was immediately suspicious and wanted to know every detail. Once, when I admitted to stopping to chat with an elderly man who was out in his yard pruning his rosebushes, Peter twisted my arm up behind my back until I cried out in pain.

"You'll be sorry if you ever cheat on me," he threatened.

Eventually, when his physical abuse became a regular part of our lives, I knew I had to get away from him. But that was when I realized, for the first time, just how trapped I really was. Since Peter kept strict control of our money, paying the bills himself and doling out small amounts to me when the mood struck him, I had no money of my own. I didn't even have a family I could turn to for help. My mother had died when I was still in junior high, and Dad had remarried and started a second family a few years later, which was one of the reasons I'd married so young. I knew there was no room in his new life for me.

Still, I was determined to find some way to get out from under Peter's domination. I'd have to find a job, of course. I had no experience or job skills, but I was young and healthy and should be able to support myself somehow. My biggest worry was that Peter would force me to quit before I could earn enough to get away from him. But I made up my mind that I'd just have to stand up to him. Nobody had the right to control another person's life that way.

Then, to my despair, I found that I was pregnant. Peter actually seemed pleased. But I knew it was really because he now had a way of keeping me tied to him, not because of any desire to be a father. As for my own feelings, I was angry and resentful and felt more trapped than ever. At least until Carla was born. When that tiny bundle was placed in my arms, all my resentment magically evaporated, replaced by a surge of protective love so powerful that it almost frightened me.

Peter hardly paid any attention to Carla. His abuse toward me increased, however, after Carla's birth. It was like now that he felt I was inescapably tied to him, he no longer had to keep up any pretense that we had a normal marriage.

By then I was too drained to even feel hatred toward my husband. The only thing left was a dull despair. I think I might actually have considered suicide if it hadn't been for my daughter. She was all that made my life bearable, and I put all my time and energy into making her life as normal and pleasant as possible.

I still hadn't given up on my plan to leave Peter. Now that I had Carla, I'd just have to wait a while—at least until she was old enough to go to school. I knew it was unlikely that I'd find any kind of job that would pay enough to support both of us and also pay for child care. Meanwhile, I'd just have to bide my time.

For the first year or two after Carla's birth, I lived in fear of becoming pregnant again. Then I found out about a family-planning clinic where I could obtain free birth-control pills, so that was one less worry to contend with.

As time went by, Peter and I made love less and less. My only reaction to the knowledge that he was seeing other women was dull apathy. You have to care about someone before you can be jealous. Peter no longer made any attempt to hide his affairs, and actually seemed to enjoy flaunting them before me.

A sound from Carla's room brought me back to the present, and a few seconds later she came into the kitchen.

"Did you have a good nap?" I asked.

She nodded as she snuggled into my arms. Then she looked around furtively. "Is Daddy here?" she asked.

I felt her small body relax when I assured her he wasn't.

Peter was home for two weeks before he went out on another run, and during that time he seemed to go out of his way to make life as unpleasant as possible for Carla and me. He criticized everything, from my cooking and housekeeping to my looks and the way I dressed.

"You've got about as much sex appeal as a dishrag," he sniped, "the way you go around all hunched over and scared looking. And do you have to keep wearing the same old clothes day after day? For Pete's sake, why don't you fix yourself up, Darlene?"

The reason I wore the same clothes was that I never had the money to buy anything new. Peter knew that. He was just trying to goad me into an argument.

He was also continually picking at Carla. She was such a good child that I seldom had to correct her, but Peter found fault with everything she did. By the end of the two weeks she was tense and jumpy.

It was a relief when Peter left on his next run. The first day he was gone was bright and sunny, so I fixed a picnic lunch of sandwiches and fruit, and Carla and I took off for the park. Although we didn't come right out and call it a "celebration," that's what it amounted to.

How long can we go on this way? I wondered as I watched Carla skipping ahead of me. When Peter was away she was a cheerful, happy little girl. When he was home she became moody and withdrawn. I knew that somehow I had to find a way to get both of us out of this trap.

While we were eating our sandwiches, Carla said, "Look, Mommy, there's the man who took our picture."

I looked up to see Reese Carter, camera slung over his shoulder, making his way across the park toward us. "Hey, I'm glad I found you," he said with a friendly grin. "I've been hoping you'd come into the shop to see those pictures."

"I—I've been pretty busy these last few weeks," I stammered, feeling flustered.

"Well, come in and take a look when you get a chance. They turned out great." He sat down at the other end of the picnic table, but he did it so casually while he continued talking, that it didn't seem like an intrusion. "You and your little girl photograph well, and I really think I have a chance at winning first place."

He was so excited about this photography contest that I found myself responding to his enthusiasm. "Have you always been interested in taking pictures?" I asked.

He nodded, and then explained that photography was his hobby and he often came to the park in search of interesting subjects. Gradually, our conversation turned to hobbies in general, and then drifted on to other topics.

When Carla finished her sandwich, she ran to the swings and called, "Mommy, come push me!" Reese and I both got up and walked over, still talking. We continued our conversation as we took turns pushing Carla.

After a while, he glanced at his watch and said, "Hey, I've got to be getting back to the shop so my assistant can take his lunch break. It was nice talking to you, Darlene. Come in and take a look at those pictures soon."

As I watched him leave, I couldn't help thinking how nice it had been to talk to another person about ordinary, everyday things. I knew Peter would immediately jump to all the wrong conclusions if he knew I'd been talking to a man, but I couldn't bring myself to feel guilty over a casual conversation. Rather than feeling as if I'd done anything wrong, I felt strangely elated, and I knew it was because I had so little contact with other adults. Peter even discouraged my making friends with other women. And anyway, I wasn't too anxious to get close to anyone because I was ashamed to have others know what sort of marriage I had.

Carla twisted around in the swing and looked up at me. "He's nice, isn't he, Mommy?" she commented, with something like surprise in her voice.

"Yes, sweetheart, he is." I was glad she was getting a chance to see that all men weren't bad tempered and abusive like her father.

The following week there were several days when it was too cool to go to the park, so one morning Carla and I decided to take a walk through the mall. We could look at all the new things in the store windows, and then we'd stop and see those pictures.

Reese was waiting on a customer and he glanced up casually when we entered the shop. Then he took a second look and a smile lit his face. "Don't go away," he said. "I'll be with you in a minute."

When he was finished with the customer, he ushered us into the back room of the shop and introduced us to his assistant, Johnny. Then he poured me a cup of coffee and got Carla some juice from a small refrigerator before turning to rifle through a file cabinet in one corner of the room.

"Here they are," he told me, pulling several photographs from a large manila envelope. He spread them out on a table, and I caught my breath in surprise as I picked up the one on top.

"I can hardly believe that's really me!" I cried.

The person in the picture didn't look like the image I had of myself—the image Peter had done his best to encourage. In the picture, I wasn't skinny and washed out like Peter often described me. I was I slender and graceful, and even my faded jeans and worn cotton shirt seemed to have a casual style. And Reese had captured the very essence of the special relationship Carla and I shared. He'd gotten us in an unguarded moment, and the camera had caught a glimpse of our own little world of make-believe. Carla's expression, so childish and innocent, was charming to look at. And my head was tilted slightly, with my hair falling over one side of my face, hiding half of my smile.

Carla came up and peered at the pictures with interest. "That's you and me in the park!" she cried.

As I looked up, Reese's eyes met mine anxiously, as if my opinion was important. "You're a very good photographer," I murmured, suddenly embarrassed.

"That's because I had such good subjects," he said quietly.

There was a moment of slight awkwardness as neither of us seemed to know what to say next. Reese was the first to break the silence, asking, "Would you like to have copies of these pictures?"

"How much are they?" I asked, knowing that whatever the cost, I probably wouldn't be able to afford them.

"Oh, I wouldn't charge you. I should be paying you for being such good models," he teased.

When we left Reese's shop, I was carrying an envelope with copies of all the pictures, and I felt really lighthearted, as if something exciting had happened to me. I saw myself in a whole new light in those photographs, and I have to admit, it did wonders for my self-esteem.

I put the envelope in a safe place when we got home, a place where I knew Peter wouldn't find it. I felt guilty for keeping a secret from my husband, but I knew he'd never understand. He'd twist the whole episode into something ugly.

Peter returned the following week with his usual criticisms and complaints. After almost six years of this kind of life, I'd learned to retreat to a private corner of my mind when his physical and emotional abuse became too much to bear. I'd simply close that part of my mind and focus on something pleasant. Now, when he started to go on about my many shortcomings, I'd remember the attractive person in those photographs I had hidden away, and I'd know the things he said about me weren't true. By this method I managed to escape the dreary hopelessness of my life—at least for the time being.

A couple of times, Carla and I ran across Reese in the park when he was looking for subjects for his photographs. We chatted briefly, and once when he saw us looking at pictures in the window of his shop, he insisted we come into the back room and see his latest shots. It was all very casual, but it made a bright spot of color in our lives.

On one of Peter's trips home, he'd become angry over some imagined wrong I'd done and he'd lashed out with his fists, like he sometimes did. Carla and I had to skip our trips to the park for several days even after he left on his next run, because I didn't want to face the curious stares I knew would come my way at the sight of my bruised face. Finally we went out again, when the purple swelling around my eyes had almost disappeared.

"Haven't seen you in the park for a while," a deep voice said as I sat watching Carla play. I looked up, shading my eyes from the sun, and saw Reese standing there. Then he sat down on the grass beside me.

"I—I haven't been feeling well lately," I said.

"Nothing serious, I hope." He sounded really concerned.

"No, I'm fine now. How's the photography coming along?" I asked, trying to change the topic.

"I've taken a few animal pictures. Ducks and squirrels in the park. But other than that I haven't run across any really good subjects. You and Carla made such good models that I guess I'm spoiled now."

126

Although I knew he was teasing, I felt myself redden, and I looked down at my hands in confusion. I was relieved when Carla ran up just then and wanted me to come and play on the slide with her. Reese made no move to leave, and as I joined my daughter I was aware that he was watching us with an expression on his face that I couldn't read.

I could tell he'd noticed the faintly visible bruises on my face, although he'd tried to conceal his surprise. The fact that I was married had come up briefly in one or two of our conversations, and I wondered if Reese was perceptive enough to sense my reluctance to discuss the subject. I was sure he'd figured out by now that my husband was abusive, and it embarrassed me that he knew. He was such a nice, open sort of person that it was probably hard for him to understand why any man would treat a woman that way. Or, for that matter, why a woman would put up with such treatment.

Because I was ashamed to have him know that I'd gotten myself into such a situation in the first place, and that now I didn't have the ability to get myself out of it, I began avoiding Reese. For the next few weeks, Carla and I stopped visiting the park, going instead to a smaller park in the opposite direction from our apartment. And when we went to the mall, I made a point of staying away from the shop.

"Mommy, let's go look at the pictures in Reese's window," Carla said once, pulling in that direction.

I held her hand tightly. "No, honey, we don't want to bother Reese."

She looked puzzled. "But he's our friend. He likes to have us bother him." Then one day as we were walking through the mall, I heard a voice calling my name. I turned to see Reese hurrying to catch up with us.

"I've been wanting to see you," he said, taking my arm. "Come with me. I have something for you."

Surprised, I let him lead us back to the shop and into the back room. He rummaged around in a drawer and then handed me a folded piece of paper. I opened it and my mouth dropped open. It was a check for five hundred dollars. And it was made out to me!

"I don't understand," I began.

"I told you I'd split the prize money with you," he said with a broad grin.

"Reese, you won the contest!" I cried. Without thinking, I threw my arms around him excitedly. At first he seemed unsure of what to do. Then I felt his arms close around me. I was so unused to any kind of human contact, except for Carla's hugs and Peter's fists, that his touch brought a wave of emotions rushing over me. I was shocked at the warmth that flooded through me, and I pulled away in confusion.

Reese released me and stood looking down at me with a strange expression.

"Thank you, but I couldn't accept this," I said, recovering my composure. "You won the contest, and it's your money."

"But I couldn't have won without the two of you as models," he insisted, ignoring the check I held out to him. "Please keep it. I wouldn't feel right if I didn't share it with you." His tone was serious, and I knew that he really meant for me to keep the money.

When Carla and I left the shop, my head was full of plans for what I could do with this windfall. Why, this would be the basis for getting away from Peter. I decided to go to the bank in the mall and open a savings account so it could draw interest while I made my plans. Never having had any money of my own, I had no experience with banks, and the idea of walking into one as if it was something I did every day scared me half to death. I had to remind myself that I had as much right as anyone else to be there.

Gripping Carla's hand tightly, I took a deep breath, pushed open the big double doors, and headed for a sign that read, "New Accounts." If the attractive young woman behind the desk had any idea of my inexperience, she gave no indication as she patiently explained about the different kinds of savings accounts and helped me choose the one that was best for me.

There was a spring in my step as I walked home, and I felt like a completely different person. I was no longer shy, washed-out Darlene Ventor, without a penny to her name. I was a woman with a bank account, and it made all the difference in the world. Oh, I knew that five hundred dollars by itself wouldn't be enough to support Carla and me for very long, but it would certainly help until I found a job—which I intended to do as soon as Carla was in school.

Even Peter's return the following week failed to dampen my spirits, even though he was just as critical and overbearing as ever. Just knowing that my goal of getting out from under his domination was in reach made his treatment of me easier to bear. He seemed to sense that his ugly remarks weren't reaching me, and I could tell that angered and frustrated him.

Peter was due to go out again on a Monday morning. On Sunday evening, after an afternoon of restless pacing and harping at Carla and me for a hundred different things, he stormed out of the apartment, saying he was going out to get something to eat.

"A man can't eat the garbage you dish up!" he'd yelled.

Since I'd fixed an especially nice dinner, I knew he was just using that as an excuse to go out—probably to see one of his girlfriends. I'd long ago stopped caring what he did as long as he left Carla and me alone. So I was relieved when he left.

But when he returned late that evening, I could tell something was terribly wrong the minute he walked in. His whole bearing gave off an air of suppressed rage. He was carrying a newspaper, and when he slammed it down on the table I saw the reason he was in such a mood. It was a Sunday paper, and it was folded open to the leisure section.

"Prizewinning Photograph," the caption read, and below that was one of the pictures Reese had taken of Carla and me on the monkey bars. To one side were a few lines giving Reese's name, along with the names of the second- and third-place winners and the runners-up. Although the quality of the reproduction was grainy and my face was half hidden, there was no mistaking that it was a picture of me and Carla.

"Who is this Reese Carter?" Peter demanded.

"He—he's just a man who was taking pictures in the park," I stammered. "He took a few pictures of Carla and me, and then said he'd like to enter them in the contest."

"Oh, yeah? What other kinds of pictures has he been taking of you?" Peter asked accusingly.

"No others!" I insisted.

"Don't give me that, you little tramp!" He hit me across the face so hard that I staggered backward. "I want you to tell me what's been going on with you and this guy."

When I swore that there was nothing to tell, he struck me again, then went on to describe exactly what he thought was happening between Reese and me. Having to listen to his filthy accusations was almost as painful as his blows. He took the friendship I had with Reese, one of the few bright spots in my life, and turned it into something dirty and disgusting.

"Peter, it's not like that!" I protested tearfully.

"All this time you've been acting so meek and good, while you've been running around behind my back! Who else have you been sleeping with?" he demanded.

I tried to make him understand that I hadn't done any of the things he was accusing me of, but he was like a wild man.

"Don't lie to me!" he shouted, calling me dirty names. His huge muscular arm struck me again, knocking me across the room. I think I must have blacked out for a few seconds, because the next thing I knew I was on the kitchen floor and Peter's hand was entangled in my hair, pulling my head back.

"I'll fix you so no man will look at you," he spat out, and I saw that he had a pair of scissors in his other hand.

Terror washed over me and I tried to twist free, but my struggles were no match for his brutal strength. I closed my eyes as I saw the scissors coming near my face. I screamed. There was a sharp cutting sound and then my head dropped forward.

"There," Peter grunted with satisfaction as he stood up and threw the scissors down. They landed with a loud clatter on the floor. Then the door slammed and I knew he'd gone out.

I don't know how long I lay there frightened and crying. My head felt strangely light, but it didn't seem to be from Peter's beating. When I finally dared to move, I reached up to rub the back of my neck. Then I ran my hand through my hair in shocked surprise. I pushed myself up to a sitting position and turned my head slowly.

There on the floor next to the scissors, in a tangled heap, lay the remains of my long hair.

I felt something wet fall on my hand, and I realized I was crying again. I told myself that it was silly and childish to be crying about my hair when everything else in my life was so drastically out of order. I knew Peter might return at any time. And immediately I knew Carla and I couldn't be there when he came back. I'd hoped to be able to put up with his abuse, at least until Carla was old enough to go to school. But this last crazy act of his had made me realize just how dangerous he really was. I couldn't sit around crying over hair when my daughter and I were in danger.

I dressed hurriedly in jeans and a sweatshirt, and then ran into Carla's room. "Wake up, sweetheart," I said gently.

At first she struggled to get her eyes open, but then she sat straight up in bed and stared at me. "Mommy, what happened to your hair?" she blurted out.

"I had it cut," I said matter of factly. "Never mind that now. Get up. We're going for a walk."

"In the dark?" The idea obviously intrigued her.

I got her dressed quickly, grabbed up her jacket, and hurried her out of the apartment. We could come back later to get whatever else we needed, after I was sure Peter had left on his run.

We headed for the park, because I had no idea where else to go. Although it had always been such a friendly, welcoming place in the daytime, our footsteps now echoed eerily in the silence and sinister shapes seemed to lurk behind each bush and shrub. For Carla's sake, I tried to hide my fear. We found a bench in a deserted section of the park, and I pulled Carla into my lap and held her close in my arms, rocking her gently until she fell asleep.

As I sat there in the dark, tensing nervously at every sound, I tried to force my mind to calm down so I could decide what to do next. We couldn't go back home until I was sure Peter had left on his run. But then I'd have two weeks to start over. Surely in that time I could find some sort of job. Although I wasn't in a position to be too choosy, it had to pay enough so that I could afford day care for Carla. Once I found a job, I'd look for a place to live and use the money I had in the bank to support us until I started getting paid. We'd be on a tight budget, but I was used to doing without. I'd gladly live in one room just to be free of Peter.

I tried to stay awake, but at last my weariness took over and I dozed. When I opened my eyes again, the sun was beginning to break through the curtain of mist. A tall form stood in front of me, silhouetted in the early morning light. My first thought was that Peter had found us, and my arms instantly tightened around Carla as I prepared to jump up and run.

"Don't be afraid," a familiar voice said, and I realized with relief that it wasn't Peter standing there; it was Reese. He had mentioned once that he often came to the park early in the morning. "That's when I get some of my best pictures," he'd explained.

Wordlessly, he sat down on the bench and reached over to take Carla from me. She stirred slightly, then leaned her head against his chest and went back to sleep. It felt good to stretch my arms and legs. They were cramped and aching. I knew I must have been a terrible sight, but Reese's face betrayed nothing except a quiet concern.

"You look like you could use some breakfast," he commented. "My car is right over there. Want to see if we can find a restaurant that's open this early?"

"Oh, I—I couldn't go in anyplace looking like this," I mumbled, feeling ugly and ashamed.

"Then we'll go to my place. I'm pretty handy with a frying pan," he joked.

Reese stood up and, still carrying Carla, led me to his car. She woke up just as we reached his apartment. At first she looked frightened, but her face brightened into a sunny smile when Reese said, "Well, hello, sleepyhead."

When Carla and I were seated at the breakfast bar in Reese's small, neat apartment, he asked us how we liked our eggs.

"Can't I do the cooking?" I offered, embarrassed at being waited on that way.

"No, you just sit and relax," he said. "You're my guests."

To my intense relief, he seemed to sense that this was not the time to ask questions. I knew that soon I'd have to explain what was going on—I owed him that much. But for now, his casual, matter-of-fact air was just what I needed.

After we finished eating, Reese settled Carla down in front of the TV in the living room to watch cartoons, poured me another cup of coffee, and took a seat across from me in the kitchen.

"Do you feel like talking about it?" he asked.

Although I was reluctant to involve him, Reese had a right to know what was going on after he'd been so kind to Carla and me. It was obvious that the bruises on my face weren't accidental. And the crooked way my hair was cut off clearly pointed to an act of violence. Still, I couldn't seem to find the right words.

"Who did this to you?" he asked softly.

"My husband," I murmured, looking down at my hands.

He put his finger under my chin and gently tilted it upward so he could study my face. "I'd like to help you if you'll let me," he said.

All at once the tears that had been so close to the surface began to flow. Once I got started I couldn't seem to stop, and Reese waited patiently until I was all cried out. After I dried my eyes, I found myself telling him the whole story of my marriage to Peter, including what had brought on last night's outburst.

He looked at me, obviously upset. "I feel responsible," he said. "I should have asked your permission before allowing that picture to be printed."

"Oh, no!" I cried, afraid I'd given him the impression that I blamed him. "It wasn't your fault."

"What are you going to do now?" he asked.

I told him of my plan to find a job and an apartment. "I won't go back to him," I said. "I've had enough."

He stirred his coffee as if he was deep in thought. "Would you consider working for me?" he asked at last. "Winning that contest has made me think I just may have what it takes to be a serious photographer, and I'd like to spend more time working at it. That means I'll need someone to look after the shop."

His offer took me by surprise. "I don't know anything about cameras and photographic supplies," I protested.

"That's all right. I'd rather have someone who's inexperienced that I can train my way. I'll teach you everything you need to know. The position would carry a lot of responsibility."

"But what about your assistant, Johnny?" I asked.

"He's already told me he'll be quitting at the end of the month. He's opening a camera shop of his own across town. So you see, I really need a replacement," he added.

He was looking at me expectantly, waiting for an answer. Although the idea of taking on all that responsibility was frightening, I knew I couldn't afford to pass up an offer like this. "Thank you," I said. "I'd like to work for you." And I vowed to myself then and there that I'd become the best camera-shop assistant anyone could be.

"Well, that's settled," he said with a grin. "Now that you've got a job, the next step is to find you a place to live. But first, let's see what we can do about that haircut."

Reese rummaged around in a drawer until he found a pair of scissors, then he trimmed the back of my hair. His touch was gentle, like he was being extra careful to not make any sudden moves. He seemed to sense that I was still on edge and frightened, and that it wouldn't take much to scare me away. I was startled when I looked in the mirror. I had to admit that this short cut was attractive, kind of cute, now that Reese had fixed it up.

Next, he called Johnny and told him he wouldn't be coming into the shop that day. "Something's come up," I heard him say.

Reese spent most of the day driving me around to look for a place to live. I could tell some of the apartment managers weren't too happy about showing me their rentals, and I couldn't blame them. After all, I didn't look like the ideal tenant with my face all covered with bruises. But Reese just turned on the charm, and when he flashed his smile, most of them—especially the women—would have agreed to almost anything.

I finally settled on a small, comfortable apartment that was just right for Carla and me, and Reese helped me pack up our things and move in. I used the money that he'd given me as my share of the contest prize to pay the security deposit. Reese talked the landlord into waiting for the rest of the rent until my first paycheck.

"There's no way in the world I can thank you for everything you've done for me," I said to Reese when I told him good-bye that evening. "I don't know what we'd have done without your help."

"You don't need to thank me," he said. "Everybody needs help now and then."

When he left and Carla and I were alone, I looked around our new home in amazement. Everything had happened so fast that I wondered if I'd wake up and find that the events of the day had been a dream. But it was all real. I had an apartment and a job and I was free of Peter at last!

Reese had told me to take my time getting settled before starting my new job. But I was anxious to start earning a paycheck, so I went in to work two days later. I'd spent the day before looking for a good day-care center for Carla, and luckily I found a nice place within walking distance of both the shop and my new apartment.

Because Reese had said it would be all right to bring Carla to the shop with me sometimes, occasionally I did. She played quietly in the back room, or followed Reese around like an adoring shadow. And he was so patient with her. Since she'd received only criticism from Peter, the only other man she'd ever known, this was a new experience for her. And she positively bloomed.

But things didn't stay perfect for long. Somehow Peter found out where I was working, and he came into the shop one day and demanded that I leave with him. "You're my wife. I'm taking you home where you belong!" he shouted, making a grab across the counter for me.

I stepped back out of his reach and stared at him defiantly. Out of the corner of my eye I could see Reese watching us from the back room, ready to help if I needed him. Although his presence was reassuring, I knew I had to handle this on my own. In some way that I couldn't quite explain, I was aware that this was an important step in regaining control of my life.

"This is a place of business, and you have no right to come here and cause trouble," I said calmly, although my insides were churning. "If you don't leave immediately, I'm calling the police."

At first his mouth dropped open in surprise. Then his eyes narrowed angrily and he took a step toward me.

"I mean it, Peter," I said, reaching for the telephone.

He glared at me, swore loudly, then turned and stormed out of the shop. I breathed a huge sigh of relief. When I glanced over at Reese, he grinned and gave me a thumbs-up sign.

Everything stayed quiet for a while, but I should have known Peter wouldn't give up that easily. I'd filed for divorce the day after he came into the shop, knowing it was the right thing, the only thing, to do. Apparently, Peter didn't see it the same way.

Two weeks later he came into the shop again, waving the divorce papers and shouting that he would decide if we would get a divorce or not. I could have laughed at his stupid arrogance if I hadn't been so scared. Peter was as mean and angry as he'd been on the night he'd cut off my hair. I nervously thanked God that Carla was at the day-care center that day, and then I hid my trembling hands under the front counter.

Peter slammed the papers down in front of me. "Who do you think you are?" he yelled. "You can't do this!"

"I can and I am!" I shot back, trying to hide how scared I was. Reese had stepped out of the shop to get lunch and there were no customers around. I felt sick with fear, but I couldn't let him see that.

"You won't! You're a loser, Darlene. You're nothing without me!" he shouted. "Tear up these papers now!"

"You're wrong," I told him. "I'm everything without you! You and your miserable accusations and your put-downs and your fists!"

Before I could say anything else, Peter reached out to grab me. I fell against the back counter as his arm whipped past, missing me but shoving everything on display onto the floor with a loud crash. That didn't stop him, though. He climbed over the counter and had me by the throat in an instant, choking me and shouting like a crazy man.

I struggled wildly as I felt the breath leave me, trying desperately

134

to pry Peter's hands from my throat. But I could barely breathe and I knew I couldn't possibly get away from him like that. So I reached out blindly around me, groping the counter for anything at all. When my hand grasped a camera Reese had been fiddling with, I didn't think about it, I just brought it up hard against Peter's head.

He yelled out in pain, releasing his grip on me. I stumbled from behind the counter just as two mall security guards and Reese came rushing into the shop.

Reese took me in his arms as the security guards handcuffed Peter. The camera hadn't hurt him that badly, because he was still struggling and swearing as they dragged him away. Reese and I followed at a distance, ignoring the crowds staring at us as they took Peter to the mall security office and called the police. I'd told them that I would definitely press charges.

Peter was arrested that day and later let out on bail. But he never came around Carla and me again. At the trial, I testified against him. He was given a suspended sentence, two years probation, and fined for the damage he'd done to Reese's shop. I felt like asking the judge why he didn't fine him for the damage he'd done to me.

My divorce came through uncontested last week. I haven't seen Peter since that day in the courtroom. I can only hope that I'll never see him again.

While all this was going on, Reese patiently instructed me in all phases of my new job. My confidence and self-esteem soared when I discovered I had a genuine talent for keeping careful records, ordering stock, and dealing with customers. Eventually I began taking over more and more of the responsibilities of running the shop, leaving Reese free to pursue his photography.

With more time to devote to taking pictures, he soon earned a reputation as a first-rate photographer. I was pleased with his success, and I felt that I'd contributed to it, at least indirectly.

Very soon now, Reese and I will be married. Although I have a lot to be grateful to Reese for, he didn't take advantage of that gratitude by trying to rush me into anything before I was ready. He was caring and patient enough to give me time to make sure of my feelings, and to allow our relationship to grow into a mature, lasting kind of love.

The memory of my marriage to Peter is fading away like a bad dream. Now my life is full of love and trust and sharing. It's a whole new wonderful world for Carla and me!

THE END

ENEMIES WITH MY NEIGHBORS!
The streets are war

No sooner had I turned the corner of Kennedy Street when violence erupted all around me. Two boys, who couldn't have been much older than my own son, were scuffling in front of the candy store on the corner. One of them pushed the other so hard that he fell heavily against me. "Oh!" I exclaimed. "Watch what you're doing!"

The one who had fallen against me turned, snarling, "Why don't you look where you're going!"

I gasped and walked on, but it seemed to me that I had walked into a nightmare. People brushed rudely against me; a man pushing a high-wheeled handcart full of ice, shouted, "Watch it, lady!" as he rattled past me, and a ball coming straight at me made me freeze in sudden panic. At the last moment, a small boy appeared out of nowhere and caught it. The boys playing ball shouted; the men, selling vegetables from pushcarts lined up at the curb, shouted; women, hanging out of upstairs windows, yelled down to their children in the street.

I stood perfectly still, staring with unseeing eyes at the slip of paper in my hand. Slowly, my eyes focused; slowly, I got command of myself and moved on, searching for the address I wanted. Most of the tenement buildings had small shops on the street floors. The number I was hunting for was over an Italian grocery store. Through the windows I could see vats of wrinkled black olives, and big pale chunks of cheese. I glanced down at the slip of paper and then up again at the building to check it, and suddenly I was staring into two unblinking black eyes. In my intentness to find the address, I hadn't realized I had stopped directly in front of a woman sitting at the grocery store entrance. She was old, but her hair was as black as the raven-haired cat sprawled across her lap. The cat, the woman's eyes, the unexpectedness of the encounter sent a stab of fright through me. I turned quickly and fled into the building. I located the superintendent's door and rang the bell. He showed me the apartment that was available.

In spite of my horror at the neighborhood, I knew that the apartment was right for us. It was the best I had seen for the money in all my days of searching. We moved in a week later. After we had pushed the furniture into place, I insisted on sitting down, not because I was tired, but because I wanted Bart to rest. We could hear Andrew whistling as he puttered around his little cubbyhole of a room. With a sixteen-year-old's ability to find adventure in every change, he was cheerfully arranging his room.

136

"I don't know how you do it, Mrs. Tinsley," Bart said, "but you have a genius for turning a place into a home!"

"Why, thank you, Mr. Tinsley," I said, smiling. I couldn't help contrasting this cramped apartment and raucous neighborhood with the home we'd just come from in a quiet, tree-lined residential section of the Bronx. But Bart had had a heart attack six months ago. The soap factory, where he'd been a supervisor, had given him two months' salary, but that sum and all our savings had gone to pay the hospital bills. The doctor had given him strict orders not to work for a year. So we had to sell our home, move to a cheap apartment, and live carefully on the money from the house.

"I'm only sorry about one thing," Bart said. "I'm sorry we couldn't bring your piano."

"Well, I'm not. I'm glad," I said. "That piano would have been as out of place here as a chandelier in a telephone booth!" Then for Bart's sake, I added, "Besides, you know I haven't been playing much lately." The piano was in storage. I was glad we couldn't bring it. It represented something tangible of our old life, something that would not be tainted by the new life I secretly dreaded.

"I hope you won't be too unhappy here," Bart said.

I saw how gray he'd grown since his illness, and my heart went out to him. "Now, honey," I said briskly, "don't you worry about me." I got up, moved behind Bart's chair, and laid my cheek against his. "I could be happy anywhere, now that I know you're going to be well." The sounds from the street swelled through the open window. "Only, I do worry about Andrew. A sixteen-year-old, growing up in this neighborhood."

"I wouldn't worry about that," Bart answered. "This neighborhood isn't dangerous; it's just different."

Then and there, I knew I would have something else to hide from Bart. So I didn't tell him about seeing ten-year-olds playing cards for money under street lamps at night, or about the foul language I'd heard at the candy store, or about the glimpse I'd caught of boys Andrew's age bending over the tables in a murky pool hall.

No matter how hard I tried. I could never stifle my personal fear of the street. It was so raucous, so violent. When I walked along the sidewalk, I felt as if eyes were watching me. The old woman always sat in front of the grocery store, stroking the cat that slept in her lap, fanning herself with a newspaper. I had to pass her each time I entered our hallway, and I always felt as if she were some monstrous, ominous black bird, looking through me with dark, hard eyes.

Well, I thought, at least in our apartment, we'll be safe. And then, three days after we moved in, there was a knock on the door and it seemed to me that the street was encroaching on our safety. A plump, middle-aged woman stood at the door. She was wearing a spotless housedress and her face was pleasant. "Good evening, good evening," she said, bobbing her head. "I am Mrs. Dabrowski upstairs. Look, I bring you piroshki."

I looked down at the plate, covered by a white napkin, which she was offering. She saw the look on my face and she laughed. "Ah! Ah! You do not know piroshki. Very good. Meat in the middle." I shook my head at her.

"Yes, yes." She nodded vigorously again, thinking I was refusing out of politeness. "I make for you."

"No, thank you," I said. Then I saw her disappointment and hastened to add, "My husband has been sick and is on a special diet. I'm sorry."

"Too bad," she said, shaking her head. Then she saw Andrew. "Ah, nice boy. Like my Danny. You will be friends, yes?" And she smiled.

Andrew returned her smile. "Sure, I'd like to."

As Mrs. Dabrowski turned to go, she looked down at the plate in her hands as if she didn't quite know what to do with it.

When the door had closed behind her, Andrew exclaimed, "You shouldn't have done that, Mom. She was being neighborly."

I knew he was right, and I felt ashamed. But, in a way, we were guilty of the same rudeness two nights later when Pastor Bob came to call. I guess Bart was as taken aback by his appearance as I was. The minister at our old church had been tall, thin, and white-haired, with a grave, distinguished face. Pastor Bob might have been a football player.

"You've certainly made this into a cheerful place," he said. "I've already met your son over sodas at the corner." Then he told us about his church and invited us to visit on Sunday.

Bart spoke up. "Thank you, Reverend Bob, but we plan to continue as members of the church in our old neighborhood."

I looked at Bart in astonishment. His reply to Pastor Bob was the first inkling I had that Bart, too, felt alien in this neighborhood.

"I can understand that you'd want to maintain old ties," said Pastor Bob pleasantly. He smiled again at Andrew. Then he described his hope of forming a neighborhood club for teenagers. Anyone else would have given up the thought of raising the necessary funds from this bone-poor district. But you could tell that the idea of failure had never entered his head. Part of me warmed to this man whose heart, obviously, was as big as his shoulders. But another part of me was crying out to him silently: Can't you see we don't belong here? Can't you see we don't want to be involved?

When Pastor Bob described the boys and girls in the area, victims of emotional poverty as well as of material poverty, I continued my wordless argument with him. But look at Andrew, I wanted to say, so clean-cut, so serious. He doesn't need that kind of club. And I don't want him involved with the kind of boys who do!

But I didn't say a word, and after a time Pastor Bob left, saying to Andrew, "Don't forget, I'm going to take you on at handball on Saturday."

After the door had closed, there was silence, and I realized that Andrew was looking at us. He was not looking at his father and mother. He was looking at a man and woman whom he was seeing for the first time. I felt uneasy under his thoughtful gaze. I expected him to say something, but he merely mumbled, "Well, guess I'll go to bed," and went into his cubicle off the kitchen and closed the door behind him.

Several evenings later he presented us with a surprise. He had found a job, he announced, trying not to show his pride. He was going to help out Mrs. Dabrowski in her butcher shop full-time in summer and part-time when school started.

At first Bart beamed. "That's fine, son." Then he fell silent, and after a moment he shook his head. "Summer in a butcher shop. Quite a change from summer in a camp in the mountains with your old friends."

"Now, Dad," Andrew said, "don't you worry about me. I'm going to like it!"

I was proud of Andrew, too, but I had misgivings. Danny Dabrowski was a hoodlum if ever I saw one. He swaggered like a pirate among the boys that hung around the candy store on the corner. Why doesn't Danny help his mother out? I wondered.

The very next day my misgivings were confirmed. I had had trouble over our car before. The day after we moved in, I had discovered a whole troop of kids swarming over the car, and I had chased them away. Several days later, all the air was let out of the tires. Then, one afternoon, I turned the corner of Kennedy Street and saw two boys dumping garbage on the car. "Stop that!" I screamed.

One of the boys grabbed hold of me and pushed me against the wall. "Don't worry, lady, you've still got your precious car. All it needs is a car wash now." Then he spat on the ground and let me go.

I went upstairs to get some rags with which to clean off the car. I also called the police. The police said they were sorry, but they couldn't do anything about it. It appeared that the kids in the neighborhood had it in for us, for some reason, and they could only suggest that we keep an eye on the car.

After that, I must have looked out of the window a hundred times a day. It became a kind of crusade, foolish as it sounds, for I knew how much the car meant to Bart. It was a means of getting away from our present life. We never went very far, just over the bridge to Manhattan or any place that didn't look like our neighborhood.

A few weeks after Andrew got the job with Mrs. Dabrowski, I was coming home from the market with my arms full of bundles when I saw four of the older boys around the car. One was Danny Dabrowski. He was lounging against the hood and regarded me lazily as I approached. Even in my nervousness, I was aware of his handsomeness, the luminous brown eyes, the dark curls tumbled on his forehead. The other boys shuffled a little, keeping expectant eyes on Danny.

"Please, boys," I said, "Please, stay away from that car."

"Well," drawled Danny, leaning on one elbow, "If it isn't Old Lady Tinsley, the queen of Kennedy Street!" In one lithe movement, he sprang to the sidewalk. Turning to the others in mock indignation, he cried, "What's the matter with you guys? The queen has come! Bow down to the queen!"

Danny got down on his knees and began bowing. Smirking, the other boys followed suit, all chanting, "Bow down, bow down!" But then the smirk I saw in their faces changed to a wild look as slowly they formed a circle around me. They wanted to maul me, to get even, to make me a part of their world. "We'll show you what life really is like around here," they told me. What good would it do me to scream for help? I didn't have a friend in this jungle. I wondered what they were going to do and shrank back in horror as they edged in on me. Just when I thought I could bear it no longer, Danny threw his head back and laughed wildly. All the other boys followed suit until pretty soon they were all laughing so hard I thought I'd go deaf.

They skipped down the street, laughing and jeering all the way, thrilled that they had just scared the life out of me! It was a big joke to them—to terrify me—but I couldn't feel relief that it was nothing more. My face flaming, I stumbled toward our door. Just as I reached the kitchen, a sack broke and potatoes rolled all over the floor. It was the last straw. I sat down and sobbed. How was I going to have strength to fight the jungle that was Kennedy Street? How was I going to keep Andrew uncontaminated by boys like Danny Dabrowski?

Several weeks later I read in the newspaper that two groups of teenage boys had been rounded up by the police. There had been a gang fight, and one boy had been seriously injured by a gunshot. The trouble had occurred on Carter Street, only four blocks away. At breakfast the next morning, before Andrew left for his job at Mrs. Dabrowski's butcher shop, I asked if he knew any of the boys in the gang. "I know a few by sight," he answered and then hurried off.

The street was getting to Andrew. I knew it. In exasperation I

140

turned on Bart. "Why do you sit there like a bump on a log? Why don't you try to keep him home nights? I rack my brain trying to think of things to keep him here. And you never open your mouth!"

Bart looked at me in astonishment. "Why, I don't think we have to worry about Andrew."

"Oh, don't you!" I snapped. "You heard him say he knew the hoodlums in that gang fight. How are you going to like reading about your own son in the paper some morning?" I asked.

"Now, Sarah," Bart said mildly, "I think you're worrying too much. Andrew is a good, steady boy. Why, he's practically supporting this family."

"Oh, you make me tired!" I flared. "Just because you've stopped working is no reason you should stop being a father!"

Bart blinked as if my words had been a physical blow. "I guess you think I've stopped being a husband, too," he said.

I was silent. Our discussion had taken a turn that frightened me. Some things were better left unsaid.

But Bart went on doggedly. "I love you, Sarah, as much as ever. You mustn't think I don't, just because I can't show it as a husband should. I—" He broke off abruptly.

I knew what he was alluding to. The doctor had said we could continue our physical relations, but in silent agreement we'd not been together as man and wife since Bart's heart attack. "That's not important to me," I said.

"It is to me," he replied with the same desperate doggedness. "I don't feel like very much of a man. My son has become the breadwinner. My wife works like a slave. And I—I sit and read the newspapers all day."

"Oh, Bart, you're looking for things—they don't matter—"

"They do matter! I'm useless. I'm a tired, worn old man ready to be thrown on the scrap heap."

"That's nonsense," I said sharply. Bart's self-pity made me feel impatient with him instead of sympathetic, but I tried to hide it. "That's nonsense," I repeated. "You've given Andrew and me a wonderful life. You deserve to have a year's vacation. You'll be going back to work and everything will be all right again. That's enough of that kind of talk," I said. "It's not your fault and it's not mine. It's the fault of this terrible neighborhood. But we've just got to put up with it for a year."

I attacked the dishes savagely. My discussion with Bart had resolved nothing. It had brought hurtful subjects out into the open and left barriers between us. And Bart had refused to admit Andrew was in danger.

And then, as I always did when I was upset, I started cleaning the apartment. I wielded the mop as though I were beating every young hoodlum who even passed my son in the street. When I got to the living room, Bart was sitting in the easy chair, reading. As I approached his chair, he raised his feet from the floor and continued to read. Almost before I knew what I was doing, I stamped my foot, and cried, "Can't you sit someplace else when I'm trying to clean in here?"

Without a word, Bart got up, put on his jacket and left the apartment. I was so exasperated that I didn't even try to stop him.

Later in the day, I went out to do the marketing. As I was walking along, a small hand-lettered card in a bakery window caught my eye. Clerk Wanted, it said. It had no significance, and I forgot all about it.

To get home from the shopping district, I had to pass a tiny, triangular park. My eyes wandered as I walked and, as if drawn by a magnet, stopped at Bart. He was sitting on a bench, staring at nothing. He was carefully dressed, but he seemed as shabby as the other beaten men around him, sitting in the sun, doing nothing. I turned my back so he wouldn't see me. He looked so alone, so like a derelict!

Quickly I retraced my steps, walked into the bakery and got the job. I wondered why I had never thought of a job before. A four-room apartment was too small a responsibility for a woman with my energy. Now Bart would be able to sit at home in comfort without being in danger of my sudden, uncontrollable outbursts. And I would be earning money!

In many ways, my working helped, but there were drawbacks, too. For one thing, at the end of the day my feet felt like two heavy flatirons. Another drawback was the fact that my working day began earlier and ended earlier than Andrew's. Bart and I would have breakfast together and I would leave the house before Andrew was even up. In the evenings I'd already be in bed before Andrew came home. Sundays were the only days when all three of us were together. We would have a picnic in the park or take a ride in the car. But when evening came, Andrew grew restless and would soon be gone.

It was a July day when the whole city was an oven. I did my housework listlessly, then Bart and I drove to the supermarket. When we got home, Bart insisted on helping me carry the bundles upstairs. In the confusion of sorting out the packages, we left the car doors unlocked and the keys in the ignition.

Upstairs, we put the groceries away and decided to have a sandwich and a glass of iced tea before taking a drive. The hallway was dark and musty and gave the illusion of coolness so that when we stepped out on the sidewalk, the steaming heat hit us like a blow in the face. Something else hit us like a blow, too. The car was gone!

A few cars were parked among the pushcarts, but none was

ours. The tailor came out of his shop and dumped a bucket of soapy water into the gutter. A bevy of kids swirled around us shooting each other with toy guns. The old woman sat in front of the grocery store, fanning herself with a newspaper.

Who was there to ask? Who was there to turn to? We had no friends here.

Slowly, Bart and I climbed the stairs. I listened as he phoned Andrew at the Dabrowski butcher shop on the next block. "Andrew, the car's disappeared. Yes, we left the keys in the ignition. No, I didn't expect you to know anything about it. Well, I'll report it to the police. Good-bye."

We waited about an hour before the police called back. They had located the car. They asked us to come down to the station house. I'd never been in a police station before, and I hadn't expected it to be quite so small and dark. The only bright spot was the flag spread out behind the desk lieutenant, who asked an officer to take us upstairs to the detective's office. The stairs squeaked under our steps, and the homely sound made me realize that there was, after all, nothing very upsetting about being in a police station. However, when the door to the detective's office opened, I thought I was going to faint. I heard Bart gasp and I groped for his hand.

Andrew was seated in front of the detective's desk, talking vehemently. "Andrew," I cried, "what have you done? You're not in trouble?"

Bart's grip on my hand tightened, not in support but in warning. Andrew swung his head around, startled. Quickly, he got up to give me the chair he'd been sitting in. I sat down feeling as if I had made a terrible mistake somewhere. I was so bewildered that I couldn't face any of the people crowding the room.

My eyes went to the window, which was cross-hatched by heavy wire, then up to the fan, lazily turning on a small platform near the ceiling, and finally down to a soda can and several stained coffee containers in the waste basket. Finally, I made myself look at the three boys sitting on the bench by the wall. Two of them I recognized as Danny Dabrowski's cohorts, the third was Danny himself.

He was lounging on the corner of the bench, one knee crossed over the other, one arm stretched along the back of the bench, as relaxed as though he were about to watch a play unfold. His remarkably beautiful dark eyes looked directly into mine, and he raised his eyebrows quizzically.

"I'll tell you why I asked you to come down," the detective said. His head was round, as was the bald spot on top of his head, and his face was round and rosy. But his mouth was thin and his eyes held no amusement. "Just about the time you reported your car was stolen, it

143

was located in a traffic tie-up outside Yankee Stadium. This one," the detective pointed to Dan Dabrowski, "was driving and had hooked bumpers with the automobile ahead of him. Since Dabrowski here could not produce a license, the officer brought all three of them to the station."

At this point the detective looked directly at Bart and me. "When they arrived at the station house," he continued, "they found your son hanging around outside. Now, your son maintains that you, Mr. Tinsley, have given him permission to use the car whenever he wants. He also maintains that he had arranged that these three would take the car, go to the doubleheader at Yankee Stadium, and that he would meet them there after he quit work, in time for the second game—all with your knowledge and approval. Is that true?"

His words bewildered me. I felt I had to set him straight, but Bart put a warning hand on my arm. "Yes," he said firmly. "That's true."

"Why—" I started to exclaim, but Bart's grip tightened on my arm. I looked at Andrew in astonishment, but his eyes were on his father.

The detective stared at Bart for a minute and when he spoke his voice was even flatter than before. "I think you should know, Mr. Tinsley, that no one is allowed to drive in the city who is not eighteen years old—with or without your permission. By allowing an underage person to drive you are guilty of a misdemeanor. And it is also an offense to leave the keys in an unoccupied automobile."

I stirred. This had gone far enough. Danny Dabrowski had gotten Andrew into trouble, and now he was getting Bart in real trouble. Bart felt my movement and he turned to me. "It's all right, Sarah," he said, a sharpness in his voice that I hadn't heard for many months. Turning back to the detective, he said, "I'm sorry, I didn't know about that, sir. I'm responsible, not only legally but morally, too. My son, and these boys, also, didn't know they were doing anything wrong. I'll—I'll take care of whatever penalties there are."

The detective scrutinized Bart for a long time before turning to Andrew. "You're one of Pastor Bob's boys, aren't you?"

"Yes, sir," Andrew answered.

Except for the lazy hum of the fan, there was silence. Slowly, the detective eyed the boys on the bench. "You three," he rapped out, "stand up!"

The three got to their feet, Danny with lazy ease, the other two, awkwardly. They could have been triplets as far as their apparel was concerned: faded T-shirts, heavy black belts with studs, and baggy blue jeans hanging off their hips. But their attitudes were vastly different. The smallest boy seemed frightened and as he stared down at the detective's desk, he swallowed constantly. The middle one was anxious, too, but he tried to hide it with a defiant slouch. Only Danny seemed at ease as he regarded the officer with expectant interest.

The detective looked up at them from under narrowed lids and his voice, dry as ever, deepened into an ominous tone. "If it hadn't been for Mr. Tinsley here, you three would be cooling your heels inside, sweating out a felony. Now, we haven't seen any of you before. You have a clear record as far as we're concerned. We don't want to see you again. So I'll tell you what I'm going to suggest to the lieutenant. A sentence of hard labor. Two days a week, from now until school starts, you'll help Pastor Bob at his club. The floors need sanding, the walls need painting."

After the detective took us back downstairs to the desk lieutenant and got his approval of the punishment he recommended, the boys left. We stayed on for another few minutes. Bart paid a small fine for his misdemeanors, and the charge against the boys was removed.

As we stepped out on the sidewalk, squinting against the sun, Danny Dabrowski detached himself from the iron railing in front of the police station and came up to us. "Say, Andrew," he began.

"Come along, Andrew," I said sharply, taking him by the arm.

"It's all right, Danny," Bart said.

I was seething. I felt so much shame, so much indignation, that it was all I could do to keep quiet until we reached the privacy of our apartment. Once inside I turned on Andrew. "How could you do it? How could you cover up for that hoodlum? You know he stole our car. Can't you imagine how I felt in the police station? I could have died with shame—putting yourself on their level, saying they were your friends. Now the police will think you're a delinquent, too!"

"Now, Sarah," Bart interrupted, "it's not as bad as that. The detective knew exactly what was going on."

I turned on Bart. "You're just as bad. You stuck up for them, too. What kind of father are you? Don't you care that Andrew is mixed up with boys like that?"

"He was sticking up for me, Mom."

"Why?" I cried, swinging back to Andrew. "Why did you have to get them out of trouble? Why did you lie to protect them? They're nothing but common, sneaking lying thieves!"

"It was a little escapade," said Bart calmly. "They wanted to get to Yankee Stadium. There was the car, there were the keys, and off they went."

"Oh!" I cried, utterly exasperated and close to tears. "It wasn't any little escapade. They did it on purpose. You don't know what Danny Dabrowski said to me the other day. They hate us; the whole neighborhood hates us. You don't seem to understand how dreadful it is. We've done our best to bring Andrew up to be a decent boy, and now this awful neighborhood is taking him away from us."

"Oh, Mom, you're getting all worked up over nothing. Nobody hates us. You just think they do because you don't know them. It works the other way, too. They didn't think so much of us, because they didn't know us. I had to learn that, too, Mom!"

I looked at him in sudden astonishment. I saw his close-cropped blond hair, his grave, gray eyes, the golden down on his cheeks, and the embarrassment tinting his clear complexion. He was so young, so vulnerable, and I hadn't realized till now that he, too, was fighting a private battle with the street. That realization frightened me.

"You mean you stood up for them just to get into Danny Dabrowski's good graces? Why, he's not worth your little finger!" My voice trembled with indignation. "Listen to me, Andrew. Tomorrow is Sunday. We'll drive you up to the mountains, to the camp. They know us well enough, after all these years, to make a place for you. What I make at the bakery will more than take care of it. You can spend the rest of the summer there and you'll be safe."

"Safe! Mom, are you crazy?" Andrew was thoroughly perplexed. "I'm safe right here in my own neighborhood!"

"No you're not, not with Danny Dabrowski and those other hoodlums around. I'll go and get started with your packing."

Now that everything was settled, now that I could do something with my hands, I felt better. But Andrew sprang up and caught me by the arm.

"Mom, hold on a minute! What's got into you? You talk as though there's some sort of danger all around. It's crazy. Honestly, it's crazy. Besides, I don't want to go away. I've got a job. And the club's just getting started." Seeing the determination in my face, he turned to Bart in entreaty. "Dad, please do something."

"Your mother may be a little upset right now," said Bart calmly, "but I think it might be a good idea for you to go to camp just as she says."

"Dad, don't you understand, either? Sure, Danny was wrong to take the car. But then you were asking for it, being so high and mighty. And if we'd been jerks at the police station it would just have made it worse. We live here. After all, we live here and they're our neighbors!"

"Yes, but we don't have to be part of it," I declared firmly.

Distractedly, Andrew ran his hand through his hair. "Honestly! You talk as though this apartment were some sort of little private heaven, and everything around it a—a jungle! Well, I'll tell you something. This place is a morgue!"

"Andrew!" I cried.

"I'm sorry, Mom, Dad." Andrew was suddenly contrite. "But I'm not going away."

146

He waited for Bart or me to speak and then mumbled, "I'll be outside," and left the apartment.

I laid out a suitcase and all of Andrew's clothes on his bed. I washed some clothes, hoping they would be dry by morning. I darned some socks. Fortunately, I had some nametags leftover from last summer, and I sewed them on the clothes that didn't already have them.

I fixed a cold supper, leaned out the window and called Andrew. We ate in silence. Afterward, we watched a television show. Then Andrew said good night and went to his room. I saw him stiffen when he saw the packed suitcase on his bed.

"Just put it on the floor," I called, going to him. He was still standing in the doorway, and I turned him around to face me, my young son who was taller than I. I wanted to hold his face between my hands and kiss him and press his head against my shoulder as I had done when he was a little boy.

"Andrew dear, I'm sure this is for the best," was all I could say.

"Sure, sure, Mom," he said.

I spent the night escaping from one violent dream after another. And every time I woke up in chills it seemed to me that Bart was awake. Once I asked him if he were sick.

"I'm all right," he answered. "I just can't get to sleep."

In the morning I prepared breakfast, called Bart, and knocked on Andrew's door. Getting no answer, I pushed open the door. The bed was still made, the suitcase still lying on top of it.

"Bart," I shouted, "Andrew's not here! He's run away!"

"I know," he said. "I heard him go."

"You heard him—and didn't stop him?"

"I couldn't. I didn't have any right."

His words made no sense to me. Nothing made sense but Andrew's empty room and unwrinkled bed. "Where did he go? Where could he go?"

"I don't think he went far. I think he went to Pastor Bob's."

"Then let's go get him," I cried.

Bart put out a restraining hand. "No. Wait, Sarah. We've got a lot to talk about before we see Andrew." He pushed the suitcase aside and sat down on the bed. "Do you know why I couldn't sleep last night? I kept thinking of what happened yesterday and what Andrew said. And the plain, unvarnished truth is that we failed him as parents. As a matter of fact, we've failed as human beings."

I looked at Bart in shock. He was hunched over, his hands clasped between his knees, but his voice was firm and quite strong.

"Andrew called this place a morgue, and he's right. Look at me—I've been going around wallowing in self-pity, acting as if my

147

life is already over. When I haven't got my nose in a newspaper, I sit like a lump, feeling sorrier and sorrier for myself. I've been some happy companion for you, Sarah. And once you said I'd stopped being a father. Well, that's true, too. I acted as though the only thing a father is needed for is to earn a living for his child. Thank God, I had sense enough to stand up for Andrew yesterday."

With this, Bart straightened up and turned around to me. He took one of my hands. "This will hurt you, Sarah, as much as it hurt me. But we've been snobs, out and out snobs. And you want to know something? We've always been snobs! I think now that one of the reasons my heart gave out was because I was pushing, always pushing, trying to get a bigger commission here, a bigger bonus there, so that we could afford a better car, a better house, better furniture than our next-door neighbor. We were even snobbish in the work we did for the church. I think we did it for prestige, for admiration, not out of any real generosity."

I felt trapped. I went to the single window that looked out on an airshaft. Bart was telling the truth, and I knew it, and it was suffocating me.

His words went on, relentlessly. "Andrew's the only one with his feet on the ground. 'We live here,' he said. It's true. We live in the world, we live with people. The question is, are we going to go on jockeying for position as we did in the past, or wrapping ourselves in isolation like mummies, as we're doing now? Or are we going to break down and really live with people?" He was silent for a minute and then his voice grew gentle. "Sarah, honey, which will it be?"

I turned away from the window. "I don't know, Bart," I cried. "This street frightens me. It seems so hostile. I'm afraid of it, afraid of the people."

He took me in his arms. "But don't you see, honey? It isn't hostile at all. It only seems hostile because you're that way. You'll see; all we have to do is relax, and we'll be happy again."

My head on his shoulder, I started to cry. I cried with relief, for now I knew it was no longer necessary to fight my bitter battle with Kennedy Street. And as my tears subsided, I began to realize now how pleasant it was to be in my husband's arms again. I hadn't known how much I missed it. I hadn't realized it, but I'd resented my husband for making us give up our home and move into this shabby apartment. How could I make myself go into his arms? I was sure he'd destroyed our marriage. Without knowing it, I had secretly blamed him—put up a barrier between us. But now at last, it was down.

A knock on the door made us spring apart. "It's Andrew! He's home!"

I flew to the door and flung it open. Danny Dabrowski faced me.

148

In surprise, he looked at my tear-stained face. "Is anything the matter, Mrs. Tinsley?"

"No, no," I said.

"Could I talk to you for a minute?"

"Oh, yes, come in," I said.

He was wearing the same clothes he had worn yesterday, but his dark unruly curls were damp and I could see comb marks through them. "Look, I want to thank you for what you did yesterday. I told my old lady—my mother—about it and she's going to come see you. But I couldn't wait. You know how it is when you got something on your mind. The thing is, I'm sorry I took your car. I took it because—" He stopped abruptly, realizing that he couldn't tell us why he had taken it.

"Because people shouldn't put on airs," Bart finished for him gently.

Startled, Danny looked at him and then flushed. "Well, anyway, thanks, for what you did. And there's something else I gotta say. I've been acting like a real jerk, and I just want to tell you I'm sorry— especially for the way I treated you, Mrs. Tinsley."

"That's all right, Danny," I said and swallowed. Suddenly I felt that I should be the one to do the apologizing.

But he ducked his head to me in a touching, awkward little bow, and then strode over to Bart and thrust out his hand. Bart took it in one hand and placed his other on top, clasping Danny's hand. "You're a fine boy."

Danny waved his words away with something of a return to his old lordly manner. Then he walked over to the sofa, sat down, crossed his legs and remarked, "You sure fixed this place up nice. Say," he said, "where's Andrew?"

"We think he's at Pastor Bob's," Bart answered. "We're going there now. Would you like to come along?"

"Yeah," Danny said, "I'll tag along."

When we got to the church, the services were over and little groups of people stood on the sidewalk exchanging Sunday pleasantries. Pastor Bob spied us right away and hurried over. "Good morning," he said. "I expect you've come to have Andrew show you around the club."

I was grateful for the tactful way in which he had told us that Andrew was here. Then he clapped Danny on the shoulder. "How are you, Danny? Look, you know the way I'm tied up here. Why don't you take Mr. and Mrs. Tinsley to the club?"

Danny led us to an old store, several buildings from the church. The big room, which we entered first, was empty except for a folding chair, some cans of paint on a newspaper, and an old battered leather sofa. That must have been where Andrew had slept, I thought with a pang.

"Hey, anybody here?" Danny shouted.

Andrew emerged from a doorway in the rear holding a paintbrush in a coffee can full of turpentine.

"Hi," Danny said.

"Hi," Andrew returned the greeting. He looked at Bart and me and grinned.

That casual, friendly greeting brought tears to my eyes. "Well," said Bart, a little huskily, "this is going to be quite a nice place."

"It's a rat-trap right now," Danny remarked, already showing a proprietor's offhand pride, "but it'll be okay when we fix it up. Now, if you'll excuse me, I gotta begin my hard labor."

Andrew, seeing the tears in my eyes, exclaimed, "Ah, Mom, I didn't mean to upset you. I just had to get away for a little while."

"It's all right now, Andrew. I understand why you did it. I—I understand now."

With his free arm, Andrew hugged me, then looked shyly at his father.

"Well, son," he said, "when you come home, I think you'll find that your mother and I have stopped being—er—jerks."

"Oh, Dad," said Andrew, embarrassed. Then, with a rush the two of them gripped each other by the arms.

Danny and his mother came to dinner that night. At first the evening limped along. But suddenly, magically, under the spell of friendliness, all uneasiness dropped away and we were having a wonderful time. Later, when Mrs. Dabrowski was helping me clean up in the kitchen, she told me about her sons. The eldest had been killed in the Army and the middle son had recently joined the service. Danny was all she had left, and she spoiled him.

"I say yes to everything. Not good, I see it now. I work hard all my life. Why should I think my son is too good for work? I made a mistake." She stared for a while and then went on. "And Danny has no father. Maybe it's a good thing what happened yesterday. Now he has Pastor Bob and your husband for friends."

"Good things happened to us, too," I said.

The next day, I woke up with a little tune running through my head, and that was unusual. At the bakery, I found myself talking to the clerks and the customers, and that was unusual. And at the end of the day, my feet didn't hurt at all!

Walking home I spied the old woman sitting on the hard-backed chair in her customary place in front of the grocery. I said that it had been a pleasant day and looked into her eyes. They were not hard and black, as I had always imagined. She seemed so happy that I had

150

stopped to talk to her. Then with all the spryness of a young girl she bounced up—and suddenly let out a cry of pain. "Oh, are you hurt?" I said. "Is there anything I can do for you?" I noticed then, although she was wearing a long black dress, that her legs were terribly swollen and that she could hardly stand up.

"I forget my old legs have no springs no more," Mrs. Arnez said. "I make hard landing on moon!" She gave the merriest laugh I'd ever heard in all my life. Then she explained that she had a very bad case of arthritis and that it was unbearably painful for her to walk. Sitting on that stoop, watching the passersby, had been her only amusement for the last five years.

"Where's your big cat?" I asked her trying to distract her.

"Oh yes, yes," she said. "You wait—take me little while because I walk slow, but I be back right away." I tried to stop her because it seemed such an effort for her to walk, but she wouldn't let me. I watched her disappear slowly into the dark hallway walking with such purpose, as if she had something very important to do. Within a few minutes she was back with a basket of the blackest little kittens I'd ever seen. "I can't walk so good, but my Pronto—she walk good and fast. Look what she give me! Now I give you! Which one you want?"

"Oh, they're lovely," I said. "How nice of you to want to give me something! That little black one over there—the one that's yawning. She looks as if she just woke up and likes it here!" I laughed. Mrs. Arnez put down the basket and gently placed the small kitten in my arms.

"Next time you pass, you stop to talk to me again. Maybe you have something to tell me—about kitten, I mean," she said shyly.

"Oh, I will stop to talk again," I said, putting my hand on her shoulder. I was so happy. "I'm sure I'll have lots to tell you now!"

THE END

BROKEN PROMISES, BROKEN VOWS
My affair ended in murder

A month had gone by since that terrible night in the woods, yet the memory of it filled all my waking moments. No matter how I tried to blank out what had happened, each ugly detail persisted in stark relief. The darkness was filled with horror pictures, too. Night after night, I lay beside my husband, listening to his quiet breathing, my mind racing frantically, refusing to allow my body any rest.

"Oh, God," I prayed desperately. "Please don't let them find out I was the woman in that car. Please, please don't let that happen." I knew my marriage would come to an abrupt end if my sin were exposed. Bill would leave me and take little Emily and the whole world would know what kind of woman I was.

Why had I gone out with Hank McKay in the first place? What primitive urge had drawn me into his arms and aroused such a passionate desire to taste his kisses, to know his touch and his nearness? Remembering the accusations my mother and husband had thrown at me, I wondered if I really was oversexed.

My mother, a tiny, fragile woman with a tight, unsmiling face, is very rigid and self-contained. Her only interest in life seems to be housework. She always kept our house immaculate, but there was no more warmth in its interior than there was inside her. I have never been able to figure out why Dad, who died when I was fifteen, married her, unless her coldness challenged his manhood and made him determined to put some life in her. I've found it impossible to imagine my mother responding to any man in a loving way, least of all my father, whose down-to-earth attitude she probably never attempted to understand.

Mom always said I reminded her of Dad, and I don't think she understood me any better than she had him. In my teens I had many boyfriends, more than the other girls I hung out with in high school. I wasn't the prettiest girl in our crowd, but boys seemed attracted to me for some reason. Mom would eye me suspiciously while I got ready for a date. "Just remember, Margaret, boys will try almost anything. You have to be one step ahead of them all the time," she'd caution.

I'd been one step ahead, all right, but not the way she meant. The mild petting sessions we kids indulged in made me want to go further, to find out what real love was like, and I guess the only thing that held me back was the fear of becoming pregnant. I knew I'd never be able to face my mother if that happened.

Mom used to wait up for me when I went out, and one night she must have been looking out the window because when I came into the house, breathless from the kisses I'd just shared, she let me have it. "You'd better watch your step, Margaret Taylor!" she cried. "I saw how you let that boy kiss you and touch you. You're oversexed, just like your father was, and if you're not careful, no decent man will marry you!"

I managed to keep a rein on my desires until I was eighteen and met Bill Rance. Mom approved of him right away. "That young man has both feet on the ground," she said. "He'll go far, make no mistake about that."

But I'd been more interested in Bill's exciting good looks than what kind of future he might have. Tall and slim, his shoulders were surprisingly broad, and he had deep blue eyes and a blond crew cut. I fell in love with him after our first date. When he asked me to marry him, I didn't hesitate a minute before saying yes. I could hardly wait to be his wife.

After a two-month engagement we had a quiet wedding and went to Canada for a honeymoon. If Bill was a little surprised at my ardent response to his lovemaking, he was also glad. "You're the kind of wife a guy dreams of, honey," he told me that first night.

After a delightful week we returned to Newport, where we found a darling little house in the suburbs.

It wasn't long before I realized how important Bill's job as assistant sales manager for a large paper company was to him. He made it clear the first week after our honeymoon that nothing must interfere with his getting ahead, not even me.

We'd gone to bed early that night, and as soon as the light was out, I'd snuggled close to Bill and twined my arms around his neck. To my surprise, he'd unclasped my arms and moved away. "Not tonight, honey," he said. "I have a big day tomorrow, and I'm bushed."

"You mean you're too tired to make love to me?" I asked, bewildered.

"I mean I can't cope with a little sexpot like you unless I'm in darned good shape," he replied. "And tonight I'm bone tired."

But I wasn't easily discouraged. I moved close to him again and kissed him full on the mouth. "Maybe I can revive you," I whispered.

"Cut it out, will you?" he said then, clearly annoyed. "I can't afford to go to work looking as if I've been pulled through a knothole. Can't you understand that?"

I felt as if he'd slapped me in the face, and when I started to cry, Bill got even angrier. "What's the matter with you?" he demanded.

That made me cry even harder, and he grabbed his pillow and stomped off to sleep in the living room, muttering angrily. Of course, we made up the next morning, but from then on, I was careful to wait for him to make the first move. And on the nights he didn't, I lay awake wishing God hadn't put so much love and longing inside of me.

When I became pregnant, a different kind of love grew in my heart as the child grew in my body. I was speechless with joy just looking at Emily that first time. I examined her tiny hands and feet and touched her corn-silk hair, twining a strand of it around my finger. Brushing my cheek against hers, I marveled at how perfectly beautiful she was.

Bill was as crazy about her as I was. "Our tiny woman," he called her, and he was a devoted, affectionate father from the day we brought her home. I'm sure most people would have said he was a devoted, affectionate husband, too. And he was, from all outward appearances. He never looked at another woman; he brought home every penny of his earnings; he never failed to compliment me on my cooking, and he made love to me once or twice a week. But that was the problem. Once or twice a week wasn't enough for me. Yet nothing I said or did made Bill understand this.

During the first three years of our marriage, he did well at his job. Mr. Farnsworth, Bill's boss, had taken a real interest in him and taught him more about the business, even included us in their social life. One night, after they'd been to our house for dinner, Bill put his arm around me and held me close. "Wonderful dinner, honey. I was awfully proud of you."

I laid my head on his shoulder. "I'm glad things went so well. I know how much Mr. Farnsworth's approval means to you. I think he and his wife had a good time."

Bill kissed me on the top of my head. "You can say that again! Do you know he's thinking of retiring in another year? If he does, I'll move right into his job. We'll really be on top then, Margaret."

"Oh, Bill, how wonderful!"

"Well, you've helped me do it," he replied. "A man needs the right kind of wife to get ahead, and you've been that and more."

Knowing I had contributed to my husband's success made me feel good and, although I was still dissatisfied with our routine lovemaking, I had to admit my marriage was nearly perfect in every other way. We'd been blessed with a wonderful daughter, our future was secure, and we loved each other very much. So I made up my mind to stop worrying about our sex life.

I might have been able to keep that resolution if I hadn't met Hank McKay and forgotten everything else in my instant awareness of him as a man. I knew right away he spelled danger, but I was drawn to him by a force too strong for me to overcome. Instinctively I realized we were two of a kind, that he had the same hot blood running through his veins that ran through mine. He must've recognized it, too, and that's why he couldn't leave me alone.

A month before our fourth wedding anniversary Bill told me at dinner one night, "I saw a beautiful sedan and, from what the salesman said, I think it would be a good buy. He promised to bring it over in the morning . . . take you for a test ride. If you like the car, we'll get it. The salesman's name is McKay. He should be here around eleven."

I arranged to have Mindy Gray, my next-door neighbor, take care of Emily, and I was dressed and waiting when the shining new blue car rolled into our driveway the next morning. Just looking at its deep red upholstery and white-walled tires excited me.

The man sitting behind the wheel climbed out and grinned at me.

"You look like a kid on Christmas morning," he teased. "But I don't blame you a bit. It's a great car."

"Oh, it's a stunning car!" I exclaimed. "I can hardly wait to see how it runs."

"That's what I'm here for," he replied. "I'm Hank McKay. I guess your husband told you I'd be here this morning."

I managed to take my eyes off the car long enough to look at the salesman. He was big, powerfully built. His eyes were deep-set and very dark, and when he smiled, I was conscious of flashing white teeth, made even whiter by contrast with his olive-toned complexion. He was strikingly handsome and absolutely radiated a male sexiness that sent waves of excitement up and down my spine.

He helped me into the car, and when he sat beside me, I was even more aware of his terrific physical appeal. Driving down the street, he pointed out some of the car's special features, but I heard only his vibrantly thrilling voice, nothing that he said. His large, well-cared for hands fascinated me. I trembled inwardly, because I couldn't help wondering how they would feel touching me.

He interrupted my little fantasy by saying, "Want to take the wheel yourself so you can see how easily she handles?"

When I nodded eagerly, he pulled over to one side of the road and got out, and I slid into the driver's seat. Just as I was about to pull away, he said, "You should use your seatbelt. It's a good habit to get into."

I was all thumbs as I tried to buckle it. "Here, let me help you," Hank offered.

He slipped one arm around me and buckled it quickly. For a second his face was so close to mine I could feel his breath on my cheek. As he was about to move away, I turned suddenly and looked into his eyes. A startled look came over his face as our glances held.

As if he knew what his nearness was doing to me, his arm tightened around my waist, and he drew me closer. "No," I whispered faintly. "No—"

Instead of answering, he put his free hand under my chin. I thrilled at the strength of his fingers as he forced my face upward to his. Then his mouth came down on mine, seeking, demanding, and giving until my whole body responded to the mounting, unrestrained passion in his kiss. My great longing, my unfulfilled hunger blotted out everything else. My own heavy breathing mingled with his and only when his hands fumbled with the buttons on my blouse did my sanity return. I tore myself out of his arms. The enormity of what I had done hit me full force, and I burst into hysterical tears. "I—I must have gone crazy. I d-don't know what I was thinking of!" I stammered between sobs.

"I do. I know damned well what you were thinking of," Hank said bluntly.

Shame took over. I felt cheap and degraded. I was afraid to look at him, and when I started the car, my hands shook so much, I zigzagged all over the road.

"Better let me drive back," he said. "You seem a little shook up."

Neither of us spoke a word until we were back at my house. Then he said, "Look, there's no need to be so upset. If it'll make you feel any better, I apologize. Maybe I tagged you wrong—but I thought you wanted me to kiss you back there."

I did want you to kiss me, I thought. I wanted you to do more than that. You know. You know exactly how I feel.

But all I said aloud was, "My husband will be in touch with you about the car. Thank you for showing it to me."

As I walked toward the house, I felt Hank's eyes boring into my back. Inside, I collapsed into a chair and covered my face with my hands. How could I have let a man I'd never seen before hold me and kiss me with the intimacy of a lover? What had come over me?

At least half an hour must have passed before I remembered to get Emily from Mindy's. I'd just finished giving her lunch and settling her down for a nap when Bill called to see if I liked the car. "Oh, it's fine. I—I like it very much," I replied shakily.

"You don't sound too enthusiastic," he said in a disappointed tone. "Would you rather look at some others before you decide?"

"Oh, no. It's really lovely," I told him quickly, trying to put some sparkle in my voice.

"Okay. I'll go ahead and close the deal. We ought to have the car in a week or so."

I hoped I wouldn't have to see Hank again, but he delivered

the car ten days later. Emily was taking a nap and I was working in my garden when he pulled up in the driveway. He got out of the car, pushed open the little gate, and walked into the garden.

"Here are your keys," he said, holding them out to me. "I hope you enjoy your new car."

But when I reached for the keys, his hand closed around mine. "I've been thinking about you a lot," he said softly. "I can't get you out of my mind."

Blood rushed to my face, and my throat felt dry and tight. I tried to pull my hand away, but he wouldn't let it go. "You've been thinking about me, too, haven't you?" he asked.

I couldn't speak for a minute, and when I did, my voice sounded ragged and unfamiliar. "Please, leave me alone. I'm happily married. I'm not the kind of woman who plays around. What happened the other day never happened to me before, and it will never happen again. Now please, go away and don't come back."

Hank dropped my hand with a shrug. "Sure," he said, "if that's the way you want it. But if you change your mind, let me know."

He handed me the car keys and walked out of the yard. A car from the agency picked him up, and a minute later he was gone. But I didn't go back to my gardening, and for the rest of the day, I couldn't keep my mind on anything.

Bill's mother called the following Tuesday and asked if Emily could visit her for a week. She lived in Spring Lake, a beach town on the Rhode Island shore, and Emily loved to visit her because Mother Rance took her to the beach every day. "It would be a good chance for you and Bill to take a little vacation," Mother Rance suggested after we decided what time she'd pick Emily up. "That boy of mine works too hard. You ought to go up to Canada for a second honeymoon. Do you both good."

Much to my surprise, Bill was all for it when I mentioned it that night. "I guess it's time I spent a little time with my wife," he said.

My hopes soared. Maybe being away from the pressures of his job for a little while would make a difference in Bill—and in our sexual relationship. Remembering how close we'd been on our honeymoon, I longed to go back to the place where our love had taken precedence over everything else.

Mother Rance picked Emily up Friday morning, and I was in the middle of packing when Bill came home that evening and told me the trip was off. "Mr. Farnsworth wants me to go to a salesmen's convention in Los Angeles this weekend," he said. "He can't make it himself, so I'll have to represent the company. Honey, I feel awfully bad about this, but I can't turn him down."

I was so disappointed I burst into tears. "He could have sent somebody else!" I cried. "Why do you have to jump every time he whistles?"

"Because he's my boss," Bill reminded me quietly. "And my whole business career depends on his good opinion of me. This is an emergency, Margaret. Don't you see how important it is for me to go?"

But all I saw were my dreams of a much-needed second honeymoon going up in smoke. I knew I couldn't afford to be separated from Bill at this time. I was afraid of what would happen if he left me home alone, and I guess that's why I fought him so unrelentingly about going to Los Angeles.

"You don't need a wife as long as you have your precious job!" I cried. "You don't know what it means to really love someone. You're too involved with selling your darned old paper to remember I'm a woman who needs you! You—"

"Cut it out, will you, Margaret? I'm trying to make a good living for you and Emily. Maybe you'd rather have some guy who's ready to jump into bed with you morning, noon, and night. All marriage means to you is a free license to indulge your sick desires. I think—"

"I don't care what you think!" I was yelling at him now. "I only know I'm a human being, and you make me feel like I'm some sort of freak! You have the idea that sex is a once-a-week special, like corned beef hash in a restaurant, but I'll bet other men don't feel that way! I'll bet other men find the time and energy to make their wives happy in bed!"

Bill's face reddened with anger. "Why are you bringing up our sex life now?" he demanded.

"Because I was hoping if we could go away together, you'd forget about your job and act like a husband for a change. But I guess that'll never happen. I guess you'll always be as cold and sexless as a—a fish!"

His mouth set in a cold, furious line. "Are you through?" he asked. "If you think you are, I'm going to bed—to sleep." We slept in the same bed that night, but we were further apart than we'd ever been. Neither of us made any attempt at reconciliation the next morning, and Bill went to the office without kissing me good-bye. The following morning I drove him to the Newport airport and I don't think we said ten words the whole time. I didn't stay to see him off. Instead I went home and felt sorry for myself.

The empty house seemed to echo my angry thoughts, and loneliness made me restless. I missed Emily, so I decided I'd drive to Mother Rance that same day and bring her home. Bill would be gone at least a week, and I didn't want to be alone all that time.

I hadn't left the city limits when the engine developed a rattle. I knew I should take the car to the agency's service department instead of our regular mechanic, but I was afraid I'd run into Hank and, in the bitter, frustrated mood I was in, I knew that would be a mistake.

Still undecided, I drove a few more miles, but the rattling got worse. This is plain silly, I reasoned with myself. We have a perfectly good guarantee on the car, so why should we pay somebody to repair a brand-new car? Besides, even if Hank is there, I needn't exchange more than a few words with him.

Armed with this defense, I drove to the agency. "I don't think it's anything serious," the mechanic said after he'd looked at the car. "But I'd suggest leaving it overnight so we can check it more thoroughly. You can pick it up tomorrow or the next day."

I sighed. "I guess I don't have much choice. I was planning to drive to Spring Lake, but I'd be afraid to take a chance under the circumstances."

"We can lend you another car," the mechanic suggested, but I said I'd rather postpone the trip. "I can manage without a car for a couple of days. And Mr. Rance is in Los Angeles."

"But you'll need a ride home, Mrs. Rance. I'll be very glad to take you."

I knew whom that voice belonged to, and the sound of it made my knees weak. "I—I can take a cab, thank you," I said desperately, afraid to turn and face him.

"They're hard to get this time of day," Hank said, coming from behind me. "My car's right here."

Not wanting to make a big deal out of it, I gave in to Hank, and all the way home, I was intently aware of his every movement. Each time his arm brushed against mine or a sudden bump in the road brought him close to me, my spine tingled as if it had been stung with electric wires.

When we stopped in front of my house, he said, "Do you still want to go to Spring Lake this afternoon? I'm free, and I could drive you there."

"No, that won't be necessary. I was only going to my mother-in-law's to get my daughter. I can wait a few days," I said, trying to open the door and get out.

He caught hold of my arm. "Well, since you're all alone, maybe you'd like to have dinner with me tonight?"

"No," I said sharply. "I wouldn't think of such a thing. I told you before, I don't play around."

His dark eyes opened wide. "Who said anything about playing around? I just asked you to have dinner with me."

I shook his hand off my arm. "No. I won't have dinner with you."

He didn't try to stop me from getting out of the car, but once again I had the feeling he was watching my every step as I walked toward the house. I closed the door quickly and leaned against it, breathing fast and hard as if I'd just run a long-distance race. But I was glad I'd had the good sense to refuse his offer.

Bill called as I was about to eat my solitary dinner. "I hope you've come to your senses by now, Margaret," he said. "I hope you realize how childish you've been about this whole thing."

He didn't say he missed me, he didn't say he'd rather have gone to Canada with me than to the convention. Instead, he talked about the speech he was supposed to make that night and the dinner he planned to attend the next day. "Taking Mr. Farnsworth's place is a big responsibility. I hope I can live up to it."

"You will," I told him bitterly. "You'll do just fine, Bill. And you'll love every minute of it, too. It's right up your alley."

"Why shouldn't it be?" he retorted. "It's part of my job!"

"And your job is the biggest part of your life," I said. "Nobody knows that better than I do!"

I heard Bill curse softly under his breath, then the line went dead. He'd hung up on me! Too upset to bother about dinner, I went out for a walk instead.

Daylight had begun to fade slowly into soft summer evening. The smell of freshly mowed lawns, mingled with the heady scent of flowers from the neighborhood gardens made my loneliness even more acute. This was an evening to be with a man, walking close, stopping for lingering kisses, forgetting the rest of the world. Instead, I was alone, depressed because the man I wanted wasn't here, and the man who wanted me I didn't dare say yes to.

I walked until I was tired and when I got back to my empty house, the phone was ringing. My heart pounded as I ran frantically to answer it, hoping it was Bill.

"I thought maybe you'd changed your mind about dinner," Hank McKay said. "I promise to bring you right home afterward. How about it?"

"All right," I said recklessly, surprised at my nerve. "I will have dinner with you."

We arranged to meet a few blocks away from my house so that no curious neighbors would see him pick me up. I hurriedly showered and dressed, anxious to get out of the house before I changed my mind. Hank was waiting in his car when I reached our meeting place.

He took me to a small, obscure restaurant that was practically empty.

"Nobody's likely to spot us here," he said, helping me into a chair. "I wouldn't want you to get in trouble."

He ordered cocktails, and as I looked at him over the rim of my glass, I thought: How crazy it is for me to be sitting here with a man I know nothing about.

"Are you married?" I asked suddenly.

He shook his head. "Nope. No ties of any kind. That's the way I like it."

He stared at me for a minute. "I have a hunch you were putting me on when you said you were happy. Am I right?"

"I ought to be," I said slowly. "My husband's a wonderful man. I guess he can't help putting his job first. But—"

Suddenly I was telling him the whole story. "I suppose I acted like a child when he had to call the trip off, but he didn't even seem to be sorry about it."

"I get the picture," Hank told me, caressing my hand. "You need more love than most women. Your husband must be some kind of a nut not to appreciate you."

"I shouldn't be discussing my personal problems," I said, flushing. "I hardly know you, and—"

His eyes burned into mine as he said softly, "I wouldn't say that. I think we know each other pretty well, and I think we're going to know each other even better before very long."

I hardly ate a mouthful of the delicious smelling dinner he ordered, so the brandy we had with our coffee went straight to my head. By the time we left the restaurant, I was more relaxed. A few blocks away from my house, Hank suddenly put his arm around my waist and drew me close to him. "May I come in with you?" he asked.

"No. I—I couldn't do that," I whispered.

"Then let's take a little ride. You don't want the evening to end just yet, do you?"

Without waiting for my answer, he turned off the main road and headed for a wooded area where the trees stood like sentinels in the bright moonlight. He stopped the car and took me in his arms. "I want you," he said huskily. "I want you more than I've ever wanted any woman."

I collapsed against him, raising my face to his. Our lips met in a kiss that made me feel as if the very life was being drained out of me.

Hank let me go and opened the door of the car. "Come on," he whispered, getting out.

He guided me through the dense growth of trees to a small clearing, where the moon shone down with an almost unearthly light. Spreading his jacket on the ground, he drew me down beside him. We reached for each other hungrily and our lips met in a searing kiss. As I felt his hands on my body, my pulse raced wildly in anticipation of release from the intense passion consuming me.

Suddenly his whole body stiffened; his head swiveled fearfully. "What was that?" he demanded in a hushed voice.

161

I heard it then—branches snapping under the heavy crush of feet plodding through the dense underbrush. My blood froze in my veins when, looking over Hank's shoulder, I saw a man standing over us—a giant with a long, jagged scar on his face and maniacal eyes. Then I saw something that terrified me even more—his gun! Pointing it directly at us he roared in a terrifying voice, "Sinners! Servants of the devil! God has sent me to rid the world of your rotten souls!"

"What the hell—" Hank muttered, starting to turn around to see what was happening. Then, with no warning, the man shot Hank! Just like that! I watched in horror as he rolled over and lay on his back, his eyes wide open in a look of shocked disbelief, blood gushing from his head. Terrified beyond all thought or movement, I closed my eyes and waited, sure the maniac would kill me, too.

But some quirk in his deranged mind stopped him, and he just stood there cursing me for a minute before he ran back into the woods.

The awful stillness that comes with death descended around me, and I lay there, my eyes squeezed shut, shocked into immobility. The first thing I saw when I opened my eyes was Hank's rigid, lifeless body lying near me in an ever-widening pool of blood. I crawled away from the horrible sight, fighting the nausea that threatened to overtake me. Holding onto a tree trunk, I tried to pull myself up, but my legs gave way, and I fell down again. After a few more tries, I finally managed to get to my feet, only to fall against the tree, sicker than I'd ever been in my life.

I stumbled toward Hank's car and got in, but when I realized the keys were still in his pocket, I got out and started to walk the two miles to my house. I couldn't bear to touch or see Hank's body again.

I felt like a hunted animal as I slunk along the edge of the road, hiding behind trees whenever I saw the lights of an oncoming car. I was on the verge of collapse by the time I got into my house. I fell into a chair and sobbed in wild, uncontrollable hysteria. "Oh, my God!" I kept saying. "Oh, my God!"

I sat there all night, crying, praying, and worrying. How soon would someone find Hank's body? Would the police be able to track down the crazy man who had killed him? Would he remember me? My terror of being involved was so great I felt no grief or sense of loss for Hank. I hadn't been in love with him. Sex alone had drawn us together, and with his violent death, that feeling had died, too.

Exhaustion finally drove me to bed at dawn, but I slept only a few hours, and the minute I awakened, terror descended upon me again.

The first item of news I heard on the radio was about Hank. Two children had discovered his body and the car. "The only clue to the lovers' lane killing is a woman's compact found near the body," the

162

announcer said. "A citywide search is being conducted to find her."

I jumped up and grabbed my purse, dumping its contents in wild disarray all over the bed. My keys, lipstick, wallet, and identification papers were all there, but my compact was missing! It's the kind of compact anybody might have, I told myself, pacing the room feverishly. They won't be able to trace it to me.

After all, I was Mrs. Bill Rance, a respectable, suburban housewife. Hank McKay was simply the auto salesman who had sold us our car. Nobody knew I'd gone out with him. Nobody knew of the crazy attraction we'd felt for each other—or did they? Had he talked to anyone or bragged about the possibility of a conquest?

The next few days were a hideous nightmare. The papers were full of the grisly murder and people talked of nothing else. I stayed in the house, too terrified to venture out into the street. The man from the automobile agency who delivered my car had his own ideas about the case.

"Hank was always fooling around with married women," he said. "I had a hunch some guy would let him have it one day. I bet that's what happened, too. I bet some husband got wise and followed them to that place. You wait and see if I'm not right."

Bill came home from Los Angeles a few days later, and I nearly went to pieces when he took me in his arms and said he'd missed me. "We'll take that trip soon, honey," he promised. "I'm sorry I said those rotten things to you."

I hid my face against him so that he wouldn't see the agony in my eyes. If he knew what had happened. . . .

We drove to Spring Lake to bring Emily home that evening, and all the way there and back the news broadcasts were full of new leads, and the commentators spoke of the "mystery woman" who still hadn't been located.

"I wouldn't want to be in her shoes," Bill remarked. "She must be really sweating it out. Maybe she's the one who killed him. Who knows?"

I clenched my hands together in my lap. "What makes you think that?" I asked.

Bill shrugged. "He looked like a pretty smooth customer to me. He probably had a lot of women friends, and one of them found out he was two-timing her and shot him. It gives you a funny feeling, though. A couple of weeks ago we bought a car from the guy—now he's the victim in a murder case!"

Another week went by. Then two, then three. By the end of the month, the murder had faded from the front pages of the paper, and the radio and TV newscasters had other things to talk about. But my own panic hadn't diminished. Instead, it had grown steadily until it seemed like a monster bent on destroying me. I lived each day, wondering if the next would bring the discovery of my terrible secret. And the hardest part of it all was the deception I had to practice to keep Bill from noticing the strain I was under.

And then something happened that pushed everything else out of my mind. Emily became violently sick. It was several days before her illness was correctly diagnosed, and by that time she was worse. "Spinal meningitis," the doctor said. "She must be hospitalized immediately."

While the doctors worked frantically, Bill and I spent two agonizing days in the hospital waiting room, begging God to spare her. And when the turning point came, we cried together in a great surge of thankfulness that brought us closer than we'd ever been before. After looking in on our sleeping daughter, we left the hospital. Bill kept one arm around me and drove all the way home with one hand. As soon as we got inside the house, he took me in his arms and kissed me.

"I had to come close to losing Emily before I realized what marriage is all about," he said unsteadily. "It means so much to have a wife to share the bad moments. I couldn't have made it alone, Margaret. I never needed or loved you more than I have these past few days."

I was crying as I reached up and touched his face. And after that I could have found everything I hungered for in his arms, but my guilt kept getting in the way. Dear God, please let me forget about Hank McKay, and I'll never do anything to jeopardize my marriage again, I prayed.

But I should've known you can't bargain with God. Shortly after Emily came home from the hospital and was recuperating nicely, the bottom fell out of my world.

Bill and I were watching the late news one night when the announcer said there'd been a break in the lovers' lane murder case. "The police have arrested Arnold Harris, fifty-five, and are holding him on charges of manslaughter. He is unemployed and lives in a squatter's shack near the scene of the murder. He was arrested in a bar and grill when he tried to trade a gun for a few drinks. Later, the gun was found to be the same weapon that killed Hank McKay. Here is the scene which took place outside of the courthouse where Harris was taken to be arraigned."

My eyes were glued to the television screen. At first I got only a glimpse of the shabbily dressed man, flanked by several detectives, as he was hurried out of a police squad car and up the steps of the courthouse. Then there was a close-up of him entering the building, and I stifled a scream. The police had arrested the wrong man!

My hands began to shake, and the TV screen swam in front of

164

my eyes. I didn't see nor hear the rest of the news broadcast. When it was over, Bill turned off the set. "I'm glad they caught that guy," he said. "I've felt a little uneasy, knowing he was still on the loose. That piece of woodland where the murder took place is too close to our house for comfort."

I heard the clock strike every hour through that terrible night as I lay writhing in my own private hell. And when morning finally came, I dragged myself out of bed, white-faced, exhausted, and sick inside. I waited until Bill left for work before looking at the morning paper. The whole front page was devoted to the story:

"Arnold Harris had lived in a little shack in the woods for years without bothering anybody. What sudden impulse made him kill a man he apparently didn't know and had no grudge against is hard to figure out. He keeps saying, 'I didn't kill nobody. Honest, I didn't. I found that gun in the woods.' So far, nobody believes him. District Attorney Brown is sure he has his man, but he's also hoping to locate the one witness who could clinch the case by positively identifying the suspect as the killer of Hank McKay. So far, there were no clues to her whereabouts."

The paper dropped from my nerveless fingers. I knew what I had to do now. Even though it would wreck my marriage and destroy my life, I'd have to go to the District Attorney and tell him the truth. I couldn't let this man die for a crime he hadn't committed.

I dressed Emily and took longer than usual to give her breakfast. She was such a darling little girl, and I loved her dearly. I was sure Bill would take her away from me once he found out what I'd done. He'd say I was an unfit mother and nobody would blame him.

I asked Mindy Gray if she'd keep Emily while I attended to some business downtown. "I hope she won't give you any trouble," I said.

"Are you kidding?" Mindy replied cheerfully. "She's a little angel compared to most kids her age."

Because Bill had taken the car that morning, I had to travel by bus to the District Attorney's office. I was told he was too busy to see me unless my business was urgent. "It is," I said. "I have evidence about the Hank McKay murder."

I was taken to Mr. Brown's private office immediately. The minute the door closed behind me, I said, "I'm Mrs. Bill Rance. I was with Hank McKay the night he was killed. I came to tell you—"

My superficial composure suddenly left me, and I burst into tears. "You've arrested the wrong man," I managed to tell him. "Arnold Harris isn't guilty; I will swear to it."

Mr. Brown stared at me without speaking for a minute. Then he walked over and took hold of my arm. "You'd better sit down," he said brusquely.

I sank in a chair and gripped the edge of the desk until my knuckles showed white. "Now, let's have that again, lady. And you'd better be telling the truth. You'll be in plenty of trouble if you're lying."

"Do you think I'd be crazy enough to come here and tell you this if it wasn't true?" I asked in a hoarse whisper.

"Where have you been all this time?" he demanded. "You knew the police were looking for you. Why didn't you come forward before?"

"I was too ashamed and frightened. I'm a married woman with a little girl. I—I hoped nobody would ever have to find out I'd been with Hank McKay that night."

Mr. Brown grunted, and there was no sympathy in his face as he said bluntly, "You were playing around with the guy, is that it? Well, go ahead. Let's have the rest of your story."

Hearing myself talk about how I'd met Hank and later gone out that night made me feel even more ashamed. When I finished, the District Attorney said he'd fingerprint me to see if my prints matched those found in the abandoned car.

The fingerprints matched, but my ordeal had just begun. Next I had to look at mug shots of known criminals and sex deviates, in hopes I might recognize the killer. "No," I said after I'd looked at all of them. "I don't recognize any of them."

Mr. Brown asked how I could be sure what the man looked like. "It must have been dark in the woods. How could you see him so plainly?"

I bit my lips so hard my teeth almost sank through them. "The moon was full that night. The man stood right over me. He was a big man, with a long scar on his face and his eyes—" I shuddered— "his eyes were like those of a mad man. I'll never forget them as long as I live."

A police artist made several sketches of the killer as I described him and finally came up with one that resembled him closely. "Well, we have something to go on," the D.A. said. "Now I want you to look at the prisoner and give us your sworn statement he isn't the man who committed the murder. Once you do that we'll have to release him and start searching all over again."

I thought they would be through with me then, but they weren't. "You're a material witness for the State, Mrs. Rance. You didn't expect to just walk out of here, did you? We have to be sure you'll be available to testify against the real murderer when we find him."

"I won't run away," I said desperately. "I promise. Please, let me go home now."

"Not until Judge Reynolds sets bail for you," Mr. Brown said.

In the judge's chambers everything seemed to close in on me. Dimly I heard him set my bail at ten thousand dollars and tell me I could call my husband or my lawyer. That's when I fainted. When I opened my eyes, I was lying on a couch in a small room off the District Attorney's office. Bill was standing beside me, his face chalk white, and his eyes sick with horror and disbelief.

"Margaret! In God's name, what's this all about?" he demanded. "You must have lost your mind, coming here with this crazy story! You—"

I looked up at him, and he must've read the truth in my face because the disbelief faded from his eyes.

"Oh, God," he moaned. "It's true. You are involved in this rotten mess. My God, my wife—my own wife!"

He turned away and walked into the District Attorney's office. "I'll arrange bail for her," he said tonelessly. "And then I'll take her home."

He didn't speak or look at me all the way home. As soon as the front door closed, he said, "Pack Emily's things. I'm taking her to my mother's, and if I can help it, you'll never see her again. From now on, she has no mother. Do you understand that?"

"Bill, please, listen to me."

The hate in his eyes was the worst punishment I'd faced so far. "Listen to you? For what? To hear you say you're sorry for pulling the whole world down around my ears? To hear you say you didn't mean to go sneaking around with a no-good punk like McKay?" He threw back his head and laughed. "What do you take me for anyway—a poor slob without any brains?"

His face tightened with rage. "It makes me sick to my stomach to be in the same room with you," he said, "I want to get Emily as far away from you as I can. And if you try to see her or talk to her I swear I'll kill you!"

He made Emily sit in the car while I packed her clothes; he wouldn't even let me say good-bye to her. I heard the door close behind him, and I watched from the window as the car pulled away from the house. I was all alone now. I'd never see my husband or my little girl again. All the meaning was gone from my life.

I was spared any sensational publicity, being referred to as the mysterious woman witness whose testimony led to Arnold Harris' release. I knew I'd be called to testify against the real murderer at his trial, and as much as I dreaded that, it was nothing compared to the grief and remorse I suffered over the breakup of my marriage and the loss of my child. I didn't care what happened to me now, because I had nothing left to live for.

I tried to get through each day and night without too much thinking, because only by making my mind a blank, could I keep from going crazy.

I was staring blankly out the window one Sunday about a month

167

later when Bill brought Emily back to me. I couldn't believe my eyes when I saw him walking up the front steps, leading her by the hand. I opened the door but didn't dare make a move toward her until she broke away from her father and came running to me, her little arms outstretched, crying, "Mommy! Mommy! Mommy!"

Kneeling down, I fell apart as I hugged her to me. Tears streamed down my face as I whispered, "Emily! Oh, my darling! My baby! Mommy's so glad to see you!"

"She was making herself sick crying all the time, because she missed you so much. I couldn't stand seeing her cry. I had to bring her back," Bill mumbled.

"I don't deserve her," I said tremulously, looking up at him. "But thank you for giving her back to me." Throwing myself completely at his mercy, I begged, "I wish you could forgive me enough to give me another chance. I must've been crazy that night, but I know it will never happen again. I love you, Bill, more than anybody else in the world."

He reached down and drew me to my feet, an undecided look in his eyes. Emily tugged at his coat. "Please don't go away, Daddy," she pleaded. "Please stay here with us."

Tears in his eyes, Bill gently patted her curly head. "I guess that settles it. I guess I'll have to stay now," he said, looking at me.

God must have decided I'd been punished enough for my sins, because a few days after Bill and Emily came home, the District Attorney sent for me.

"We've caught Hank McKay's murderer, Mrs. Rance," he told me.

My face must have turned gray, because he added quickly, "You won't be called to testify against him. The police were about to arrest him as a Peeping Tom when he decided to shoot it out. He died in the hospital a short while ago, but not before we got a complete confession from him. He was some kind of religious maniac, as well as having sex on the brain. Anyway, his story ties in one hundred percent with yours, and we've closed the case."

When I walked out of his office, I felt as if I had gotten a reprieve from death that would allow me to begin life all over again. And I thanked God for letting me off so easy.

Bill and I have been slowly rebuilding our marriage. I know it will be a long time before he can trust me again, but I won't worry because we have Emily to keep us together. "A little child shall lead them" is a truth I've learned to believe. And I hope that her love and faith in us will help to bring about the miracle I'm praying for. Somehow I believe it will.

THE END

168

Family Nightmare:
LOVE SEALED OUR LIPS!

It was one of those dry December days that you get in Upstate New York. A wind off Lake Erie propelled me back home from a late morning shopping expedition. Only a woman who has been separated from the man she loves for three years can understand how I felt at the sight of my husband and sons around the electrical train. Vince was becoming reacquainted with five-year-old Andrew and getting to know three-year-old Christopher, whom we called "Chris."

There may have been a time when we intended to call Andrew by a nickname, but it just never took. He had been named Andrew for my father. He had the light coloring and blond hair that my father gave to me. From Vince, little Andrew had inherited piercing black eyes. This unusual combination of Saxon-Latin physical characteristics made him impressively beautiful.

I was depositing my groceries on the kitchen table when Vince jumped up from the floor to help me on with my coat. "Hands are cold," he said, taking me in his arms and finding my lips. "I can't have too much of you."

"It's morning," I joked, noticing the compelling, hungry passion that hovered about his full lips, the unbelievable smoldering effect of his eyes, and the great mass of tiny jet black curls that covered his head.

Chris, who had been born while Vince was in the service, toddled up to study us. Maybe he was still wondering about this strange man who had come into our home a few days ago and now was kissing Mom. A look of complete happiness covered the child's face as though he approved. We returned his smile, and when I glanced back at Vince, he winked. "That young man believes in love."

"It makes them secure to realize that their parents love each other," I said.

"Let's show him how secure he is," Vince whispered, running his lips over mine. It may have been then that I realized how happy I was, and remembering those long, lonely, fear-wracked nights when Vince was moving along the Middle Eastern desert in sandstorms, my arms tightened about him.

As we clung to each other in our immeasurable happiness that morning, how could we have known that within hours each one of us would be tortured by terrible doubts and suspicions, devouring our very beings? We were enjoying this second honeymoon in our own home until after Christmas. Then Vince would go back to working for his father. The Bellagio family, a hardworking family of Italian extraction, had their own sanding and sandblasting business.

I had met Vince in college. That was seven years ago, when I had just turned eighteen and he was twenty. My father didn't want me to marry an American, especially one whose religion was different from my own.

But Vince and I fell in love. Since my own mother had died when I was a child, Vince's mother took a hand in our romance, formally inviting me to spend a weekend with her in New York.

Chris must have decided that there was too much loving going on between his parents and reminded us that he wanted to be kissed, too. Vince swept him up into his arms, this little black-haired replica of himself, and I made some offhanded remark about how they looked like two peas in a pod.

"Do you mind?" he asked facetiously, nuzzling his nose into Chris's neck.

"Mind? Didn't I pick you because of your good looks?"

It was then I turned to see what Andrew was doing. He was ignoring the train, just sitting there quietly studying the three of us. When he saw that I was looking at him, he smiled that winning smile and I reached out my arms to him.

"You're part of this family, too, Andrew." I hugged him.

Later, when Vince was helping me prepare lunch, we heard one of his father's trucks pull up in front of the building. I could tell that he was itching to see what was going on in the family office downstairs. "Remember," I said, "you promised me you wouldn't go back to work until after Christmas."

"I'll just mosey down and see what they're up to," he said, scooping Chris up into his arms. "I'll take my boy with me."

"Not unless you dress him properly."

"Oh, Rosie, it's only downstairs. He's a healthy kid."

"But it's drafty down there, hon." We lived on the third floor of the building. The office occupied the first floor and Vince's brother, Sal, lived on the second level with his family. Vince put Chris back on his feet next to Andrew. As though he were going on another long journey, he kissed me intensely. For some inexplicable reason, I walked with him to the door, watching him take the stairs by twos. I would remember this gesture and probably attach all manner of strange meanings to it in the days ahead. Because neither Vince nor I could ever be quite the same again.

I was reaching into the kitchen cabinet when I realized that Andrew was standing behind me. He had a way of lingering near me silently with some question on his mind.

"Mama, Daddy loves Chris more than me."

"Oh, of course not, darling. We love you and Chris the same." Slightly concerned, I put the flour canister down. "You have to remember that Daddy has been away for more than three years in the Marines. It will take him time to get to know you and Chris." I reminded him of the letters he used to help me write Daddy and about the packages we used to send him. I felt the need to explain again that he was less than two years old when Vince went to the Middle East.

"But Chris wasn't even here when Daddy went away, Mama."

"Well, that's it, Andrew. Daddy feels that he knows you, but he never saw Chris until a few days ago."

It wasn't like Andrew to argue, but now he said, "He's always picking Chris up."

"Chris's just a baby, honey. You're two whole years older."

"Daddy wanted to take Chris with him. He didn't want to take me. And you said that when he came home he would be taking me on outings. Yes, you did, Mom—that day Aunt Charlene was here eating lunch."

"Sweetie, it's wintertime. It's going to snow. Outings are for summer."

"Maybe Daddy will only take Chris on outings, Mom."

"Now really, Andrew, don't you think you should give Mom time to make lunch? You can go into the dining room and take those nice Christmas candles out of the middle drawer, and when I get a chance I'll put them on the table."

"But you said they were for Christmas. There are still ten more shopping days till Christmas. You said."

"But we want to make the table festive for Daddy, honey. Remember, he's been away from home so long, eating in drab mess halls."

He thought about this for a moment and then went into the dining room.

As I breaded chops, I caught snatches of the children's conversation. They were arguing over the train. Generally, Chris was content to follow his brother's lead, but today he seemed to be insisting on some new rights. But I didn't think too much about this because my own personal happiness was blotting all else out of my mind.

"Mom," Andrew was saying to me with that sense of dignity that seemed strange in so small a child, "Chris is being very bad! Just because Daddy is home now, Chris won't do as I say. He wants to be engineer instead of a passenger. He's real mean, Mom. He used to play nice until Daddy came home."

How did I answer? I think I dismissed Andrew, telling him to go and play. Later, I heard another tiff taking place between the kids, and then Chris was laughing in that uncontrollable good humor of his. Ever since he had discovered how well he could laugh and how much his laughter meant to grownups, he'd been given to these great outbursts.

I could afford to leave the kitchen a few moments later. I walked into the dining room, noticing that Andrew had set the Christmas candles on the table for me. The children had left the train and were playing in their bedroom at the front of the apartment.

Back in the kitchen, I started the coffee perking. Since Vince had returned, I kept a mirror in the kitchen. Between basting chops and cutting large leaves of spinach, I glanced at myself. I decided to apply another round of lipstick. I was doing just that when I saw Andrew in the background. His lips were moving fretfully. I turned to smile encouragement into that lovely little boy's eyes. "You caught Mom in the act of trying to make herself pretty, didn't you?"

"Chris fell out the window," he announced.

It was another second before I took in his words. A thousand drums began to beat about my head. I heard—or thought I heard—shouting from the front of the house. Pushing the boy aside, I rushed into the bedroom. The window was open; Chris wasn't there. I didn't trust myself to glance out the window at the crowd gathering below. Somehow, my legs got me down the two flights of stairs. Vince's brothers held me back.

"No! No!" I begged, fighting their restraint.

When I broke free, I saw Vince cradling the little body in his arms on the sidewalk. About us, people were milling. I heard the words "ambulance, doctor—" magic words at such a time and some old Italian woman muttering a litany of prayers.

But this couldn't be, this wasn't happening to me, not to my little boy, lying there beneath some stranger's coat. And mother-like, I wanted to grasp that little bleeding body from my husband. They were tugging at me as the ambulance whined around the corner.

Mute, wanting to be deaf at that moment, I watched the two young men in blue take over. A great gasping awe generated itself from the throats of the crowd, as one paramedic shook his head. I saw the lips of the doctors move, but I couldn't hear their words as they transferred my baby to the vehicle. But Vince heard as he crouched there on his knees, and the restraining arms of his brothers couldn't keep him from letting his head fall to the December sidewalk, great gasps of pain shaking his body.

Eternal optimist that I was, I kept telling myself that Chris would be all right. But then the full import of Vince's crying invaded my brain. He was saying over and over, "He's dead, dead, my little boy is dead!" And in time I would learn that one of the paramedics had pronounced Chris dead a second after examining him.

Vince's sisters and mother got me to bed and they sat with me all night. I would cry myself into a doze, only to awaken to ask for Andrew, Vince, to insist that I be taken to the funeral parlor. And the women would assure me that Andrew was all right. He had been taken to Maria's house, where there were children to play with. Maria is Vince's oldest sister. He and his brothers were out making funeral arrangements.

Vince's sisters, Maria and Concetta, tried to comfort me. "You have to accept the fact that Chris is dead, Rosalyn," Concetta told me softly. "You have so much to live for. Remember, Vince loves you and you're fortunate to have him."

His sister, Maria, who had married young, could only say to me over and over again, "I don't know what I would do if it happened to my Donny. I'd want to die." And like all young mothers in our town, she made sure all the windows of her home were locked.

The pills Doctor Benino prescribed must have been stronger than I suspected, because I slept through the night. When I awakened, my mother-in-law was dozing by my bed. I explained that I had to go to Chris. In her broken English, she argued that there were no cars, buses, taxis, and that I had to stay in bed like the doctor had said. When I brushed past her into the dining room, Maria was awakening out of a doze in the rocking chair. She told me that the funeral parlor would not be open or ready for us until ten o'clock.

"Where's Vince?" I asked, shocked that he hadn't come home.

Maria explained that their brother, Hal, had taken Vince home with him. "Poor Vince is terribly broken up, Rosie. I talked to Vince on the phone an hour ago. Please. . . ." There were tears in her eyes. "Try to help him."

Ignoring her, I insisted on going to the funeral parlor. Maria called her brother, Sal, from downstairs, and the three of us battled the snowdrifts in the middle of the streets, where cars were stalled, in order to cover the twelve city blocks to the funeral parlor.

All evidence of a violent end had been erased from Chris's sturdy little body, and the reality of his death was now upon me. We were standing there, numbed by cold and sorrow, when Vince came in with Hal and Maria's husband. Our teeth were chattering as we embraced. Vince broke away from me to put his head upon the tiny casket that Chris was in, dressed in a short-sleeved white suit. "He's cold," Vince cried out, "cold."

Maria and his brothers tried to breathe warm sympathy into Vince's deep, impenetrable sorrow, but my husband was adamant. Maria gave in to him and called Concetta, asking her to bring over a woolen sweater for Chris.

Neither Vince nor I left the funeral parlor until we followed Chris's casket the following morning to the cemetery. Mercifully, the snowplows had done their work and in the cemetery's bleak whiteness, the undertaker had a tent erected over Chris's grave. Since Vince was in a state of almost complete collapse, he rode in the second car with his brothers, who had difficulty supporting him on their arms. I rode between Maria and Doctor Benino, a family friend. Carlo Benino had delivered almost all the Bellagio babies of the younger generation, including my two. He had always been very kind to me. When he delivered Andrew, he had jokingly suggested that he be the baby's godfather. I didn't know that he said this to all the young mothers. I thought it a good idea. At the christening party, I learned that I had been the first of his patients who had taken him up on his suggestion. Andrew had been his favorite patient ever since.

My own father came to visit us the following week, carefully checking in at a local hotel so that he wouldn't be any bother. It was he who talked me out of my guilt feelings about having left that window open. And it was he who cited the most important reason for my pulling myself together. "Rosalyn, I've noticed that Vince is near the breaking point. You know they talk about delayed combat fatigue. . . ."

I looked up instantly at his words. Yes, Vince was withdrawing more and more; he was silent now, unapproachable, brooding, not eating or sleeping, finding within himself no bridge upon which he could walk to the sympathetic understanding of his wife, his other child, his family. I stood up with resolution. "I should go to him," I said.

Dad also stood up, placing a hand on my arm in one of his rare loving gestures. "And you have to think of Andrew, too," he said. "Leaving him off with Vince's relatives isn't fair, not after all the boy's been through."

"But I have to think of Vince first," I argued weakly. "After all he's been through in the service, and now coming home to this. Andrew is all right with Maria. There are children for him to play with; they'll help him forget. And over there he can have some semblance of a Christmas."

"No, Rosalyn, you have to have Christmas here. You have to put up a tree for Andrew. Life has to go on. Both Vince and Andrew need you. I'd be very disappointed in my daughter if she couldn't rise to this difficult challenge."

His face seemed impassive, without feeling, but I knew then what it had cost my father to develop that mask. I knew what he must have suffered when my mother died giving birth to a stillborn child; when his only brother was killed in a hunting accident.

"I'll be strong," I promised him.

174

Despite my urging, Vince refused to see a doctor. About a week after the funeral, he just showed up at the office downstairs one morning, intent on going to work. It was then that I decided to bring Andrew home from Maria's house. She told me that Andrew, too, had become withdrawn, refusing to play with the children, calling out in the middle of the night for Chris. "He's brooding something terrible," she said.

What she called "brooding," my father referred to as, "Andrew's tortured awareness that he has lost his little companion." My first thought now was of my little boy. I had to envelop him with a sense of total security. I was developing guilt feelings toward Andrew. After all, I had left that window open. Had I exposed him to emotional problems that might prove worse in the long run than the death Chris had met?

I couldn't forget the way Andrew had stood there that day, his mouth working and trying to form the words, "Chris fell out the window!" Had this reaction been one of shock? I knew that I needed to steer his mind away from that tragedy, getting him so involved in new ideas and new pastimes that he would soon forget.

Vince was solving his own personal grief by working twelve hours a day. He seemed to fail to see Andrew and me in a room at times. One night I followed him into the bedroom and in the dark had to ask the awful question that was eating into my being: "Do you blame me, Vince? Are you telling yourself that I should have locked that window?" But he only reached out to me in the darkness, squeezing my arm.

My Christmas efforts were a dismal failure. I tried, but whether it was shopping for toys for one child, setting table for one less person, trying to evoke for Andrew's sake an interest in the holiday I didn't have, the image of Chris was always there. And, try as I might, I couldn't keep my feelings from Andrew. One night when I was undressing him, he asked, "Are you never going to stop crying for Chris, Mom?"

To see that little boy so perplexed by the grief surrounding him went to my heart. "Yes, honey, Daddy and I will soon stop crying for Chris. Because our Chris is safe in Heaven, a little angel, where God loves him so very much."

"Can he see us down here, Mom?"

"I think so, honey."

"He can't talk to us," Andrew said.

"Well, not the way people on earth talk, honey, but he's with God, and that gives us an angel all our own in Heaven. And in some ways, he'll talk to us."

"What will he talk about? Will he tell us how he fell and if it hurt him?" Since I was trying to turn Andrew's thoughts away from the tragedy, I changed the subject.

One afternoon I took Andrew into church. We walked up to the side altar, where the crèche rested amid a cluster of fir trees, a large angel holding forth the Christmas star. Sitting there in the front pew of that almost deserted church, peace seemed to come to me. I could pray that Vince and I would rise above this tragedy and be husband and wife again. Andrew's active mind was manufacturing a dozen questions, going all the way from the Three Kings to the nature of Heaven itself and even to the mercy of God and the forgiveness of sins.

I had difficulty answering him. As we walked down the aisle of the church, I noticed in one of the back pews Mrs. Harrison, an older woman who lived across the street from us. I remembered that she'd sent flowers when Chris was buried. Now she was coming out of the pew.

"I hope you're feeling somewhat better, my dear," she said.

Although I barely knew her, I realized instinctively that her feelings were genuine, but I questioned why she would cling so tightly to my hand, as her eyes moved from Andrew's friendly smile and back to my own unhappy expression. "I intend to visit you and your husband one evening," she said in a strangely meaningful way.

I forgot to mention this encounter to Vince, and January passed slowly. He was usually too tired at night to do more than pick a little at his dinner. Sometimes I would wake up to his deep sobs. On each occasion during late January, he seemed annoyed that I was also awake. But as February moved along, he would take me into his arms, holding me quietly without the conversation that once had been so much a part of our ardor.

Vince had already retired that night in February when Mrs. Harrison tapped on the kitchen door. I was cleaning up after having put Andrew to bed. I was really glad to have her companionship. I had a kind of ingrown respect for her age and for the fact that in her widowhood she had taken a sick sister into her home.

"I'm sorry Mr. Bellagio has already gone to bed," she said, glancing at her watch. She was slipping out of her coat. "Would you mind very much calling him, my dear?"

I turned abruptly from the stove, where I was putting on the kettle, noticing how dark were the half moons beneath slate-gray eyes. "I don't understand."

"I have to talk to you and your husband. I assure you I haven't breathed a word of this to another soul."

"Talk? But is it something that has do with my husband?"

She fell into a chair at the table. "God, I didn't know what to do.

There's nobody over there now but my sister, and she's not the kind you talk to. And I didn't want to break in on your grief right after the tragedy, but it's been terrible carrying this around."

I sat down opposite her, more baffled than ever by her words. People talked to Mrs. Harrison when a husband was unfaithful. "What is it, Mrs. Harrison?"

"I think I should speak to your husband, Mrs. Bellagio. After all, he's the boy's father."

I got up from the table to close the door between the kitchen and the rest of the apartment. "What about Andrew?" I asked.

She looked away from my fear because she knew that it was composed of two-thirds anger. "I saw them at the window that day and I should have phoned you. I'll never forgive myself for not calling you, Mrs. Bellagio. I saw Andrew lift the child up onto the window sill."

I broke out into cold perspiration.

"Mrs. Bellagio, I saw Andrew lift Chris up onto the window sill!"

The teakettle began to whistle. I stepped to the stove to turn off the gas and gather my inner resources.

"Andrew began carrying Chris about a year ago," I said. "Naturally, I discouraged this, but Chris seemed to expect such help from his brother." I poured water over the teabags in two mugs. I turned and smiled at her, trying to put on a brave face.

She heaved an enormous sigh. "I had to tell you. You see, it happened so quickly that day. I was dusting Bonnie's bedroom, and I looked out the window. The boys were at the window, looking out. I should have gone right to the phone that instant, but Bonnie needed me just then. I saw Andrew lift that child up. And then. . . ."

"Then what?" I asked coldly, fear tugging at my heart.

"When I looked again, I could see there was a commotion. Oh, I've blamed myself every day, starting out to tell you, and then not able to bring myself to it."

I brought the teapot to the table. "You know, Mrs. Harrison, right after it happened I tried to blame myself. I left that window open. But it had been open morning after morning for months, and nothing had ever happened.

"Doctor Benino said I was trying to assume a harmful and false guilt. Now I can say it: Chris died, and if I hadn't left the bedroom window open, perhaps it wouldn't have happened. If Vince hadn't come home from the service a few days earlier, it wouldn't have happened. If Vince hadn't gone downstairs to the shop that morning, perhaps it wouldn't have happened. Oh, Mrs. Harrison—if Vince and I had never met and married, then there wouldn't have been any Chris to fall out the window."

"I know how you feel, Mrs. Bellagio, but it's better for parents to know what a child is capable of."

"Please, Mrs. Harrison, I can believe that Andrew fell into the habit of helping Chris climb. It isn't as though you saw Andrew push—" I dropped my cup.

"Did you burn yourself, my dear?" I shook my head dumbly and she continued, "You were so revolted by the idea, weren't you?"

I was drawing the tea towel across my dress. Suddenly I looked deep into her eyes. "That was all you saw, all that happened." That idea must be implanted in this woman's mind.

Mercifully, she nodded. I continued, "It was a frightful thing, Mrs. Harrison; you can imagine how my husband and I—"

"I know, my dear, I know. I must be getting back to Bonnie." I asked her how her sister was, and we discussed the woman's ailment for a few minutes.

I didn't mention her visit to Vince. After she left I sat there at the kitchen table, running my fingers along the blocks in the tablecloth. I forced myself to remember the events in our happy home that had been a prelude to stark tragedy. I was remembering Andrew's numerous complaints about Chris. And it was true, dear God, that Chris had suddenly become ultra-independent of Andrew that morning.

It was almost a week before I could bring myself to carry my measuring tape into the bedroom. Chris had been thirty-five inches tall when he died. Now I measured thirty-five inches from the door to the windowsill. Only his eyes would have been above the sill. But he could have been standing on something.

I wished that I could remember how this room had looked. I glanced around, seeing large books, boxes, and even two small chairs. He could have been standing on any of these. I had closed the door when I came into the room, leaving Andrew playing with his blocks in the dining room. Should I call him in now and question him for the first time since Chris's death?

Everybody who had any opinion on the subject seemed to think it was important that Andrew forget. But he hadn't forgotten. He asked questions about the possibility of Chris's return from Heaven. He had gone off on this tack because his Grandmother Bellagio had told him that new babies came down from Heaven. Andrew had accepted the fact that dead children went automatically to Heaven, and putting two and two together, he had some idea that Chris would be coming back. Only this time, he would come in the guise of a new baby. During the weeks since Chris's death, Andrew's natural curiosity had taken an ultra-religious bent.

I had my own ideas about life and death and the way man might be rewarded or punished. I didn't know much about the Catholic

Church in which Andrew would be reared. But he would be going to school soon and learning his church's views. I didn't want to clutter his mind with any of my own personal conclusions. I tried to describe Heaven as a very lovely place where Chris had become an angel.

Remembering these question-and-answer sessions and the strong religious bent that Andrew was developing, I disliked the picture I must have made, kneeling on the floor, tape measure in hand like some prying detective, trying to find that one clue that would condemn Andrew. And at that moment he opened the door, that lovely, innocently provocative smile on his face. I reached for him and he buried himself in my arms.

When he looked up, I saw a shadow of fear in his eyes. Burrowing himself against my breast, he sobbed, "I don't like this room anymore, Mom."

"Would you like to sleep in Mom's bedroom and have Mom and Daddy move their bed in here?" I asked.

"Let Daddy sleep in here. I want to sleep with you in your room."

I pointed out that all mothers and fathers had their own bedrooms. He told me, "Sometimes, I dream that Chris is falling out the window again, Mom, and I hear him shouting."

I forced myself to ask, "Shouting, darling?" We had never discussed any such thing.

"He shouted, 'Mama!' just before he went over," Andrew said. My imagination may have been playing tricks on me. At that moment, I could have sworn that Chris's last cry, imprisoned in these walls for almost three months, was suddenly set free, that last conscious breath of my little boy—"Mama!" So sure was I, so intent upon answering that call, that a terrible chill passed over me. I held Andrew so tightly in my arms that he gasped for breath.

That evening, I suggested a transfer of bedrooms to Vince. He asked, "Was this Sir Andrew's idea?"

"It was my idea. We should have thought of it earlier."

"How did this come up, Rosalyn?"

"What do you mean? It's a simple transfer from room to room. Why should this require a major decision?"

"If you want to change the rooms," he said tiredly, "I will."

Throughout that spring I kept asking myself what I'd said, what Andrew had said, what Chris may have said, what Vince said. Just how had Mrs. Harrison really looked when she made her announcement that night in February? Where was Andrew when we were down in the street watching Chris die? And it dawned on me during these painful self-analysis periods that I had been deliberately avoiding any possible meeting with Mrs. Harrison, actually checking the street first like a sneak thief before leaving my home.

Perhaps I could have found relief if I had discussed my fears with Vince or talked about that day to Andrew. Perhaps I was trying to slip some of my own guilt feelings off my back onto Andrew. Didn't Doctor Benino tell me that the mind would play strange tricks? Didn't he tell me that I shouldn't dwell on that day? Didn't my father scoff at my guilt feelings? It was all in my mind, never in Andrew's capability. I had to pull myself together before my mind cracked.

My father came to visit us in late April, bringing birthday presents for Andrew. The boy was six and would be entering first grade in September. I became aware of my father's intent glances from time to time. Finally he asked, "What's wrong between you and Vince? Rosalyn, as much as I opposed your marriage, I want to see you happy."

He pried, and I tried to be evasive. I agreed to visit him that summer at his little cabin in the north woods.

While Andrew, my father, and I were relaxing one July afternoon in front of the cabin, my father's cat showed up with a brilliantly colored bird in his mouth. The cat wanted us to see his prize. Andrew was horrified, "The beautiful bird, Mom, the beautiful bird—and Prince killed it!"

"Andrew," my father said, "It's one of the laws of nature that the strong prey upon the weak."

"Pray upon?" Andrew asked. I knew that the word, pray, had only one meaning to my ultra-religious little boy.

"Yes, Andrew. It's right for Prince to catch a bird, just as it was right for the bird to catch and eat a worm this morning. Man hunts and kills larger birds, such as partridge, and then he eats his kill. Prince is doing no worse than man. This is the way of nature."

"I don't like nature," Andrew said, "not if you have to eat what you kill."

"Well, now, there are some who say that a gentleman only hunts for the thrill of it, but you and I, being more practical men, will hunt only for necessity—and we will eat what we kill."

"No, no, no!" the child cried. Although he loved his Grandfather Bale as he loved few others, Andrew wriggled away from my father's lap.

"Do you have to talk like that?" I asked with annoyance. "He's only six."

"It's terrible, Mom," Andrew said, just as Prince paraded past us again in proud triumph, actually flipping the bird above his nose and catching it to show us what he had. "God shouldn't let Prince catch that bird."

"Oh, come now," my father said. "God controls nature. Perhaps He is nature."

"Please, Dad," I implored. "Can't we drop it?"

"On the contrary, Rosalyn. Andrew is a brilliant child, and these questions should be explained fully. You shouldn't allow him to have ideas he'll scorn in the years to come."

"But why does God let Prince catch the bird, Mom?"

"I don't know, honey, but your grandfather is right: This is the way of nature that God made all the animals and birds the way they are."

"Did He make me the way I am, Mom, if I kill Prince, the bad, nasty cat?"

"Nonsense!" my father said. "Prince should be rewarded for making that fine kill. Look at the gorgeous plumage, Andrew." Prince was eating noisily. I stood up, wanting to lead Andrew back into the cabin. But he was fascinated, his eyes glued on Prince's feasting.

"Grandmother Bellagio says God always punishes you when you do wrong," Andrew told my father.

"Well," his grandfather said sarcastically, "she must know, since she has a private telephone line going into Heaven."

"Does she?" Andrew asked.

"Please, Father," I broke in.

"It would be a pretty big order for God to punish my beloved Prince," my father said to Andrew, both of them ignoring me.

"That mama bird and daddy bird are going to be sick tonight and cry and not be able to eat," Andrew told his grandfather, "because the Chris bird is dead."

I felt my hand closing tightly on the doorjamb. Without looking at the two of them, I walked into the cabin. Andrew remained with my father another half hour; I could hear the rise and fall of their voices. Finally, they came inside.

Andrew seemed to be over his earlier worries. He marched up to me with the announcement, "My grandfather says that God has already forgiven Prince. He says God put another egg in the mama bird's nest already to show that he has forgiven Prince."

When Andrew was napping, I walked out into the sunshine. My father followed, his crossword puzzle in hand. We were silent for a few moments, and then he said, "Andrew is positively brilliant. You have to challenge his mind with increasing knowledge." I didn't answer. "I'm sorry, Rosalyn, if you disapprove of the nonsense I told him about God forgiving Prince, but your little boy is oppressively religious. I'd watch that if I were you. I suppose Vince's mother is some sort of religious fanatic."

"She's very sane," I answered coldly.

"Well, if you say so . . . but I'd still watch this streak in Andrew."

I looked at him, his head bowed over his puzzle. I wished I could discuss my concern for Andrew with him. But I couldn't even bring myself to tell him the good news that I was now sure I was pregnant.

Back home, I waited for that precious moment after Andrew was sleeping to give my wonderful news to Vince. I was in his arms on the living room sofa, and we had been discussing my train trip back from Canada. I told him that I was pregnant. He didn't answer and I couldn't see his face. I turned abruptly, half sitting up to look at his strange silence. Deep in his eyes, I saw an uncertain fear crouching as though my announcement were driving him into some corner. And he had been so happy on the other two occasions when I made similar announcements. Now there was no joy; there was no sense of pride.

"You're not happy," I said.

He bounced back to reality. "Of course I'm happy. Sure, I'm happy." He stood and ran his hand through his hair and walked around the room as though he might find some refuge. He made it as far as the bedroom door; then he glanced directly at me. But he couldn't bring himself to say the words. I knew then that I wasn't alone in my suspicions. Our eyes met, imparting something of that same love that sealed our lips.

In September, Andrew began school in the first grade of our local parish school. Despite his strange, grownup ways, he proved a diligent student. In October his teacher, a young woman named Mary Ellen, sent a note home with him that she would like to see me. She suggested that Andrew was able to do second grade work. Naturally, I was pleased and I admitted that I had been helping him, "because he seemed so anxious to be able to read." We agreed he could be moved up on trial. He began concentrating on his catechism also, because if all went well, he would be receiving the sacraments of confession and Holy Communion the following spring. Now he became especially concerned about the state of his soul and sin. Again I had difficulty answering many of his questions, but Maria and Concetta were helpful.

He also was learning many formal prayers in class, and it was difficult to get him off his knees at night and into bed. I had kissed me good night at seven-thirty one evening in early November, and when I casually glanced in his room an hour later to make sure he was covered properly, I found him praying on his knees on the side of his bed. Vince was out of town on a job. I sat down on Andrew's bed, running my hand through his silky hair. "So many prayers, Andrew. You're going to keep Heaven working overtime."

"Mama, Sister says that when we sin, we hurt God because He taught us how to be good."

"But when we know sorrow for our sin, Andrew, then God is kind and forgives us."

"Mom, when I go to confession next time, I'll have to tell all the sins of my life."

"Do you have so many, honey?"

"Oh, Mom, I want to be good."

"I'm sure you do, Andrew, and maybe we can help each other."

"Mom, I'm so lonely for Chris. I'd give anything if he could come back."

"Well, honey, then I have to tell you my good news. We're going to have another baby."

His response was electric, his arms wrapping around me. "I prayed, Mom. I've been praying that God would send Chris back to me."

I heard myself telling him that we had to take what God sends us. Remembering my father's insistence that Andrew's mind be challenged with increasing knowledge, I heard myself answering his questions in greater detail than I intended. I told him that parents cooperated with God in producing children. And for each of my sentences, he had still another question. He placed the palm of his hand on my stomach, wanting to feel life. My stomach stretched slightly as he put his face against it, and he murmured, "Chris, Chris," believing the child I was carrying to be the reincarnation of his dead brother.

At breakfast the following morning, he asked me if it had hurt when I gave birth to him, to Chris. "It's like in the Christmas story, Andrew; the pain is nothing compared to the joy a mother feels when she holds her child in her arms."

I told him that I not only felt joy then, but even now when I held him. When he asked if I felt similar joy when Chris was born, I nodded.

"Greater than when I was born?"

"The same," I answered.

He didn't respond to this for a moment and then his next comment surprised me, "I wish you knew greater joy when Chris was born."

"Why, honey?"

"Because Chris was better than me."

"But that's not true. Andrew, tell me why you think Chris was better than you?"

He looked out of the window where snow again covered the backyard, reminding him, perhaps, of that tragic day. Was he just a simple little boy without any answers? Or was he a monster changeling, who manufactured murder, deceit, and lies in his head?

"Because he's dead," he blurted out, "and I loved him so much."

In that instant, I hated my devious mind that could entertain such sinful doubts about this loving child. I hugged him to me, saying, "Oh, honey, I do love you so much."

Like Vince, Andrew took great pains for my comfort, making sure that there was a pillow behind me and bringing me extra glasses of milk. One night when I found him on his knees in front of his bed, long after I expected he would be sleeping, he said, "I know you'll get Chris back when you go to the hospital, Mom, I just know it. I've been asking Saint Anthony and Saint Joseph to intercede with God for me."

"There, there," I said, wishing I had the words to comfort him. "God knows what will be best."

"And you'll call the baby 'Chris,' won't you?" This subject was becoming taboo in our home because Vince disliked hearing Andrew talk this way and Vince's mother had argued with the child on this matter. The old woman said the baby should have a new name—Michael, Angelo, or Peter.

"Now, Andrew, you know parents never call two children by the same name." He was touching my waist frantically, and I knew that it was the child within me that he was loving. My hand at his forehead detected a slight fever, but he insisted he felt fine. I called Vince from his newspaper, asking him to take Andrew's temperature. It was slightly above normal.

"Daddy," he pleaded, "we can call the baby 'Chris,' can't we?"

Vince was glancing at Andrew in a strange way; again, I had the feeling that my husband missed Chris so much that he almost resented the presence of this child who looked so different from the Bellagio family. "No, we won't call him 'Chris.' Grow up and stop being a silly baby yourself!"

"But this baby will be Chris come back from Heaven to us," Andrew insisted, "I know, I know."

Vince ran a hand across his forehead, looking a little helplessly at me. He turned out the night light before saying, "Your mother and I will think of some name you'll like."

When Vince and I returned to the living room, I said, "Under the circumstances, I think we should call the child 'Chris,' that is, if it's a boy."

He let the newspaper fall from his lap. "No, we will not call him 'Chris.' "

"But, Vince. . . ."

"It isn't right, Rosie. We had our Chris and he died. Do you think any other baby can ever take his place here?" He bumped a fist against his heart.

"What is this, Vince? Do you feel some need for loving the dead more than the living?"

"I didn't say that. I'll love this new child just as much as I loved Chris, and you know it. But he won't take Chris's place—not in my home, my heart, my memory. Chris has that special place with me; he was conceived and born at a particular time in my life. That means a lot to me. Chris was the child that I wanted and needed when I felt cheated out of Andrew by your father and you."

"Vince, that's silly."

"Chris was conceived that time you came to visit me at the fort, after we had been separated for months, and my life was one long hell. I was unsure of myself. I wasn't the type who liked to be away from home. And you came to visit me, even though my family was against it. How can you forget that weekend? Chris was the child of my fears, of my deepest love, when I so desperately needed a link with home and with the future."

It was the first time I had ever heard Vince use the word "fear" in connection with himself, but I could never forget how much he wanted the second child. My face fell to his shoulder. "Were you afraid you were going to be killed in the service?"

"I knew I was going to be killed, Rosie. I had that awful conviction all through it. And I knew that I'd never be afraid for myself again. Call it crazy, but you sent me a picture of Chris just when I needed something to help me go on. What I was looking for was right there in the eyes of my little boy, the little son I wanted, the little boy I had dreamed about. Sure, your old man says I'm superstitious—okay, so I am. But I found it in Chris's eyes in that little old snapshot that has never left me since, torn, bloody, muddy, but to me—sacred!"

Because I'm the kind of woman who can accept the unexplainable, I said, "I can understand your feeling that way, Vince."

"Ah, Rosie, how do I know? I wanted marriage early and children. And I love you very much. I didn't want to bum about when I was in the army, having affairs here and there. Your coming to camp that time had something to do with holding the right doors open for me, and you seemed to make everything right when Chris was born. And, Rosie, you always knew what to write to me. I think you must've known when you sent me that snapshot. Can you understand then why I loved Chris so much, why he has to go on being special to me? Because how do I know that it wasn't agreed in Heaven that I could live, but Chris had to die?"

"I don't know what to say, Vince. Doesn't Andrew bring any comfort to you? Don't you love him?"

Vince broke away from me. "Of course, I love Andrew. But I can't claim to understand him. We have nothing in common. Maybe he's a genius like you and your father say, but he's a strange bird. I didn't expect anything like him. Andrew is a genius, okay, but I'm just an ordinary guy with an ordinary mind."

"And you had Chris for so few days," I said a little forlornly. "But, Vince, what you've just told me convinces me that we should name this child after him."

"No, name him Joseph, Michael, Roger, anything you like."

"But Andrew has his heart set on—"

"Well, Sir Andrew can go fly a kite!"

185

"Vince, remember, he's only six and he feels so badly about Chris's death."

"Does he?" Vince stormed.

"Yes, he does."

"Rosie I don't want to talk about it. It's too horrible. Sometimes I think I can't live with this thing in my mind. . . ."

"It's about Andrew." He nodded, looking away. "Vince, have you been unsure all these months about Chris's death? Have you been unsure about the way Chris fell?"

"I don't think you should be talking about that. Not now, when you're pregnant. And even if my worst fears were true, what could we do about them? Nothing." He looked directly at me to whisper, "You don't send children to death row."

I clutched his face in my hands. "Oh, yes, we are going to talk about it, and don't you look away from me, Vince Bellagio." But even now I couldn't bring myself to say the words.

"Forgive me, Rosie. Maybe I am out of my mind."

"You've wondered about that day. Haven't you, Vince?"

He broke free of my grasp, kicking the table furiously. "God forgive me, but I've wondered—wondered how Chris managed to get up on that windowsill—wondered every day since it happened—wondered in the middle of the night about the power of jealousy, if I weren't to blame for maybe showing partiality to Chris—wondered, wondered, wondered. Are you satisfied now that you've gotten me to say it?"

There was no emotion in my voice, fortunately, when I answered. "But you never saw Chris climb, Vince. You were overseas." My sentences must be strong, convincing, swinging into lies that would give Vince peace of mind and protect Andrew from his smoldering wrath. "I saw Chris climb up onto chairs, his little cheek enough of a lever to propel his hardy body." I heard myself breaking into semi-hysterical laughter. "I used to say to Chris, 'What kind of monkey do I have?'"

"But Andrew was there that day," Vince said between his teeth. "If he's such a genius, why didn't he protect Chris?"

"Come now, Vince. What do you expect from a baby?"

"But Maria said—"

"What did Maria say?" I demanded, a new fury in my voice, which was intended to cover up my uncertainty.

"Only that Andrew was very vague about that day. You remember Maria took him home with her right after. . . ."

"Is that all? And she's a teacher. Well, she should know that five-year-olds can be very vague, especially while in shock. Remember, Andrew was there. He bore the full brunt of that terrible scene. He

186

saw Chris fall; you and I were at least spared that. And now you're still trying to throw some diabolical suspicion on that sweet little angel."

"I'm sorry, Rosie. And you're working yourself up. It isn't good for you. I've been half out of my mind all year."

I knew that there was nothing to forgive Vince, for my own private suspicions were worse than his, fed by his words tonight. But I had to keep them from Vince, from the world, even from Andrew. My child had to be permitted to forget that day.

When Christmas approached, I moved into the eighth month of pregnancy. Though it was hard for me to get around, I realized that Andrew shouldn't be denied the chance of seeing Santa Claus. Also, I saw an opportunity to bring him and Vince closer.

He had come in from school, that same pained expression covering his face again when he noticed how difficult it was for me to move around. He rushed toward me, as was his custom during this pregnancy, to hug my waist.

"Andrew, I think you should suggest to your daddy that he take you Christmas shopping one of these afternoons. You'll want to see Santa Claus."

He hesitated a moment, studying my face. "Mom, I don't believe in Santa Claus anymore." He brought me a glass of milk, explaining that he began doubting Santa Claus because the idea of the Easter bunny was so foolish. "When Grandmother Bellagio kept talking about an Easter bunny bringing eggs, I began to think that it was a fairy tale. And then I knew that big people told silly stories."

I asked him again about doing his Christmas shopping with Vince. "Daddy wouldn't like to take me," he said.

"How do you know if you haven't asked him? After all, you and he have been Christmas shopping lots of times. But you and Daddy haven't been since you were a tiny baby and he carried you in his arms."

My words seemed to surprise him. "Did Daddy carry me like he carried Chris?"

"Of course. And he was so proud."

At dinner that night, Andrew asked Vince if he would take him Christmas shopping. Vince glanced at me, then said, "I think it would be a very good idea."

They went Christmas shopping the following afternoon, staying out much later than I expected. When they returned, Andrew kissed me, whispering his love to the life that beat beneath my heart. Since he had eaten earlier, he went off to bed.

"Would you like to see the newspaper, Vince?" I asked.

"No, no, I'm kind of pooped." He looked away from my

searching glance. After a few seconds he walked into the kitchen, closing the door behind him. I followed.

"What happened, Vince?"

"Nothing, we just walked and walked."

"I noticed Andrew didn't do much shopping," I said.

Vince shrugged his shoulders, sitting down at the kitchen table. "No, he's a strange little Scrooge, pricing things and deciding against them. He's saving to buy lots of presents for the new baby."

"I hope you enjoyed it, honey. You spend so little time with him."

"Rosalyn, I happen to work ten hours a day and I don't want to argue."

"I don't either, sweetheart. If only you knew how happy I was to see the two of you go off together."

"But there should have been three of us," he said in a whisper that was fierce and angry.

"You talked to Andrew," I accused, "you talked about that day; you probed and dug. . . ."

He threw me one of his dark scowls. But in a second there was sympathy for me on his handsome features. "Yes, I talked. . . ."

"You mean you hectored and probed."

"I talked to him. Rosie, I don't know what to say. He knows something."

"Vince, can't you see how tortured Andrew is, unable to forget the horror of seeing his brother fall? Do you want to drive that child out of his mind?"

My husband was staring at me with the full force of his own terrible doubts. "Rosie, that's a terrible thing to say to me. Yes, I can see that he's tortured—as tortured as I am."

"But he's just a child, Vince, hurt, without the strength that you have to sustain you." And on that note, I heard my voice breaking. I looked around the room as though there might be some refuge from my own anxieties. Never by word or by look did I want Vince to suspect that I, too, was tortured by uncertainty.

"It was Andrew," Vince said, "who brought up Chris's name this afternoon, not me. He was talking about how we should always keep our windows locked when we get the new baby. So I asked him in a gentle way if he had anything else to tell me about that day. Oh, I tried to assure him of my love, my protection—and so help me, God, at that very moment, I think I would have breathed a sigh of relief if he'd told me he'd picked Chris up bodily and threw him out the window! God forgive me, Rosie." Vince was crying into his hands in a subdued way. "I wanted to hear him say it once and for all, because that's how I dream it happened."

Guardedly, I remained silent. Should I feign shock? Should

188

I attack my husband's fears with a fierce anger? Should I merely sympathize with his pain of not knowing and wanting to know? Should I throw myself into his arms, admitting that I, too, had fears and doubts greater than his? Should I tell him what Mrs. Harrison had seen that day, knowing that when I mentioned there had been a witness who saw Andrew actually lift Chris up, that it couldn't stop there?

Not with Vince, tortured as he was. He would have to know everything then. Even about Chris's last call, "Mama!" and how hurt he would be that the child hadn't called for him.

Andrew would be harried, poor boy, driven, hounded like an animal. And for what? So that we could see it, analyze it, weigh it, smack our lips over it, maybe even feel fine inside ourselves because we had never given way to an impulse to shove somebody we were jealous of out the window. Sure, thrust Andrew into the limelight, mark and brand him a monster for all time, a Cain, with never a chance of vindication, for Cain's sin was the unforgivable one.

"Vince, Vince, you're going to have to handle this breakdown of yours at once or turn yourself over to a doctor."

Something like a gasp escaped him. Maybe he realized that I was sacrificing him to save Andrew, and I wanted to cry out, tell him how much I loved him, needed him, begging him to forgive Andrew, to forgive me for choosing the boy at that awful moment of truth.

"You're insane, Vince, insane, bothering that child! What could be more cruel? Beat him physically if you have to, but don't destroy his spirit."

"I've never beaten him in my life," he insisted, and this was the truth.

"No, you don't beat him—you just play cat-and-mouse with his mind and soul."

"Not like that," he told me meaningfully, shaking an index finger at me, "and you have no right to say it. It's because I love him that I follow these fears of mine.

"Because I love you. There's another child on the way, Rosalyn, remember that. I want to think of this new baby in the house. I want to be sure that when my back is turned that this child will be safe."

"You fool! Don't you see that Andrew is welcoming this child even more than we are?"

For a moment, I thought I heard Vince mutter something about monsters needing new victims, but he was saying, his voice low, "Rosie, try to understand that I talk to you about it because I could never bring myself to discuss these things with another soul."

I went to him. "I understand, darling, I understand."

Long after Vince was asleep, I heard his words again, wondering if I dare feel safe with another helpless baby in the house. What if Vince ever showed, as he was bound to show, some deep affection for this child? I had to face the fact that Andrew had been jealous of Chris.

No full-time maid could have helped me get through the month of January any better than Andrew did. Whenever the unborn baby kicked, he was aware of the movement, rushing to me to whisper his endearments to "Chris."

Maria was present one afternoon when this happened. Later, when Andrew had left on an errand, she said, "It's uncanny how that boy seems to feel what you feel, Rosie."

"Never did a child so welcome a brother."

"You seem awfully sure that it's going to be a boy."

"Andrew is sure, in his strange little way, so sure that he has me believing it. He's even convinced my father that Chris is being reincarnated. It will be a boy, Maria, and no matter what my Vince says, we're calling him Chris."

Maria nodded. "Perhaps that will be best; perhaps this new child will wipe out the memory of that awful day."

"He has to, Maria. He has to."

My baby was expected the eighth of February. Because of this, I identified my pains in late January as false indigestion, gas, some voice in the back of my mind still making me wonder. Andrew noticed that I was exceptionally uncomfortable that morning and insisted on remaining with me. "But Andrew, it will be another week. You don't want to miss school. Besides, there are people in Grandfather Bellagio's office if I need help."

"Mom, I won't leave you. I have to be here." He flinched with me, as though each pain that cut through me was being absorbed by his little body. I agreed then that he could remain at home.

By noon I couldn't ignore the strange reverberations in my body. I called Doctor Benino, mentioning that this labor, if it was labor, was different from what I had known the other times. He said that he would be in the neighborhood in a short while and would drop in and see me. When he arrived, my body was tightening in the grip of pain. Andrew cried out and the doctor turned to see the child twisting and contorting. Oh, God, I was thinking, what is happening to my little boy?

Doctor Benino, Andrew's godfather, led the child away from me into the living room. When he returned I hoped that he would give me some explanation for Andrew's strange actions. "He's been like that all morning, Doctor."

"Rosie, I'm going to have Vince take you to the hospital."

I stood up to get my overnight bag, but he discouraged me from walking around. "I want Vince to take Andrew along with you."

"But, Doctor, they have rules at the hospital."

"Don't worry about that."

Andrew came out of the front bedroom, carrying my overnight bag and his own coat. He directed a wave of deep appreciation to Doctor Benino, who was calling Vince on the phone. The doctor noticed how I was staring at Andrew. He spread his hands in the air in front of him in a fine Italian expression. "Who knows? He apparently is so close to you, Rosie, so involved in this birth, that he's identifying."

Vince came bounding up the stairs as Doctor Benino was leaving. He told Andrew to go downstairs to his Aunt Charlene and stay there. "No, no," the child screamed, seizing Doctor Benino's hand, "I'm going with Mom."

Just then I felt another wave of pain and Andrew had to grip Vince's legs for support. I saw the shock of Andrew's behavior registering itself on my husband's face and he looked to the doctor for some assurance.

"Take Andrew with Rosie," the doctor said.

At the hospital, a nurse wheeled a chair for me to get into. Vince reached down to kiss me. Andrew must have believed that he could accompany me even from that point on, and as I reached the elevator and the nurse turned my chair about, I saw that Vince had picked up our protesting son and was cradling him in his arms. Rather than accompany me during the birth of our child, Vince would be staying with our son.

I felt the need to explain: "Doctor Benino seems to think it will be all right if Andrew waits downstairs."

I was in labor almost two more hours, listening to the loudspeaker locating one doctor after the other.

Another woman was wheeled into the labor room. "There's a sweet little blond boy downstairs," she said.

"That's my son," I told her.

"Well, honey, I've heard of husbands having labor pains at the crucial moment, but this is the first time I've seen a little boy going through them."

I was hoping that Andrew's seizures were fairly normal, nothing serious. But I found myself thinking more about him than about the baby trying to be born. In another ten minutes, I was taken into delivery. I gave birth to a little boy, his head a mass of black hair.

When I awakened in my room, I saw Vince looking more haggard than I had ever seen him. He was holding my sweaty hand, his eyes beckoning me back to reality, but there was no happiness on his face when I said, "A little boy . . . looks just like you and Chris."

He nodded, and I became aware of pressure on my feet, looking down to see Andrew spread across the end of the bed, enormous tears on his face, but steady, stable, resigned and almost relaxed in his quiet crying. "Oh, Mom," he began, lifting himself off my feet and moving to the head of the bed where he could look into my face, "Oh, Mom, God has given us back Chris, and I'll love him and protect him." But his words gave no peace or joy to my husband, who was dropping his head, staring at the floor between his knees.

"Of course, you'll protect him, Andrew, because you're my good son, my good helper during all these months."

Andrew brushed past his father to kiss me, keeping his head on my breast a moment, "Oh, Mom, my daddy said I shouldn't bother you today, but God has forgiven me." I heard Vince's ghastly intake of breath. He looked at me, begging me to be kind, to be understanding, to be able to take it now. His hands were supporting our son.

"Mom," Andrew managed in an almost-steady voice, "God has forgiven me for pushing Chris out the window," and I knew at that moment that those are the last words I shall hear when I die.

When I could speak, I said, "And I forgive you, Andrew, just as your daddy does." I looked at Vince's bowed head and added, "For who are we to deny forgiveness that God finds so easy and right?"

Later that evening, when Vince returned to the hospital alone, he told me, "Rosie, I knew downstairs while you were in labor that Andrew was at a breaking point. I had him alone in the waiting room, his body was retching something terrible. At one point, he cried out in pain as though he were giving birth to the baby instead of you. And when his shock subsided, I knew then that you must have given birth. Just before the doctor told me the news, Andrew said, 'Chris has come back, Daddy, and God has forgiven me.'

"I held him tightly, Rosie, saying, 'You mean God has forgiven you for something you did that was bad?' and he was nodding, Rosie, admitting then the horrible truth of it, perspiration pouring from his little body. And, Rosie, he was looking to me for an understanding I had to manufacture at that moment. To me, who suspected all along and at times almost hated myself as much as I hated Chris's death. What my feelings for Andrew were at those times—I don't dare admit, even to you."

I was tightening my feeble grasp of Vince's hand. "But you have found it in your heart to understand, Vince?"

"Yes. All I could do was hold Andrew in my arms, trying to pour out to him everything in me that smacked of good and kindness and love, knowing that he's my son and that I shouldn't fail him, his problems had to be my problems. Maybe I'll never be as close to a human being as I was to Andrew at that moment. But I am going to be his father, Rosie. And I'm afraid you and his Grandfather Bale are going to have to move over a bit. I mean that."

Later, Vince agreed that we could name the new baby "Chris." But we hadn't taken into account what had been going on in Andrew's mind. The very night that I brought our baby home from the hospital, Vince was putting Andrew to bed. When I finished with the baby I walked into the bedroom, hearing the rise and fall of their conversation there in the dark.

When Andrew noticed that I was in the room, he didn't slip from the arm Vince had about him. He said, "Mom, I know that the new baby isn't really Chris, and I think we should name him 'Vince' for Daddy. But my daddy says that Vince is a good name only for a bull or a goat."

I laughed. "It's a king's name." I wouldn't mention to Andrew that Vince had never liked his own name, which actually was meant to be Vincenzo. But for the first time, Vince wasn't protesting.

"If that's what you want," he said to Andrew. And so the baby was named Vince.

But it is not my imagination or wishful thinking that little Vince is a replica of our Chris, even to the joy of laughter that the dead child knew and indulged so often. It was some time before Andrew trusted me completely with the baby. He watched my every move, fearful that I might forget a feeding, horrified that the child might fall from his bassinet. And as little Vince learned to sit up, shout, smile, and walk, Andrew sloughed off some of his fear and worry.

Andrew's tragic and terrible revelation to Vince and me that afternoon in February remained our secret, something we didn't share with anybody else. Nor did we speak of it with Andrew until the following May, when he would be confessing his sins for the first time in order to receive Holy Communion. Without any prompting, he knew that this sin must be confessed, but he knew even more that God had already forgiven him.

It was on the advice of the priest that we took Andrew to see a psychiatrist. If we thought that our revelation would shock Doctor Orlando, we were certainly surprised at the understanding and help that we received from that kindly man.

I know that Andrew met responsibilities outside the province of other children. Recently he spoke to me about the special religious order he hopes to enter one day. I recognized the name as that of a particularly difficult order whose members deny themselves all comforts, other than the comfort of hard labor in the interest of others. It was then I felt compelled to ask, "Andrew, are you sure there isn't some sense of guilt still bothering you?"

"Mother," he said, quietly, studying me before smiling

193

encouragement, "I'm twenty years old and I've thought this thing out fully. Please believe me, I have no sense of guilt, other than a recognition of having done wrong. When you've been forgiven sin, Mother, it's wrong to doubt the forgiveness of God. Besides, they wouldn't take me in the monastery if they believed that I was merely administering to some selfish guilt. Guilt can be selfish."

"I don't know these things, Andrew," I said, "but I trust you to do the right thing when the time comes."

His answer was simple. "I promised Dad and Vince that I'd help them on the McPherson Building job." And as I watched him swing agilely out of the house with a faith in himself that has been one of the staunchest pillars of our home, my heart leapt with pride. As it always must, because I remember the enormity of his suffering, and the way he worked, step by step, out of the awful maze of terror and guilt when Vince and I could only stand by with our suspicions and doubts.

Now I watched Andrew step lively behind the wheel of Vince's car, and as he turned it from the country place we bought some years ago, I was warmed once again by the rightness of this life. Love sealed my lips unwisely perhaps, but love opened Andrew's heart.

THE END

THE DAY I DISCOVERED
THE TRUTH
ABOUT MYSELF

I stared at my mother in shock and disbelief! I tried to stay calm and keep my voice low for her sake, though I was trembling inside. "Mom, are you saying Dad is not my real father?"

Her dear face was gray with pain against the white hospital pillow. "I'm sorry, dear. I should have told you before, but I was so afraid it would hurt you and it might change your feelings for me. But I can't die with it on my conscience!"

"You're not going to die, Mom. You can't die!"

Her voice was weak, but firm with determination. "Dora, we've known for a year it was only a question of time. The doctors are amazed I've lived this long. I must tell you the truth before it's too late."

I held her hand gently, fighting back my tears. "Mom, whatever the story is, I'll always love you!"

She smiled, and I felt the faint pressure of her hand. "I was thirty-five when I met your father at the coffee shop, dear. He was twenty years old, such a handsome, vibrant young man, and I was so attracted to him! I'd never married. I devoted my life to your grandma and grandpa before they died, and ran the coffee shop for them. I desperately wanted a child. You can understand that, can't you, dear?

"I thought about it, and made the deliberate decision that this young man would be the father. Marriage was out of the question—he was so young and not in love with me, although he thought he was. Luke had been my partner for years, and when I became pregnant, I told him the whole truth, turned the coffee shop over to him and stayed home for a year. I didn't know it, but Luke had been in love with me for a long time. He asked me to marry him, and I did, six months before you were born."

I heard Mom's story as if in a dream—dear, kind Luke, waiting outside, the only dad I'd ever known, was not my father!

Mom's voice was an exhausted whisper now. "I came to really love Luke, dear He's been the sweetest, dearest husband and he loves you like his own daughter. He and I own the coffee shop and the land. It's very important to us, and we've left it to you in our wills. It's a good inheritance—take care of it! When you finish high school, learn the business so you can take it over when Luke retires. Please discuss it with him."

"Mom," I said, "I promise you I will, but please tell me my real father's name!"

"Luke's the only one who knows," she said, "and he kept my secret. Your father married a year after you were born, dear, and he has two sons. He doesn't even know he has a daughter. Maybe you should keep it that way. He has a lovely wife, and it could cause a lot of unhappiness!"

"Mom, it sounds like you know a lot about him! Have you seen him recently? Does he still come into the coffee shop?"

She closed her eyes without answering me, and I could tell she was drifting off to sleep again. She was smiling, as if her memories were happy ones.

I tiptoed out of the room, trying to absorb the pain of Mom's impending death and this revelation about my parentage. I joined Dad in the waiting room, and he looked at me despairingly. "Your mom told you about your father, didn't she? She said she was going to."

"Yes, she did. But she didn't tell me his name."

"I didn't think she would. This must be a terrible shock, but try to understand your mother's desperate need for a child, and always remember how much she loved you."

"Dad," I said, "would you leave me alone for a little while? Will you get me a cup of coffee?"

"Sure, dear."

After he left, the tears I'd been fighting streamed down my face. This was all too much for me to bear! Mom had gone to the doctor a year ago about her blinding headaches. Tests disclosed a brain tumor, too far advanced to be removed. The last year had been a nightmare of pain for her, and I'd be selfish to deny her the right to die at peace with herself. But dear God, how it hurt! It wasn't fair—she was only fifty-three. And, now, this horrifying news that Dad was not my real father. . . .

When Dad came back with the coffee, I pulled myself together. I should be helping him. He looked so pale and tired, much older than his fifty-six years.

"Honey, I'm glad your mom told you about your father. It always bothered me that you never knew."

"Dad," I said, "you've been a wonderful father to me—you'll always be my dad. You know who my real father is, don't you?"

"That was a long time ago, dear. Please forget it!"

Forget it? My mind was already on a feverish journey back in time to that twenty-year-old boy—my father! Who was he? Mom had practically no contacts outside the coffee shop, and most of our business came from the big assembly plant across the street.

"Dad," I burst out, "is he one of the men who still works at the assembly plant?"

Dear, honest Dad—he couldn't hide his feelings from me. I'd hit close to the truth. "Please, dear," he pleaded, "don't try to figure out who he is. If your mom wanted you to know, she'd have told you."

Mom died that night without uttering another word. Dad and I were with her, thankful that her suffering was finally over.

Dad closed the coffee shop for a week, and we both tried to cope with our grief. I don't know what I would have done without my boyfriend, Bo. He was such a comfort to me. I'd been going with him for a year. We were both seventeen and deeply in love. He was sweet and understanding when I told him Mom's story about my real father. "It doesn't matter to me, darling. You're the girl I love!"

Three months after Mom died, Bo and I were engaged. He gave me a ring, which I flashed around proudly. It seemed so romantic to be engaged in high school.

When I showed Dad the ring, he was very upset. "Honey, you and Bo are too young to be engaged. Both of you need more life experience before you make such a commitment."

I didn't listen to him. I loved Bo, my grief over Mom was still very deep, and being engaged gave me such a good feeling of security.

After Bo and I finished high school, I went to work full-time at the coffee shop, to learn the business. It was what Mom, Dad, and I all wanted.

The coffee shop was a real moneymaker, right across the street from a big automobile assembly plant. Our busiest time was weekday breakfasts and lunches, when the men from the plant came over.

I missed Mom terribly and tried to forget about finding my real father by concentrating on Bo. I loved him so much! After graduation, he floundered around, trying to decide what to do about his future. Then, one day, he came into the coffee shop looking very upbeat.

"I've got a job at the assembly plant. I start tomorrow!"

I felt good about it. He'd be close to me, and it was an obvious choice—many of our classmates worked at the plant.

"Why don't we get married now?" Bo asked. "We love each other, and with two salaries, we can start saving for a down payment on a house."

That sounded fine to me, though I felt sad that Mom couldn't share our happiness. "I'd love to marry you right away," I said, "but I want a quiet wedding—because of Mom, you know."

"Okay with me," said Bo. "So let's elope! But first, there's one thing we should talk about. I hope you don't want kids right away. I'd like us to enjoy our marriage for a few years first. We're both young!"

I was disappointed. I longed to have a child as quickly as possible! Mom's death had left a void in my life, the doubt about my father made me feel rootless, and I wanted a baby badly. I agreed to wait though, since it was what Bo wanted.

He went home to tell his parents, and I broke the news to Dad. He shook his head doubtfully. "Honey, why don't you wait? Bo's a nice boy, but he's pretty immature—I don't think he's ready for the responsibilities of marriage."

Neither Bo nor I could be talked out of it! We were of age, we loved each other, and we both had good jobs—why wait?

We decided not to elope, and settled for a justice of the peace wedding. After the ceremony, Bo's mother kissed me and wished us the best, but his dad didn't even shake my hand. He did not approve of the marriage or me.

Bo and I had already rented an apartment and started furnishing it, and after a short honeymoon, we moved in. We'd waited until marriage for sex, and I quickly learned the ecstasy of complete fulfillment. I was more in love with Bo than ever.

Now that I was all settled in my marriage, the need to know my real father began to obsess me. Every day at the coffee shop, I found myself watching all the older men who came in. It seemed so hopeless! There were just too many men; it could be anyone!

I was waiting on the lunch tables one day, when a man I'd never seen before walked in. He was tall, handsome, in his late thirties, with eyes the exact color of mine! They say we women are very intuitive. My nerves started tingling, and I had a peculiar, twisting feeling in my stomach. Could he be my father? He sat down at one of my tables and kept staring at me. I came over to take his order.

"I have a strange feeling we've met before." He smiled. "Don't I know you from somewhere?"

I felt as if I were choking. "I don't think so."

"Oh," he said, "I know what it is. You look so much like Antoinette, who used to run this place."

"She was my mother," I said.

"Ah, so that's it! I came in here regularly for years, though I haven't been in for a while. The men at the plant told me Antoinette died. I'm so sorry! We were close friends before she married Luke."

I had to know more about him. "You work at the plant?" I asked casually.

"Yeah. I've been there about nineteen years. I'm a foreman now."

"You have a family?" I asked.

"I have two sons, fifteen and thirteen." Mom had said my father had two sons—this couldn't be a coincidence!

"My name's Kevin Crane," he continued. "And yours?"

"Dora—Dora Evans. I'm married to Bo Evans, at the plant."

"Bo? I don't think I know him, but I'll make it a point to look him up."

I was too scared to ask any more questions. "Do you want to order now?"

"Sure. Nice talking to you."

I was in shock all day. I couldn't be positive, of course, that Kevin Crane was my father, but all the facts seemed to fit together! I didn't tell Dad my suspicions—he was still so broken up over Mom. I told Bo as soon as I got home.

He listened in amazement. "Wow! That's quite a story. But you could be wrong. It might be one of a hundred other men."

"I don't think so, Bo," I said. "It all adds up."

"What are you going to do about it?"

"I don't know what to do," I said, "so for the time being, I won't do anything."

"What's the big deal, anyway?" he asked. "Luke's been your dad all these years, and a darned good one. It's hard enough living in the present, without digging up the past."

I flared up in anger. That was easy for him to say! He knew who both his mother and father were. He just didn't understand. Bo was very loving, but I'd detected a streak of impatience and restlessness in him lately, nothing I could pin down in my mind.

Kevin Crane started coming in for lunch several times a week. He always sat at one of my tables. I watched him so eagerly.

"I enjoy knowing you, Dora," he said to me one day. "I always wished I had a daughter like you."

I felt hot blood rushing through my veins. How I longed to tell him he could be my father, but the words died in my throat.

We often talked about Mom. "I knew Antoinette so well when I was a kid of twenty," he told me. "She was so wonderful to me. I'd just joined the company and felt lost in that big plant. I never could understand why she broke off our friendship so abruptly. She left the coffee shop, married Luke, and I didn't see her again for a year. I heard she'd had a baby. I guess that was you. I always thought she was the warmest, most attractive woman I'd ever met."

Every word he uttered reinforced my belief that he was my father!

"And, by the way," he said, "I introduced myself to Bo at the plant. I'll keep an eye on him. I'd like to help him."

Bo had never told me Kevin had talked to him, and that night I asked him why. He looked annoyed. "I felt very awkward—you and your ridiculous belief that this guy is your father. I was embarrassed."

"Honey," I said, "it's very important to me. Can't you understand how I feel?"

199

"All I see is that finding your father is an obsession with you. It's ruining our marriage! Why can't you leave it alone? I mean it!"

Kevin hadn't come into the coffee shop for a week, and I was really worried. "What's happened to Kevin Crane?" I asked one of the men. "I haven't seen him around."

"Oh, he took a two-week vacation."

I was so relieved. I didn't want to lose touch with the man who could be my father. I felt inexpressibly happy when he came in the next Monday for lunch, and sat at one of my tables as usual.

"I missed you," I said. "I understand you were on vacation. Did you have a good time?"

"A depressing time," he said. "Can I talk to you for a few minutes?"

"Sure," I said. "Did something happen?"

"I feel very low," he said. "My wife and I separated about a year ago, and we went away together to try and patch things up. It looks pretty hopeless. She's really alienated from me. The boys and I are so disappointed."

"Sorry to hear it," I said. "Where are the boys living? What are their names?"

"They're living with my wife, Una, and their names are Peter and Matt. I see them over weekends. I'm going to keep trying to win Una back. I love her!"

I wondered what the trouble had been between them, but was afraid to ask such a personal question. "I hope it works out for you," I said. "Do you want to order now?"

"Yeah. A hamburger the way I like it and coffee. I feel better after talking to you, Dora. You're just like Antoinette—she could make a guy feel really special!"

He finished his lunch and waved good-bye, looking much more cheerful. "See you tomorrow."

I was more convinced than ever that Kevin was my father, but in view of this trouble with his wife, how could I possibly tell him now? It would complicate matters and hurt his chances of getting her back. I was so frustrated and confused. I couldn't discuss it with Bo. He was fed up with the whole subject and would only get angry at me.

I decided to talk to Dad and ask his help. We'd never mentioned my father since Mom died, and I'd have to approach it carefully. It was such a sensitive subject!

"Dad," I began, "you know I love you, and I'll always think of you as my own dear dad."

"I hope so, dear!"

"You know Kevin Crane? He's been in the coffee shop so much lately, and you've seen me talking to him, haven't you?"

"Yes, I have."

200

"Dad," I pleaded, "please tell me! Is he my father?"

Dear, honest Dad. I saw the struggle he was having with his feelings.

"You're not betraying Mom's secret," I said. "I already know it in my heart. I need your help."

He tried to hide his pain, but it was there in his eyes. "Your mom hoped you wouldn't find out, dear," he said sadly, "but she suspected you'd never rest until you knew. Since you've figured it out yourself—"

"Dad," I gasped hysterically, "he is my father, isn't he? I knew it!" He nodded, looking so unhappy. I threw my arms around him. "Thank you so much, Dad! You don't know what this means to me."

"What do you plan to do?" he asked uneasily.

"That's another reason I had to talk to you. I can't do anything about it! Kevin's having trouble with his wife, and I don't dare tell him I'm his daughter—it would only create more problems with her. But, Dad, it's helped a lot to share my feelings with you."

It grieved me not to tell Bo about my father, but I knew it would provoke a bad argument. Besides that, I was beginning to worry about his behavior. He was unhappy, quarrelsome, dissatisfied with his work, and complaining all the time.

"I get all the dirty, unimportant jobs."

"Honey," I said, "you're still an apprentice. It takes time to learn skills."

"I'll never like working there," he said resentfully, "it's too boring!"

I don't know exactly when Bo's drinking began to be a problem. It started slowly—a few extra beers at night, maybe. Then he brought home jugs of wine, drinking every night and over weekends, moderately at first, then heavily. I felt he was getting too dependent on alcohol, but he wouldn't listen to me.

"I'll drink as much as I want, when I want! It's none of your business!"

He developed a passion for clubbing, and wanted me to go with him every night. I was tired from working at the coffee shop all day, but I wanted him to be happy, so at first, I went with him, getting home very late and suffering for it the next day. I begged Bo to stay home weeknights.

"We both need our rest, dear. I'll go with you on weekends—isn't that enough?"

He was sullen about it. "Well, if that's what you want, but you're getting to be no fun at all."

He stayed home, grudgingly, and by bedtime every night, he was drunk out of his mind. I'd told Dad what was going on, but didn't know what to do about Bo's parents. His mother and I had a close relationship, but his dad was still a distant figure. He'd never forgiven me for marrying Bo!

Vera, my mother-in-law, often dropped by the coffee shop. This time, she told me that she and her husband were aware of Bo's drinking.

"He's been to see us a few times, reeking of liquor. Is his drinking getting to be a problem?"

"Worse than that," I said. "I think he's becoming an alcoholic, and his personality's changed, Vera! He used to be so warm and loving. Now he's bitter and resentful and he hates his job."

"You'll stick by him, won't you, honey?" she pleaded. "He needs you!" I promised her I would.

Kevin came into the coffee shop every day for lunch. We'd become close friends. He and his wife were still separated and now she was talking about divorce. I had to swallow my yearning to tell him he was my father, but it was beginning to eat me up.

One day, Kevin said he had good news for me. "Bo's been transferred to my department. I'm glad about that. He's a good worker! I'll keep a special eye on him."

Thank heaven, Bo's drinking hadn't affected his work! I told Kevin I appreciated his interest, and when I got home Bo seemed genuinely pleased.

"I finally got a decent job," he said, "and I'll like working for Kevin. He's a nice guy. I hope you still don't have that crazy idea he's your father."

I had to tell him the truth. "He is my father, Bo. Luke confirmed it, but I don't want Kevin to know. He's having marriage problems and it could hurt his chances of getting back with his wife."

Bo's face flushed with anger. "That's just great," he said furiously. "Now I'll be embarrassed every time I see him."

"Please don't tell him, Bo!"

"Don't worry—he'll never hear it from me. It's the last thing I want him to know."

I prayed Bo's promotion would make him happy, and he'd cut down on his drinking, but it got steadily worse. He came home very late every night, always drunk and spoiling for a fight. I didn't know what to do! Putting up with Bo's destructive behavior was destroying my own self-respect! I had such guilt feelings that I'd let him down. I felt like such a failure as a wife and a woman.

At times, I got so frustrated and angry but it never occurred to me to leave Bo. I believed in the binding nature of my wedding vows. I prayed for some miracle to change Bo.

It was incredible to me how he never let his drinking interfere with his job. Every morning, he'd be sick and shaking, but he always managed to go to work. But when he started taking a few drinks in the morning, before he left the house, I knew Bo was in even more desperate trouble.

I still saw Kevin every day at the coffee shop. We were closer friends than ever. I couldn't tell him about Bo's drinking—it might jeopardize his job! However, Kevin knew more than I thought he did. "Bo has a drinking problem, hasn't he?" he asked me one day.

"How do you know?"

"I've been watching him for some time. He's been coming to work with liquor on his breath, and he sneaks drinks during the day. I figure it's just the tip of the iceberg. He must have a real problem."

"You're not going to fire him, are you, Kevin?"

"No, he's too good a worker for that. I'm going to help him."

"How?"

"Well," he said, "alcoholism is a big problem at the plant, and management has set up an alcohol counseling center run by ex-alcoholics. Everyone with a drinking problem is sent there. I'm one of the counselors."

"You?" I asked in amazement. "Why you?"

"Dora, I was an alcoholic myself. I've been sober five years. I controlled my drinking for a long time before I became an alcoholic, but Bo's going to pieces fast. He'll be lucky if he recognizes his problem now."

I was stunned to learn that my father—my ideal man—had once been an alcoholic! Then I saw God's hand in all this.

"Kevin, please help Bo! I love him, and when he's not drinking, he's a wonderful husband!"

"I promise you I'll try to help, but you understand it's up to Bo. He must want to stop drinking, otherwise it won't work!"

Bo resented Kevin insisting that he go to the alcohol counseling center. "I'm not an alcoholic! I can stop drinking anytime I want to!" he insisted. He made no effort to stop, and drank more heavily than ever.

My day at the coffee shop ended at four o'clock, and I looked forward to going home, cooking supper, and spending time with Bo, but that was getting to be a grim joke. He was never there for supper, and he kept coming home later and later, always drunk and belligerent. One night, he didn't show up at all. I was frantic with worry.

The phone rang at eleven o'clock—Kevin! "I just had a call from Bo—he's in jail for drunk driving. He asked me to come down and bail him out."

I was horrified, and hurt at first that Bo hadn't called me. Then I was glad he trusted Kevin enough to call him. "Kevin, is he all right?"

"He's drunk, but okay. I told him I would not bail him out."

"Oh? Kevin—why not?"

"Because a night in jail may be just what Bo needs to bring him to his senses! You shouldn't rescue an alcoholic when he gets into trouble."

"It seems so heartless, Kevin!"

"It really isn't—I'm doing him a favor. However, he said he'd call his parents to bail him out. He was sure they would. I hope they don't."

"I'll go down there right away, Kevin. I have to help him!"

I dressed in a rush, and then drove down to the police station, only to find Bo had already been bailed out by his father. I rushed home and waited for him. He didn't come home—he didn't even call! I had a sleepless night, knowing Bo's father blamed me for his drinking and would encourage him not to come back to me!

I called Kevin at his home early the next morning, and told him what happened. "I'm sure he's with his parents now," I said. "Bo's father thinks I'm the cause of all his problems. I'm so afraid he'll influence him to leave me!"

"Knowing Bo," Kevin said, "he'll be at work this morning. I'll find out what's going on."

"Kevin, will being arrested affect his job?"

"No, I'll see to that. We don't fire a good worker until we absolutely have to. Bo reminds me so much of myself! I was a bright, ambitious kid, and thought the assembly line was a dead end. I kept asking myself if this was all there is to life? I hated to go to work in the morning, and I drank to escape what I considered to be grinding boredom. But I've learned, and Bo will learn, too, that it's not what you do for a living that counts—it's your attitude about your job and your good self-esteem. You can take pride in a job well-done, whatever you do."

That night I came home and found all of Bo's clothes and personal possessions gone. He'd left a note: Dora, I'm staying with Mom and Dad to think things over about us. What I'd feared had happened.

I don't know what I'd have done without Kevin's encouragement and my dear Luke's loving kindness. They kept me going. But worse was to come! Bo went on a long drinking binge. Kevin told me about it after it was all over. He didn't want to worry me, and there was nothing I could have done.

"When Bo didn't show up for work on Monday," Kevin told me, "I called his parents. They hadn't seen him since he left for work Friday morning. I checked with some of his pals at the plant. They told me he got very drunk Friday night, and they'd taken him to a motel. I called the motel, and they said he'd been in his room most of the weekend."

"Did you talk to him on the phone?"

"Yeah. He was drunk—on a real bender. I told him when he was ready to stop drinking, to call me, and not before. He missed work Tuesday and Wednesday, but he called me Wednesday night asking for help. I found him in such bad shape, I took him to a rehab center. He's as sick as a dog, Dora, but it could be the best thing that ever happened to him. I think this is Bo's last fling."

"Dear God, I hope so, Kevin! Can I see him?"

"No, dear. Bo's in no condition to see anyone. I have a lot of hope for him now. He's really hurting, and he says he wants to stop drinking. When he's discharged in a few days, I'll take him home with me for a while. He's bound to be confused and depressed, and I can help him."

A week passed—a dark and tormented time for me! I had such fears about Bo's future, and I still didn't know whether he'd left me for good. Then Kevin gave me a piece of news that lifted my spirits. "Bo stood up in a rehab meeting and admitted that he was an alcoholic!"

"He did?" I gasped. "That's a tremendous step. Has he stopped drinking?"

"He hasn't taken a drink since that last binge. He's still pretty shaky, but he's back at work, doing his usual good job."

"Has he talked to you about me, Kevin?" I asked anxiously.

"He has, indeed. He still loves you—he's ashamed of the way he treated you and he'll come back to you as soon as he feels strong enough."

"Why can't he come back to me now? I love him—I need him now!"

"Let him stay with me for a while. Our talks are helping him. Bo's shocked to realize how emotionally immature he's been. He's taking a long look at himself, and he doesn't like what he sees."

Fortunately for my peace of mind, I had another friend and ally in Vera, Bo's mother. She came into the coffee shop thrilled that he had stopped drinking. She told me Kevin had been over to talk to her husband and her about Bo.

"That Kevin's a wonderful man!" she said. "He's so understanding and compassionate. He even changed my husband's mind about you. He told him you were one of the finest girls he'd ever met."

How I longed to tell her, and the whole world, that Kevin was my father! But I couldn't—it would hurt Kevin's chances of getting his wife back, and Bo was so violently opposed to the whole idea. . . .

While I waited for Bo to come home, Kevin became even more dejected over the separation from his wife and family. "I've just about given up hope," he told me bitterly.

I'd never known the reasons behind the breakup, but I felt we were good enough friends for me to ask. "Kevin, was it your drinking that started the trouble between you and your wife?"

"Not really. She stuck by me during those bad years—I give her great credit for that. Our real marriage problems began after I stopped drinking."

"What were the problems, Kevin?"

"Well, Una accused me of being uncaring, cold, aloof, and not sharing my feelings with her. She said I didn't even know how to be tender and affectionate, and she felt rejected, cheated, and deprived of love. Then, a year ago, she told me she couldn't take it anymore."

"That doesn't sound like the Kevin I know!"

"I've learned a lot about myself since then. I've seen the plant psychologist a number of times. I wanted to find out what was wrong with me. He told me I was a strong, self-sufficient man, and like many husbands, I thought if my wife knew I loved her that was enough." He paused, and a look of pain crossed his face.

"Please go on, Kevin," I urged. "What else did he say?"

"He said it was quite common for men to have trouble saying, 'I love you' and showing warmth and tenderness. Many wives are hungry for affection. They need to be told they're loved and desired. I also discovered that I'd patterned myself after my parents. I loved and respected them, and I'm sure they loved me but nobody ever displayed any emotion in our home. I never once saw my parents kiss or even touch each other."

He smiled wryly. "I used to wonder how they ever got close enough to have me! Somehow, this left me with a deep fear of intimacy, of getting too close to others, even my wife. The psychologist said one of the reasons I drank was to feel comfortable with people."

"Kevin, you're so different now."

"Only recently. Dora, one of the hardest things to do in life is change the pattern of one's behavior! It's a slow and painful process, learning what love and loving are all about, and then expressing love in words and actions."

"I still don't understand why Una can't see the change in you."

"I hurt her badly, Dora. She's afraid to take a chance. There's something else: she says I'm too involved with my job—I spend so much time and energy helping other alcoholics, I have nothing left for her and the children."

"Is she right?"

"Yeah, I'm a pretty driven character."

"Well," I said, "you've changed in other areas. Can't you work on this one?"

206

"Oh, sure, I could slow down, but what good would it do? Una says she doesn't love me anymore."

"You can't give up, Kevin!" I exclaimed passionately. "I believe in miracles. Something will happen to make her change her mind."

Bo called me on Friday to say he was ready to come home—if I still wanted him. He sounded so different, mature, warm, loving! "All I ever wanted was you, darling," I said. "Hurry home! I'll have supper ready."

I took special pains to fix Bo's favorite supper: southern fried chicken and mashed yams. When I heard his key in the lock, I ran to open the door. Bo stood there, smiling, rosy with health, handsomer than ever! We rushed into each other's arms, tears in our eyes, so hungry for each other after all this time.

"Well"—he grinned—"how do I look?"

"Just great, darling," I said, "but more important, how do you feel?"

"Like a different man! I'm sorry for everything I did to hurt you, Dora!"

"You couldn't help it," I said. "Kevin explained you were sick, the victim of a disease."

"That may be," Bo said, "but I have so much to make up to you."

"You don't want to drink anymore?"

"No," he said confidently. "When I admitted I was an alcoholic, attended AA meetings, and had all those talks with Kevin, it was like a miracle—my compulsion to drink was completely gone.

"But I'm not taking my sobriety for granted. I'll have to keep going to meetings and helping other people stop drinking. I have to give back what was given to me. And I'll ask God to help me stay away from that first drink—that's the one that starts all the trouble!"

I looked at him proudly. Bo had really grown up. "Bo," I said, "we owe so much to Kevin. He's a remarkable man."

"He sure is, and such a good friend." He hesitated a moment. "Dora, I told him you were his daughter!"

I felt the blood draining out of my face. "Oh, no, Bo! I'm sorry you did that!"

"Honey, I had to. I gave you such a bad time over Kevin, and I felt he had a right to know."

My stomach twisted in nausea. "How did he take it?"

"He was stunned at first, and then he said he'd always had a strange feeling about you. He remembered being a little suspicious when your mom came back to the coffee shop after a year, saying she'd had a baby—Luke's child."

"When did you tell him, Bo?" I asked anxiously.

"Last night."

Last night! I hadn't even heard from Kevin since then! Was he having trouble dealing with this bombshell? I got myself together, served supper, and tried to forget Kevin in my overwhelming happiness at having Bo back. I waited all day Saturday and Sunday, and when I left for the coffee shop early Monday morning, I still hadn't heard from Kevin. I was so fearful and apprehensive.

He called me at seven-thirty. "I just got to the plant," he said. "I'm sorry I didn't call you before, but you'll understand when I see you. Are you and Bo free for supper tonight?"

"Of course! Oh, Kevin, I'm longing to see you."

"I'll be at the coffee shop at four o'clock. Dora, my dearest daughter, I have so much to tell you!"

Time seemed to stand still until four o'clock. I'd told Dad what was going on, and he had a hard time controlling his feelings—he was so afraid of losing me!

Kevin came in promptly at four o'clock. He stopped to chat with Dad for a few minutes, and then he and I sat down in a booth. I glanced over at Dad behind the counter, trying to keep busy, pretending everything was all right. I could imagine what was going through his mind. I hoped Kevin had said something to comfort him!

Kevin stared at me intently, as if he were really seeing me for the first time. "Dora, I guess you wondered why you didn't hear from me."

"Yes," I said, "I wondered."

"I was so proud and happy to learn you were my daughter. I've always felt so close to you! Then the full impact of what it meant hit me, and I was torn by so many agonizing emotions! I needed Una! I knew I had to tell her the whole truth, and I was deeply concerned about her reaction. I was so afraid she'd be angry, and more determined than ever to divorce me. I worried about it all day Saturday, and on Sunday, I went to see her."

"What happened?" I asked uneasily.

"Dora, when she opened the door I—I broke down completely. I cried—yes, I cried, for the first time since I was a kid."

"Oh, Kevin, how hard it must have been for you!"

"Una was wonderful, Dora. She sat beside me on the couch, put her arms around me, and asked what was troubling me. I told her everything, from the time I knew Antoinette, her death, meeting you, getting to know you, and how I learned the truth from Bo. I told her I felt overcome with shock, guilt, and shame, and I couldn't handle it alone."

"How did she take it?"

"Dora, she started to cry! She kissed me, and said she'd seen a vulnerable, human side of me she'd never known before—and she loved me more than ever!"

"She didn't mind that you had a daughter?"

"Mind? She wanted to know everything about you! She felt very sorry you'd lost your mother, and said it was only right that you should know your real father."

"That was very generous of her," I said. "But I hope it hasn't widened the breach between you."

"Widened? It brought us closer together! Una said she was deeply touched that I'd told her the full story and shared all my pain with her. For the first time, she felt I really needed her. She's come back to me, Dora. I waited until the boys came home and told them the whole story—I believe in being honest with children."

"How did they react?"

"Kids can handle anything if you tell them the truth. They're thrilled that we're a family again, and excited about having a sister! Everyone wants to meet you and Bo—you're having supper with us tonight. I've already told Bo what happened, and asked him to meet me here after work. He'll be along in a little while. Una and your brothers are waiting for us right now."

I felt overwhelmed by total joy! I couldn't take my eyes off Kevin's handsome face, his eyes the exact color of mine! I kept thinking of Mom—how happy she'd be for Kevin and me.

"It seems so right, Kevin," I said joyfully, "that we should be sitting together in the coffee shop, both of us knowing we're father and daughter for the first time!"

"That's why I wanted to meet you here. What more appropriate place could there be? This is where I met your mother. I have such happy memories of her!"

Bo came in, his face wreathed in a smile. I rushed over to him. "Oh, Bo, I'm so happy!"

"Well," said Kevin, "are we ready?"

I asked them to wait outside. I wanted to talk to Dad. He'd been watching from behind the counter, and I knew what this must be doing to him. I went over, kissed him, and put my arms around him. I was thinking of all the years he'd given me—all the love and devotion a true father gives a child.

"Dad," I said gently, as I kissed him, "I'm still your little girl, I always will be. Just be happy for me that I've found my family! Darling Daddy—nobody will ever take your place. I'll always call you Daddy!"

I gave him a big hug, and he hugged me back. "Thank you, darling! You don't know what that means to me."

Not every girl is as lucky as I am to have two wonderful fathers!

THE END

343/
671-8313

affordable Housing units

(844) 893-0211

www.H our thome.

PWAPT.com

I com aTwoSe Crown

Equal housing opps

3 y 4 bedrooms

2 1

Made in the USA
Middletown, DE
05 April 2016